BRENDA NOVAK

Come Home to Me

HARLEQUIN® MIRA®

Recycling programs
for this product may
not exist in your area.

ISBN-13: 978-0-7783-1591-9

COME HOME TO ME

For questions and comments about the quality of this book, please contact us at CustomerService@Harlequin.com.

Printed in U.S.A.

PRAISE FOR THE WHISKEY CREEK NOVELS OF
NEW YORK TIMES BESTSELLING AUTHOR BRENDA NOVAK

"[The characters'] heartwarming romance develops slowly
and sweetly. The sex is fantastic, but the best part is how
Simon and Gail tease and laugh as they grow closer."
—*Publishers Weekly* on *When Lightning Strikes*

"Novak delivers a lively, sparkling series debut…
romantic gold by a superior novelist."
—*RT Book Reviews* on *When Lightning Strikes*

"It's steamy, it's poignant, it's perfectly paced—
it's *When Lightning Strikes* and you don't want to miss it!"
—*USATODAY.com*'s Happy Ever After blog

"In this sensitive, passionate, and heartbreakingly poignant
second installment of her Whiskey Creek series,
Novak masterfully explores what happens when a woman
whose entire life has been consumed by playing a variety of roles
casts off her suffocating masks and, with the support of
an unexpected lover, embraces who she was, is and can be."
—*RT Book Reviews* on *When Snow Falls* (2012 Reviewers' Choice
Winner and Nominee for Book of the Year)

"With a great supporting cast of characters Novak fans have come
to know quite well, *When Summer Comes* is a magical addition to
the already heartwarming Whiskey Creek series."
—*Fresh Fiction*

"[*Home to Whiskey Creek* is an] engrossing, character-rich story
that takes a hard look at responsibility, loyalty and the results
of telling (or concealing) the truth."
—*Library Journal*

"Rate [*Home to Whiskey Creek*] A+ for story and writing….
The book scores as a winner on many levels."
—*Yahoo! Voices* (Mary Beth Magee)

"Affecting, painful, sometimes funny, but ultimately satisfying,
this engrossing tale of love and forgiveness takes on real problems
and gives its characters the strength and compassion to
come through with flying colors. Real people—
with all their virtues and vices—live in Whiskey Creek,
and Ted and Sophia will be two more you'll be glad to have met."
—*Library Journal* on *Take Me Home for Christmas* (Starred Review)

Look for Brenda Novak's next novel
THE HEART OF CHRISTMAS
available soon from Harlequin MIRA

To my father.
Although I lost you when I was barely twenty,
your love has carried me through.

Dear Reader,

I've heard from so many of you requesting a story about another one of Whiskey Creek's "Fearsome Five"— the five hell-raising brothers who are "bad boys" on the outside but have tender hearts underneath. So I'm excited to present you with Aaron's story. (He's the brother of Dylan from *When Snow Falls,* which won *RT Book Reviews* magazine's Best Contemporary Romance Novel of 2012).

I love making my characters earn their happily-ever-afters, and these two characters—Aaron and Presley—do just that. Although they both have troubled pasts, they dig deep to overcome their problems and build something with their lives, and it was enjoyable for me to watch them realize just how much in love with each other they are. Another Amos brother falls to the right woman! Yay!

I've really enjoyed writing stories set in this fictional town. Since this is my sixth Whiskey Creek book (not including the prequel novella), the town is feeling very much like home to me. I hope it's feeling as comfortable and familiar to you—and that you'll look forward to returning to Gold Country for Eve's story in *The Heart of Christmas,* which will be coming up next.

I love to hear from my readers. You can write me at P.O. Box 3781, Citrus Heights, CA 95611, or contact me via my website at www.brendanovak.com, where you will also be able to enter my monthly draws, learn more about this series and the other books I've written, or sign up to participate in my annual online auction for diabetes research. Together with my generous supporters, I have raised more than $2 million for this cause so far, and I'm hoping to keep pushing forward until we have a cure for my son, as well as all the other people who suffer from this terrible disease.

All the best,

Brenda Novak

WHISKEY CREEK Cast of Characters

Major Characters

Aaron Amos: Second-oldest Amos brother (one of the "Fearsome Five"); works with Dylan and brothers at their auto-body shop. Had a relationship with **Presley Christensen.**

Cheyenne Christensen: Helps Eve Harmon run Little Mary's B & B (formerly the Gold Nugget). Married to **Dylan Amos,** who owns Amos Auto Body.

Sophia DeBussi: Jilted Ted Dixon years ago to marry investment guru Skip DeBussi—later revealed as a fraud. Mother of **Alexa.** Reconnected with Ted and now engaged to him.

Gail DeMarco: Owns a public relations firm in L.A. Married to movie star **Simon O'Neal.**

Ted Dixon: Bestselling thriller writer.

Eve Harmon: Manages Little Mary's B & B, which is owned by her family.

Kyle Houseman: Owns a solar panel business. Formerly married to Noelle Arnold.

Baxter North: Stockbroker in San Francisco.

Presley Christensen: Former "bad girl" who left town two years ago and has just returned. Mother of **Wyatt.**

Noah Rackham: Professional cyclist. Owns Crank It Up bike shop. Married to **Adelaide Davies,** chef and manager of Just Like Mom's restaurant, owned by her grandmother.

Riley Stinson: Contractor.

Callie Vanetta: Photographer. Married to **Levi McCloud/Pendleton,** veteran of Afghanistan.

Other Recurring Characters

The Amos Brothers: Dylan, Aaron, Rodney, Grady and **Mack.**

Olivia Arnold: Kyle Houseman's true love but married to **Brandon Lucero,** Kyle's stepbrother.

Joe DeMarco: Gail DeMarco's older brother. Owns the Whiskey Creek Gas-n-Go.

Phoenix Fuller: In prison. Mother of **Jacob Stinson,** who is being raised by his father, Riley.

1

Aaron Amos was in the bookstore, too. Presley Christensen could tell by the prickle that skittered up her spine. Maybe she'd subconsciously recognized his voice amid the babble of the others, or there really was such a thing as a sixth sense, because when she turned and glanced across the crowded room, she confirmed what her body had already told her. He was standing off to one side, looking right at her.

It'd been two years since she'd seen him, and almost the same length of time since she'd shared his bed. But it felt like much longer. Her pregnancy and the first eighteen months of her son's life had been hard, harder than anything that had come before—which was saying something for a girl who'd lived out of a car or a motel for most of her childhood.

Although she'd known when she decided to return to Whiskey Creek that she might bump into Aaron, and had tried to prepare herself for that moment, her eyes locked with his as if he held a high-powered magnet that drew them there against her will. Then it was all she could do not to stumble back; the sight of him hit her like a blow to the chest.

Damn it! Her reaction—the way her breath jammed in her throat and her stomach knotted—was ridiculous. *Why* couldn't she get over him?

Gritting her teeth, she jerked her gaze away and slipped behind the people standing in line to get Ted Dixon's autograph. She was a big fan of Ted's work. Once she'd moved to Fresno to start over, his thrillers, along with a lot of other novels, had helped keep her mind occupied so she wouldn't fall back into her previous lifestyle. And after she found work at the Helping Hands Thrift Store, which was the best job she could land with so little education, books—second-hand, mostly—had provided the only entertainment she could afford. They'd especially been a blessing after Wyatt was born and she was up walking the floor so often with a colicky baby.

Still, Ted was local. It wasn't as if she wouldn't have another chance to see him. She'd wanted to come but probably wouldn't have if not for the urging of her sister. Cheyenne had insisted on watching Wyatt so Presley could get out for a few hours. She said it was important for her to take a break. And Presley was grateful. After the effort she'd put into cleaning her small rental house, getting settled and finding the perfect retail space to lease for her new yoga studio, she'd been eager for the chance to clean up and feel like something other than a mom.

But that was when she'd believed, as Cheyenne and Cheyenne's husband, Dylan, had believed, that Aaron would be a hundred and forty miles to the northeast. He planned to branch off on his own and open a franchise of Amos Auto Body, the collision repair shop he owned with Dylan and his other brothers. According to Cheyenne, he'd been spending a great deal of time in Reno looking for the best location.

"Excuse me." She pressed against the closest bookshelves in an attempt to squeeze past two men who were deep in conversation.

"Presley!"

She'd been so intent on her escape that she hadn't even looked up, but this caught her attention. Kyle and Riley, two of her sister's closest friends, were standing there. Ted Dixon, the author, belonged to their clique, so it was no surprise to see them here. If she searched hard enough, she'd likely find a handful of the others who'd hung out with Ted since kindergarten.

"Hello." She managed a smile, although her heart was pounding. Was Aaron, at this very instant, threading his way through the people standing between them?

There wasn't any reason he should feel uncomfortable approaching her. Maybe they hadn't kept in touch while she was gone, but there'd been no expectations along those lines. Their former relationship hadn't involved any commitment or obligation. They'd partied a great deal, and they'd had the hottest sex she'd ever experienced, but as far as *he* was concerned it was all in fun. They hadn't even had a fight when she left. The death of her mother and the knowledge of her pregnancy had set her off on a self-destructive odyssey that led her to an abortion clinic in Arizona. She'd felt sure that ending her pregnancy was what Aaron would want if he knew about it, which was why, when she decided to keep the baby, she didn't feel she owed him anything, even notice that Wyatt was his.

"Chey told me you were moving back," Kyle said. "How long have you been in town?"

She checked behind her, but at only five feet two inches tall she couldn't see over the people surrounding her—and it was so packed she couldn't see through them, either. "Just a couple of weeks." She paused to be polite, but she wasn't about to hang out and talk for more than a quick second, not with Aaron ten feet away and possibly closing the distance between them. Unfortunately, she couldn't leave. Ted had already signed and personalized her book, and there was a huge line at the register.

Riley spoke before she could actually say the goodbye that hovered on her lips.

"It's great to have you home. You look *amazing,* by the way." He gave her a low whistle. "Must be all that yoga."

Presley felt too anxious to enjoy the compliment— or to tell them that yoga had done a lot more for her than help her get into shape. That would prove to be too long a discussion. "Have you ever been to a class?" she asked instead.

Kyle and Riley exchanged a look. "Can't say I have," Riley drawled with a smile that told her he probably wouldn't, either.

"Once I get the studio open, you'll have to give it a try," she said.

"If you'll be there, *I'll* do it," Kyle volunteered.

Presley hadn't expected either of them to flirt with her. When she'd lived here before, she'd always had the feeling that they considered themselves too good for her. They'd been popular and well-adjusted from the beginning; she'd been a lost and lonely outcast who'd made some very poor choices. She might've been flattered at how her reception had changed, but she was too worried that she was about to be confronted by Aaron. She didn't want to speak to him. It made no difference how many times she told herself that he wasn't the right man for her, that their relationship had been unbalanced and unhealthy; she couldn't stop longing for his smile, his laugh, his touch.

Not that the difficulty of getting over him should have come as any surprise. Her whole life had been a series of struggles.

"Great. I should be open for business in another week." She *had* to open soon. She couldn't go without income for much longer. "See you there."

She could feel their eyes on her as she moved away, could tell they were startled she'd brushed them off. But with Aaron in the room…all she wanted to do was melt into the background. Just the sight of his perfectly sculpted face, which was almost *too* pretty despite the scar he'd gotten in a fight, was enough to drag her to a place of weakness and craving.

He was like the crack cocaine that'd taken control of her life before. She had to avoid him as avidly as all the other things that had nearly destroyed her.

It wasn't until she stepped through the curtain and into the dark storeroom where Angelica Hansen, owner of Turn the Page, received her inventory that Presley relaxed. She'd reached safety, a hidden corner where he'd be unlikely to look for her. Once Aaron left, she'd pay for her book and get out of there.

But when she turned, intending to peek out at those

in the front of the store, she collided with his hard, unyielding chest as he came through the curtain.

He grabbed her before she could fall over the stack of books at her feet, drawing her up against him. "What are you doing back here?"

Breaking his hold before the smell or feel of him could erode her resolve, Presley stumbled, which sent the books flying. She was lucky they didn't trip her as they almost had before. "I…needed room to breathe. It's so…crowded out there. I thought I'd wait here for a few minutes, until the line was shorter."

His eyes narrowed slightly at the way she'd scrambled out of reach so quickly. Or maybe it was her reason for seeking the storeroom that gave him pause. Did he think she was trying to steal Ted's book?

Or had he figured out the truth? He'd always been perceptive—too quick-witted for his own good…and hers. He was the sensitive Amos brother, the one who'd taken the loss of his mother and everything that'd happened after her suicide the hardest. But he didn't comment on the fact that she was still backing away.

"I heard you moved into the old Mullins place two weeks ago," he said.

She had to tilt her head to look into his face. "I did."

"Then…where have you been?"

Was he asking why she hadn't contacted him? "I've been busy."

"That means you're *never* home?"

Her stomach muscles tightened again. "You've dropped by?"

"I didn't bother to knock. I never see a car in the carport."

"I don't have a car anymore." She'd sold her new Hyundai several months ago so she could get out from under the payments and save enough to be able to lease a studio. She would've stayed in Fresno and kept saving to give herself a bigger financial cushion—would've opened her studio there, too—but when she found some strange marks on Wyatt, she was afraid his home day-care provider was mistreating him and decided to return to Whiskey Creek. Her sister had offered to help with child care, and once Aaron had told Cheyenne and Dylan he was relocating, going home was finally a possibility.

He hesitated. "How do you get around without a car?"

"For the most part, I walk." Chey's house was down the street and around the corner from hers. Her studio was two blocks in the other direction, along with the rest of downtown, making it easy to get wherever she needed to go.

"The exercise has obviously been good for you."

She wished that compliment didn't evoke the pleasure it did. But during the past two years, she'd judged everything by how much he'd like what she was doing, how she was changing herself. She supposed the desire to finally be admired by him was too powerful to overcome. "The owner of the thrift shop where I worked introduced me to yoga. That made the difference, more than anything else."

"Flexible *and* toned." His teeth flashed in an appreciative smile. "You look better than ever."

"Thanks." There were other things to explain the

physical improvements—like her strict eating habits—but she didn't want to engage him in any more conversation than she already had. He wouldn't care what she was doing with her life—not after he realized they weren't going to pick up where they'd left off and fall into bed.

"How have you been?" he asked. "It's been a long time."

And she'd felt every painstaking minute of it. She couldn't count how often she'd almost broken down and called him. Only the risk that he might find out he was Wyatt's father stopped her.

"Fine." She wiped sweaty palms on her jeans. "You?"

"Hangin' in."

He seemed to be faring well. He'd put on a few pounds, nicely filling out his large frame, which he'd needed to do. He'd been muscular but too wiry that last year when they'd been seeing each other. According to Cheyenne and Dylan, he'd also quit using drugs. Now that she had the chance to see him, she believed it.

"Good," she said. "I—I'm glad to hear it." She wished he'd leave it at that, but he didn't move out of the doorway, and she couldn't go anywhere while he was blocking her in.

"I was shocked to hear that you rented the Mullins cottage. That place was a cesspool when they lived there." He grimaced. "Talk about trashy people."

"It's taken some serious work to make it livable." She'd rented the two-bedroom because it was cheap and centrally located. Fortunately, where the house was concerned, a little elbow grease could make a big difference. "It's clean now. I just have a few things still to do."

"Like what?"

"Paint the porch and fix the fence. Plant some flowers out front."

He hooked his thumbs in his pockets. "Flowers?"

"Anything wrong with flowers?"

"Sounds like you're planning to stay for a while."

"I am."

"You weren't that domestic when you left."

She hadn't had a child then, but she didn't want to draw his attention to that, since he didn't know he was the one who'd made her a mother. "It's tough to be too focused on everyday concerns when all you care about is getting high."

"Yeah, I guess you're right." He rubbed his jaw. "I take it you've changed."

"Completely."

"I can see that."

No, he couldn't. Not yet. He assumed the changes were superficial, that she'd eventually fall at his feet the way she had before.

"I would've helped you clean up the rental," he said. "You should've called me."

She cleared her throat. "It wasn't necessary. I managed."

His eyes became guarded and inscrutable. He was figuring out that the "changes" he'd noticed included an unwillingness to associate with him. "Couldn't have been easy to get all that done, not with a baby."

Tentacles of fear slithered around her heart and squeezed. This was his first mention of Wyatt. She had to be careful, had to handle his perceptions carefully from the start. Any hint of suspicion on his part could destroy her happiness. "No, but I could've had Wyatt's father come and help. He would have, if I'd needed him."

"Doesn't he live in Arizona?"

Cheyenne had supplied everyone with this information, even Dylan. "He does, but he *could* come here. He has money, and he cares about Wyatt."

"You're in touch with him, then? He's a stand-up guy?" He sounded hopeful, as if he wanted that for her. There was no reason he wouldn't. To her knowledge, he'd never wished her ill, never done anything *purposely* to hurt her. He'd been too self-absorbed, but that was simply a byproduct of the fact that he'd never really cared about her, not like she'd cared about him.

"We don't have a relationship beyond Wyatt," she said, "but…he's a great father."

"That's got to make a big difference."

If Wyatt's father helped out to any significant degree, she wouldn't have had to clean the worst property in town in order to have a place to live but, thankfully, Aaron didn't seem to make the connection. "It does," she said. "And soon I'll be earning good money myself."

"As a yoga instructor, right?"

"And a massage therapist," she added so no one would be surprised when she advertised her services. She wanted everyone to understand from the beginning that she'd be doing both. She needed all the legitimacy she could establish.

"How'd you get into that?"

"I met someone at yoga who became my roommate. He was a massage therapist."

"He..."

"We've never been together, if that's what you're asking. Roger was gay. He paid half the rent and got me into massage."

"I see. Do you have a license or...whatever it takes?"

"I did some yoga-teacher training. And I'm a certified massage therapist." Luckily for her, a government grant had covered her schooling and Wyatt's day-care expenses while she attended class.

"You've got big plans. When will you be open for business?"

"In a week, if everything goes well." After she'd painted the interior of her studio and built her own tenant improvements, like the reception counter. She didn't know much about construction but with the price of supplies she couldn't afford to hire anyone, so she'd just have to learn. Dylan would do what he could, and Cheyenne would help when she wasn't working at Little Mary's B and B, but her sister and brother-in-law had their own lives, and she was in a hurry to get it done.

"Great." He winked at her. "I'll be your first customer."

She knew he thought he was being charming, but she stiffened all the same. "Excuse me?"

He stared at her. "I said I'd become a client."

"But... It's not what you think."

His smile faded at her affronted tone. *"What* do I think?"

"I'll be running two legitimate businesses, Aaron.

I don't…I don't party anymore. Or do anything else that might interest you."

He scowled. "Because you know so much about what interests me after being gone for two years?"

"I know the only thing *I've* got that interests you. It's all I've ever had. And I'm no longer willing to… to be one of your many sex partners. That's not the life I've chosen for myself."

"*Many* partners? Are we counting?"

She shook her head. "I'm not judging you."

"How generous."

That hadn't come out right. She had no grounds to criticize anyone, and she knew it. "I'm not the same person I was, that's all."

A muscle flexed in his cheek. "You're saying I took advantage of you before?"

He'd had a few brushes with the law, so his reputation wasn't any more sterling than hers. The Fearsome Five, as he and his brothers had been called, were used to being blamed even for things they *didn't* do—although she doubted that would continue. The last chief of police had recently been fired for misconduct; the new one didn't seem quite so drunk on his own power.

"No." She shook her head again for emphasis. "What happened before was entirely my fault. You never asked me to follow you around like a puppy or to crawl into your bed whenever I had the chance." She laughed as she rolled her eyes. "It must've driven you crazy to have me hanging on your every word, your every move. I'm sorry I was so annoying."

He didn't laugh with her. "Yeah, that was pretty miserable."

She could hear the sarcasm in his statement. He'd probably forgotten how much she used to irritate him, but *she* remembered. When her mother died, she'd instinctively gone to him for comfort, but he'd turned her away with a few sharp words for waking him in the middle of the night.

Still, she didn't hold that against him. Not really. She just wanted the next man in her life to care a *little* more.

"I'm sure it was," she said, taking his words as if he'd meant them literally. "But I won't bother you this time around. I—I'm looking for other things."

"So you've said." Jaw hard, lips tight, he leaned one shoulder against the door frame. Obviously, he wasn't happy with the way this was going. She could tell because of the badass attitude he'd adopted. It might've made her uneasy—that cutting glare made most people nervous—but she couldn't imagine he'd get angry just because she preferred to keep her distance. He'd never wanted her to begin with. So why would it matter now if she refused to have any contact with him? He could have practically any woman he wanted. Even those who pretended to be too good for him sometimes cast longing glances in his direction.

"And what, exactly, are these other 'things' you're looking for?" he asked.

"A husband for me and a great, uh, stepfather for Wyatt. A committed relationship." Which counted him out. "So…if you'll excuse me…"

He didn't react. He was too busy searching her face with those hazel eyes of his. Maybe he was hoping to find the old Presley, but she hadn't been lying when she said that person was gone.

When she stepped closer, indicating that she expected him to get out of the way, he shoved off from the wall and waved her past him with an exaggerated flourish. "Be my guest."

Gone was the flicker of excitement she'd seen when he first addressed her. His expression had turned implacable, stony. But she had no reason to regret her words. She'd only done what she had to do. And *she'd* taken responsibility for the past, laid nothing at his feet.

"Thank you," she said softly, and walked into the front, although it felt as if she were dragging her heart on the floor behind her.

Now she wouldn't have to worry about running into him in the future, she told herself. They could both work to avoid each other—cross over to the other side of the street, if necessary. That would make the next few weeks or months, however long it took him to move to Reno, easier.

So why did her eyes sting with unshed tears and her throat feel like she'd just swallowed a grapefruit?

She was standing in line, face hot and pulse racing, when Kyle and Riley stopped Aaron as he strode toward the front of the store. They greeted him, and he responded, sounding perfectly fine. Her rejection hadn't stung at all—which proved he'd never really cared about her to begin with. He'd used her, but the way she'd thrown herself at him made it equally her fault.

"Hey, Presley's here," Kyle said. "Have you seen her?"

She curled the fingernails of her free hand into her palm, praying she wouldn't have to hear Aaron's response. But there was no missing it. She couldn't have kept herself from listening even if she'd had the power to do so.

"From a distance," he said.

There'd been very little distance between them when he saved her from falling over those books, but she didn't begrudge him a white lie. She just wished the line would move faster so she could get out of the bookstore.

"She's opening a yoga studio one store down from Callie's photography studio," Riley informed him. "She'll be doing massage there, too."

There was an undercurrent in that statement, as if they all considered it pretty amusing. No doubt everyone was wondering if there'd be additional services she couldn't advertise. But that was her fault, too. It would take time to live down what she'd been like before.

"One-stop shopping," Aaron said dryly.

Assuming he was playing into those suspicions, Presley flinched.

"She'll have no trouble coming up with paying customers," Riley said. "Not the way she looks these days."

"She looks about the same to me," Aaron said, and moved away.

He was leaving. Presley's internal "Aaron radar" tracked him to the door. Then, in spite of her efforts to keep her eyes on the person in front of her, she glanced over to catch a final glimpse of him—and found him looking at her again. This time his expression wasn't inscrutable as much as it was bewildered.

But that hurt-little-boy pout disappeared beneath a mask of indifference as soon as he realized she was watching, and he stepped out.

2

Aaron stood on Cheyenne and Dylan's doorstep, next to the baby stroller parked on the porch. Waiting for someone to answer his knock, he heard Cheyenne's voice from inside the house. "Mommy's here, Wyatt," she cooed.

A few seconds later, she swung open the door and did a double take.

Aaron had imagined she was holding Presley's baby, but she wasn't. She must've said what she did as she left him in the other room.

"Aaron! I wasn't expecting you."

He hadn't planned on coming over—until he ran into Presley at Ted Dixon's signing. Ever since he'd learned she was back, and even before that, he'd been hoping for an opportunity to apologize for his behavior the night her mother died. He hadn't been able to deal with the level of emotion involved. That kind of tragedy carried him back to his own mother's death, something he avoided at all costs. But he felt bad for being such a callous jerk and would never forget how frightened he'd been when Presley went missing right after she left his place and didn't turn up for several days. He blamed himself for everything that happened in the interim; he knew she'd been through a lot. Whatever she'd experienced was so awful that neither Cheyenne nor Dylan would talk about it. For a long time, he'd wanted to tell Presley he was sorry, but she hadn't given him the chance. Whenever he asked for her number, Cheyenne told him she didn't have a phone. And Presley never called him. Even in the two weeks she'd been home, she hadn't tried to reconnect. If not for his customers at the auto body shop alerting him, he would've had no idea she was back in town, not until he ran into her at the signing. Dylan hadn't mentioned it. Dylan rarely talked about Presley in Aaron's presence.

"Dyl home?" he asked because Cheyenne was still blocking the doorway, and he didn't know how to inspire a warmer welcome. He'd guessed Presley would be stopping by to pick up her baby. Wyatt had to be somewhere if he wasn't with his mother, and this was the logical place. The stroller confirmed it.

His sister-in-law began to fidget. "Dyl?"

"Yeah. Your husband and my big brother—remember him?" Presley couldn't assume he was merely looking to get in her pants if her sister and his brother were around when he spoke to her. That would make the contact legit. Then maybe they could strike up some of their old camaraderie, and he could walk her home and offer an apology, since things had gone badly at the bookstore before he could work his way around to what he'd really wanted to say.

Cheyenne ignored the sarcastic jab. "Of course he's here. He's watching TV."

When she glanced past him, at the drive, he realized why she was reluctant to invite him in. She didn't want him here when Presley arrived. But Cheyenne was too polite to make it any more obvious. With a pleasant smile, she stepped back. "Come on in."

He understood that she didn't feel he'd treated her sister right. He *hadn't* been the best for Presley. But he'd never hurt her intentionally. And he wasn't the same person he used to be. Why did they think only she could change?

When Cheyenne grabbed a sweater off the hall tree instead of following him toward the living room, he stopped. "Where are you going?"

"Nowhere." She waved a hand. "I'm just taking Wyatt for a walk."

"It's cold and dark." It had also been raining an hour ago and could rain again. Spring usually came early in Gold Country, but the first week of March had been a week of full winter.

"We won't go far."

A dark-headed little boy toddled out of the living room, holding a rubber block, the corner of which he had stuffed in his mouth.

"This must be Wyatt."

There was another pause on Cheyenne's part, but he understood why. She didn't want anything, or any-*one,* to come between Presley and her recovery, and that included him. "Yeah. That's Wyatt, her pride and joy."

It was motherhood that'd changed Presley. Aaron felt certain of it.

Wyatt stared up at Aaron with round eyes the color of melted chocolate—just like his mom's.

"Cute little bugger," he said. "Seems big for his

age. Kind of surprising coming from a half-pint like Pres."

"Presley says his father was tall." Cheyenne moved as if she planned to sweep the baby into her arms and head outside, but Aaron was closer and stooped to pick him up before she could.

"Hey, you," he said. "What a chunk you are. Doesn't look like you've ever missed a meal."

The baby pulled the block out of his mouth and gave him a gummy smile that revealed several Mini-Chiclet teeth. "Ma-ma-ma!" he chanted, hitting the block with his free hand.

Aaron shifted his attention to Cheyenne. "Doesn't seem to be afraid of strangers."

"No. He's a happy, trusting little guy."

When Aaron used the baby's own fist to tap his nose, Wyatt gave an infectious belly laugh and tried to shove his toy into Aaron's mouth.

"That's okay, dude," Aaron said, twisting his head. "That block's got more than enough spit on it already."

"Aaron? That you?" Dylan called, and Aaron let Cheyenne take the baby.

"Yeah, it's me."

"How'd it go in Reno? You find the right location?"

Aaron walked into the living room to see Dylan sprawled on the couch, his hair wet. He'd worked late and must've just showered. They were slammed with business, which was another reason Aaron thought it was time to open a franchise. "Nothing I'm in love with. I'm considering Placerville instead."

"I wouldn't go there."

"It's closer, only forty miles away."

"But it's a smaller market. When'd you get back?"

Aaron fell into one of two leather side chairs and propped his feet on the coffee table. The L.A. Lakers were playing the Miami Heat, and it looked like a close game. "Couple of hours ago. I promised Mr. Nunes if he gave us another day to finish his Land Rover I'd get Ted's new book autographed for him."

Dylan sat up. "You went to the signing?"

"For a few minutes." He hadn't gotten the book. The line had been too long. Then he'd spoken to Presley and ended up walking out. But he could go over to Ted's later and pick up a copy.

"How'd it go?" his brother asked.

Why did Aaron get the feeling that this was a loaded question? Was there some underlying concern about him attending the book signing? "Fine. Why wouldn't it?"

His brother forwarded through a commercial break. "No reason."

"Because Presley was there?"

"Chey's been nervous about the two of you running into each other," he explained.

"Why?" Aaron asked. "What's going on? Everyone's acting as if we should be enemies. As if I'll do something terrible if I get the chance. But I've never mistreated Presley. I mean...I wasn't always as nice as I could've been, but I was never seriously out of line. We were friends," he added with a shrug. "We had fun together. That was it."

Dylan didn't seem particularly swayed by this speech. "You know she's had a rocky past. We don't want her getting mixed up in the things she used to do, that's all."

"*I'm* one of those things? You're blaming *me* for her drug use?"

Drawing up one leg, Dylan rested the hand that held the remote on his knee. "You partied with her a lot."

"But it's not like I introduced her to drugs, or even encouraged her to take them. She was a coke-hound. She would've partied with someone else if not with me."

"Maybe, but you weren't in the best place back then, either. It's not like you ever *dis*couraged her. You both played fast and loose. But whatever. That's in the past. We're hoping it'll stay there. Life's difficult enough for a woman trying to support a kid all on her own."

Aaron frowned as he remembered his conversation with Presley at the bookstore. "She's not doing it 'all on her own.' Wyatt's father helps out, doesn't he?"

Dylan made a sound of disbelief. "You kidding? She knew Wyatt's father for…what? An hour or two? He was just some prick who took advantage of her when she was high and running from everything she didn't want to feel. If there was any hope of finding him, I'd rearrange his face. But she's not in contact with him, doesn't know how to reach him. When I asked, she couldn't even give me a name."

"She told me he pays child support," Aaron said tightly.

"Pride talking. She doesn't want you to realize how desperate she's been, that she's barely getting by."

"Why would she feel she has something to prove to *me?* I've never looked down on her."

"She's putting on a brave face, what else? People do that."

"Not people who know each other as well as we do."

"Things have changed, Aaron."

That was the second time tonight he'd heard essentially the same thing. "To hell with change. Why does everything have to change?"

"Just let go of the past. The two of you aren't good for each other—especially now that she has a child."

The old anger welled up. "Wait a second. Who the hell are you to make that decision?"

Dylan shot him a dirty look. "Chey and I were here when you were together, remember? We know what the two of you were like."

"So what? You have no right to tell me who I can and can't see. Even after all these years, you're *still* trying to be my father?"

Dylan paused the Lakers game. "Don't start on that tired old argument—"

"I'll start on it if I want to. I've had enough, Dyl. There's only three years between us. It's time you remembered that."

Fortunately for Aaron's peace of mind, Dylan didn't deny that he had the tendency to be too controlling. "Old habits are hard to break, I guess," he grumbled. "Anyway, when will you finally get past whatever you hold against me? We can go over my mistakes until we're blue in the face, but that won't fix them. The bottom line is this—Chey and I care about you *and* Presley. We want to see you both continue to—"

"What?" Aaron broke in, throwing up his hands. "Live our lives as *you* see fit?"

"Stay off drugs, if you want the truth, damn it!"

Aaron got to his feet. "I shouldn't have come by."

Dylan tossed the remote on the coffee table and stood up to follow him out. "Maybe you don't want to admit it, but you have one hell of a chip on your shoulder. It's time to grow up. Time to understand that I did the best I could. I was eighteen when Dad went to prison. Do you think I *wanted* to take his place? Hell, no! But I didn't see anyone else who was willing to do the job. Were *you* going to do it? At *fifteen?*"

"Kiss my ass," Aaron muttered, and that was all it took to snap Dylan's restraint.

"Shit, you know how to enrage me like nobody else!" he roared, and smashed his fist through the wall.

Aaron felt his jaw drop. They'd gotten into some gnarly fights in the past, but he'd never seen Dylan lose control with so little provocation. This spat was minor in the overall scheme of their relationship. "Aren't you overreacting a bit?"

"I don't care if I am!" Dylan yelled. "You think *you're* sick of a few things? Well, *I'm* sick of them, too—and tired of your damn resentment!"

Aaron didn't respond. He just slammed the door on his way out.

It wasn't until he was back at the rambler in the river bottoms where he'd grown up and still lived with his younger brothers that he cooled off enough to realize all the baby gear in the hallway and the stroller he'd seen at Dylan's house were gone when he stormed out. Cheyenne hadn't taken Wyatt for a walk; she'd taken him home to his mother.

When Cheyenne came back from bringing Wyatt to Presley's and saw that Aaron's truck was no longer parked in front, she breathed a sigh of relief.

"He's gone," she said into the phone. She'd used her cell to call Eve Harmon, whose family owned the B and B where they both worked, as soon as she left her sister's. Eve was the only person in the world with whom she'd shared the truth about Presley's baby. Even her other close friends didn't know.

"I'm glad to hear it," Eve said.

Cheyenne unzipped her coat. Thanks to the brisk walk, she wasn't cold enough to remain bundled up. "At least now I won't have to go back in and smile while we chat about Presley and Wyatt as if I'm not betraying my brother-in-law *and* my husband." Because of Presley's recent return, her name would definitely have come up if Aaron *was* still there.

"Are you sure Aaron has no clue that Wyatt is his?" Eve asked. "Or could it be that he suspects but prefers to leave the situation as it is?"

"I have no idea. I just know how hard it is for *me* to keep this a secret. Sometimes Wyatt's paternity seems so obvious that I can't believe Dylan hasn't guessed."

"Why would he? You told him Wyatt's dad was some guy from Arizona, so he accepts it."

She paused on the sidewalk. She didn't want to go any closer to the house, didn't want her husband to overhear what she was saying. "Is this you trying to make me feel better? Because pointing out how much he trusts me only makes me feel worse."

"We've talked about this before. What else can you do?"

Dylan might be her husband but he was also Aaron's brother, and for all the differences between the two men, they loved each other with the kind of ferocity that stemmed from surviving great hardship together. She had no doubt that Dylan would tell Aaron—eventually, if not right away. He wouldn't be able to help seeing the situation from his brother's perspective, just as she couldn't help seeing the situation from her sister's. She could plead with him, of course. Tell him that Presley had never had her life so together, that they couldn't risk sending her into another tailspin like the time she'd run away from Whiskey Creek and gotten mixed up with a sadistic man. But that would only be effective for so long, until the loyalty he felt toward his brother prevailed.

"Maybe it would be different if Presley wasn't a great mother," Cheyenne said. "But she's completely devoted to Wyatt. I feel terrible admitting this, but she's done a lot better with him than I ever expected."

"It would also be different if Aaron wasn't so unpredictable," Eve added. "But you have no way of knowing how he might react—whether he'll be fair and reasonable or angry and overpowering."

Cheyenne stared at the lights glowing from inside her own house. "He can be so large and in-charge. And he has more resources than Presley does. If they ever battled over Wyatt…" She shuddered at the thought. No one wanted to fight Aaron. But Presley would do just that. She'd never give up, not if she were fighting for her child. "How could I ever put my sister in that precarious a situation?"

"You can't. Presley deserves *some* happiness. And she is happy these days, isn't she?"

"Happier than I've ever seen her."

"Then that's proof you're doing the right thing."

"Still, if Aaron or Dylan ever find out…" She felt heartsick at the prospect, but she couldn't open her mouth, couldn't risk telling because of what it could destroy.

"You have to hope they don't," Eve said matter-of-factly.

"What a mess." Someday what she and Presley were doing would not end well; the thought of that terrified her. "Anyway, I'm home now. I should go."

"Okay. You're on tomorrow?"

Cheyenne had recently scaled back her hours so she could help with Wyatt. Neither of them were quite used to her new schedule. "Yeah."

"Then I'll see you in the morning."

As they disconnected, Cheyenne tried to push her concern into the back of her mind, as she'd done so far. But when she went inside and turned to hang up her coat, she saw the hole in the wall—proof that she couldn't tell Aaron about Wyatt. He had an anger problem. That alone suggested they'd better not second-guess the decisions made two years ago.

"What happened?" she called out to Dylan. "Don't tell me you and Aaron got into it again."

There was no answer.

Unhappy with the damage that had been done to her house, Cheyenne hurried into the living room. Her husband sat on the couch with the TV on pause, holding his head in his hands.

"Dylan, what is it? He didn't hit you, did he?"

She grew even more alarmed when he glanced up at her with a hollowness in his eyes.

"No, he didn't hit me."

"What made him punch the wall?"

Dylan shoved a hand through his hair. "Aaron didn't do that. I did."

"What?" She'd never known Dylan to do such a thing. Like Aaron, he had a temper. Heaven help any worthy opponent who pushed him too far. But he'd always been able to control himself—at least since she'd come into his life. Before that, he'd had a reputation for being reckless, even dangerous, but that was understandable. He'd felt he had to do whatever he could to survive, and to make sure his brothers did, too.

"I'll patch it," he said in an attempt to mollify her.

"I'm not worried about that so much as I am about *you*." Sitting down next to him, she rubbed his back, trying to soothe him. "What got you so upset?"

"Aaron infuriates me. You know that."

"But you can usually cope with it. What did he say or do to set you off tonight?"

His beard growth rasped as he rubbed a hand over his jaw. "I was trying to tell him to stay away from Presley, and he got belligerent, as he always does."

The guilt she'd been feeling burrowed a little deeper. "Don't fight with your brother over Presley. That makes me feel I'm the one who dragged you into it, because I'm so concerned about her."

"There's no need for him to screw up her life. If he loved her and was willing to step up and marry her, I wouldn't feel like this. But…he doesn't want anything she's got to offer. Not now. She has a kid, and that's entirely too much responsibility for him."

Dylan adored Wyatt, felt protective of him. "Are you sure? That Aaron's not ready for—" the way he looked at her made her adjust what she was about to say "—for someone who might be interested in a more serious relationship?"

"Hell, no. He's never been able to maintain a serious relationship. What makes you think he could start now? I wouldn't want him to get involved with Presley again, anyway. That's all we need. You know how volatile he is, how their relationship could potentially affect ours."

But Aaron wouldn't ask permission. No one could tell him what to do; no one could make him see reason if he didn't want to. If Dylan tried to step in, to influence him, Aaron could do exactly the opposite just to prove his autonomy.

"It's too bad that she had to come back before he left," Cheyenne lamented.

"I'd rather have her here in Whiskey Creek than depending on people she can't trust to take care of Wyatt."

Dylan had been as livid as she was when Presley found those marks on Wyatt. The owner of the thrift shop had let her bring Wyatt to work three days a week, but she still had to leave him on the weekends, because it was busier, and when she went to massage school at night

"I agree Wyatt's better off here," she said, "but…"

"What?" he prompted.

But he didn't know nearly as much as she did. "Having the two of them in town for even a month is too long." She gave him a rueful smile as she checked his hand. He'd bruised and scraped his knuckles. "Do we need to take you to the hospital? Have that X-rayed?"

He shook her off. "No. It's not broken."

"You're sure?"

"Positive. I've broken it often enough to know the difference."

She mussed his hair. Although he was as tough as a man could be, there was a childlike innocence in the way he cared for her that formed the foundation of her happiness. "I love you so much, *too* much. Even when you punch holes in my wall." She stood up. "Let's wash off your hand before you get blood on the couch."

"Chey?" He caught her wrist, pulling her back to him.

"Yes?"

"Does it ever make you…envious to see Wyatt?"

The gravity of that question gave her an inkling of what might be causing Dylan to act out. It didn't have to do with Aaron. Not completely.

"Why would it make me feel envious?" She could guess, but wanted to draw him out. He rarely put a voice to his fears and concerns; instead, he expressed them in some physical act, by making love to her, going to the gym he and his brothers had set up in their barn or—tonight, anyway—punching a hole in the wall.

"We've been married for a while now and…no baby." He studied her. "Despite how badly you want one."

He felt he had to provide something she wanted

that much. He wasn't used to being unable to give her what would make her happiest. Since he was eighteen, he'd been taking care of the people in his life. He always took on added responsibility; it was just who he was.

"I *do* want a baby," she admitted. "I want *your* baby. But if we can't have one, we can't. Nothing could ever make me regret marrying you."

"What if it's me—my fault? You wouldn't resent it someday?"

"Of course not."

"Because it's got to be me," he said. "You've never done anything physically damaging."

"You think fighting might've hurt your…equipment?"

"If I had a dollar for every time I got kicked in the nuts…"

He'd started in MMA when his father, grief-stricken after losing his children's mother, stabbed a man in a bar and went to prison. Dylan had had to do something to augment what he could earn from the family's auto body shop, which wasn't exactly a success back then. Without the money he made fighting, his younger brothers would've been split up and placed in foster care.

"If that's the way it is…we'll accept it," she said.

"Accept less, you mean."

"Accept *reality*."

His troubled eyes met hers "I should get checked out."

She'd wanted him to see a doctor—until she'd gone to a doctor herself and learned that it wasn't her. "No."

He reared back. "Why not?"

"Because it doesn't matter." She laced her fingers through his. "We'll keep trying. You like that part, anyway," she teased, but he didn't let her levity distract him. He didn't even smile; he was too intent on the conversation.

"And if it doesn't work?"

"We'll adopt."

"But thanks to your mother—or, rather, Anita—you've missed out on so much already. I want you to have your *own* baby. I want you to experience pregnancy and childbirth and see yourself in the child you're raising. And I want your real mother, now that you've found each other, to see her family grow."

"We don't always get what we want," she told him.

"That's just it. You've had to settle for most of your life. I can't bear the thought that you might have to settle now because of me."

"Dylan, I can love an adopted child just as much. Anyway, even if we never get a baby, I'd give up *anything* for you."

He stared at her as if trying to decide whether she meant it. Then he kissed her deeply, tenderly, and led her into the bedroom, where he made love to her as though everything was fine and they'd get beyond this. But she could tell when she started to doze on his chest afterward that he was wide-awake and staring at the ceiling.

3

Presley couldn't sleep. And she knew why. But she refused to obsess over running into Aaron at the bookstore. She also refused to toss and turn all night.

Kicking off the covers, she got up, threw on a pair of holey jeans and a sweatshirt and lifted her baby from his crib. Wyatt stirred but didn't wake when she put him in his stroller. She almost hoped he *would* wake up—otherwise, he'd be ready to play when she needed rest. A single mother had to sleep when her baby did or go without.

But he didn't make a peep as she hurried down the street to her studio. There was so much work that needed to be done. She figured she might as well get started, take advantage of this time.

Once she let herself in and stowed Wyatt in what she planned to use as her massage room, where it was dark and quiet, she walked through the place, studying it with a skeptical eye. How could she make the studio more appealing on such a limited budget?

The little she'd had in savings had dwindled fast, and she was concerned that she wouldn't be able to pay her rent. If she didn't get enough appointments, she'd have *no* hope....

"What-ifs" churned like acid in her stomach, but over the course of her life she'd been through much worse than financial uncertainty. She could remember as a girl rummaging through Dumpsters, hoping to find a cast-off burrito or hamburger that might be edible. Her mother had taken off whenever it suited her, leaving Presley and Cheyenne on their own, often for days, without heat or even food if they were in the car.

Fortunately, those years were behind them. Pancreatic cancer had taken Anita, releasing those closest to her from the obligation of caring for her. Presley was taking a leap of faith by opening her own business, and fear sometimes threatened to paralyze her. But she could make it work. She could overcome anything as long as Wyatt remained healthy and happy.

At least here in Whiskey Creek she didn't have to worry about his day-care provider hurting him. She hated that *she* was the one who'd left him vulnerable to that. But it wasn't as if she'd left him to go off with some strange man so she could trade sex for money as Anita so often had. She'd had a legitimate job, and she'd kept him with her whenever she could. She'd do the same here. Otherwise, Cheyenne or a girl named Alexa, the fourteen-year-old daughter of Ted Dixon's fiancée, would help out. Alexa wasn't someone Presley knew well, but she seemed very sweet. Cheyenne was confident that she'd be nothing but kind to Wyatt.

A knock on the glass made her jump. It was after midnight, and she wasn't expecting company.

It could only be Cheyenne coming to check on her, she thought. Cheyenne was trying so hard to be supportive. But when Presley turned, she saw Riley Stinson, Cheyenne's friend whom she'd spoken to at the book signing, standing on the sidewalk in front of her store.

He waved. Then he blew on his hands to keep them warm as she walked over to let him in.

"Riley! What are you doing out and about at this hour?"

"I was on my way home from Ted's and saw your light. Figured maybe I'd catch you working."

"You did. Well, I haven't really begun yet. But I intend to." She glanced toward the street, where he'd parked. "Where's Jacob tonight?"

Riley had a fifteen-year-old son he was raising, with a little help from his parents. Jacob's mother wasn't in the picture. She'd been sentenced to twenty years in prison for running down his next love interest with an old Buick just before they all graduated from high school. The last thing Presley had heard about Phoenix Fuller was that she was due to be released around the same time as Aaron's father.

Presley wondered how Riley felt about his ex-girlfriend coming home at last, but she didn't know him well enough to ask such a personal question.

"Jacob's staying at a friend's." He whistled as he took in their surroundings. "So this is the new studio, huh?"

She felt herself flush. It wasn't much to look at. But it was more than she'd ever had. "So far. There's still a lot to do."

"What do you have planned?"

"Repairing the drywall and painting, to begin with." She folded her arms against the chill, wishing she'd brought a coat. Until Wyatt was up and no longer under a blanket, she was hesitant to turn on the heat, since she, and not her landlord, had to pay the utility bill. "After that I'll create a reception area where I can book my appointments and clients can check in."

She indicated the door leading to where Wyatt was sleeping. "That will be the massage room." She also showed him the larger area on the other side. "This will be the yoga studio."

"Nice."

He seemed to approve, and that made her less critical. "There's even a small kitchen in back," she said, feeling some of the excitement she'd experienced in Fresno when she'd lain awake so many nights, dreaming and planning for her future.

"This space has everything you'll need."

"It's a bit run-down," she admitted. The shop had once been an antiques co-op. The individual co-op members rented booths in which they displayed whatever they could scrounge up to sell. From what Presley remembered, most of it was junk, and no one had done much to maintain the property.

"There's nothing here a little work won't fix," Riley said.

"Work *and* money," she added with a rueful smile.

"I've got some extra wood lying around my backyard. I'd be happy to donate it to the cause and build that reception desk you mentioned."

She shook her head. "Oh, no! I wasn't hinting for you to do that. I don't have the money to pay you. Not right now. But Cheyenne told me you're a good contractor. I'll keep you in mind if things go well for me."

He studied her. "Why not work out a trade?"

She raised her eyebrows. "Construction for yoga lessons?"

"No." His grin slanted to one side. "Construction for *massage*."

How had she guessed? "You don't even know if I'm any good."

"I'm willing to take that on faith."

She might've thought nothing of his willingness to do so much work in the hope that he might like her massages, but she wasn't used to that kind of generosity. She felt certain *something* had to be behind this, something other than what he'd stated. And because of the exchange she'd overheard at the bookstore, she suspected she knew what it was. Cheyenne's friends—hopefully Aaron, too—weren't aware of what she'd done when she took off two years ago. But it wasn't a secret that she'd never been particularly circumspect. At times she wondered just where she'd be if she hadn't had her sister to counteract her mother's example. At least now, without the drugs, she could see herself as she wanted to be, as she *could* be, and thought she might eventually get there—if she stayed the course.

"I doubt you'd be interested in the type of massage I'm offering," she told him.

He seemed taken aback by the flatness of her voice. "Because…"

She gave him a look that said he could stop pretending. "It's just a massage, Riley. Nothing to get too excited about."

His eyes widened. "I wasn't expecting… I mean, I didn't think you were offering anything more."

Maybe that was true. Maybe it was her own insecurities that made it difficult to trust even a guy like
Riley. But, to be safe, she figured she'd be better off
carrying her own burdens. "I'd rather do the work
myself. But thanks."

"O-kay," he said, drawing out the word.

When she didn't soften her refusal or make conversation, he started for the door. "I'll get out of your
way, then."

She couldn't help going after him. "Wait, I'm sorry
if I assumed the wrong thing. But that doesn't change
the fact that I have too many sharp angles for someone like you, so there's no point in becoming friends."

He lowered his voice as if to add gravity to his
words. "Who says you have too many sharp angles
for someone like me?"

"I do."

"You barely know me!"

"And yet I know I'm not what you want. I could
never be what you want. If...if that's what you were
considering."

"I hadn't decided. But...why *couldn't* you be what
I want?"

Because she'd made too many mistakes. Was too
jaded. Too suspicious and distrustful and defensive.
She had a sordid past, an unfortunate upbringing,
too much experience. He deserved a girl who'd once
been prom queen, not a one-time addict. "I might be
Chey's sister but I'm nothing like her."

"The panther tattoo on your arm gave that away
at first glance," he said wryly.

"So...why are you here? Because you're tempted
to take a walk on the wild side? If so, you need to un-

derstand that nothing comes cheap or easy with me anymore. If you heard otherwise, it would've been true…in the past. But I have a kid now."

"People change. And I have a kid, too. That's partly why I'm interested in getting to know you. I understand what it's like to be a single parent. Or have you forgotten?"

The silence stretched out as they stared at each other.

"I'll build your reception desk tomorrow," he said. "After I get some sleep. And you don't have to pay me anything."

She grabbed the door as it swung back. "Why would you do that?" she called after him. "What's in it for you?"

"It's called friendship, Presley. Maybe it's time you became acquainted with it," he said, and got into his truck.

Presley was up all night, plastering over the cracks and holes in the walls. Although intent on finishing before Wyatt woke up, she wasn't quite that lucky. The baby monitor alerted her when he began to stir. It was early—not yet six—and she had another hour of repairs. So she took him out of the stroller, changed him and put him in the playpen she'd set up in one corner several days ago. But less than thirty minutes later, he was tired of his toys and getting hungry. She was just lifting him into her arms when Riley showed up, carrying a sawhorse.

"Cute kid," he said as he let himself in.

Somehow, in her hurry to get started last night, she'd forgotten to lock the door after he left. It was fortunate that she lived in Whiskey Creek these days and not the dumpy neighborhood she'd had to brave in Fresno, or that could have been a much bigger deal. Here, a lot of people didn't lock their doors at night—which was probably why Riley didn't comment on the fact that he could stroll right in.

"Thanks." She watched the muscles ripple under his T-shirt as he put down the sawhorse. He was good-looking, and he had a nice build. Maybe he wasn't as breathtaking as Aaron. Few men were. But neither was he as troubled.

"No problem." Dusting off his hands, he examined her work. "You've made some great progress."

Presley couldn't believe he'd really come back, especially so early. "What are you doing here?"

"You know what I'm doing here. I told you last night that I'd be building your reception area this morning."

She shifted Wyatt to her other hip. "You're either a really nice guy—or a glutton for punishment."

"Are you asking me? Because if you are, I'm a really nice guy."

Wyatt, interested in this newcomer, had stopped crying. She wiped the tears from his face as she said, "You're still going to be disappointed when I won't sleep with you."

She refused to feel obligated, not when she'd warned him. She wouldn't let anyone pressure her into making choices that were detrimental to her, no matter how grateful she felt for his friendship. That was the old Presley.

He put a hand to his chest as if she'd wounded him. She expected him to accuse her of being too brash.

Cheyenne would never have blurted out something like that. But she'd been frank on purpose, to highlight the truth: she wasn't his type.

Surprisingly, his response wasn't what she'd predicted. "Who said you won't sleep with me?"

She gaped at him. "I told you—"

"That you won't trade sex for money. If I get a massage, I get only a massage."

"That's true."

He nodded. "Then we're fine. Because when we have sex, I don't plan on paying you."

He'd said that with a straight face, but she could see a mischievous twinkle in his eye. "*When* we have sex?"

"I'm not saying it'll happen, so don't get mad. I'm just not ruling it out. In other words, if we ever reach that point, I'm open to getting physical. In case you were wondering."

She didn't know how to respond. She'd accepted long ago that she'd never be able to attract the kind of solid citizens her sister did. So why was popular, handsome, someone-who-should-know-better Riley Stinson even giving her the time of day?

He chuckled at her stunned silence. "Don't tell me you're that easily embarrassed. *You* started it."

She'd been trying to scare him off; she hadn't expected him to say something equally shocking. "But…you're my little sister's friend."

"What difference does that make?"

"I'm older than you are."

"There's two years between us. Two years hardly makes you a cougar."

She jiggled Wyatt, who was getting fussy again.

"It's not just the age difference I'm worried about. It's the other differences."

"And those are…"

"Vast."

He tilted his head as he peered into her face. "Isn't that the case with most guys you meet? Not many people have been raised the way you were."

"And Cheyenne turned out all right. That's what you must be thinking. But you have to understand that Cheyenne is special. She could've been raised in *any* circumstances and survived them." Somehow her sister had navigated their crazy childhood without ever screwing up. She'd left all the bad stuff to Presley, who'd tried everything once—and the most damaging things a lot more often than that. "She never made the mistakes I did."

"Which makes you…what? A bad person?"

"Some people might see it that way." *His* crowd typically did.

"Well, I appreciate the warning. But Chey says you've gotten your life under control." He searched her face. "Is that true?"

Wyatt was struggling to get down, but she couldn't let him because of all the tools and nails and wet plaster. "It is. I haven't done anything wrong in two years."

"And 'wrong' includes…"

"I haven't had sex. I haven't taken drugs. I haven't even had any alcohol, other than an occasional glass of chardonnay."

"Then I'd say your recent track record's better than mine," he quipped.

In what way? It had to be sex or alcohol; no one

in Cheyenne's group would risk the damage drugs could cause.

"But two years isn't that long," she argued. "It's not enough time to be able to trust me." Lord knew she didn't trust herself. That was why she had to stay away from Aaron. With one touch, he could make her forget everything she was striving to be.

"Tell me this, what are you looking for in life?" Riley asked.

He was no longer joking, so she sobered, too. "Someone who'll love me—for *me*—at last."

That wasn't something a girl usually admitted to a guy who was interested in asking her out. But she wasn't a teenager anymore, and they were having an honest conversation. Why hide the truth? Presley had been trying to warn him off from the beginning. If this didn't do the trick, he deserved whatever disappointment she proved to be.

To her surprise, her words didn't seem to make him uncomfortable. He pursed his lips as he considered them. Then he nodded. "I'd like to see if I'm the right man for the job," he said, and walked out to get more of his tools.

4

Aaron located what had to be Presley's yoga studio from its proximity to Reflections by Callie. He had pictured the old antiques emporium as soon as Kyle and Riley mentioned it. But it was worth coming by to see how far along she was in the process of opening. He was curious about her and everything she was doing; he hadn't been able to get her off his mind since running into her last night. So he'd told himself he'd swing by on his way to Reno. If she happened to be alone, maybe he'd stop and say something, get what he was thinking and feeling off his chest. It didn't seem fair that she suddenly seemed to believe the worst of him. Not when he'd been convinced that she was one of the few people who truly understood him.

But then he saw Riley Stinson's truck parked in front and he pulled over—even though she clearly wasn't alone. She wasn't open for business yet. So why was Riley hanging around?

He decided to find out.

The high-pitched whine of an electric saw cut through the air as he crossed the street, and he could see a ladder and some paint tarps through the wide storefront windows.

The door had been propped open for ventilation. For a moment, he stood at the threshold, watching Riley check the length of a piece of wood he'd just cut. Presley wasn't around. Maybe she was in another room. That he was glad she was out of earshot, glad he had the chance to confront Riley alone, told him he shouldn't be here. He'd been in a terrible mood ever since he'd encountered her at the bookstore. The fight with Dylan hadn't helped and neither had the sleepless night he'd spent trying to convince himself that he didn't care if Presley no longer wanted him in her life.

He'd let her go easily enough two years ago, hadn't he?

Not *that* easily. He *had* thought about her a hell of a lot, at odd hours when it was late and the house was quiet. He'd missed her, missed the fun they used to have and the excitement she'd brought him in bed. But missing her didn't really explain why he was so out of sorts. He should be *glad* she'd moved on. There'd been plenty of instances when he'd wished she would. He'd known all along that she cared more than he did, and that kind of thing never ended well.

"Hey!" he called.

Riley whipped his head around. Then he turned off the saw and lowered the goggles protecting his eyes. "How's it going?"

Still no sign of Presley. "Where is she?" Aaron asked.

Riley didn't ask who. That was obvious. "Had to take her little boy home. She was up all night, patch-ing the walls in here, so I'm hoping she'll catch a nap, too. But, stubborn as she is, she'll probably come right back."

He was talking as if he knew Presley well—but he didn't. Not really. No one in Whiskey Creek, except Cheyenne, knew her as well as Aaron did. Like him, Presley had always been an outsider, someone regarded with distrust. He'd never cared much about what other people thought. He didn't let their opinions bother him. But Presley hadn't grown the same thick skin. "So you're working alone?"

Using a measuring tape, Riley marked the board where he wanted to make his next cut. "For the moment."

Aaron kicked a loose nail that'd fallen to the tarp back and forth between his feet. "I didn't realize she'd hired you to build her tenant improvements. You didn't say anything about it at the bookstore."

"I didn't know I'd be doing this."

He sauntered closer, eyeing what Riley was building. "Receptionist's station?"

Riley blew the sawdust from his hands, then brushed off his white T-shirt. "That's right."

"Does she have the money to pay for all this?" He gestured at the work that'd been done so far. Dylan had told him Presley wasn't in a good financial situation. "It's tough, being a single parent."

"Tell me about it," Riley muttered.

He and Presley were both single parents, but the similarity between them ended there. "You've always had the support of your folks, and a decent way to earn a living. She's never had either." Riley had also had a lot of other things Presley didn't, but Aaron felt he'd said enough.

"She has Chey in her corner. And I'm hoping her yoga and massage businesses will be successful. But I'm not arguing with you. She's in a tight spot, especially while her son is so young."

Aaron jerked his head toward the saw. "Maybe you should let me finish up."

Riley straightened, finally giving Aaron his full attention. "Excuse me?"

"It won't be as nice as if you'd done it, but I can manage a hammer and nails--and it won't cost her a cent." Maybe that would make up for how he'd behaved the night her mother died; maybe it would finally ease his conscience.

Riley positioned the wood he'd prepped on the sawhorse. "There's no need for you to take over. I'm not charging her."

"Why not?" Aaron spoke before Riley could turn on the saw. "This may not be a big job, but it'll take the better part of your weekend." Wasn't that a lot to ask of a mere acquaintance?

Riley shrugged and raised his goggles. "I don't mind helping."

The saw blasted again, forcing Aaron to talk above it. "Since when did you two become friends? When she was here before, you barely knew her."

Riley's blade bit through the two-by-four and the end dropped onto the scrap heap. "I knew her," he said as the sudden silence rang in their ears. "I've hung out with Cheyenne for years."

That didn't mean he'd spared a glance—or a thought—for Presley. "So that's it? You're just doing a good deed?" Aaron met his gaze. "Or are you making some sort of play for her?"

Riley turned around to confront him, and the goggles came off again. "You're acting a little…territorial, Aaron. Which I didn't expect. According to Cheyenne, whatever you and Presley had when she lived here before is over. Was Chey wrong about that? Is there something going on between you two that I should know about?"

Aaron couldn't say there was. Presley had told him, in no uncertain terms, that she wasn't interested in getting involved with him again. But he didn't see why that meant they couldn't be friends. She'd needed his friendship once. "I'm sure Cheyenne would love nothing more than to see her sister with such an *upstanding* guy. Is that what this is about? Is she behind it?"

Riley scowled. "Aaron, there's never been any trouble between us, so why are you trying to start it now? Chey's not pushing me at Presley."

"She just happened to catch your eye at the book signing last night?"

"Does it matter? I thought you'd moved on. If I remember right, I've heard your name linked with Noelle Arnold's."

Aaron had bumped into Noelle at Sexy Sadie's once or twice and taken her home, but only because she'd let him know she wanted to sleep with him, and he'd had nothing better to do. He didn't particularly care for her. He'd never been in love with Presley, either, but he liked her a lot more than Noelle. At least Presley was real, down-to-earth. Noelle was the most shallow, vain creature he'd ever met.

"Noelle and I are friends, that's all."

Riley picked up another piece of wood and began to examine it. "For your sake, I'm glad to hear that."

Without a doubt, Noelle was the most hated person in town. That alone made Aaron feel sorry for her. But she didn't seem to understand what she was doing to evoke that reaction, so there was nothing he could do to help her.

Still, he didn't like Riley acting so superior. But maybe he had a right. He'd never screwed up the way Aaron had, that was for damn sure. "I don't need you to warn me off. I'll choose my own women."

"Good. Enjoy Noelle all you want, because you aren't what Presley wants anymore."

"And you are?" he snapped.

Riley didn't get the chance to respond. A female voice, shocked and slightly outraged, interrupted.

"Aaron...what are you doing here?"

He and Riley had been so focused on each other that they hadn't seen Presley walk in. She came toward them, clutching the hand of her son, who was doing his best to keep up. She wasn't wearing makeup, but going natural was a great look on her. With smooth, café-au-lait skin, wide brown eyes and a short, choppy haircut, she reminded him of Halle Berry.

He wasn't happy that she'd probably heard what they'd said. But the only thing he could do was shrug and act as though it didn't matter. Indifference could cover almost any uncomfortable situation —because it wasn't uncomfortable if you didn't care.

"I dropped by to see how the improvements are going," he said.

Their eyes met. He wondered if she could tell that he wasn't as emotionally detached as he was pretending to be. But she looked away before he could guess at her thoughts. "They're going fine."

Aaron made a point of gazing around. "Seems to me you could use some help."

"I've got it." Riley scowled at him. He no longer held a piece of lumber or any tools. He was keeping his hands free. Just in case?

"You've got the receptionist area under control," Aaron said. "But that leaves the painting. If I help, it'll go that much faster. I'll run over to the paint store. What color should I get?"

Presley's lips parted in surprise. "It's Saturday. Don't you have to work at the shop?"

"Not till Monday." So much for his appointment with the real estate agent in Reno, but he could cancel. He'd already seen about all there was to see. The only thing left was to decide on a location.

"You don't want to spend your time off doing... *this*," she said.

Was it really so inconceivable that he'd make that kind of sacrifice?

Part of him felt he should get the hell out of there. He knew when he wasn't wanted. But the other part refused to let her toss him aside so easily. He hadn't meant to hurt her two years ago. Who'd been better to her? Certainly not *Riley*. Cheyenne's friends had pretty much ignored Presley's existence. She could forgive him that one night when he couldn't face her pain without having to swim through a whole sea of his own, couldn't she?

"Sure, why not?" he said. If she wanted to get r

of him, she'd have to tell him to go. But he didn't think she'd do that. Her heart was too soft. And if Riley tried to force the issue, he'd be sorry he'd ever stuck his nose in Presley's business....

Fortunately, Riley didn't react the way Aaron expected. A smile suddenly curved his lips. "Yeah, why not?" he said. "Everything will go faster with an extra pair of hands."

Presley seemed startled by his capitulation. "But... I don't have the money to pay either of you! And I don't want to feel I'm taking advantage. I can do this on my own. Really. I'd *rather* do it on my own."

She'd grown cautious, protective, since she'd left Whiskey Creek, which made Aaron feel even guiltier for turning his back on her that long-ago night.

"There's no need to do it yourself." Riley's smile widened. "We're happy to help—aren't we, Aaron?"

Riley was making it clear that he didn't consider Aaron a threat. *You aren't what Presley wants anymore,* he'd said. Was he cocky enough to think he could prove it?

Far be it from Aaron to resist a challenge. "Absolutely," he said. "We'd never let you do this alone."

Presley might've continued to argue, but Wyatt was trying to escape so he could play in the sawdust and wood scraps.

"You could get hurt," she murmured as she struggled to restrain him. She looked tired. It was tempting to pick up the baby for her, but she'd been acting so skittish around him that he didn't dare, not in front of Riley.

"Why don't you take him home and let him play where it's safe?" Aaron suggested. "We've got this."

She glanced from him to Riley and back again. "But…"

"What will you be able to accomplish with him here?" Riley asked, throwing his support behind Aaron's suggestion.

"I could put him in his playpen," she began.

"Where he'd only last a short time," Aaron said.

She sighed. "That's true, but…"

"Go!" Aaron said.

Riley gestured for her to take off, too.

"I'll do what I can to make it up to both of you," she told them. Then, in spite of a crying and wiggling child, she somehow managed to pull a paint swatch and some cash from her purse. "Here's the shade I picked out. If this isn't enough money to cover it, I'll reimburse you later."

5

Presley hated leaving other people to do her work. She didn't want to feel indebted to Riley or Aaron. *Especially* Aaron. But she was terrified that if Aaron and Wyatt had any interaction at all he'd suspect the truth. If Aaron hadn't always been so vigilant about birth control, or if there'd been a specific incident when they'd noticed a broken rubber—which there wasn't—he would already have questioned her or Cheyenne about the circumstances of Wyatt's conception.

Fortunately, she had those two things going for her.

She'd made the right decision in not telling him, hadn't she? Every once in a while, she panicked, wondering if she'd been crazy to make the choice she'd made. But she hadn't gotten pregnant on purpose; there was no duplicity involved. And she didn't expect child support or anything else from him. So how was the fact that she'd kept Wyatt hurting him?

It wasn't. To her knowledge, he'd never expressed any interest in having a child. Indeed, his diligence in the birth control department indicated he *didn't* want one. There were times he'd even said as much, when a friend married or had a kid. That meant she was doing him a huge favor by keeping the truth to herself. It allowed him to lead whatever life he chose without having to wrestle with his conscience.

Of course, if he found out, there was no guarantee *he'd* look at the situation so philosophically. That was what frightened her. She hated to even think of the possibility....

Wyatt, happy now that she'd let him loose to run around the house, started to empty his toy box.

"You little devil," she teased when she saw the mess he was making.

He grinned up at her, completely unrepentant, and she bent to press her lips to his forehead. Then she dropped onto the lumpy sofa she'd bought from the thrift store where she'd worked in Fresno. "You're a charmer, aren't you?" she said as he babbled and played. "Just like your daddy. Headstrong, too," she added, thinking of how willful they could *both* be.

"Mama!" He brought her his collection of cars, one by one.

Despite a long list of worries, Presley couldn't help smiling when he trundled over without a car just to plant a kiss on her face. His kisses were wet and sloppy but, for her, they were one of life's true pleasures. She loved Wyatt *so* much—and that was why she had to keep up her defenses where Aaron was concerned, no matter *how* intent he seemed on regaining her friendship.

Her cell phone rang. She tensed, afraid it might be Riley or Aaron with a question, but caller ID indicated it was Cheyenne.

With a yawn, she hit the talk button. "Hello?"

Wyatt tugged at her arm. "Pone, Mama? Pone?"

She smiled at his attempt to say *phone*. He was learning more words all the time. "That's right, baby. Phone."

"Presley? Hello?"

She could hear a certain amount of pique in Cheyenne's voice. "I'm here. What's wrong?"

"I just stopped by your studio."

Oh, boy... When Cheyenne and Dylan had agreed to help her if she moved back, they'd indicated that the quickest way to lose their support would be to get mixed up with the wrong crowd again—and they considered Aaron and his friends "the wrong crowd."

"I don't know what he's doing there, Chey," she said, preempting her sister's complaint.

"It looked to me like he was *painting!*"

Stifling a groan, she covered her eyes with one arm. "He came over this morning and offered. It wasn't as if I *asked* him."

"You could've said no! You told me you'd stay away from him. If he finds out...I don't have to tell you I have a lot to lose, too."

Cheyenne *hated* lying to Dylan. And having her and Aaron in such close proximity threatened them both with exposure.

But Presley hadn't *wanted* things to turn out like this! She'd tried to make the situation easier on everyone by leaving town. She'd planned to stay in Fresno indefinitely and would have done so if not for what was going on at Wyatt's day care. She'd lodged a complaint, knew the day care was being investigated, but those days of doubt and suspicion had shaken her trust.

"I *tried*."

"You said that you told him you wouldn't be spending any time with him."

"I did!"

"Maybe you weren't blunt enough."

The look on Aaron's face when she squeezed past him at the bookstore convinced her otherwise. "He understood."

"Then why is he painting your studio?"

She couldn't figure it out, unless… "I can only guess that finding Riley there made him…competitive." He wasn't used to being rejected or upstaged. Most girls couldn't bring him home to their mothers and expect their mothers to be pleased, but women were inexplicably drawn to the edgy, take-your-chance aura that surrounded him. Aaron dared what most men wouldn't. That, coupled with his good looks, made him almost irresistible. Although he didn't seem to take his appeal too seriously, Presley had witnessed the female attention he received and had often been surprised that *she* was the one going home with him at the end of the evening.

"Maybe *he* wants to be the one to reject *me*." She'd always felt he was more attractive than she was. And his personality? He could charm most people—or cut them with a glance. He wouldn't like losing the position of strength he'd held with her.

"Isn't that what happened the night Mom died?" Cheyenne asked.

"More or less," she mumbled, but he hadn't actually said or done anything to change the status of their relationship. Had she not been pregnant, and had she stayed in town, they probably would've gone on like before—partying and sleeping together, at least until he met someone else. But she hadn't been satisfied being a placeholder, hadn't been satisfied with knowing that he was restless and would eventually move on.

Then, in the midst of her quandary about what she should do to protect herself before she got hurt, she'd run out of time to decide. Once she found out she was pregnant, she'd had to choose quickly—have an abortion, as he'd likely prefer, or throw her whole heart into raising their child alone.

She glanced over at Wyatt. He was sitting on the floor, playing with a toy that had pop-up Sesame Street characters. His face lit up when he noticed her watching and he slammed Cookie Monster back into his cubby just to show her that he could.

She'd made the right choice, she decided. Wyatt could take all the love she had to give—and *he* had the ability to love her back.

"So why's he still interested?" Cheyenne asked. "You've always said he doesn't really care about you. Is it that he suddenly sees you as a challenge and that excites him? Or is he trying to save face? Maybe he wants to prove he can get you back in the sack—or he's out to show Dylan and me that he'll do as he damn well pleases."

"I thought you liked Aaron."

"I do. I love him to pieces. But you know how contrary he can be."

"I can't imagine he'd be willing to work that hard just to get me back in bed. He's more of a take-me-or-leave-me kind of guy. That was the Aaron I used to know, anyway."

"So, to be on the safe side, you're going to reiterate that you're not interested?"

"Of course." She had no choice, not with the secret she was guarding.

"I hope you're more effective than you were when you said he couldn't paint your studio," her sister grumbled.

"Riley was there, helping out. I didn't want to tell Aaron he couldn't do the same. What reason could I give? Why would it be more acceptable for Riley to help me than Aaron?"

"Riley's not Wyatt's father."

"Exactly my point. That's something we don't want him to guess." She rolled a ball over to Wyatt. "Speaking of Riley, you don't sound surprised about finding *him* there."

"I was surprised. At first."

Presley leaned back. "And then?"

"He told me he wants to take you out, and it made sense."

"Was *Aaron* there when he said that?"

"He was standing about ten feet away. I actually got the impression Riley was announcing his intentions for Aaron's sake, to stake his claim or...or put him on notice."

"You sound pleased."

"I am. I loved it. After the way he took you for granted, don't you?"

She supposed it did feel good that someone else might want her, and that Aaron was aware of it. She'd always suffered from low self-esteem. She couldn't feel good about herself while making the kinds of mistakes she'd made. "How did Aaron react?"

"He dropped his brush," Cheyenne said with a laugh.

"That's it? He didn't say anything?"

"Not a word."

Of course he wouldn't. Why had she even asked? Aaron wouldn't feel threatened. He'd only befriended her in the beginning out of pity. He understood what it was like to be lost and alone; they both did. "I know why he's helping," she said, finally figuring it out.

"Why?"

"He feels bad about how he acted the night Mom died. This is his way of apologizing."

"You think so?"

"That's my guess. He can be sweet. Sometimes." He could also be tender, especially in the wee hours of the night after making love, which was why sex with him was more fulfilling than with most men. Just thinking about the deep-down satisfaction he could provide made her feel bereft without him.

Don't focus on that. He's like smoke. There's no way to grab hold of him for more than a few minutes, no way to keep him close....

"How can you let him off the hook so he'll go on about his business?"

"By accepting his apology and assuring him that I have no hard feelings."

"Fabulous. Do it right away."

Wyatt was getting sleepy. Presley could see him rubbing his eyes. Thank goodness. She needed a nap herself. "If you'll watch Wyatt later this afternoon, I'll go over to the studio, thank Aaron for his help and tell him I don't hold anything against him. That should do the trick."

"What if Riley's still there?"

"I'll walk Aaron out."

"Perfect. Of course I'll babysit." Her sister didn't ask why she didn't want to take her son along; she understood that Presley was afraid for Wyatt to be around Aaron. She'd seen Aaron's baby pictures. They both thought Wyatt resembled him at that age. "How much will you have to pay him for painting?"

"Nothing."

"And Riley?"

"He's not charging me, either."

"You're kidding."

"No. Can you believe it? They're working for free."

"Well, not *free*," Cheyenne said. "Riley wants to date you. Which makes me wonder about Aaron. Is it truly forgiveness he's after? Or something that involves less clothes and more skin?"

Presley didn't answer that question. She couldn't even consider it without having her thoughts go places that weakened her resolve. "When will he be leaving town?"

"The date still isn't set."

Too bad. It would be so much simpler if she could mark her calendar, give herself a goal. She was about to say so when Cheyenne changed the subject.

"You know when…when you got pregnant with Wyatt?"

Her son squealed as he found the lever that revealed Big Bird. "What?" Presley said, returning her attention to their conversation.

"The night you got pregnant."

"What night would that be? Aaron and I always

used birth control. So I have no idea exactly when I conceived."

"Whatever night it was…somehow it happened even though you were using a condom?"

Where was she going with *this?* "Yes. Condoms aren't a hundred percent effective, Chey. That can't come as a shock to you. You're not suggesting I *tried* to get pregnant—"

"Of course not!"

Presley had always been afraid she might be accused of trying to trap him, since everyone knew she cared more for Aaron than he did for her. But she'd kept Wyatt's connection to Aaron a secret, so that argument was irrelevant. Still, she didn't want anyone thinking she'd tried to use him to give her a child, either. "Then what are we talking about?"

"Aaron's obviously capable of fathering children."

"Why would anyone assume otherwise?"

"They wouldn't, but you got pregnant, despite trying not to. That suggests he has…you know, strong, competent swimmers."

"You're evaluating the potency of his *sperm?*"

Presley regretted her shocked tone when Cheyenne immediately backpedaled. "No, never mind. Forget it."

She sat up. "Why would you have any interest in Aaron's sperm?"

"Because he has the same genes as Dylan!" her sister replied, exasperated. "Why else?"

"The rest of the Amos brothers would have those genes, too."

"But Aaron would be the most likely to cooperate

with something a little…unorthodox—and the least likely to tell Dylan."

Unorthodox? Presley wasn't sure she liked the sound of that. Switching the phone to her other ear, she stood and began to pace. "You're considering artificial insemination."

"Maybe."

"With *Aaron* as the donor?"

There was a brief silence. Then her sister said, "I'm getting desperate, Pres. What we're going through is affecting our marriage. I *hate* seeing my husband feel so bad about himself."

"How do you know Dylan's sterile? It could be you, couldn't it?"

This pause lasted longer.

"Chey?"

"No," she replied. "It's not me. I've been checked."

Presley sucked in her breath. As often as they talked—and she thought they shared *everything*—Cheyenne hadn't mentioned going to the doctor. "Did Dylan go with you?" She couldn't help wondering how he'd taken the news.

"No. I haven't told him about it. I don't think I ever will."

So she'd made the appointment and driven to Sacramento on her own. Why hadn't she asked Presley to go with her? Cheyenne had always been too damn private about whatever struggles she faced. She opened up only if she had no choice, which told Presley how concerned she was about this issue. "When did you see the doctor?"

"Last month."

"And Dylan?"

"He hasn't been checked, at least not officially."

"There's an unofficial way to do it?"

"There are kits you can buy online."

"Seriously?"

"They have just about everything these days."

"Wow. So he tested himself?"

"*I* tested him—without his knowledge. I didn't *want* him to know…just in case. But now he's talking about going to see his doctor. He mentioned it last night. And that means he'll find out he's infertile even if I don't tell him. I'd rather wind up pregnant, if I can arrange it, so he can feel *he* did it. As if there's nothing wrong with him…"

Cheyenne loved Dyl so much. She'd do anything to protect him, even concoct a daring plan like this. But she wasn't a deceitful person. Keeping Wyatt's true paternity a secret was enough of a burden for her. How would she cope with a much more personal secret?

"Dylan has been through so much, Chey. And he's always managed. He can handle this, too. I think you're selling him short."

"It isn't that at all! The question is why make him handle it? Why can't I be *his* guardian angel for a change? He's brought me so much happiness—I want to return the favor. If Aaron could lend me some sperm, Dylan would never have to cope with feeling inadequate. He won't have to feel indebted, knowing how we got the baby, or jealous or disappointed, either. I mean, God, he deserves a break, right? Who deserves a break more than he does?"

"But using *Aaron* to get pregnant? That's your solution?"

"Why not?"

"For starters, he and Dylan fight like crazy."

"Doesn't matter. Aaron would never tell a soul. I *know* he wouldn't. He loves Dylan as much as I do. He'd do whatever was necessary to ensure Dylan's happiness, especially if he understood what Dylan's going through right now—how emasculating this is for him."

Presley had to agree. Aaron had his issues, but he was loyal to the bone and, whether he'd admit it or not, he admired Dylan more than any other person on earth.

But there were as many reasons to reject Cheyenne's idea as there were to consider it.

"Are you sure it's time to resort to fertility treatments? It's only been a couple of years. Maybe his sperm count will go up."

"That's highly unlikely."

"How do you know?"

"I spoke to my doctor."

"And?"

"She said there's always a chance we could get pregnant, but in our case it would be slight. She suggested we look into alternatives."

"Are there things you can do to increase that chance?"

"We've already done everything we can. We started trying for a baby almost as soon as we were married. The past six months, I've been taking my temperature and tracking ovulation. And I've never been on the pill. I was a virgin until I slept with him, remember? So it's not as if we can blame the delay on the contraceptives we've used. If I was going to conceive in the usual way, it should've happened by now."

"Maybe not—"

"I'm out of time. This is really upsetting Dyl. I want a baby, too, of course. Badly. But he's feeling it was a mistake for me to marry him."

Presley slid Wyatt's toys closer to him with one foot. "I'm sorry about that, but there are so many risks when you're using a known sperm donor." Her mind was racing through them. "I mean, on some level, it makes sense to use Aaron. The baby will be closely related to Dyl and will look like him and all of that, so there's a much better chance he'd never find out."

"And I know Aaron's medical history, know he's healthy. Unless you think the drugs he took in the past—"

"No. He smoked pot now and then, but he didn't do nearly as much crack as I did. He's fine. But what about how Aaron might feel, looking at your child and knowing it's his? Would he be able to handle that?"

"For Dylan's sake? I think so. Aaron's tough. Once he makes up his mind, there's no changing it. He'd never go back on his word."

But he was sensitive, too. That was what so many people didn't understand about him—that his toughness protected a very soft heart. "He might regret it."

"Why would he regret making his brother happy? We'd take excellent care of the child. And he can have other kids if he wants."

Presley had made having a secret Aaron baby look easy. She hadn't even meant to get pregnant, and here she was with Wyatt. No doubt that figured into her sister's thoughts. "It would be a perfect plan if there was some way we could get Aaron's sperm without him knowing," she mused. "Like I did—by accident. But how could we ever do that?"

"We couldn't. He'd have to go to a clinic and bank the sperm, and I'd have to go there afterward."

"Without telling Dylan?"

"Yes, without telling Dylan!"

"Would a clinic do that?"

"Fortunately, we live in the most liberal state in the country when it comes to things like that. I asked an online doctor at one of those expert advice sites. According to her, there's no law that a husband has to give his consent. She also said some clinics might demand it, but that I could find one that won't."

"And if you can't?"

"Aaron has the same last name as my husband."

"You'd have him pose as your *partner?*"

"Why not? I'd just need to go to a clinic or doctor that isn't affiliated with the hospital where I'll be giving birth. Otherwise, the fact that I was artificially inseminated would be noted on my chart, and one of the nurses could let it slip."

"I can see you've put a lot of thought into this. But that brings up another point. What if Dylan found out? If not now, then later? In five or ten years? How would he feel about it?"

When Cheyenne spoke again, her voice was soft, defeated. "What am I doing? You're right. That would be terrible. It won't work."

"And yet you can't help going back to the possibility."

"It would solve *everything*," she said. "Using Aaron's sperm instead of Dylan's seems like such a...a technicality. It wouldn't make any difference to me if I had Aaron's child. Aaron's so much like my husband. I love them both. And Dylan would adore a child. You've seen how he is with Wyatt."

"He'd be a good father." There was no question about that. "But…why not adopt?"

"That comes with as many risks."

"True, but—"

"Anyway, I'm not opposed to it. I could see us adopting at some point. I just need Dylan to believe he gave me *one*."

"To salvage all that male pride?"

"It's the way he is," she said defensively. "And I wouldn't change him even if I could. Pride's one of the things that carried him through the hard times, that gave him the determination he needed to soldier on. It's—"

"You want to do this," Presley broke in, going straight to the bottom line.

"If it'll make Dylan feel better, I do. But I'm scared, too."

Now that she wasn't so shocked by the idea, Presley tried to be more open-minded. In a way, it *did* seem like a technicality that it wouldn't be Dylan's sperm. She'd want to save her husband the humiliation and anguish, too, if she had a husband like Dylan and that husband had a brother like Aaron. "I guess you wouldn't be the first person to use a known donor."

"People do it all the time."

More knowledge gleaned from the internet? "Without the consent of their spouse? I still think that's asking for trouble."

"It's not like I intend to *sleep* with Aaron, Pres. I won't be cheating. Is it really that terrible to use, with the donor's permission, some DNA that's very similar to my husband's? What Dylan doesn't know can't hurt him."

Presley sat on the edge of the couch and massaged her forehead. She'd used almost the same logic. Which led to the same conclusion. "Unless he finds out."

"He won't," Cheyenne argued. "Who's going to tell him? Me? You? Aaron? None of us! It doesn't have to be a big deal unless we make it a big deal."

"If you do this, we'll *both* have children by Aaron." She chuckled, although it wasn't funny.

"Maybe it's time to tell him about Wyatt, since that could figure into his decision."

"No. Absolutely not." Cheyenne wanted to end the anxiety that keeping her secret created. But Presley wasn't ready, wasn't willing to trade a release of anxiety for what could happen if Aaron found out. "Not yet."

"Are you sure?"

"Positive. Wyatt's too little. Maybe when he gets older, when he's capable of making his own choices."

"Okay, but…if I go to Aaron about this…donation, do you think he'll demand we tell Dylan?"

"My bet? He'd rather Dylan *not* know. That way, it can't get awkward between them." The Aaron she knew wouldn't want or need the credit. He was like that. Bighearted, magnanimous and sensitive to the delicate balance that made it possible to continue having a relationship with Dylan. Some people took home stray dogs or cats. Aaron took home stray people. She had a feeling he'd only befriended her initially because she'd been so isolated from the rest of Whiskey Creek. The night he'd sought her out at Sexy Sadie's she'd been sitting in a corner alone. He'd walked over and said something about being her neighbor before inviting her to his table.

"I should talk to him, then?" Cheyenne asked.

"If you're really convinced it'll make things better for Dylan."

"You wouldn't mind if…if I also had a child by Aaron?"

"You felt you had to ask me?"

"Because of Wyatt I thought I should."

"I have no claim on Aaron." Wyatt and her baby would be half brothers instead of cousins, but why would that matter? "Our children can grow up together here in Whiskey Creek."

"It'll be a far nicer childhood than ours was."

"No kidding," Presley agreed with a weak laugh. She especially felt sorry for Cheyenne. She would've had a very different life if Anita hadn't stolen her from her birth family. At least Anita was Presley's real mother. "So when are you going to approach him?"

"I have to do it soon, before Dylan works up the nerve to go to the doctor, or there'll be no point."

Presley tried to picture her sister asking Aaron to donate his sperm. "That should be a very interesting conversation."

6

Riley wasn't there when Presley returned. Presley considered that a lucky break. Although she'd baked two apple pies, one for each of her helpers as a thank-you, it would be a lot easier to talk to Aaron if they had a few minutes alone.

Now she had that. Because she'd walked Wyatt over to Cheyenne's before loading the pies in his stroller, she didn't have the challenge of trying to restrain her son.

This is the perfect opportunity. Aaron's just a regular man.

Except that wasn't true. He meant the world to her....

Reminding herself that that was *before* and not *now,* she summoned her courage, swung open the door and leaned against it so she could wheel the pies inside. Aaron was wearing headphones, listening to music on his iPod while he painted, but her movements must've caught his eye. He turned and pulled the buds from his ears.

"You're back," he said as he climbed off the ladder.

Would he be glad to get the pie? It was the one

thing she used to make for him. But Ruthie at Just Like Mom's served good apple pie, too, so he probably hadn't missed it any more than he'd missed her. "Where's Riley?"

"He went to take care of something with his kid."

The smile he flashed her reminded her that they were alone together on a Saturday night for the first time in twenty-six months. It also made her feel like she was clinging to a rock as the ocean tried to drag her out to sea.

Just hang on...

"Sorry I've been gone all day." It was almost eight o'clock. She'd fallen asleep when Wyatt napped and slept for three hours. Then it'd taken longer to make the pies than she'd expected, since she'd had to scrap her first attempt. She rarely ate sugar these days, was rusty in the kitchen. And once she got the pies out of the oven she was further delayed while deciding what to wear. She'd tried on four different outfits and, for the first time since leaving Whiskey Creek, she even vacillated over her selection of panties, eventually settling on the sheer black bra and thong her friend Roger gave her for her last birthday (while he tried to talk her into "living again").

Wearing lingerie was silly, since no one was going to see it. But what was the point of letting such beauty languish in the back of her drawer? Aaron made her feel sexy and young again— even if she couldn't act on the desire he aroused.

"No problem. I've been busy, anyway." He gestured at the work he'd done. "What do you think?"

She'd been rehearsing what she planned to say, had been so focused on it that she hadn't looked at what he'd accomplished in her absence. But now that he'd drawn her attention to the walls, she was so impressed she couldn't possibly start in on her "I forgive you, you didn't owe me anything" speech. Not immediately.

"It's *beautiful!*" she breathed, and meant it. She'd picked out a buttery yellow, one that reminded her of the sun. She'd wanted her studio to be uplifting and soothing, since both of her businesses dealt with stress relief. But he'd added a new element. The walls were the yellow she'd requested, but he'd painted the trim black—the baseboards, the doorframes and the window casings. It looked so stylish she almost couldn't believe *this* was the same drab space she'd rented.

"I *knew* it would be nice," he said, standing back to survey the effect.

She left the stroller in the middle of the room and moved closer to the wet paint. "Someone told you it wouldn't?"

"Harvey down at the hardware store was pushing me to call you. He thought you should go with white trim, until I showed him the picture."

"What picture?"

"The one I found in a magazine while I was waiting for him to help me."

"What magazine? *Martha Stewart Living?*"

"A Ralph Lauren paint brochure."

She pivoted to face him. "You bought *designer* paint? But…there's no way I gave you enough money for that."

"It came close," he said with a shrug. "I'm not worried about the difference. I wanted it to make a statement, and it does."

"I would've been happy with something much simpler. You're already donating the labor. Why go to the added expense?"

He held her gaze. "It's my way of telling you I'm sorry, Presley."

So she'd guessed right. Apparently, she knew him as well as she thought she did, and since he'd brought up the subject himself, she no longer had to search for a way to approach it. "I don't hold you responsible for anything, Aaron. How could I? You never made me any promises."

"But the last night I saw you…"

"Don't mention that night." She shook her head. "I don't even want to think of it."

His expression grew even more sympathetic. "It was *that* bad?"

The days she'd spent with the man who'd provided her with drugs in Arizona were mostly a blur, and she was grateful for that. She could hardly believe she'd been through the degradation she *did* remember. "It's over. There's no reason to dwell on it."

"I feel like it's my fault."

"Because you didn't love me? You can't make yourself love someone."

Lines formed on his forehead. "It's not as if I didn't *care* about you. And your mother had just died…."

"That was my problem, not yours." But she was lucky she'd survived those first few days after leaving Whiskey Creek, lucky that what she'd done hadn't damaged Wyatt. Only after she'd decided to keep him had she found the will to fight for a better life, to look after herself for his sake. Without him, she might never have changed.

"Maybe if I'd reacted differently, you wouldn't have taken off."

She would've had to do something. "You reacted honestly. That's more important. And you were right. I had no business bothering you in the middle of the night."

He grimaced. "Except that when your world falls apart, you should be able to wake someone you've been…intimate with."

"No. I understood the rules."

"The *rules?*" he repeated.

"How you really felt about me. Moving on had to happen one way or another. How else could our… arrangement have ended?"

"More gently."

He seemed to feel sincere regret, so she smiled in an effort to ease his conscience. "I'm okay," she said. "Stronger than ever."

With a jerk of his head, he indicated all the tools Riley had left behind. "And with *prospects*."

"I've finally arrived," she teased.

"So…are you going to date him?"

"I think so."

"Really."

"Is there some reason I shouldn't?"

He raised his hands. "Of course not. Riley's the best Whiskey Creek has to offer."

She didn't join in his sarcasm; she didn't feel it was fair to Riley, who'd also done a lot to help her today. The reception desk was only partly finished, but she could tell it was going to be far nicer than anything she could've built. "Did he say when he'd be back?"

"Tomorrow. He's bringing Jacob to help him finish up."

"I'll have to put his pie in the fridge, then. Or maybe drop it off at his house—if Cheyenne will let me borrow her car."

"I'd let you take mine, but I don't really care if he gets a pie."

"You don't like Riley? Since when?"

"He's fine," he said, but she couldn't tell if his indifference was real or feigned.

She pulled the stroller closer. "I made you a pie, too. It's not much but...I wanted to thank you for painting."

When she tried to hand it to him, he made no move to accept it. He just stared at her as if he was still hoping to tear off the polite mask she was trying so hard to keep in place. "You used to like my apple pie," she added lamely.

"I liked a lot more about you than your pies, Pres."

Suddenly, she was no longer grateful they were alone. The same privacy that allowed them to talk without being overheard made other things possible, as well. The spike in her pulse suggested several alternatives—all of them physical—and she knew that would only enslave her again.

"That's nice of you to say," she responded.

"Quit being so damned courteous," he snapped. "I'm not just stroking your ego!"

He was getting irritated, and she understood why. He didn't see any reason they couldn't resume the relationship they'd had before. But that was impossible.

Even if she didn't have Wyatt, why would she settle for someone who couldn't love her?

She'd rather spend the rest of her life alone. "I should explain something."

He placed both hands on his lean hips—the very picture of a disgruntled male. "What?"

"I know why you befriended me in the first place. I saw it on your face when you came up to me at Sexy Sadie's. You deserve credit for that."

"Credit for *what?*"

"For reaching out to someone who had no one else. My mother had cancer. Cheyenne was wrapped up in her friends. It was...a dark time for me, and I think you could sense that."

"I didn't view you as some kind of charity case, if that's what you mean."

"I'm not suggesting you weren't honest in your friendship, just that you can't help looking out for the underdog. But rescuing people doesn't give them the right to grab on to you the way I did." She pursed her lips, remembering. "I can see how it could be overwhelming, but you didn't complain. You took my affection in stride and did your best to tolerate all the extra attention. So while you seem to believe you failed me, I'm here to tell you that you shouldn't feel any guilt. No one else even *tried* to include me."

"I've always hated the way you see yourself," he said.

"You mean you hate that I can see the truth." She caught his hand and made him take the pie. "Neither of us has much of an education, Aaron, but we're not stupid. And I probably know you better than anyone. Who else has been more devoted to you?"

"You don't seem so devoted anymore."

If he only knew. She let her gaze linger on his lips. He had the softest lips. "You'll get over it. By tomorrow."

When she added that and laughed, his jaw tightened. "There you go again."

"I'm joking! Take your pie home and enjoy it. And please realize that I'm grateful for the work you did today, even though you didn't owe it to me to begin with. You're under no further obligation. You've already done everything that could be expected of you." She stepped away from him. "Go find another bird with a broken wing to patch up."

"You don't need me anymore."

"I don't need you anymore." But, God, did she want him.

He didn't move. "I don't understand why we can't be friends."

"Because, where you're concerned, there's no middle ground for me. I can't be friends with you, not without wanting to rip off your clothes."

"See? Nothing's really changed." His eyes slid over her, making her supremely conscious of her black lace underwear. It wasn't difficult to figure out why she'd worn them—or why she felt warm when she recognized the heavy-lidded look on his face. She'd seen that look before, knew what it meant.

"Was that so hard to admit?" he asked.

"No, it was entirely too easy. That's the problem. After spending the night together countless times, we're so conditioned to being with each other in that way, it's the first thing we think of when we see each other. But it might be a bit harder to explain to Riley, or anyone else who wants to legitimately date me, why I'm still having sex with you."

"He's not your boyfriend."

"So?"

"So I don't believe what we do should be anyone's business but our own."

Once again Presley could feel the pull of that powerful and tenacious ocean of need. But she couldn't allow herself to be ripped away from the rock of safety "no" provided. "Just walk away while you can do it with a clear conscience, okay? Now's your chance," she said, but she knew he wasn't going to when he set her pie aside, slipped his arms around her and brought her against him.

She didn't resist but neither did she respond when he lowered his head and pressed his lips to hers.

"It's been a long time," he whispered.

All the bones in Presley's body felt as if they'd dissolved on contact. But she refused to lose this battle; she wanted to be tough, defiant, unmoved. "I'm not interested."

The warmth of his breath fanned her face as his lips moved over hers again. "You're interested, all right."

Her body tingled as the memories returned— Aaron naked above her, Aaron suckling her breast, Aaron hooking his arms under her knees as he drove inside her. "How can you tell?" she asked, but she shouldn't have spoken. The quaver in her voice only confirmed his words.

He buried his nose in her neck and took a deep breath. Then he put his mouth on the tender skin there, but she stopped him before he could leave a mark. "I can taste it on you," he said. "I can even smell it."

She swallowed hard. "So? I can tell you want me, too." The truth was apparent; she could feel his arousal against her abdomen.

"I'm not the one trying to deny it."

Her mouth watered for a deeper kiss so she could obtain *some* satisfaction. But he kept his mouth a fraction of an inch away and didn't move his hands to any of the places that were throbbing in anticipation.

"We had fun," he said. "There's no reason it couldn't be like that again."

She squeezed her eyes shut. "No."

"Fine." A second later, he let go of her and recovered his pie.

"You're just going to walk away?" she asked.

A devilish grin slanted his lips to one side. "You had your chance. If you change your mind, you know where to find me."

Presley stayed where she was, gripping what had been built of the receptionist's desk as his steps receded. Not until he was gone did she remember her conversation with Cheyenne. Her sister was going to ask him to donate sperm so she could have a baby. Presley had planned to prepare him, to give him some advance warning so he could think about how he wanted to respond. It wouldn't be an easy decision. While she wanted her sister to have a baby, she also wanted Aaron to be sure he was willing to play a role.

She'd gotten too distracted to mention it, but she wasn't about to go after him. Not right now. Although she'd survived their encounter, her confidence was badly shaken. If he hadn't stopped touching her, if he'd slid his hand up her shirt instead of letting go, would she have been able to deny him?

Chances were, she would've dragged him into the back room and showed off her sexy underwear. She knew how much he liked lace panties—and she knew she'd never looked better in them, which certainly wasn't helping. She felt she finally had the kind of body he could admire, so vanity was working against her, too. That was the downside to the improvements she'd made. While they boosted her self-esteem, they didn't do a lot for her resistance.

"You have no willpower," she muttered. "Not when it comes to Aaron."

She needed to stay away from him in the future— and pray he left for Reno soon.

Damn it! What the hell was he doing? He'd received Presley's forgiveness, knew she didn't hold anything against him. He had her pie in his passenger seat to prove it. So why had he stirred up those dying embers? Why couldn't he leave well enough alone?

Because he'd missed her. And he still wanted her. Although he'd slept with several women since her, none of them had brought him the same level of fun, comfort or satisfaction.

But why would he do anything to threaten her chance of catching a great guy like Riley—someone who, if he married her, would treat her like a queen?

What she'd said was true. That night when he first approached her at Sexy Sadie's, he'd simply been trying to include a lonely woman, someone he'd seen around town for several years but who'd never quite fit in. Thanks to her mother, she was so battle-scarred that she made most people uncomfortable. But he could relate to someone who elicited distrust and hesitation. He had his own detractors, and there'd been a time when his circumstances weren't a whole lot better.

She didn't need him anymore, though; she'd said as much. He should be *glad* she was doing so well on her own. Instead, he was screwing with her head because she was screwing with *his* and she wasn't even trying. She was giving him what he'd always assumed he wanted—for her to be happy and strong and less needy, less clingy. There'd been times when he'd thought he'd suffocate beneath her adoration. So why did he suddenly feel bereft now that she'd decided she was done with him?

She'd gone too far. Did she have to cut him off completely? He could understand if she had someone else in her life, but she didn't.

"It's confusing," he told himself. Somehow it had been easier to move on when she wasn't around, easier to make himself believe he wasn't missing out on anything. Seeing her again, especially seeing her looking so healthy, reminded him of the details that made her unique, all the little things he'd pushed into the back of his mind. Her laugh. Her quirky sense of humor. The way she could roll with the ups and downs of life without growing bitter. Even some of her insecurities were endearing because she was so damn honest about them. He'd spent more time with her than any other woman....

He turned up the radio, hoping the pounding of his subwoofer would soothe his restlessness, or at least distract him. He didn't like the way he was feeling. He wasn't accustomed to jealousy, but he was pretty sure that was the emotion picturing her with Riley evoked.

Are you going to date him?

I think so.

Why wouldn't she? Riley was universally admired. After college, he'd started his own contracting business, which was successful, *of course*. He'd never been picked up by the police, never gotten into a fight, never been thrown out of a bar. He'd messed up by getting a girl pregnant back in high school—not the best girl to put in such a vulnerable position, as it turned out—but he'd redeemed himself by raising the child and proving to be a devoted father.

"Forget Presley," Aaron grumbled. "You won't be living here much longer, anyway."

But it was impossible to forget her when he could smell the pie she'd baked. So instead of going home, he drove to Jackson and went to a drive-through to get a plastic fork. Then he pulled over and dug into the pie. He was determined to eat as much of it as he wanted before his brothers got hold of it. After all, he was the one who'd spent his entire day painting, and he'd done a damn fine job, too. He deserved some of the most delicious pie he'd ever tasted, since he wasn't going to get what he *really* wanted from Presley....

He was jamming another bite into his mouth when his cell phone vibrated against his leg. He thought it might be one of his brothers, or maybe one of his friends wanting to head out for a drink. It was Saturday night, after all. He wasn't in the mood for the usual weekend revelry, but what good was it going to do him to sit around by himself?

Straightening his leg so he could get his phone

out of his pocket, he checked caller ID. The number wasn't in his contacts.

"'Lo?"

"Aaron?"

Noelle. Recognizing her voice, he turned down the radio. Music blared in the background as it was. Where was she? Sexy Sadie's? "Yeah?"

"What are you doing?"

He swallowed what he had in his mouth. "Eating."

"You could do that here with me. I've got a plate of wings, and a seat with your name on it."

He didn't ask where "here" was. "How'd you get my number?" Sometimes they hooked up if they bumped into each other, but those occasions were few and far between, and he'd been careful not to let the relationship become more than that.

"Your brothers are at the club having a drink."

Damn it! They knew better than to give out his number. He guessed whichever brother she'd gotten it from was drunk—or wanted her to leave him the hell alone.

"You should come join us," she said.

He tapped his leg. "I'm not in the mood."

"You're not in the mood to see *me?*"

If only he could go back and talk to Presley, convince her to let him touch her again. That was what had him so worked up—what he really wanted. But he refused to be the kind of jerk who'd push for that if she didn't want it, too. "I'm busy."

"Eating?"

He didn't answer.

"I have some more modeling pics to show you," Noelle added with a suggestive giggle.

He hadn't been particularly impressed with the last set. She was getting too carried away with surgeries and Botox and liposuction. Although she put every dime she made into improving her appearance—and charged the rest—in his opinion she'd actually looked prettier before. That was partly what he liked about Presley. She was so natural. She looked as good without makeup as she did with it. "Not tonight. I'm tired."

"Come on! You can't be *that* tired. I'll make it worth your while...."

She wanted a man in her bed. And because he'd been crazy or drunk or stupid enough to accommodate her a few times, she was coming back for more.

Setting the pie aside, he leaned back. "You said my brothers are there?"

"All of them except you—and the one who doesn't like me."

She meant Dylan. But there weren't many people who did like her, including her own family. Getting pregnant by her sister's boyfriend, and using that pregnancy to wrangle a wedding proposal, had sealed her fate. Aaron prided himself on being more forgiving than most. He kept telling himself that whatever she'd done in the past was *her* business. But he had yet to find anything redeeming about her. "Dylan's taken, anyway. Maybe Grady would like to see your pictures."

"You don't care if I show them to him?"

Her affronted tone made him nervous. The first time she asked to come home with him, he'd warned her that he wasn't interested in a relationship. He'd reminded her since. The fact that he wouldn't give her his cell phone number should've made that abundantly clear. But Noelle couldn't stop herself from pushing too hard for whatever she wanted. "Noelle, we've been over this."

"Never mind," she snapped, and ended the call.

With a sigh, Aaron put his phone on the console, closed the plastic container that held Presley's pie and started his truck. At this point, he knew for sure that he didn't want to go to Sexy Sadie's.

When his phone buzzed, indicating an incoming text, he almost ignored it. He suspected it was Noelle sending him the equivalent of a rude hand gesture. But he couldn't keep himself from glancing at the screen.

Noelle hadn't texted him; Cheyenne had.

Putting the transmission back in park, he picked up his phone.

Is there any chance you could get away sometime tomorrow to meet me in Sutter Creek? I need to talk to you in private. Please don't mention this to Dylan or anyone else.

His sister-in-law was probably trying to act as mediator. Even after two years of dealing with him and Dylan, she didn't realize that their arguments never lasted long. He'd see Dylan at the shop on Monday, and they'd go on as if nothing had happened. But Cheyenne loved her husband so much, she had to try and make them talk it out every time they had a disagreement.

You don't need to get involved, he wrote back. Dyl and I are fine.

This isn't about Friday.

Then what's it about?

I have a favor to ask.

Of me?

What could that be? Dylan provided everything she could possibly want. Dylan would walk through fire for her.

I'd rather not put it in writing.

I won't apologize to Dylan. I didn't do anything.

I'm not asking you to apologize.

Then what on earth could it be?

Can you come see me now?

No. Dylan's home. I can't get away until tomorrow afternoon. I'll tell him I have to help Presley and meet you at JB's Steakhouse in Sutter Creek, if you're willing.

This was turning into quite a mystery. His sister-in-law had never approached him in such a clandestine manner.

Another thought occurred to him.

Does this have anything to do with Presley?

Absolutely nothing.

I won't talk to you about her.

He was adamant that she and Dylan mind their own business.

I promise.

Why are you being so secretive?

You'll understand once I've had the chance to explain. I'm nervous about this. I'm only doing it because I trust you. Next to Dylan and Presley, I trust you most in the world.

Now she was making *him* nervous. What could it be?

He came up with a few alternatives, but didn't like any of them. Especially the ones that had to do with catastrophic illnesses. Did she have cancer?

Maybe she'd received bad news from her doctor and couldn't tell Dylan....

What time? he texted.

Dylan's planning to work on the deck he's building in back. He should be well into it by three. Will that work?

That's fine. Meet you at JB's.

I'll text you if anything changes.

Sounds good.

Thanks, Aaron. I really appreciate it.

He had to try to clarify one last time.

And this has nothing to do with Presley? You're not going to warn me off?

Didn't Dylan already do that?

He tried.

This has nothing to do with her. But let me point out that you don't really want Pres, or we wouldn't say a word.

He sat staring at her last line for probably fifteen minutes. How did she know that when even *he* wasn't sure?

7

JB's was a traditional steakhouse with branding implements on the wood-plank walls and a bar along the right side. The interior was darker than the average restaurant, particularly in contrast to such a bright, sunny afternoon, and the candles sitting on the tables did little to offset that.

Aaron stood at the entrance for a second so his eyes could adjust. Then he spotted Cheyenne in a corner booth, looking like she was about to step in front of a firing squad. Her agitation heightened his own anxiety as the hostess hurried over from where she'd been rolling silverware into napkins. This was between meals—not a busy time of day, even on a Sunday.

"Would you like a table?" she asked.

He pointed at Cheyenne. "My party's been seated."

She waved him past her. "She said she was expecting someone. I left a menu for you."

With a quick thanks, he strode across the restaurant and took the seat opposite Cheyenne, who offered him a fleeting smile. "Thanks for coming."

"No problem," he said.

She slid his menu toward him. "Would you like to order first?"

He preferred to find out what the hell was going on, but to prevent the waitress from interrupting, he scanned the menu, decided on the porterhouse and closed it. "This is all very secretive."

Color suffused her cheeks. "I'm sorry, but it's something that has to be handled in person."

"We couldn't have met in Whiskey Creek?"

"I was afraid someone would see us together."

"And do or say…what?"

"I just didn't see any reason to raise eyebrows."

He put his napkin in his lap and arranged his silverware. "We're related now. I'm not sure anyone would find it strange for us to share a meal."

She didn't have a chance to respond. The waitress came to ask what they'd like to drink. Although Cheyenne seemed too agitated to care about such mundane details, she ordered an iced tea. He wasn't really interested in eating *or* drinking—not while he was this curious—so he decided to stick with water.

"I'll give you a few more minutes," the waitress said, but neither one of them needed the time. Aaron opened his mouth to say they'd go ahead and order, but she was already walking away, and since Cheyenne didn't call her back, he figured his sister-in-law wasn't in any hurry to reveal whatever it was. Maybe she needed time to work up the nerve. The way she kept fidgeting with her purse strap told him it wouldn't be easy for her.

"If you're thinking you're going to say or do something that will piss me off, don't worry," he said. "I'd never even raise my voice to you."

This was rewarded with a sweet smile. "That's partly why you're here."

So her nervousness didn't stem from fear....

"You can tell me anything," he said. "As long as it doesn't call into question the loyalty I feel toward my brother."

She nodded. "I appreciate that. I love Dylan, too, so I would never pit you against him—unless I thought it was for his own good."

That sounded ominous. He studied her as she folded her arms, crossed her legs, repositioned her purse, took a drink of water and glanced repeatedly at the big-screen TV in one corner. A baseball game was on, so she couldn't be *too* interested. She didn't care about sports. But until the waitress returned, she acted as if that game was the most fascinating thing she'd ever seen.

Once they'd placed their order, Aaron scooted his chair back so he could stretch out his legs. "Okay," he said, "let's have it."

She bit her lip, apparently searching for the right words until he leaned forward and prompted her again. "What is it, Chey?"

"I want a baby."

The words came out so softly he wasn't sure he'd heard correctly. Or maybe he didn't see how this could possibly relate to him. "Excuse me?"

Her chest rose as if she'd just drawn a deep breath "I want a baby," she said, louder.

"Okay." Was this a joke? He looked around to see if he was being punked by his brothers but there was no sign of them. "So…why don't you and Dylan have one?"

"We've been trying."

Dylan hadn't said a word one way or the other. But neither had Aaron asked. He assumed they'd start a family when they were ready. "Are you trying to tell me you're pregnant?"

"No, I'm trying to tell you I'm *not* pregnant. Even though we've done everything we can."

How was he supposed to respond? He was fairly certain she'd just divulged information Dylan would rather he not have. He finally settled on, "Sometimes these things take time."

"It's been two *years*."

"You're not…"

"I'm fine. It's not me."

The way she said that tipped him off. "You're saying Dylan…"

"May need some help."

Aaron lifted his hands as if she held a gun. "There's not much I can do to help there."

She clasped her hands together. "Actually, there is. It's a difficult request for me to make, but…who else can I turn to?"

Other than *him?* "Go on."

"I'm considering—" she cleared her throat as she met his gaze "—I'm considering artificial insemination."

At last he understood. "And you want *me* to be the donor?"

"This is so awkward. I'm sorry I have to ask, but—"

"Why isn't Dylan here with you?" he broke in. "Shouldn't he have handled this?"

"He can't."

"Why? Because he has to build the damn deck in your backyard?"

Her voice dropped again. "Because he doesn't know I'm asking."

Aaron stiffened. *"You haven't made sure he wants to do this?"*

She sent him a look that pleaded with him to understand. Then she said, "I want him to believe the baby is his."

"Holy shit!" He stood up, turned around as though he'd walk out, then realized he couldn't leave her sitting there alone and fell into his chair again.

"This is killing him, Aaron," she said. "I want a baby so badly. And he wants me to have one. *His* baby. He feels he needs to do that for me."

"He wants you to have *everything* you want."

"Because he takes pride in how well he cares for the people he loves."

"There's a lot doctors can do these days."

"I know that, but according to a test I secretly ran, he's basically sterile. And if he finds that out, he'll feel he's let me down."

"A test *you* ran? How can you rely on that? You have to explore every option—"

"And let it destroy his self-esteem and damage our marriage in the process? Why? The test was legitimate. There's very little chance he could ever father a child."

"But if he knows it's not you…"

"He doesn't. I went to see the doctor on my own and didn't tell him."

"So…what? You want to get pregnant and let him

believe the child is his?" He was saying this in shock and incredulity, but she nodded.

"Yes. That's exactly what I want."

The waitress approached with their food. Aaron warned Cheyenne with a glance that she was coming, and they fell silent until they could speak without being overheard.

"Am I asking too much?" she whispered when the waitress walked away.

He couldn't resist the entreaty in her voice. She was Dylan's greatest blessing, the one thing he'd never had to use for the benefit of his siblings. As conflicted as Aaron sometimes felt toward his older brother, he couldn't bear the thought of how greatly Dylan would suffer if anything came between him and the woman he loved.

But Aaron wasn't sure he could go behind Dylan's back. What would Dylan say or do if he ever found out about *this?* And what would it be like to have a *child,* a child who didn't know his true father?

"You're hoping I'll help you have a baby but never say a word about it."

"To *anyone.* Yes." She didn't attempt to disguise any aspect of her plan. "You'd sign away your parental rights, be the baby's uncle, nothing more."

So he'd have contact. He could have a lot of contact. But would that make it harder—or easier?

"I'm not sure," he said. "I want to say yes, but... I'm afraid this would just give Dyl and me something else to compete over."

"Which is one of the primary reasons I think this should be done secretly. That way there'll be far less chance it would affect your relationship. He won't have to feel indebted, and you won't ever have to feel that he's being ungrateful, because you'll know he has no clue of the sacrifice you made," she said. "You'd have to do it because you love him, and you'd have to relinquish all claim and forgo all credit."

Aaron let his breath seep out as he ran a hand over his chin. "Is there a clinic around here or…"

"There are probably several. My doctor even suggested one. I just haven't contacted anyone yet because I needed to know you were on board before I moved forward."

"How would it work?"

She gestured at his food. "You should start on your steak. It's getting cold."

He'd lost what little appetite he'd had when he walked in but made a halfhearted attempt to cut off a few pieces and chew, which was more than he could say for her. She merely pushed her salad around with a fork.

"It must feel really strange to think of making a baby with me," she said, "but…if you could just look at it through my eyes. I love you as my brother-in-law, so I'd be happy to know my child came from you. Of all the Amos boys, you look the most like my husband. And, sure, he could weather this the way he's weathered all the other difficulties in his life, but why put him through that when we can so easily get around the need for it? I want Dylan to be happy. He hasn't been himself lately."

Aaron struggled to swallow the piece of steak in his mouth. "You think this is why?"

"I know it is."

Dylan *had* been uncharacteristically irritable and preoccupied. But…

"I need some time to consider it," he said.

She took a sip of her iced tea, but her manner told him she was stalling while she decided how to spring something else on him.

"Is that a problem?" he asked when she put down her glass.

"That's just it."

"What is?"

"Time. There isn't much of it. Dylan is talking about going to the doctor. And if he does…"

"He'll learn the truth."

He managed to chase his steak with a bite of his baked potato. "Maybe that's for the best, Chey. I mean…I'd be open to this if…if the two of you wanted to meet with me later. It's not that I begrudge you the… What you need to make it happen." Or… he didn't think so. He hadn't quite wrapped his mind around that part of it, either. But he forged ahead. "I'm mostly worried about keeping this a secret."

"You're not convinced it would work better that way? Since your relationship with Dylan is so…complicated? You know how humbling it would be for *him* to have to ask, and how indebted he'd feel afterward."

It was a legitimate concern. "How soon would you need my answer?"

"You guys are so busy at work that I could probably give you a few days. He wouldn't even be able to book an appointment before then. But the process will take several weeks to complete—to schedule with the clinic, to have the procedure done and see if it takes. If it doesn't, we'd have to go through the entire process again."

"Would we go in at the same time?"

"No. From what I've read online it could be completely separate."

"But…shouldn't someone be with you?"

"Presley will go."

He was glad. It was weird enough that he'd be donating the sperm. He didn't want to take his brother's place at Cheyenne's side, as well. "You and Pres talked about this?"

"I called her yesterday."

He cut off another piece of his meat before looking up. "Did she encourage you to ask me?"

"Not really."

"She doesn't think it's a good idea?"

"She's worried about how it might affect you."

Unable to keep eating, he reached for his water glass, wiping off the condensation. "Even though she no longer wants to associate with me?"

His sister-in-law squeezed his wrist. "That's nothing personal, Aaron."

"It's *very* personal," he said, "and we both know it."

Giving up on her salad, she shoved her plate away. "She had the worst time getting over you."

"From what I've seen, she's managed quite nicely. I haven't heard from her once since she left."

"I'm sure it wasn't easy not to contact you. You're a hard act to follow."

"But you think Riley can manage it."

She clasped her hands together. "Riley's looking for a wife. You're not."

He wasn't opposed to getting married. He was at an age where he *should* settle down. He just hadn't met the right woman. A guy needed to be in love to make that kind of commitment, but there were times when he wondered if his heart was even whole enough to give away. Maybe Dylan was capable of such complete devotion, but Aaron feared that part of him had been destroyed in the turbulence of his childhood.

Or he'd been defective from the beginning.

Taking out his wallet, he tossed sixty bucks on the table and stood. "I'll call you when I decide."

"Aaron?"

He glanced back.

"It's a difficult decision to make. I won't hold it against you if you say no."

With a nod, he walked out of the restaurant.

8

It was Sunday night. Somehow she'd come through the weekend unscathed. Presley could hardly believe it. After running into Aaron at Ted's book signing, then having him at the studio yesterday, he'd been on her mind so much she wasn't sure she'd make it to Monday without breaking down and calling him. She'd never dreamed it was possible to crave another person so much. Every minute had been a battle—but she'd remained strong. She could breathe a sigh of relief and pat herself on the back.

"It should get easier," she muttered even though she was alone. Earlier, Chey had called to tell her about meeting Aaron in Sutter Creek, so he was, no doubt, preoccupied with that. If luck was on her side, the artificial insemination would keep him preoccupied until he moved away.

Fortunately, she had other things to concentrate on, too. She'd spent the morning—until Wyatt's nap—with Riley and his son, helping build the reception area. After they'd finished, Riley and Jacob stopped by her house. While she was grateful for all their assistance, being with Riley just wasn't as…magical as being with Aaron.

But their friendship was new. She couldn't expect fireworks from the beginning, not even with an attractive, exceptional guy like Riley. The important thing was that she'd enjoyed herself. They'd laughed and talked while Jacob played with Wyatt, and Riley had flattered her by making a big fuss about the pie she'd baked for him.

Presley could see herself in a relationship with Riley, couldn't she? Why not? This time she was determined to choose someone who would be a responsible father instead of a man who was as broken as she was. Riley had asked her to join him for dinner on Friday, and she'd agreed. So she was at least going to give him a chance.

She rocked Wyatt to sleep—she loved having a few minutes of quiet time with her baby at night—then changed into a T-shirt and a pair of sweat shorts before curling up on the couch with a blanket and Ted's new book. *Hot and Heavy* promised to be his best work yet. But she'd read barely sixty pages when someone banged on the door.

Surprised, she glanced at the clock Riley had helped her hang: ten-thirty. Who would be coming by so late?

Carefully putting down her book, she crossed to the door and peered through the peephole.

The sight of Aaron on her porch in a pair of faded jeans and an Amos Auto Body T-shirt hit her like a defibrillator. Aaron! Why was he here?

She waited, hoping he'd leave if she didn't answer. She wasn't dressed for company. But he'd seen her like this before, many times, and when he knocked again, she couldn't continue to ignore him, especially when he said, "Pres, I know you're in there."

Cracking the door a few inches, she blocked the opening. "What's going on?"

His hazel eyes ran over her, making her even more conscious of the fact that she wasn't wearing a bra. He didn't smile but something about his expression told her he'd noticed. It probably reminded him how familiar they'd once been with each other.

"Can we talk?" he asked.

His smile made her breath catch. At one time, she'd lived for that smile. "It's late, and Wyatt's asleep."

"I'll be quiet."

When she didn't move, he raised his eyebrows, and she felt herself weaken even further. *Damn it*. He held some power over her. "Fine, come in," she grumbled, and stepped aside.

"Why are you here?" she asked as she closed the door.

He walked around the room, examining her things while she leaned against the wall.

"Aaron?"

"You've gone to a lot of work."

"The place was filthy, like you said." Even now it wasn't what she'd call *nice*. The house she'd rented in Fresno had been better, despite the surrounding neighborhood, but she'd had a roommate there to share the costs. This was clean and safe. Considering her other challenges, that was all she could ask for until she started making some money. "I'll upgrade when I can."

He gestured at the books stacked in one corner. "These yours?"

"They are."

"Since when did you become a reader?"

Since she'd given up everything else. "In Fresno."

"That's kind of a solitary activity, isn't it?"

When he'd known her before, she'd hardly ever picked up a book. Back then she'd thought life was all about partying with her friends, but once she turned her back on that lifestyle, books had provided her only solace, her only company—at times, her only hope. "It's good entertainment, and it's free—if you use the library."

He sorted through a few of the titles. "Thrillers?"

"Mostly." She couldn't read romance, not without fantasizing about him. When she'd assumed she'd never move back to Whiskey Creek, she would occasionally permit herself to remember and imagine. But she knew better than to indulge in that sort of behavior now that circumstances had changed—and the object of her obsession was so close at hand.

"Did you want to sit down?" she asked.

"If I'm allowed."

She ignored his jab at her unfriendliness, and indicated the couch. "What can I do for you?"

He threw her a look that said he didn't like her brusque tone. "Can't we just be…normal with each other? Is that too much to ask?"

She sat in her orange chair. It was comfortable, but that was the best she could say about it. "What's your interpretation of 'normal'?"

"We were friends, weren't we?"

"Maybe you've forgotten, because it was so meaningless and unremarkable to you, but we were more like friends with benefits."

"Ouch!"

"The truth hurts. I was pretty much available whenever you wanted to make a booty call."

"You made your own share of booty calls," he retorted.

That was true. She'd shown up at his place whenever she thought she might get lucky enough to catch him in the mood, which wasn't always a certainty with Aaron. "I haven't forgotten."

"Why do you keep focusing on the physical? I don't remember what we had the same way you do—I don't see our…relationship as a bad thing. But even if I'm as lecherous as you think, I haven't asked you to sleep with me since you've been back, so…where's the problem?"

"That's not what you want? That's not why you're here?" she asked pointblank.

He shifted on the couch and shrugged. "I'm not saying I wouldn't like it. But I can take no for an answer. I'll gladly pass on sex, if that's what it takes to maintain the friendship."

"Then *that's* why you're here? For the sake of our friendship?"

"I've missed you.

The fact that he spoke those words grudgingly heightened their impact instead of lessening it. Maybe she'd been handling this wrong. If she couldn't get him out of her life until she agreed to be his friend, she'd agree to be his friend. Then he'd have nothing left to fight for, especially if he was telling the truth about his willingness to accept less than they'd had before.

"Fine. We'll be friends."

He narrowed his eyes. "That was too glib to be sincere."

She toyed with a lock of her hair. "And you're *more* sincere? You missed me so much that you never tried to contact me!"

"Whoa, I asked Cheyenne for your number several times."

"If you'd really wanted to see me, you would've figured out a way, Aaron. Fresno's only a two-hour drive."

"I *should've* made more effort," he admitted. "But you could've contacted me, too. What happened there?"

"You know what happened there. I was starting over. So now I've done that, I don't understand why we're having this conversation. Is it because I've lost some weight? All of a sudden you think you're missing out?"

He grimaced. "Considering how much you used to care, you don't have a very high opinion of me."

She was as aware of his strengths as his weaknesses; she just couldn't focus on them. "You're a great guy in a lot of ways, Aaron. No one's more loyal or generous or kind to the unfortunate. But…"

"Here we go," he muttered.

"I have a kid now. I have to take life seriously, have to protect myself from the type of man who wouldn't be good for my son."

"And that's *me?*"

She'd had a few friends at the casino where she'd

worked as a dealer, but those friends had lived outside of Whiskey Creek. He'd been her only regular companion here, so she could understand his surprise. "Are you interested in marriage? In starting a family?"

"Is that the new stipulation?"

"Yes."

He seemed tempted to continue their argument, but he must've decided to let it go because he changed the subject. "I met with Cheyenne today."

Presley wondered if she'd been too defensive. Maybe he'd come to talk about the artificial insemination. It wasn't as if he could discuss it with just anyone. And that made her feel a little silly for possibly assuming too much. "She mentioned that to me," she said, backing off. "How do you feel about what she proposed?"

"I'm not sure. On the one hand, I can't see any reason I shouldn't help her out."

"And on the other?"

He scratched his head. "Don't you think it's a big deal that Dylan won't know?"

She hugged her knees because it gave her something to do with her hands and hid her chest from his view at the same time. "Wouldn't you *rather* he not know?"

"To be honest, yes. Except I hate feeling as if… as if we're going behind his back. He's my brother. Loyalty makes that hard."

She studied his troubled face. "Even if you're giving him exactly what he wants?"

"*I* would hate to find out in ten years that the son I've been raising, the son I thought was mine, actually belongs to him. I'm not convinced he'd call that 'helping.'"

The fact that the element of secrecy was such a stumbling block for him made the guilt Presley felt for harboring her own secret flare up. She'd been hard on him tonight, but she wasn't blameless. "Why would he ever need to find out? As long as he's happily unaware, everything will be fine."

She hoped the same rationale held true for Aaron. She'd certainly tried to convince herself of that—many times.

"You can never rely on a secret remaining a secret," he said. "For all we know, he and Cheyenne will divorce someday. If they end up in a custody battle, one that Cheyenne's afraid of losing, what would stop her from tossing the child's true paternity in Dylan's face?"

"That's pretty jaded, Aaron."

"I have to consider the possibility, decide if I'm prepared to face the worst."

"Cheyenne would never throw you under the bus. Besides, they love each other so much I can't believe they won't make it."

"You can't take anything for granted," he insisted. "You, of all people, know that life is uncertain. Even if they don't split up, what if the kid needs a bone marrow transplant? What if they test Dylan to see if he's a match and the truth comes out? Or Cheyenne needs to get me involved?"

"That wouldn't be good."

"Exactly." He stared at his hands, his expression pensive. "And if Dylan ever did discover the truth, he'd never forgive me, even if I did it because I was trying to help. There's too much rivalry between us, too much competition. There always has been."

"You're a lot alike," she agreed. "But that's why Cheyenne picked you. She wants a baby as close to what she'd get from Dylan as possible."

"Grady, Rod and Mack have similar genes."

"But they'd never dare to do it, not without telling Dyl."

"So *I* should step up?"

"I'd love for Cheyenne and Dylan to get what they want. But…I can't say yes, not when it might be difficult for you to live with that decision."

His expression suddenly cleared. "What the hell," he said. "How bad can it get? I should just do it."

"Only if you're sure you'll be okay with the results. Will it bother you to see the baby and know he or she is yours?" And what would Aaron do if he found out that Cheyenne's wasn't his only child? She felt terrible that he'd come to *her* to help him make this decision. She was the last person he should trust.

"How can I even guess?" he replied. "This isn't a scenario I've ever imagined."

"You need to be sure. Genetic material isn't something you'll be able to take back."

He sighed as his gaze moved restlessly around her living room. "It's tough."

"It *is* tough." She was in a real dilemma herself. She wanted to tell him about Wyatt; she just didn't dare. So when he settled on a picture of her son, she grew nervous again.

"Your little boy's really cute. I saw him at Dylan's on Friday."

"Thanks. My apartment was nicer in Fresno, by

the way," she volunteered, hoping to divert his attention before he could see the resemblance she saw whenever she looked into Wyatt's face.

"This place is adequate."

"What with starting the studio, I thought I should be conservative."

He nodded at her massage table, which was folded up in the corner. "That's got to be the deluxe version."

"It is." It had been expensive for someone at her income level, but she needed it and Cheyenne and Dylan had pitched in with some cash as part of her Christmas present.

"Are you any good?"

"At massage?" Her eyes met his. "*I* think so."

"Why don't you show me?"

She heard the challenge in those words. "Right now?"

"Why not? Doesn't have to be a full-blown deal. I'll even pay you for it."

Hadn't she just congratulated herself on keeping her distance from Aaron? "Not tonight."

"Too tired?"

Not anymore. She was too scared. But what could it hurt? He'd done all that painting for her, and refusing would make a big deal out of something that shouldn't be. She was in the massage business, after all.

"I guess I could." She got off the couch to set up the table. When he came over to help, she let him finish. "I'll be right back. I have to get the table cover, a sheet, my heating pad and some cream."

Once she entered her bedroom, she stood against the door, willing herself to return and send him home.

But the idea of getting his clothes off and running her hands over his body, just one more time, drove her like a cattle prod. Maybe this would be a safe way to get her "Aaron fix."

It wouldn't go anywhere, she promised herself, and put on a bra and one of her work smocks to prove it was strictly professional.

"You're serious about this," he said when she returned and he saw that she'd changed.

"Absolutely. It's my job." But never before had she approached a massage with her heart pounding so hard she thought it might crack a rib. She lit several lavender-scented candles. Then she turned off the lamp she'd been reading by and put on some soft Celtic music. She would've done the same for any client. Massage was about peace and quiet and relaxation. But tonight everything she did felt so…sensual. Maybe because she'd dreamed of doing this for him half a million times.

After she'd covered the table, she draped the sheet across the bottom half and stood with her back to him. "Undress and climb under the sheet, faceup. Let me know when you're ready."

"Face*up?*" he echoed.

"I'll start with your scalp. I need to give my cream a chance to get warm."

She could hear his clothes rustle as he removed them, heard them drop,

"I'm all set," he said a couple of minutes later.

She walked closer, but what was transmitted between them when their eyes met again should've warned her off. The air crackled with energy, but she was too invested, too eager to get her hands on him, to change course.

As soon as he's facedown it won't feel as risky. She'd massaged so many people since entering school. This was no different, she told herself.

He closed his eyes as she slipped her fingers through his hair. She felt less self-conscious now that he was no longer looking at her, no longer reading every nuance of her expression. But when she started to massage his scalp and he groaned, showing her how much he was enjoying it, the uneasiness she'd been feeling returned. Almost at first touch, she'd become aroused and hyperaware of every detail—the lavender scent of the candles, their flickering light, his bare chest rising and falling beneath the sheet. He must've had a similar reaction, because she soon noticed something else—the sheet lower down was tented.

His eyes no longer closed, he was watching her carefully, knew where she was looking and, possibly, what she was feeling. "Force of habit," he said with a boyish grin.

"It happens sometimes." She shifted her gaze to his chest—which seemed far safer than anything above or below it.

"You mean with other guys you've worked on?"

"Sometimes. You can roll over." She'd reached the ten-minute mark. She had her massages down to a routine, knowing precisely how long to focus on each area. Her cream would be the perfect temperature by now. But as often as she'd done this before, she'd never given a massage during which it was so difficult to breathe.

"They taught you well at that school," he said as she smoothed the cream over his back and began to knead his shoulders. "But you were always good at this sort of thing."

That reminder didn't help. They'd traded massages before. Many times. She'd just never enjoyed being on the *giving* end quite this much. It'd been so long since she'd been with him. So long since she'd been with *anyone*. Although she'd had a few relationships while she was in Fresno, they'd been flecting. None of those men had been a good enough father for Wyatt, so she'd never let her clothes come off.

Channeling her emotions through her hands, since she couldn't express them any other way, she focused on the music. She was making love to Aaron without actually making love to him, and it was such a relief. Somehow she'd managed to cross the desert of the past two years and come out successfully on the other side.

But the relief didn't last. Soon the tension began to build instead of dissipate. The feel of him was so familiar that massaging him wasn't enough. As she worked the thicker muscles along his spine down to his narrow hips, it was all she could do not to curl her hands around his tight buttocks.

"Feels good," he murmured.

She tried to ignore the slight hoarseness in his voice. But it wasn't easy. If only she could turn him over and make good use of that erection! She'd told him she didn't want anything to do with him—but it was all she could do not to climb on top of him and reveal the exact opposite.

When the image of doing just that passed through

her mind for at least the tenth time—with more immediacy, more demand—she finally pulled away. "We shouldn't have started this," she said.

He rolled onto his side. "Why not? It's what you do for everyone else, isn't it?"

"It's...not the same."

"Why not?"

"Maybe it's because we've slept together in the past."

"I don't think it has anything to do with the past," he scoffed. "I think it has to do with what we want right now."

She wiped her hands on a towel. "I don't...I don't want you," she insisted, but it wasn't a very convincing lie. She could tell he wasn't buying it when he grabbed her by the wrist and sat up.

"Prove it," he said, putting her hands on his chest. "Touch me when I can play a part in this, Presley. When I can show you how it makes me feel, and I can touch you back."

The sheet puddled at his waist, allowing him a slight amount of modesty, but it wasn't difficult to recall the size and shape of what she'd find underneath.

This was the father of her baby, the man she saw in her mind's eye whenever she looked at Wyatt. She'd missed Aaron *so* much....

"Don't," she whispered, but she didn't try to pull away.

He cupped her cheek as he ran a thumb over her bottom lip. "Don't what?"

Don't make me tremble. Don't make me mess up. Don't remind me how wonderful it feels to have your full attention.

"Stop pretending you want me," she said.

"I *do* want you." His hands circled her waist, drawing her against him. But he didn't hold her too tightly. She could tell he was being careful not to be too forceful. He preferred to entice her.

He didn't need to be forceful. She'd lost this battle the moment she agreed to give him a massage.

Some of his caution faded when she pressed her lips to his and took his tongue in her mouth. That was when she realized he had her. He gripped her tighter, with his old confidence.

The sheet fell away as he stood. He was still only kissing her, but he was growing more aggressive. She could feel it. Briefly, a final warning rushed through her head. She *had* to stop this. But the power to act was there and then gone before she could grasp it. The compulsion to possess him, and to let him possess her, was too great. So when his hands slid up her shirt, it startled them both that she jumped back.

"What is it?" he murmured. "You okay?"

Her laugh was shaky, but she nodded. "Just overly sensitive. I haven't been touched there in a long time."

"How long?"

"Two years."

"You've been celibate for *two years?*"

She nodded. She'd thought she was reinforcing her new lifestyle, being a better person during those months of abstinence. But now she had to wonder if all those good intentions had carried her to her weakest moment just when she was facing her most formidable challenge.

"Why?" he asked.

"I never met the right man." *He* wasn't the right

man, either. History had proven that. But heaven help her…

"Sounds like we need to make up for lost time."

Yes. Let him do it. Let him erase all the days and hours of missing him. If she was going down, she might as well go down in flames.

She dropped her head back as his thumbs flicked across the tips of her breasts. "God, I'm going to regret this."

She hadn't realized she'd spoken aloud until he froze. Then she opened her eyes to find him staring down at her. She couldn't tell what he was thinking but she began to fight her way through the hormones that were interfering with her own ability to think. She took hold of his wrists so she could push his hands away, but the disappointment that crossed his face made her hesitate. Then he kissed her again, and it was too late.

"You don't mean that, do you?" he whispered against her mouth. "What's to regret? It's just me. We've been together hundreds of times."

Maybe he was right. Making love once wouldn't lead to anything that could threaten Wyatt. Aaron was the king of casual. Afterward he'd continue on his way. It might even help because once he accomplished his goal he'd have no reason to give her a second thought.

He untied her smock, and the rest of her clothes were gone soon after. But she wasn't spooked; she was done trying to resist. Although she hated to admit it, he was as much her safe harbor as he was her Achilles' heel. After not having a home for most of

her life she'd latched on to him—figuratively and literally—and couldn't make herself give him up.

"No one feels as good as you do," she whispered
as her arms slid around his neck.

"That's my girl."

His girl. Although she wished it *wasn't* true, she
couldn't argue with that. But at least this time he
seemed to be equally invested. That made their lovemaking more exciting than ever before. She had to
have him right away, couldn't wait another heartbeat
after having waited for so long.

Fortunately, she didn't have to wait. He felt the
same urgency. Or he was afraid she might balk if she
had the chance. So he got a condom out of his wallet,
which he tossed aside, then lifted her against the wall
and took her hard and fast, just roughly enough....

"Yes," she groaned, "that's it."

His teeth flashed in a self-satisfied smile. "You
like this?" he asked as he thrust harder.

She clung to him as he continued to move inside
her. "Yes."

"How much?"

"*Too* much." Almost immediately the tension began
to mount. "Whatever you do, don't stop." She heard
the desperation in her own voice. She was *so* close....

"I wouldn't...leave you...hanging." His muscles
were trembling with the strain, but he proved his
words. When she cried out, he seemed relieved. Then
he took a ragged breath and let himself go

9

"That was freaking *amazing*," he gasped as he lowered her feet to the floor. He no longer had the strength to hold her; his limbs felt like rubber. The past ten minutes had been so intense it had depleted his energy. "The best."

When she said nothing, he felt a small jolt of alarm. Earlier she'd mentioned regret, but he hadn't taken her seriously. What was there to regret? They'd *both* wanted this.

But he was pretty sure she was crying. Although she was trying to keep her face averted, he'd felt a warm drop on his arm.

"What's wrong?" he asked.

She shook her head, but he wasn't reassured. "You'd tell me, right?"

"Of course."

That was the answer he'd been looking for, but those words held no conviction, so they didn't persuade him, especially when she immediately moved out of reach. He was so concerned about her reaction, it wasn't until she went to wash up that he realized the condom he'd used was broken. Then panic shot through him, and he wondered if maybe he'd misinterpreted disappointment or sadness for fear. Had she noticed? Was that what was wrong?

If so, she had every right to be frightened. He was frightened, too. He'd never had anything like that happen before. "I didn't come over to…to do what we just did," he said when she returned to put on her panties. Now that he was standing more than two inches away from her nude body, he could see how much she'd done to get in shape. She looked great, but she seemed to be in a hurry to cover herself, which added to the unsettled feelings he already had. It'd never been like this between them.

He didn't bother going after his own clothes; instead, he leaned a shoulder against the wall and watched her. "You believe me, don't you? I mean…I really wanted to talk to you tonight." This was especially important for her to know, given the state of that damn condom, which he'd removed and thrown away. He had to tell her, of course. He just wasn't sure how to start out.

"Don't worry about…what happened here," she mumbled. "It was as much my fault as it was yours."

She was good at taking responsibility. She'd done that before—at the book signing. But her reaction only made him feel worse. What if she got pregnant because he wouldn't leave her alone? "Does it have to be anybody's 'fault'?"

"No," she said, but she spoke as if she was forcing the word through her teeth, and she wouldn't look at him. It disturbed him even more that she moved quickly, erratically, as if her life depended on getting dressed and gathering up her massage stuff.

"You had fun, too. I felt you climax. You seemed to like it."

"Yeah. You were as accommodating as ever. Thank you."

He hadn't been seeking praise, and *accommodating* wasn't the word he would've hoped to hear even if he had been. That made him sound like he'd merely been *servicing* her. There'd been a lot more to it than that. They had too much history to make love without *any* emotion. He'd felt a great deal beyond pleasure—relief, satisfaction, a sense of resolution. So why was she upset?

"You know about the rubber?" he asked.

She finally glanced over at him. "What about it?"

She didn't know, he realized. At some point, he had to tell her.

Or maybe not. Maybe he should just wait and see if she missed her next period. Maybe they were in the clear, and there was no reason to worry about it.

Damn the risk he'd taken! His brother, his sister-in-law—even Presley—had asked him to keep away from her. He'd come over here despite those warnings, and things had gone further than they should have, just like everyone had been afraid they might.

"At least say we can still be friends," he said. "I don't want you to feel bad, especially about this. And I definitely don't want to feel as if...you know, as if I pushed you into something that wasn't good for you."

"You didn't push me into anything."

"So you're not angry?"

"No."

"You *are* angry." He knew her too well for her to deny it.

"Not at you," she clarified. "I'm mad at myself. I didn't even make it until Monday. This wasn't the direction I wanted to go."

"Meaning…"

She sighed. "I have a date with Riley next Friday."

He didn't like the idea of Presley seeing someone else. It wasn't often that a woman he'd just made love to brought up another man. He supposed that was why he felt a sudden surge of possessiveness, a desire to touch her again, to drag her into the bedroom until he could find the person he used to know amid all this resistance. "And this makes you feel… what? Guilty? Like you cheated on him? You don't owe Riley anything. You barely know him. A date is just a date. Besides, Friday will be your *first* date."

"I'm aware that there's no commitment between Riley and me. But I'm sure he's not expecting *this*. And I'd rather be the type of person a guy like Riley can admire, okay? I'd rather be the type of person *I* can admire."

He shoved a hand through his hair. "A guy *like Riley?* Is he somehow different from other guys? From *me?*"

"You know what I mean. You told me yourself he's the best Whiskey Creek has to offer. He has his shit together."

"He's not *that* great," he said. "I was being sarcastic. And just because you had sex with a partner you've slept with a hundred times before—after two years of celibacy—doesn't make you a…" He didn't want to say *whore*; he didn't even want to introduce that word into the conversation. "Lowlife," he finished.

"Having a one-night stand with someone who's already made it clear that he doesn't want me for anything beyond physical pleasure doesn't exactly make me a pillar of the community."

He didn't attempt to defend his position. His feelings were too complicated for that. He couldn't definitely say what they encompassed. She wasn't merely a friend; he wanted to sleep with her too badly for that. And she wasn't his girlfriend; he wasn't in love with her. She was somewhere in between. But despite a few instances where he'd fallen a little short, he'd always tried to be kind to her. "A pillar of the community? That's what you're shooting for?"

"Why not?"

"I think a 'pillar' would be too boring for you. For both of us."

"At least I wouldn't lose my self-respect. This isn't something I want Riley to know. I finally have a chance at the kind of life my sister has, and…look at me." She covered her face as if she was too ashamed to show it. "I've already fucked up."

Aaron hadn't seen this coming. Grabbing his boxers, he jammed his legs into them. "Quit beating yourself up. Riley's not your type, anyway."

She whirled toward him. "Why not? What's that supposed to mean?"

He struggled to come up with a reason they wouldn't be compatible but couldn't immediately land on one.

"You think he's too good for me?" she asked.

"Of course not! It's just that…you can do what you want when it comes to men. Riley has no claim on you. Maybe *he's* with another woman right now."

"We both know he's not. He's not like that."

"He could be." He buttoned his pants. "So what? Now you're hoping for a ring from *Riley Stinson?*"

"He's a good man."

"And I'm not?" Aaron gaped at her. In the old days, she'd never made him feel like anything less than the moon and stars. What was going on?

"Stop twisting my words," she said. "I just... I need you to go so I can think straight."

"Come here..." He reached for her. But then her son started to cry in the other room, and the second that happened, whatever chance he'd had to reconcile with her was over. She scooped his shirt and shoes off the floor and thrust them at his chest while propelling him toward the door.

"I—I'm sorry I let this get out of hand," she said, suddenly polite—*too* polite. "Please forgive me if I've said or done anything to offend you. But...I need to take care of my baby now."

"This is crazy, Pres. Can't I wait until you've done whatever you need to do with your kid so we can say goodbye? Does it have to end this way?"

"How else can it end?" she asked, and the next thing he knew, he was standing on her porch half-dressed.

Aaron sat in his truck for probably fifteen minutes before driving away. He hadn't even bothered to put on his shirt and shoes before he got behind the wheel; he'd tossed them in the passenger seat. He wanted to go back into Presley's house. Somehow he'd upset her, but he hadn't meant to. He'd come here hoping to reestablish their friendship. Like he'd told her, he honestly *hadn't* come to get laid—not consciously. He'd been hoping to relieve a certain…sense of loss.

He shouldn't have suggested the massage, but she'd been acting so remote. He hadn't known how to break through that icy reserve. And then, once she touched him, the memories came tumbling back and…he'd never felt such lust. She seemed to feel the same thing.

So why would she be sorry afterward? She didn't know about the broken rubber. And he'd made sure she had an orgasm. As excited as they were, it hadn't even taken much work. Climax had come quickly for both of them. The whole encounter was exceptional—except for the part where he realized they hadn't had the protection they'd assumed. And the part where she shoved him out the door. Why had she done that? She used to curl up beside him and spend the rest of the night. Sometimes she would stay far longer than he wanted her to.…

If he didn't know her better, he'd think she was trying to punish him. But she wasn't a conniving person, and her reaction had been so heartfelt. She'd exhibited genuine remorse. Maybe that was why her reaction upset him even more than the broken condom—although that was a serious concern.

"Shit," he muttered, and smacked the steering wheel. He'd come here to make things better; instead, he'd made them worse.

As she rocked Wyatt back to sleep, Presley couldn't seem to stop crying. She wasn't sobbing, but she was so disappointed in herself that the tears kept falling. What was wrong with her? She'd gone back on everything she'd told herself she was, everything she'd told herself she'd do and be.

Aaron was too big a temptation for her.

So now what?

She put her baby in his crib and went to get her phone. She wasn't worthy of someone like Riley. She'd tried to tell him that from the start.

After wiping her cheeks, she sent him a text.

It was great to see you today. Thanks for everything. But I'm afraid I can't make it Friday night.

Presley heard her cell phone ring early the next morning and was so afraid it would wake Wyatt that she sprang out of bed and grabbed it. She didn't want him up this early, not when that extra thirty minutes of sleep made such a difference.

"Hello?" she said, her voice raspy but purposely low.

"Don't tell me I woke you."

Cheyenne. "What time is it?" She combed her fingers through her short bangs. After tossing and turning for most of the night, her hair was going every which way. She didn't even want to *see* the damage crying had done to her eyes.

"Eight-thirty. Don't tell me Wyatt's not up."

"It's unusual for him to sleep so late, but he had a rough night." She could only guess he'd sensed her turmoil.

"I'm sorry I disturbed you, then."

"No problem." Cheyenne was probably calling to talk about her artificial insemination plans; it was

Monday and Dylan was out of the house. "Have you heard from Aaron yet?"

Chances were slim that Aaron had contacted Cheyenne since they were together last night, but Presley was trying to give her sister the lead-in she assumed Chey was looking for.

"Not yet, although it would've been great to wake up to a text from him this morning."

Presley could've volunteered that he was seriously considering it—that she'd talked to him—but she wasn't going anywhere close to that. Just the mention of his name brought back every physically exquisite but bitterly regretted detail of what she'd done. Things better kept to herself. "Did he say when he'd have an answer for you?"

"Not specifically, but I told him we don't have much time, so…I'm hoping he'll decide fast."

She slipped under the covers again, craving a few more minutes of comfort and relaxation. "Will you be too disappointed if the answer is no?"

"I want to say I won't, but…you know I will be."

Presley heard someone in the background and realized that Cheyenne was at work. "Is that Eve?"

"Yeah."

"Tell her I said hi."

There was a slight pause while Cheyenne spoke to her best friend and employer. "She said you should come over for lunch," Cheyenne said when she came back on the line.

"At the B and B?"

"Why not? We have a wonderful chef. We'll be able to make a small feast with the leftovers from breakfast—and this morning we're having crab and cream cheese omelets."

Presley thought of everything she had to do at the studio. Now that her reception area had been built and the place had been painted, she could finish cleaning up the debris, take her massage table over and start looking for a few chairs for the reception area. She couldn't afford much, but she had a knack for finding quality secondhand items. She didn't need a lot of furniture, especially for the yoga side. Until she could afford to add a few bells and whistles, she was planning to ask everyone to bring their own mats, towels and drinks; she had the music, the experience and the room.

But she'd been so focused on taking care of Wyatt and getting her business launched that she hadn't seen Eve or any of Cheyenne's other friends, except those she'd bumped into at the book signing. For that matter, she hadn't seen any of *her* old friends from the casino where she used to work. But she *couldn't* see her friends, couldn't risk being tempted back into her old lifestyle. That was part of the reason she was supposed to stay clear of Aaron.

"I could carve out an hour or so. What time?"

"Mama!"

Wyatt was awake. She could hear him calling to her from the other room.

"Ma-ma!"

With a yawn, she went to get him. "There's my boy."

A toothy grin bunched his fat cheeks, and he wiggled in excitement as she approached.

"I wish just waking up in the morning made me

as happy as it does you," she told him, and held the phone to her ear with her shoulder so she could change his diaper.

"Eleven okay?" Cheyenne asked.

"Eleven works for me."

"See you then."

"Bye," she said, but Cheyenne interrupted her before she could hang up.

"How'd it go with Riley yesterday?"

Presley thought of her text to him late last night. Cheyenne wouldn't be pleased to learn she'd canceled. She hoped Riley wouldn't mention it, that the fact he'd asked her out in the first place would simply fade into the past. "Great. He finished the build-out."

"And you like it?"

"*Love* it." The work Aaron had done was equally good, but Cheyenne wouldn't want to hear that. And Presley didn't really want to say it. It just seemed unfair to focus so much on what Riley had done.

"It was nice of him to help."

This was her chance to say that she'd decided not to go out with him. She couldn't let him pay for her dinner after the way she'd behaved with Aaron last night. But she wasn't going to volunteer a word of that, either. Suddenly, she felt as if she was holding back a lot, which felt deceptive, but she wanted to move ahead with her business, look after her baby and avoid all the emotional turmoil.

So that was what she decided she'd do.

"He's a nice guy," she said, carrying her son into the kitchen.

"I can't wait to see what he's done. We'll walk over after lunch and make a list of decorating ideas."

Presley put Wyatt in his high chair and got out the oatmeal. "A yoga studio doesn't need much decoration. I was thinking of putting up some posters with motivational quotes but that's about it." Twenty or thirty bucks was all her pocketbook could withstand.

"But you've got to have one of those relaxing water-falling-over-rocks things that most day spas have."

She took a frying pan off the shelves that served as her cupboards. "I do?"

"No self-respecting massage therapist would be without one," she teased. "So I'm going to get you one."

Presley laughed. "Are you sure?"

"What else makes such soothing sounds for under a hundred bucks?"

"Nothing I know of," she said as she fastened Wyatt's bib. "I'll see you at eleven."

She fed her son hot cereal for breakfast, cleaned the kitchen and put him down to play while she straightened the rest of the house. But as she was vacuuming the living room, she nearly ran over something that had previously blended in with the color of the carpet—a brown leather wallet.

She didn't have to look inside to know it belonged to Aaron. Riley and Jacob wouldn't have had any reason to take out their wallets at her house. But Aaron had gotten a condom from his and then thrown the wallet aside.

"Oh, God."

"Mama?" Wyatt, who loved the vacuum, grabbed hold of it now that she'd turned it off and tried to push it himself.

"Mommy made a big mistake, Wyatt," she said, and checked inside the wallet to confirm that she'd guessed the correct owner.

Sure enough, it belonged to Aaron—which meant he'd be looking for it.

10

It was three o'clock Monday afternoon. Although Presley had been nervous that Aaron might call while she was at lunch with Cheyenne—or afterward, when Cheyenne and Eve had come over to see the studio— she hadn't heard from him. He was probably wondering if he'd left his wallet someplace else. Or he was caught up at work and wouldn't think about it until he returned home and wanted to go out for the evening.

Curiosity had consumed her all day, but she hadn't let herself act on it. She refused to look at what he carried inside. They weren't going to be part of each other's lives. But once she put Wyatt down for his nap in the playpen at the studio and relaxed for a minute herself, that curiosity grew even stronger. If they *weren't* going to be part of each other's lives, it didn't matter if she knew what he kept in his wallet. She flipped it open.

He had over five hundred dollars in cash, which was half her monthly rent. She was envious but not remotely tempted to steal. Thankfully, theft was one vice she'd never found difficult to resist; she felt too much empathy for the victims. And his financial situation played no part in how she felt about him. She knew she'd love him just as much if he were jobless and penniless.

"There's no hope for me." She sighed. Invading his privacy had turned out to be a waste of time. What she'd found didn't tell her much. He kept his credit cards and driver's license in there, of course, but no pictures, no notes, no phone numbers. These days most people kept all of that on a smartphone, so it didn't come as any surprise.

She was about to close his wallet so she could slip it inside her purse when she noticed a compartment she hadn't checked. It was flat, so she assumed it would be empty, but it wasn't. He carried a picture, after all—a photograph of his mother. Presley recognized Wynona because she'd seen a different picture of her on his dresser.

Mrs. Amos was such a pretty woman, and her two oldest sons looked a lot like her. Presley wondered how different Aaron would be had he not lost her when he was so young. If she hadn't taken her own life, maybe their father wouldn't have fallen into depression and turned to alcohol. And if J.T. hadn't turned to alcohol, maybe he wouldn't have stabbed a man in a bar and gone to prison. And if he hadn't gone to prison, Dylan wouldn't have had to take over as head of the family when he was barely eighteen....

Not many kids had a less conventional upbringing than the Amos boys. They understood, as few could, what loss felt like, but at least they'd had Dylan. She and Cheyenne hadn't had a savior; they'd had to muddle through on their own.

Her cell phone vibrated. She'd turned off the ringer

when she'd managed to get Wyatt to sleep, but the interruption reminded her that what she was doing was wrong.

She slid the picture into place before digging her phone out of her pocket. She feared it might be Aaron calling to get the wallet she'd just snooped through, but it was Riley. He hadn't responded to her text. Apparently, he wanted to talk about it.

"Hello?" She went outside so she could speak in a normal tone of voice without disturbing Wyatt. Because he hadn't gotten enough sleep last night, he'd been cranky and tired, but he hadn't been able to nap as soon as she would've liked. She'd hate to have anything wake him. This was her chance to make some real progress on cleaning up the studio.

"Presley?"

She sat on a wooden bench a few feet from her storefront. "Hi, Riley. How are you?"

"A little disappointed, if you want the truth. I thought we had a date."

She gazed down the street in the direction of Amos Auto Body, where Aaron would be working—if he wasn't looking at real estate in Reno. She couldn't see his business. It was located off Sutter Street, not Main, but she'd been there often enough when they were hanging out that she could easily picture the whole place. They'd even had sex in the office once, after hours, when they were both high.

"I'm sorry about that," she said.

There was a slight hesitation. "Did something come up?"

"No, I just... I don't feel I'm the right type of woman for you."

"You didn't like it when Jacob and I came to visit yesterday?"

"Of course I liked it. This has nothing to do with that."

"Then…what is it? You got cold feet? A date is too much of a commitment—not casual enough for you to feel comfortable? What if we had Cheyenne and Dylan join us?"

No way. Then she'd have her sister evaluating her behavior all evening and telling her she needed to be less aloof and more warm and friendly. She was who she was, would never be like Chey. Some things couldn't be changed.

"I don't need Dylan and Cheyenne to be there. But I'd like you to understand something."

"And that is…"

Part of her felt she should tell him about Aaron. Her conscience dictated it. But she was afraid he'd tell Cheyenne what she'd said. "I've done some things in my life that you wouldn't approve of. I'm not proud of them myself."

"We've been over this—"

"You're not getting it! I thought I was ready for someone like you, that I'd become…better. But that's not really the case." She hadn't intended to blurt that out, to reveal her honest doubt, but there it was: maybe she wasn't capable of changing as much as she'd hoped.

"Presley, it seems to me that you're trying very hard to be a good person."

"I am," she agreed. She'd tried *so* hard. She'd given up drugs and alcohol and, until Aaron last night, even sex. After her mother died, she'd moved away and started over, had rebuilt her life step by painstaking step without any support, except for what Cheyenne could offer from a distance. Now she worked out on a regular basis, watched what she ate and lived a neat and organized life. Most importantly, she did everything she could to take care of her child. But she was powerless to resist Aaron—much as she'd hoped otherwise when she moved back. And that was a fundamental flaw that would interfere with dating other guys.

"Then I don't understand the problem," he said.

"You're better off with someone else." She hit the End button, but he called right back.

"That's bullshit," he said. "I'm picking you up on Friday at six, so make sure you're ready."

She blinked in surprise when he disconnected before she could respond.

"That's the second time I tried to warn you," she said with a sigh. But it was only dinner.

When Aaron saw Presley pushing a stroller toward him, wearing a white shirt with a pair of cutoffs, he felt his chest tighten. She looked so wholesome and healthy, so in control of all the demons that had once defeated her. He couldn't help being proud. The transformation couldn't have been easy, yet she'd done it in two short years. And she'd done it because of the love she felt for another person—her son —which said a lot about her as a person.

Of course, she still had her panther tattoo and a hard "I've walked through fire and lived to tell about it" edge, but she'd had to be tough to survive. As far as he was concerned, that only made her sexier.

He'd suggested picking up his wallet at her place, but she'd refused to let him come by. Instead, she'd arranged to meet him at the park, next to the giant statue of a forty-niner panning for gold. He got the impression she was afraid to be alone with him.

She gave him an uncertain smile and pushed her sunglasses higher on the bridge of her nose as she parked the stroller and stepped around it. "Hey."

He couldn't stop himself from checking out her legs. She wasn't very tall but she'd always had shapely legs. "Hey."

"It's nice out tonight, isn't it?"

He squinted at the setting sun. "Finally. It's been so damn cold this year."

"Feels like spring. I hope it lasts. I think I'll have a bigger turnout for my grand opening if it does." Wyatt squealed and tried to wriggle out of his seat belt, but she got him a toy from the basket on the stroller to mollify him. Then she rummaged in her purse, coming up with Aaron's wallet.

"I went through it," she announced as she handed it to him.

He straightened. "You...what?"

A blush tinged her cheeks. "I'm sorry. I couldn't help myself. I was too curious."

"About..."

She shrugged. "What you keep in there."

Maybe he should've been mad but he found himself laughing. "Why would you immediately confess? That hadn't even occurred to me."

"I don't want to feel creepy about having done i I'm sorry," she said again.

Her lack of artifice was endearing, despite her invasion of his privacy. "Find anything interesting?"

She hesitated for a second, then shook her head. "Just the usual. And nothing's missing, of course. I hope I didn't worry you by saying I went through it."

"No." He slid his billfold into his pocket without inspecting it.

"Good. Well, I'll see you around," she said with a parting smile. She started to leave, but he called her back.

"About last night..."

She parked the stroller again, glancing to either side to make sure they couldn't be overheard. "Do we really have to talk about last night?"

"There's something you don't know. I haven't wanted to tell you, but... It's possible I'm worried for no reason. At the very least, though, you should be prepared."

"For... What's this about?"

"The condom we used."

She licked her lips as if she suddenly felt self-conscious or perhaps anxious. "What about it?"

"I'm not sure how it happened... I mean, it's never happened to me before, but...it was obviously..."

"What?" she prodded again, her eyes round and fearful.

"Broken."

The color drained from her face.

"I'm sorry. We were...rougher than usual. Maybe that's why. Or else it was defective to begin with."

She covered her mouth with one hand but said nothing.

"Are you okay?" he asked.

"Oh, God."

"You didn't notice?"

"No. I wasn't thinking about anything except..." She caught herself, but he would've liked to hear the rest of that sentence. Would it have been "you"? "How you made me feel"? "The best climax of my life"? "Getting you out of my house"? What?

He pinched his lips as he tried to evaluate her body language. "How worried should I be?"

"I'm not on the pill, if that's what you're asking. I was telling you the truth when I said I hadn't slept with anyone in ages."

Wyatt threw his toy on the ground and Aaron retrieved it for him. "So, no...IUD, or whatever those things are called, either?" He knew that if she wasn't sexually active, she wouldn't have one, but he couldn't help hoping.

She shook her head.

He kicked at a tuft of grass before meeting her eyes. "Are *you* concerned?" She was already a mother. He doubted she'd want a *second* surprise pregnancy. The thought that it might be too late terrified him. He'd stand by any kid he helped create, if she went through with the pregnancy, but this wasn't the way he'd planned to start a family—if and when he got around to it.

"Of course."

His anxiety went deeper. "So it might've been...a fertile time of the month?"

She lowered her voice even more. "To be honest, I have no idea. These days my periods just come and go. Because they don't interfere with my nonexistent sex life, I don't pay much attention."

He let his breath go. He'd been hoping for more definitive news. "I'm sorry if you're upset."

"It takes two," she said.

Grateful she wasn't placing all the blame on him, he shoved his hands in his pockets. "You'll let me know when...when you're in the clear—or even if you're not?"

With a nod of confirmation, she wheeled Wyatt back in the direction from which she'd come.

Feeling the same disappointment and dissatisfaction he'd experienced while sitting in his truck last night, after she pushed him out the door, Aaron began to go after her. He didn't see why their relationship had to be so damned strained. He cared about her as much as ever. So why couldn't they go to dinner now, like they would've done two years ago? Wouldn't she enjoy a nice meal and maybe a movie?

He didn't get two steps before he heard another guy call out to her from the edge of the park, where there was parking for nearby shops. It took him a second, but he eventually identified Kyle Houseman. As Kyle walked over to say hello to her, he seemed to be teasing her about something, because she slugged him in the arm and they both laughed.

Inexplicably irked that their exchange seemed so uncomplicated, so genuine, Aaron stalked to his truck and drove away.

Several hours after he arrived home from the park, Aaron sat in the easy chair that used to be his older brother's, back when Dylan lived with them. He was staring at a sports channel, loosely holding the television remote. Grady and Rod were sprawled on the couch, looking tired after a long day at the shop. Their youngest brother, Mack, who was twenty-three, was out somewhere with his girlfriend. Two basketball teams in the Sweet Sixteen were battling it out, and Mack was missing it, but Aaron wasn't paying much attention, anyway. He owed Cheyenne an answer, so he had to figure out what that answer was going to be.

"You're quiet tonight," Grady said when the game cut to a commercial. "Have you settled on a location for your franchise?"

He hadn't made a decision there, either. Since he'd learned that Presley was back in town, he hadn't been able to concentrate. First, he'd been intent on catching a glimpse of her and had kept driving by her place. Then he'd run into her, and things had gotten a whole lot more complicated. "Not yet."

"What's taking so long? Aren't there any good options?"

Part of the problem was that opening a franchise in Reno sounded better in theory than it was likely to be in practice. If he moved away from Whiskey Creek, he wouldn't be working with his brothers anymore. He wouldn't live with them, either; it didn't make sense to commute that far. So while he felt that leaving Whiskey Creek and the business he'd helped build—ever since he was a teenager—would defuse the ongoing tension between him and Dylan, the prospect of starting a new shop on his own was beginning to feel more lonely than appealing. None of his brothers wanted to leave the area. So without the people in his life, he'd only have work—lots of it if he wanted the franchise to be successful—and he spent enough time at the shop as it was.

"There are a few options," he mumbled, gesturing with the remote. "I just haven't settled on one."

His brother took a drink of his beer. "Want to show me the final three sometime this week? Maybe we can decide together."

Aaron was grateful for the offer, but if he went that far, he might actually have to choose one and take the next step—which was where he made the financial commitment. Once he signed a lease and wrote that check, it would be too late to back out. "It might make more sense just to…expand."

"Here?" Rod and Grady both turned to look at him.

"Why not?" he said. "We have more business than we can handle. We could add another couple of paint bays, train a few new techs…"

Grady eased back. "Sounds good to me. I've never liked the idea of you leaving."

"Me, neither." Rod shot him a grin. "What would you do without us?"

Aaron knew he was about to get razzed about something. "Excuse me?"

"Who'll be around to get your ass out of trouble?"

"You've gotten me *into* more fights than you've ever gotten me out of," Aaron said, but since he was the black sheep in the family, the reverse was actually true. *He'd* been the biggest pain in the ass; they should all want to be rid of him.

"Not quite," Grady responded. "But I will say that if I ever *do* get into a situation, you're the one I'd want to have my back."

"You mean you'd want Dylan. *He's* the professional."

"Dylan might be a hell of a fighter, but these days he's too…mellow to hit anyone."

Rod chuckled. "Ain't that the truth! Cheyenne's got him so whipped he'd have to ask her for permission first."

They teased Dylan mercilessly about how tame he'd become, but deep down they were all jealous that he'd found such peace—not that they'd ever want to see him lose it.

"Yeah, but heaven help the man who threatens *her*," Aaron said. "He'd tear the dumb bastard limb from limb."

"Used to be the same with us," Rod pointed out a little nostalgically.

Grady crushed his beer can. "We don't need him to fight our battles anymore. He'd be there if we did."

"So are you going to mention the expansion idea to Dylan?" Rod asked. "Or do you want me to do it?"

"I'll talk to him, if I decide that's what we should do." He wasn't sure his older brother would be happy to have him stay. Maybe Dylan was relieved by the thought that they wouldn't be working together anymore, at least not so closely. They'd refer clients back and forth, pool their buying power and share business contacts. They'd agreed on that much. But it wouldn't be the same. And that could be a good thing. If Aaron was going to donate his sperm to Cheyenne, it would probably be best for everyone involved if he got the hell out.

Rod went to the kitchen as a few seconds later, the front door opened and shut. Aaron turned around, expecting to see Mack, but it was Dylan. Dylan had lived with them for so long he hardly ever bothered to knock. His name was still on the deed to the house.

"Hey, Dyl," Grady called out. "We were just talking about you."

"What were you saying?" he asked as he came up behind the couch.

Grady sent him a daring glance. "That you're a pussy these days."

Dylan swatted him upside the head. "Come on outside, little brother. I'll show you how much of a pussy I am."

Grady wasn't stupid enough to give Dylan the chance. He laughed as Rodney, who returned with a couple more beers, said hello. Then they both encouraged Dylan to sit down and watch the game.

Aaron remained silent throughout the exchange and kept his eyes on the TV. He'd been at the shop today but had managed to avoid Dylan. Aaron hadn't spoken directly to him since Dylan punched a hole in the wall on Friday night.

"I can't stay," Dylan said. "Chey's at home. She's on the phone with Eve, but she'll want me home with her once she hangs up."

Grady nudged Rod. "See what I mean?"

"What?" Dylan snapped.

A wry smile twisted Rodney's lips, but he didn't needle Dylan again. "It's not like you to leave her behind. What's up?"

"I have a few things I'd like to say to Aaron." He shoved Aaron's recliner into a sitting position. "You got a minute?"

Aaron was tempted to tell him to go to hell. But he swallowed a sigh, handed Grady the remote and followed Dylan out back, where the yard fell away to the river. It wasn't that Aaron didn't want to make things right. He loved Dylan even more than he loved his other brothers—loved him like a father, in some ways. They just couldn't get along. To make matters worse, he felt guilty for doing exactly what Dylan had been afraid he'd do. Presley certainly wasn't better off for the visit he'd paid her. There was even a possibility that she was pregnant.

He scratched his neck. "If this is about the other night..."

"I was out of line on Friday, Aaron. I'm sorry."

His brother was a proud man; rarely did he apologize. So Aaron appreciated the effort and was willing to admit that maybe he'd overreacted, too, especially now that he'd proven Dylan had been right to worry. "No big deal. I understand you're concerned about Presley."

"It wasn't only that."

Aaron's thoughts turned to Dylan's inability to father a child. But he should've known Dylan would never talk about something so private. To him, being infertile would be almost as bad as not being able to get it up in the first place.

"I had a letter from Dad last Wednesday," Dylan said.

Aaron studied his brother's face but, as usual, Dylan wasn't giving much away. Dylan's emotions were complicated when it came to J.T.—Aaron's, too. Only their younger brothers seemed capable of having a relationship with him. Not that it was much of a relationship. They wrote him a letter now and then or went down to Soledad once in a blue moon to visit.

"What'd he have to say? He still getting out this summer?"

J.T. had been scheduled for release last year, but several months before that, his cell mate ratted him out for having a shank hidden under his mattress and he got another twelve months for possession of a deadly weapon.

"He is. And he expects to come back here, to stay in the house and work at the body shop, until he can get on his feet."

They sauntered closer to the river, which would soon swell with the spring runoff coming out of the Sierra Nevada Mountains. "We knew we'd have to deal with that eventually. Where else would he go? Not only that, he thinks what we have belongs to him. He's the one who initially bought this house. He also started the business."

Dylan selected a flat rock and skipped it across the water. "He signed both over to me when they put him away."

"Only so you'd have some chance of keeping a roof over our heads and taking care of us."

"Most men would *want* to provide for their children, but he acts like he did us a big favor. He's already said it would've been better for him if he'd had a Realtor sell the house and the business to someone else."

"How generous. Aaron skipped a rock of his own. But he's forgetting that there wasn't any equity in this place when he went to prison. And after Mom died, he let the business fall to crap."

"I don't think he deserves to waltz in and take over now that we've made Amos Auto Body a success."

Dylan was being kind in saying "we." Aaron didn't feel he could take much credit for the shop, at least not in the early years. It was Dylan who'd saved the business from bankruptcy while trying to keep all of his brothers in school. He'd managed to stay afloat until he could do that by augmenting the shop's trickle of income by fighting professionally on weekends.

Aaron glanced over at the barn. These days, they kept their weights and other workout equipment in there. But all those years ago, he and a friend had been spending the night in the loft when his father stabbed Mel Hafer at a local tavern for saying he'd done a shitty job fixing his car. Mel had also told J.T. that his poor dead wife would be disgusted by what he'd become. "Is Dad assuming he'll just take over?"

"He's not coming on too strong right now. His letter was…humble, conciliatory. He hopes we can see our way clear to including him. Shit like that. But this is a man who was hiding a deadly weapon under his mattress a year ago. What'll he be like in a few months when he regains his confidence? We don't even know him anymore." Dylan cursed under his breath. "And there's another wrinkle," he added.

"You mean it gets worse?"

"He's married, Aaron."

Aaron dropped the rock he'd picked up. "*What? To who?*"

"Some woman he met on a hookup site for prisoners."

"You've got to be kidding me! What kind of woman goes to a *prison* website to find a mate?"

"Do you really want an answer?"

"No." He could guess.

"Someone by the name of Anya Sharp has been writing and visiting him the past few months. They got married three weeks ago and, according to him, they can't wait until he's released so they can start their lives together."

"Here?" Couldn't their father just leave them alone? Hadn't he done enough? "Why didn't he tell us he was getting married?"

Dylan skipped another rock. "The lapse in communication isn't entirely his fault. We don't exactly keep in close touch."

"Grady, Rod and Mack have exchanged a few letters with him. He could've told *them*."

"Knowing Dad? He didn't think it would make him look as helpless and downtrodden as he'd like to appear. He's constantly at them to put money on his books. If they knew he had her doing the same— that he'd been enjoying conjugal visits, no less—they wouldn't be as likely to trouble themselves."

Aaron shook his head. Their father had been in prison for nearly twenty years. They'd felt his loss when he left but certainly didn't need him now, when they'd finally outdistanced the past. "He's being released just in time for *us* to take care of *him,* and he's setting us up for it, too."

"He's still capable of working," Dylan said.

"For how long? Anyway, what are you going to tell him?"

"I figure we should buy him off and ask him to go somewhere else. I don't see how having him in Whiskey Creek will help any of us. And now that he's got a wife, maybe if we gave him some money he'd go peacefully."

"Sounds good to me."

"I thought it might. But I'm worried about Mack. He always gets defensive when we talk about Dad."

"He feels we should forgive him. But Dad screwed up about as badly as a guy can screw up, and he did it when we needed him most. As far as I'm concerned, we don't owe him anything. The shop wasn't worth jack shit when you took over. It's worth something now, but it's taken nearly two decades of hard work to build it—*our* hard work, not his."

"And the house?"

"Maybe he could've sold it. Or maybe he would've lost it to the bank. Who knows? The only thing we do know is that you're the one who made the payments. We're here because of *you,* not him. So we shouldn't have to give him much—just enough to make a fresh start. He *is* our father, but I won't let him take advantage of us."

Dylan seemed torn. "I can't imagine we'll get rid of him unless we make it worth his while."

"And getting rid of him is important," Aaron concurred. "Not so much for you and me. We know not to trust him. But Mack and the others? The letters he's sent them make me sick. He's always whining about something and pleading for more money."

Dylan toed the ground, looking for another smooth stone. "What if we give him seed money and he wastes it? Winds up on our doorstep anyway?"

"Whether he does anything with it will be up to him."

Aaron caught sight of the house where Presley used to live and thought of what had happened there when her mother was dying of cancer. He and Presley had both been through so much when they were neighbors. They'd supported each other, forged a bond. Maybe that was why he couldn't forget her.

"I guess you're right."

"What does Chey think?" Aaron asked.

Dylan's expression grew more inscrutable. He was acting as if he'd revealed everything, laid it all out, but he was holding back. He always tried to carry the heavy end of whatever problem they faced. Aaron hated that tendency as much as he admired it. It made him feel so indebted to Dylan. "I haven't discussed this with her," he said.

"Why not?" Aaron pressed. "She's part of the family now. Shouldn't she have a say?"

"I don't see any point in upsetting her. She's got enough going on in her life right now."

"You mean with Presley moving back."

He pulled some weeds they'd missed when they were working in the yard over the weekend. "That and other things."

Like the fact that she wanted a baby but couldn't get pregnant? That she was coping with her own disappointment while worrying about her husband and how he'd take the news that *he* was the reason?

Aaron studied the river rushing over the boulders not far away. Dylan had been asked to deal with enough. At least one thing of real importance to him should come free and easy. And that could happen, if Aaron agreed to go down to the clinic Cheyenne had mentioned.,..

"That and other things. I just want her to be happy," Dylan muttered.

She will be, Aaron thought.

11

The moment Aaron's text came in, Cheyenne nudged Presley and held out her phone. "Look! He's decided!"

"'I'll do it,'" Presley read. "Oh, my gosh! He's in!"

Wyatt stopped trying to reach the coasters on Cheyenne's side table, plopped on his butt and stared up at them as they squealed and embraced. Fortunately, Dylan was out—Cheyenne hadn't said where—so they didn't have to worry about being overheard.

"I can't believe it," Cheyenne breathed. "I'm *so* excited—and scared."

"It'll be okay."

Cheyenne pulled away, a pensive expression on her face.

"Do you *really* think so?"

It wasn't often that Cheyenne needed reassurance, especially from *her*. Cheyenne had always had her life more "together," but Presley figured Cheyenne had a genetic advantage. She had been born to intelligent, attractive and wealthy parents in Colorado. She should've had the easiest life in the world. She would have, had she not fallen victim to Anita. Fortunately, a couple of years ago she'd managed to unravel the truth behind all those odd memories of people she no longer knew, and now had a close relationship with her birth family. She went to visit them once every few months.

Presley, on the other hand, had the misfortune of being Anita's true daughter—and who could say what her father had been like? He couldn't have been *too* admirable, not if he was willing to pay for sex with Anita. She wasn't what most men would consider a desirable prostitute—just a cheap one.

"I think you're going to do it, anyway, so you might as well approach it with hope and faith and try to enjoy the process," she said.

Cheyenne must've liked her answer because her smile relaxed. "I'm going to get my baby!"

Another text came from Aaron, which they read together.

In case you're hopping on the computer to make our appointments, Dylan's on his way home so be sure to clean out your browser history and delete these messages from your phone.

"How does *he* know Dylan's coming home?"

"They must've been together," Presley said. When she arrived, Cheyenne had been on the phone with Eve and merely shrugged when she asked about Dylan.

"He didn't say he was going over to the old house. Why wouldn't he wait and take me with him?"

Was he over there? Cheyenne typed to Aaron.

Presley waited with her for the answer.

For a few minutes. He came to apologize, but don't let on that I told you. You know how private he is about that kind of stuff.

And you know how private I want to be about this stuff, Cheyenne wrote back. I won't say a word if you won't.

Deal. Just promise me you'll never change your mind on that, not without speaking to me first.

I promise, Cheyenne replied.

"Why would Dylan owe Aaron an apology?" Presley asked. "Have they been fighting?"

"They kind of got into it on Friday night—enough that Dylan had to patch and paint a hole in my wall on Saturday."

"Aaron punched the wall?" Presley caught her sister's elbow to get her attention because she was staring at her phone with a sort of dumbstruck expression.

"No, Dylan did."

"What'd Aaron do to make him mad?"

"Who knows? Dylan isn't one to go into detail about that sort of thing."

"But you asked Aaron to be your donor *after* that."

"They have these flare-ups occasionally. It's nothing new. That's just the nature of their relationship."

"And it doesn't bother you?"

"Sometimes, but I'm happy right now so don't ruin it." She held up her phone to indicate she was going to text Aaron again.

Is that why you said yes? Because you're not mad at him anymore?

Aaron's answer came almost instantly.

I said yes because he deserves it. And so do you.

Cheyenne smiled wistfully. "Aaron can be a real sweetheart when he wants to be."

Didn't Presley know it! He was also damn good in bed. But she made no comment. That she might be pregnant—for the second time—with Aaron's baby made her feel like the biggest fool on earth. She'd *narrowly* escaped the bad decisions she'd made in the past and was somehow managing to build a life with the one child she had. Why would she tempt fate to make her challenges even more difficult?

She watched as Cheyenne sent Aaron a grateful You're the best brother-in-law ever!

Just give me my jacking-off instructions when you get them, he replied, and they both cracked up.

"Leave it to a guy to sum it up so frankly." Cheyenne grimaced as she erased their texts so that Dylan would never see them.

"I think I'll take your Prius and clear out before Dylan gets home," Presley told her. She'd stopped by to borrow one of their vehicles so she could transport her massage table and other items to the shop now that it was clean. "Then you two can have celebratory sex, although he'll just think he's getting lucky, and neither of you will have to be polite to the sister who keeps interrupting your life."

"Quit it! You're not interrupting our lives. Wait

and take his Jeep if it'll be easier to fit your table inside. Dylan cares about you, too. He'll even help you load up. Or I can."

"There's no need for that. And the Prius will work fine. I'll drop it off later, but it might be late so I'll leave the keys under the mat and walk home."

"That's fine." Cheyenne changed the subject to where her mind was, anyway. "Think of it…a baby. I'll be a mother," she said, but then her forehead puckered with fresh concern. "I wonder how long the process will take."

"Nothing to do with doctors happens overnight," Presley said. "Nothing even happens in a *reasonable* time. So be prepared."

"But it has to happen before Dylan goes in to be checked, or there'll be no point."

"You'll have to stall him—and try to hurry the insemination process along. Speaking of which…how will you pay for it? I doubt insurance covers something like this."

"No, but it's not as expensive as you might think. The procedure itself is only four hundred dollars."

Presley stopped Wyatt from pulling over a lamp. "Wow, that *is* a surprise."

"But there'll also be meds, lab work and ultrasounds so…in total I may have to come up with as much as two to four thousand dollars."

"Do you have that kind of money?" A mere thousand was a fortune in Presley's world.

"I have a small savings account that's separate from the one I share with Dylan. I can swing it if I have to. If I don't have enough, Eve or Ted or one of my other friends would help, but I'd rather not include them in this."

"A wise decision." Presley gathered up her diaper bag. "The fewer people who know, the better."

Presley was grateful to Aaron for making this possible, but she didn't like the way his role in this kept him front and center of her life. It was hard enough for her not to think of him *without* it. "Sounds like you're committed to your decision."

"This is the only crazy thing I've ever done—except get involved with Dylan in the first place. And look how perfectly that turned out."

Presley smiled despite her concern. Dylan had been the best thing to ever happen to Cheyenne. But that was part of the reason Presley was so worried about the deception. She knew from experience that such secrets weren't easy to keep.

When Wyatt saw that she was getting ready to leave, he toddled over. He liked Cheyenne but didn't want to be left behind.

She kissed him as she pulled him into her arms and headed to the door.

She was out front, holding Wyatt while Cheyenne strapped in his car seat, when Dylan arrived.

"Where'd you go?" Cheyenne called as he got out.

"Had to take care of a few things."

"You came home just in time," Presley told him, jumping into the conversation before Cheyenne could accidentally mention that she knew he'd visited his brother. "Otherwise, you wouldn't have gotten to see me. *Again,*" she said with a laugh.

He came over and took Wyatt away from her,

tossed him in the air and caught him. "What's happening with you tonight, little man?"

Wyatt squealed and kicked. "Mo!" he demanded, and Dylan threw him again.

Cheyenne, finished with the car seat, stepped out of the way. "Presley's borrowing the Prius so she can move a few things tonight," she told Dylan. "You don't mind, do you?"

"Not at all." He gave Wyatt back so she could put him in his seat. "Need a hand?"

"No, I'll just be puttering around doing small stuff." She tightened her grip on Wyatt when he said, "Unca," for Uncle Dylan and suddenly lurched for his idol. "I'll have it back before morning."

"No need to bring it back." He tweaked Wyatt on the nose. "I can walk over and pick it up before work if that's easier."

Impulsively, she grabbed her brother-in-law and hugged him as well as she could while holding a baby. "You're special, Dylan Amos. I'm *so* glad my sister has you, and that Wyatt has a good man in his life."

Dylan seemed to be taken off guard. He'd always been a little rough around the edges, wasn't used to receiving such effusive praise. And she wasn't the type to deliver it. She'd never told him how much she liked him, let alone *loved* him. But she felt it. He added so much strength and support to her life. Before Dylan, Cheyenne had been all the family she had. Besides Anita, of course…

"You can borrow one of our cars anytime," he called after her. Although she could hear the grin in his voice, she was too embarrassed to look back.

"Riley's a good guy, too," Cheyenne chimed in.

But, as good as Riley was, Presley didn't want him. The only man she'd *ever* wanted was Aaron.

Getting the rest of her things moved didn't turn out to be as easy as Presley had expected. Wyatt was usually cooperative about sleeping in his stroller or playpen if they weren't home, but he wasn't having it tonight. He wanted his crib, and he was letting her know it. So Presley gave up before she was finished and took him home. She hadn't accomplished as much as she would've liked, which was a shame since she had a vehicle to use, but as a mother she had to be flexible.

Besides, she was tired, too. It was nearly eleven— and yet she couldn't sleep. She kept thinking about Aaron and the fact that he'd agreed to help Cheyenne. She wanted to tell him that she appreciated the happiness it would bring and the generosity behind his decision, but she hesitated to dial his number because she wasn't sure if that was just an excuse to hear his voice.

She picked up her phone and put it down two or three times before she decided to go ahead and say what she had to say. Even then, she would've ended the call as soon as she heard the sleep in his voice but he already knew who it was.

"Pres?"

She winced as the memory of how he'd reacted the night her mother died rose in her mind. Damn caller ID. "Sorry, I didn't mean to wake you," she said, then clicked off.

"Shit," she muttered, and buried her head beneath

the covers, but he called her right back. And when she didn't answer, he called again. And again.

Finally, she picked up.

"Presley, are you okay?"

"Yes. Of course. We can talk later. I thought you might be up watching TV." He'd never gone to bed so early before. "We can connect in the morning. Or some other time."

"Whoa, don't hang up. It's fine. *Please* let me re-deem myself for…what happened two years ago…"

"There's no need for that. It's okay." Without that rude awakening, maybe she never would've had the impetus to take her life in another direction. Maybe she would've aborted Wyatt. Maybe she would've settled for hanging on to Aaron's coattails as long as he allowed it. Then where would she be?

Granted, her life had gotten worse before it got better, but look where she was today.

"So…do you have news?" he asked.

"About?"

"Are you pregnant?"

"I don't know yet." She could get a test from the grocery store, but had no idea if they were accurate within twenty-four hours of a possible conception. And if they weren't, why spend the money? Besides, she didn't want to be seen buying something like that in such a small town—didn't want word of it cir-culating among the gossips when she was trying so hard to convince everyone she'd changed. She could only imagine what Cheyenne would say if word got back to her.…

"When will you find out?" he asked.

"I can't give you an exact day. There are over-the-counter tests I could buy, and I have Cheyenne's Prius, but Dylan's planning to pick it up in the morning and nothing's open at the moment."

"I can get a test tomorrow. It doesn't have to be your responsibility."

"Don't bother. I'll take care of it when I can and give you the results."

"Okay."

She swallowed against a dry throat. "Anyway, I called to thank you for helping Cheyenne."

"That's all?" He sounded disappointed.

"I already told you I have no answers on…that other issue."

"An answer wasn't the only thing I was hoping you were calling about. I'll be more careful this time if you want me to come over."

She closed her eyes. Of course he expected what he'd gotten last night. She knew that was the one thing he associated her with. But if she didn't hold out for more, for real love instead of mere sexual gratification, she might never have a relationship like the one Cheyenne had with Dylan. And she wanted that, wanted to raise her life to a higher level.

Don't accept less!

"I'll let you go back to sleep," she said, and hung up.

Since Presley had called him once, Aaron thought he might hear from her again. She hadn't moved on as completely as she wanted him to believe, or she wouldn't have contacted him on Monday night, especially so late—and Sunday wouldn't have been as explosive and satisfying as it was.

But Tuesday, Wednesday and Thursday passed, and he didn't see or hear anything. He drove by her house and studio a few times hoping to catch a glimpse of her, but all he saw was a sign that said her grand opening would be Saturday. If she noticed him or his truck in the vicinity, she didn't convey it. He figured she was too busy to think of anything besides her business.

On Friday, he decided he was a fool for trying to outwait her. Here he was, constantly checking his phone, looking for a voice mail or a text and getting upset when he didn't receive one. What was the point? Why was he suddenly playing games with her, letting his pride get in the way? If he wanted to see her, he should call and ask if she wanted to go out with him tonight.

So he did. But she told him she had a date with Riley.

"Where's he taking you?" he asked.

There was a slight pause.

"Is that classified information?" He regretted the jealous edge to his voice, but she didn't call him on it. She was obviously too convinced that her being with another man wouldn't disturb him.

"He said I could pick my favorite restaurant."

"Generous of him. So you're going to Just Like Mom's?"

"It's not fancy. He'll probably laugh when I tell him, but…there's just something about it, and I haven't been since I got home."

Just Like Mom's featured home cooking the likes of which she'd never had as a child. And Ruthie, the owner, represented the nurturing, motherlike figure she'd always craved. He understood, because he liked the local restaurant for the same reasons. They used to go there together and order open-faced turkey sandwiches, spaghetti and meatballs, meat loaf and mashed potatoes or grilled pork chops with a fully loaded baked potato. And, always, apple pie à la mode for dessert. They'd been like lost children eager to pretend they'd found a home.

"I guess you've forgotten, but *I* like it, too," he said.

"I know."

"*I* would've taken you there. We could've ordered the chili fries with extra chili and cheese for old times' sake."

"I'm sorry, Aaron. You might be right, maybe Riley's not the one I'm looking for, but I'm going to give him a chance," she said, then ended the call.

Presley was nervous. She'd never been on a date like this—not with someone so...*suitable,* someone she could settle down with who'd actually make a good father for Wyatt. The guys she'd dated in Fresno generally had a record, no interest in marriage or kids, let alone taking on the responsibility of someone *else's* child. Or they didn't have a job.

"How do I look?" she asked Cheyenne when she went over to drop off Wyatt. She hadn't known what to wear. Her wardrobe was getting sparse; it had never been elaborate to begin with. She spent all her money on living expenses.

Her sister handed Wyatt to Dylan and pulled her into the bedroom, where she had Presley change out of her jeans, boots and leather jacket and put on a pretty sheath dress with strappy sandals, smaller earrings and a few bangle bracelets.

"Where did you get this stuff?" she demanded, surprised to find that it was all her size instead of her much taller sister's.

"I bought it for you."

"You knew you wouldn't like what I chose?"

"I got it for your birthday in June."

"That's two months away!"

"I plan ahead."

She was going to look silly so dressed up at Just Like Mom's, but Cheyenne didn't seem to care where they were going. She even dragged her into the bathroom and added a bit of curl to Presley's short cut.

Soon, Presley scarcely recognized herself. She stared into the mirror, thinking she'd never looked more like her completely unrelated sister than she did at that moment—despite the difference in their size, coloring and hair length. But she guessed Riley would like the classy vibe she was sporting tonight. He might be a contractor, but he wasn't like the belly-scratching beer hounds she'd known in the past.

"Well?" Cheyenne awaited her response with glittering eyes.

"I look whiter than I ever have. That's for sure."

"*Whiter?* What are you talking about? Pale?"

"No. I'm saying I look like a middle- or even upper-class white woman."

"You *are* a white woman."

"Partly. Maybe. Who knows?"

"Stop. What does the color of your skin have to do with anything, anyway? You're beautiful. Nothing else matters."

Presley wasn't sure why she felt uncomfortable, but she didn't want to disappoint Cheyenne after her sister had gone to so much trouble and expense, so she didn't try to describe her feelings. "I like what you bought. Thanks."

"You're welcome." Cheyenne gave her a hug. "I hope you have a *really* nice time."

"I'm sure I will," she said, but with the way her nerves were acting up, she doubted she'd be able to swallow a single bite. She was going to get her first free meal in ages—since the last guy she'd dated never had the money to pay for dinner—yet she wouldn't be in any condition to enjoy it. How ironic.

Cheyenne touched her tattoo. "Have you ever thought about having this removed?"

Presley glanced at the jaguar slinking down her right arm. "No." She had some Chinese characters that represented truth and courage on her side, too. But they couldn't be seen unless she was naked, so there was no reason to mention them.

"Just a thought," Cheyenne said.

A wish, more likely. Cheyenne hated tattoos on women. She felt they were tacky.

The doorbell rang, signaling Riley's arrival. Presley had texted him to let him know she'd be at Cheyenne's.

Presley remembered Aaron's reaction to her date, the way he'd said, *"I would've taken you there."* Lounging in a booth, eating overladen chili-cheese fries while laughing with the man she loved sounded like fun. "Is it too late to back out?" she asked.

Cheyenne scowled at her. "Stop. You're all set, you're gorgeous, and you're going to have a blast."

Dylan quit playing with Wyatt long enough to whistle at her as she came through the living room. "Wow! Riley had better watch out."

She rolled her eyes. "You only like the way I look because I resemble your wife—as much as I can, anyway."

"You always look good," he told her.

"Sure I do." She infused those words with so much sarcasm he couldn't mistake it. "But thanks for trying."

He winked at her, then chuckled as she answered the door.

12

Presley had a lot more fun than she'd expected to. For starters, Riley was surprisingly easy to talk to. And the fact that they both had a son, even though Riley's was so much older, gave them plenty of common ground.

They didn't end up going to Just Like Mom's. Presley had been hesitant to name it as her favorite restaurant while sitting in his car wearing the elegant dress her sister had bought. So when he suggested they drive to San Francisco, she agreed. She had her grand opening in the morning and didn't want to get home *too* late—San Francisco was an hour and a half away—but he looked so handsome sitting there, all scrubbed and polished, that she couldn't refuse.

Why *not* go fancy? She was wearing high heels, wasn't she? That alone made it a special occasion.

He took her to a famous seafood restaurant on the pier, but it wasn't in the least pretentious. She felt comfortable there. Although she was planning to order the salmon or another entrée that wasn't particularly pricy, Riley insisted she get lobster since she'd never tried it. Between the sweet meat and salty butter, the wine and the engaging conversation, she was glad she'd come. She hadn't done much on a social level since she'd moved away.

After dinner, they strolled along the wharf, taking in the beauty of the moon sparkling on the bay and enjoying the street performers. When Riley gave her his coat, saying the breeze was too cold for her to go without one, she felt like a fairy princess. She was wearing beautiful clothes in a beautiful city with a beautiful man who had taken her hand to guide her through the crowds. She'd never felt further from the white-trash image she'd always had of herself.

It wasn't until they drove home and he walked her up to Cheyenne's door that she grew self-conscious again. Was he going to kiss her? Did she want him to? Would there be a second date?

"I had a great time," she said as they reached the doorstep. "Thank you for a fun night."

"I had fun, too. You seem so grateful for everything, so excited about even the small stuff. It's... refreshing."

"Eating lobster for the first time in San Francisco isn't small stuff."

He leaned against the porch railing. "The view wasn't anything I paid for, and yet it seemed you liked that best."

She'd liked *all* of it. She was beginning to believe—*truly* believe—in a future that was very different from her past. All those nights spent cuddled up with Cheyenne for warmth in Anita's rattletrap car, or some fleabag hotel, scared and alone—or tolerating the presence of a strange man in their mother's bed—had never felt so far away. Even the nights that had come much later, the nights she'd checked out, using drugs to escape her memories, her fears and her self-loathing, seemed like they'd occurred in another lifetime. She felt so much more positive about herself, and associating with people like Riley gave her confidence that she wouldn't regress.

"Maybe it's because I'm seeing the world in a new way—or at least the possibilities of it," she said.

She wondered what he'd make of that. She expected him to question her but he didn't. Maybe he understood her better than she'd given him credit for.

"I like showing you those possibilities," he said. Then he bent his head and kissed her lightly on the lips. "Good night," he murmured, and walked back to his car.

Presley watched him drive off before going inside.

"I'm here for Wyatt," she whispered into the entryway of her sister's bedroom. Because she wasn't sure how she felt about Riley, she'd been hoping to take her baby and slip out. She'd thought she might be able to, since everyone was asleep. But Cheyenne got up, pulled on a robe and followed her into the guest room, where she'd put Wyatt to bed in his playpen, which she'd picked up earlier.

"So? How'd it go?" she asked.

Although Presley spotted Wyatt's diaper bag in the corner, all packed up, and slung it over her arm, she didn't approach her baby. She wouldn't disturb him until she could carry him straight out to his stroller. "It was fun."

"Where'd he take you?"

"San Francisco."

"Sounds romantic."

Presley smiled as she replayed the evening in her head like the melody of a music box. "It was."

"Do you think you'll be seeing him again?"

"I'm sure I will, considering the size of this town."

"You know what I mean."

"If he asks me."

"He didn't give you any indication?"

"No. He just said he had a nice time," she said with a shrug.

Her sister lowered her voice. "Did he kiss you?"

Presley felt herself blush. This conversation made her feel like a teenager. "Sort of."

"What does that mean?"

"It was a very chaste kiss."

"Is 'chaste' a turnoff?"

"Not at all." Presley gave her a gentle nudge. "Go back to bed. We can talk about this later."

"I wasn't sleeping that well to begin with," Cheyenne admitted.

"Worried about the artificial insemination?"

"Among other things."

"Like…"

She sighed. "Dylan and I had an argument tonight."

They didn't fight often. "Why?"

"I found a letter in one of his pockets from his father. J.T's remarried. Can you *believe* that? Dylan has a stepmother, and he didn't even tell me."

"Why?"

"He said he didn't want to upset me."

"But he had to realize you were going to find out eventually."

"He claims he *was* going to tell me. He just hadn't gotten around to it yet."

If Dylan had a new stepmother, so did Aaron and the others. Presley considered what that might mean to the Fearsome Five. "Who is she? Did you learn anything about her?"

"Only that he met her on a singles site for prisoners."

"You'd have to be seriously out of options to shop for a man there."

"Or you're addicted to the thrill of danger."

"Does Aaron know?" Presley asked.

"I'm pretty sure he does. Remember when we got the text from him saying he'd—" she checked behind her to make sure Dylan wasn't standing in the hallway "—do what we want him to?"

"Of course. That was a few days ago."

"I think he and Dylan discussed it that night."

"I'll bet you're right. But you're not going to let the fact that he didn't tell you about his father cause a problem between the two of you...."

"*He* caused the problem by shutting me out. He says he did it to protect me from worrying that maybe his father's marriage will end before he's released. But if *he's* worried about something, I want to know about it. I'm his wife, the person who loves him, so I *should* know about it."

"Like he knows what's going on in your life?" she countered.

"Stop. I don't have any choice about how I'm going to get pregnant. I'm doing that for him."

"And he was hoping his father's marriage would end, and he'd never have to tell you or anyone else."

"Thanks for taking his side."

"I'm not taking his side."

"You don't like that I'm keeping the truth from him."

"I just want you to understand that it's a choice but…to be honest, I'd probably make the same one in your shoes," she admitted.

"Thanks for that, at least. Anyway, I'm glad it went well with you and Riley, and that he's taking my advice."

"About?"

She grinned. "I told him to go slow."

Presley grabbed her arm. "Hey, I don't like you coaching him."

"He's a great guy, Pres. I don't want you to overlook him."

"I won't. I like who I am when I'm with him, if that makes sense." Maybe that was more important than the powerful lust and the giddiness she felt around Aaron. Maybe a relationship based on mutual respect instead of sexual attraction would keep her on an even keel, make her capable of achieving more than she otherwise would. It would certainly give her more power in the relationship, which was important after having such a one-sided experience with Aaron.

"He didn't ask to see you again, though?"

"No."

"I'm sure he will."

"I'm not stewing about it one way or the other. With my opening tomorrow, I can't really think about anything else."

"Right. You're probably nervous. I don't know if

I remembered to tell you, but I took some flyers to my friends when we met for coffee this morning."

"Was the one I posted in the coffee shop still there by the register?"

"It was."

"How did your friends respond?"

"Several of them said they're planning to come."

She was offering free ten-minute massages as well as cookies and punch. "Hopefully, they'll like what I can do enough to become clients."

Her sister squeezed her arm. "I'm betting Riley will."

"I owe him. He spent a lot tonight. And he did all that work on the reception area."

"Which looks great, by the way. He must really like you."

When Wyatt began to stir, Presley waved Cheyenne to silence. She was afraid he'd wake up too completely and not be able to go back to sleep. She had to get *some* rest to face such a big day. But that didn't become a problem. Cheyenne took the diaper bag, put it down and pulled her out of the bedroom.

"Leave him for tonight," she said. "It doesn't make sense to move him if you have to bring him back first thing in the morning, anyway."

"Are you sure?"

"Positive."

Presley smiled in gratitude. She hadn't been blessed with a good mother, father or extended family. But, quite by accident, since Cheyenne was just a little girl when it all happened, her mother had stolen her the best of sisters—not that being raised by Anita could ever be construed as a blessing to Cheyenne. "Thank you. I appreciate it."

"What are sisters for? I'll see you tomorrow. Wyatt and I will stop by to check out the grand opening, so leave me the stroller."

"Dylan won't be coming to get a free massage?"

"He's got to work."

"Tell him I'll give him a massage some other time, then. Longer than the ten-minute samples I'll be doing tomorrow. He's earned it."

She carried her clothes home with a smile, but as she approached her house, she saw Aaron sitting in his truck across the street and realized her night wasn't over quite yet.

Presley had never looked less like her old self than when Aaron saw her coming down the street in a pretty cocktail dress and high heels. If he hadn't known better, he would've thought she was some classy stranger—a small, compact woman with short, choppy hair and dark eyes as big as saucers.

It was partly the dress that made her seem different. She'd never worn anything like that when she lived in Whiskey Creek before. He'd seen her in a sundress or, when they went clubbing, far sexier clothing. But this simple sleeveless number...

He liked it. A lot. It enhanced her improved figure, something that was quite evident since she wasn't wearing a coat. Speaking of which, what was she doing meandering down the sidewalk as if she was in no hurry whatsoever when it was only forty-five degrees outside?

This wasn't how he'd been hoping to find her. From

all the signs, including that dreamy smile, her date with Riley had gone well. Where the heck was her baby? There'd been no one at home when he knocked, and she was obviously coming from Cheyenne's but didn't have him with her.

"Hey," he said as he got out.

Her smile had disappeared the moment she noticed his truck. She'd also come to a stop. Now her expression was...wary.

"Hey." Her response held far less enthusiasm than he would've liked. Somehow, *he'd* become the bad guy. He wasn't sure how. For years, he'd been just about her only friend.

He grabbed the sack he'd tossed in his passenger seat and closed the door before crossing the street. "I expected you to get home ages ago."

He shouldn't have said that. He had no reason to be monitoring the time she spent with Riley.

She smoothed her dress. "How long have you been waiting?"

"Not long," he replied. But it had been an hour or more. He hadn't been able to make himself leave. The later it grew, the more frightened he'd become that she'd gone home with Riley, that Riley was touching her the way *he'd* touched her, and that had bothered him so much he'd driven over to Riley's. When he didn't see Riley's truck where it was usually parked, he'd returned to her house, but the sick feeling in his gut hadn't dissipated.

It wasn't until he'd finally spotted her, alone, that his anxiety eased. But that flash of relief turned out to be short-lived. The way she was dressed and walking on air indicated that the date had convinced her Riley had *potential*.

She's looking for a husband...

"So how'd it go?" he asked.

She hugged herself, rubbing away the chill bumps that had sprung up on her arms. Apparently, now that she was face-to-face with *him,* she could feel the cold. "Fine."

"What'd you do?"

"Went to San Francisco."

He almost took off his jacket and slipped it around her shoulders, but he was afraid she'd think he was making some kind of move on her. She'd already told him that she didn't even want him coming over.

At least he had a good reason for being here tonight.

"For dinner?" he asked. "I thought you were going to Just Like Mom's." He'd figured out that they hadn't gone to the local diner hours ago—he'd checked when he and Grady went to the drive-in down the street. But she didn't know that.

"We decided to do something different, get out of town. I tried lobster for the first time," she added with a touch of wonder. "And the moon over the bay was so full."

He refused to let his smile wilt. Riley was putting some effort into pursuing Presley; Aaron had to give him that. "Nice. So you like him?"

"Of course. What's not to like?"

That didn't tell him much. "He's not your type."

"Then who is?"

Someone who could understand her. Someone who could relate to the life she'd led. Someone more like *him.* But he knew he couldn't say that; it wouldn't come out right, since he wasn't really interested in the kind of relationship she was looking for. "No one from around here."

Her gaze shifted to the bag he was carrying. "What's that?"

He opened it to show her the pregnancy test he'd purchased.

"Of course. I understand now."

"What?" he asked. "What do you understand?"

"Why you're here. Where did you get that, by the way?"

"Jackson. Don't worry. I wasn't stupid enough to buy it here."

"Come on in. It won't take long."

"Where's Wyatt?" he asked as she led him to the porch and pulled out her keys.

"Cheyenne's keeping him overnight. I have my grand opening in the morning."

"Are you excited about that?"

She pushed the door open. "A little. Nervous, too."

"Why would you be nervous?"

"I'm afraid no one will show up," she said as they went in. "It's a small town, and I wasn't exactly popular when I lived here before. I wasn't even considered *respectable*."

"You've always been a nice person. You were just confused."

"No one cares about the reasons." She closed the door with a bang. "But Riley said he'd bring some people, and Cheyenne asked Eve and some others to come, so…maybe there'll be a decent turnout."

Riley was certainly doing all he could to win her

over. Aaron had never disliked the guy before, but that was beginning to change.

"I just hope I get some real clients out of it." She gestured at the sofa. "Would you like to sit down?"

He shook his head. "You're afraid there might not be a market here for yoga and massage?"

"That's a very real possibility."

"You could've gone to a big city. What made you come here?"

"I wanted to be close to Chey and Dylan, wanted Wyatt to have some family around. And I figured, if I worked hard enough, I should be able to establish *something*. This place is the closest thing I have to home."

"It'll work out." At least, he hoped it would. She deserved it.

"You're probably right," she said. "I'm just feeling a little jittery, since I've sunk everything into a business that involves so much risk."

He could understand why she might be nervous. She'd never had much of anything go her way. He wanted to support her grand opening, too, but he wasn't sure whether or not to offer. He doubted she'd want him there. Besides, Riley had beaten him to making the commitment, so it would just seem like he was trying to compete.

"You're good. The massage you gave me was incredible."

She blanched. "That's not the kind of massage I'll be giving everyone."

"I wasn't suggesting that. I only wanted to reassure you. I hate…" He let his words trail off when he couldn't decide how to say what he wanted to say.

"What?" She tossed her keys on the coffee table and looked up.

He hated that she regretted being with him. But she was so convinced that he didn't care about her, she wouldn't take him seriously even if he said he did.

"Never mind."

She didn't press him. She actually seemed relieved that he'd backed off. "Okay. I'll be right out," she said, and disappeared into the bathroom with the sack.

Presley's hands shook as she removed the pregnancy test from its box. She already had one child by Aaron. What would she do if she was pregnant with another? And how would *he* react? It certainly wasn't a secret she'd try to keep a second time. If she was pregnant, he was going to hear about it. But after having Wyatt, she knew she could never get an abortion. It just wasn't an option for her. Which meant she might wind up raising *two* children alone....

"This is what happens when you screw up," she breathed. "It's your own fault. You *knew* better." She *had* to keep chastising herself; otherwise, the desire to be with Aaron again would take control. The second she'd seen him sitting in his truck she'd forgotten all about her date with Riley, all about everything, except him. *Them.* For her, the pleasure he could provide went far beyond the physical. And since Cheyenne had kept Wyatt the whole night stretched before her without any of the responsibilities of motherhood. That made her even more vulnerable.

"Did you say something?" Aaron's voice came through the door.

"No."

"Well? What's the verdict?"

"Sorry. Working up the nerve."

There was a brief silence. Then he said, "I won't leave you to face the consequences alone—if there are any. Maybe that'll make it a *little* easier."

That was a nice thing to say, but what *exactly* did it mean? He'd pay for an abortion? Drive her to the clinic? How would he respond when she told him she wouldn't get one?

"Thanks," she said dully. She had no real hope of his support. Not the kind she wanted, anyway.

Gathering her courage, she read the information included with the kit so she'd know what she was doing.

The test strip would read the levels of hCG, the pregnancy hormone, in her urine. It could detect a rise in these levels as early as six days from fertilization. She'd been with Aaron last Monday, which meant it hadn't been quite that long.

Maybe she'd be smart to wait another few days.

"You done yet?" he asked.

He was nervous, too, of course—and impatient to alleviate his concern. So she decided to go ahead. Her period was due any day. If it didn't come as expected, she'd buy another test in a week or so—and if it turned out to be positive, she'd just have to tell him later.

"Takes three minutes," she said.

"Are you timing it? Or should I?"

"I will."

"I could use the stopwatch on my phone. But…is there any chance I could come in?"

"No." Absolutely not. She certainly didn't plan

on keeping the truth from him, but she felt vulnerable enough.

"Why? I've seen every inch of you, touched every inch. So what's with the sudden modesty?"

"It's not sudden," she told him. "It's taken two years." Besides, she wanted to be the first to see the results. If the answer was yes, she'd need a moment to recover.

"Hurry up, then."

After she performed the test, she set the plastic tray on the sink and held her breath while she waited. It would turn pink if it was positive, blue if it wasn't.

Was that pink she detected?

"It's time," Aaron announced, startling her.

Her phone indicated the same thing. She bent closer, staring at the results.

Blue. Thank God. Sinking onto the toilet, she let her breath go. "You don't have anything to worry about," she called out. If the test could be trusted. "According to this, I'm not pregnant."

He didn't respond right away, but she imagined he was out there thanking God as much as she was.

She threw everything away, washed her hands and opened the door to find him waiting in the hallway.

"That was a close one," he said.

"Too close."

"Are you relieved?"

"Aren't you?"

He looked chagrined. "Sorry for the scare. I can't tell you what I did wrong—if anything."

"That sort of thing happens sometimes."

Silence fell as they stared at each other. Aaron was the first to break it. "So…I guess I'd better go."

"Okay," she said as he straightened. "Thanks for buying the test."

"No problem."

She expected him to cross to the door, but he didn't.

"They had this big makeup case at the drugstore," he told her, turning back. "I almost bought one."

"You want makeup?"

He came close enough that she could smell his cologne. "Of course not. I thought *you* might like it. It has all these layers and tons of stuff inside. With a mirror."

"Sounds interesting. I'll have to check it out." Or not. She wouldn't have the money for something like that for quite a while.

"I'll pick one up next time."

"That's okay. Don't get it for me."

"It looked like the sort of thing a girl could use."

"There's always Cheyenne."

He scowled at her. "Dylan can get one for Cheyenne. I'm trying to be nice."

"You don't need to be," she said. "I can't return the favor."

"Why the hell not? You're being pretty damn nice to Riley."

She braced one hand against the wall. "Riley's different."

"In what way?"

"We have no business talking about this."

"You're right. Good night."

She thought she'd said good night in exchange, so she had no idea why he didn't leave. Or how, a split second later, she came to be plastered against him, kissing him openmouthed and wet, as if she needed his tongue more than oxygen. One second he was walking away from her; the next an invisible force took hold—and it didn't seem to be her fault any more than his. The sudden kiss was...mutual.

"We can't do this," she gasped as his lips moved down her neck.

"Okay," he said, but neither one of them stopped. If anything, the intensity grew. Soon, he was suckling her breast while his hand worked pure Aaron magic between her legs.

Presley wanted him so badly, *too* badly to stop. She clung to his broad shoulders, instinctively thrusting in response to what he was doing with his fingers.

Why was he so different from every other man? *Why* couldn't she resist him?

She couldn't concentrate long enough to answer those questions. She was already charging down the road that led where she wanted to go. But she forced herself to stop responding, to stop *feeling,* and caught his face between her hands. "Are you going home? You *have* to go home."

Suddenly, he withdrew, leaving her blouse open and her clothes disheveled. "Is that what you *really* want?"

Anger glittered in his eyes. He didn't like the mixed signals he'd been getting, the confusion, the frustration, the disappointment—and then the surprise of her giving in. But she wasn't any happier with the situation. She was involved in such a battle. Sometimes she gained ground; sometimes she lost it.

"Okay. You can stay. But it's only for tonight," she told him. "You have birth control?"

"I do. Plenty. And they're brand-new. Not like that old piece of shit I used the last time."

"Fine. Then we've got tonight. That's all. And you can't act possessive afterward or tell *anyone,* especially Dylan."

He hesitated, seemingly torn. It wasn't like Aaron to accept less than everything he wanted. He didn't like that she wasn't allowing him back in her life with all the rights, access and privileges he'd had before, didn't like that she wasn't letting him call the shots.

She could sense his resistance, his inclination just to walk out.

Part of her prayed he would. She needed him to remove the temptation he posed. But he seemed to be entangled in the same ropes of desire that held her fast, which was a surprise. Why didn't he head over to Sexy Sadie's and pick up some other girl?

"If you want me to be your dirty little secret, you'd better make it worth my while," he growled, and the next thing she knew, he was carrying her into the bedroom.

13

By morning, Aaron was so exhausted he could hardly move. He'd never made love so many times, and so rigorously, in a single night. He and Presley had both wanted to get their fill of each other so they could move on.

He hoped they'd accomplished that. He didn't want to be responsible if she regressed; for one thing Dylan and Cheyenne would blame him. Neither did he want her to become as infatuated with him as she'd been before, because he couldn't bear the thought of hurting her. He'd felt bad for two years, thanks to his behavior the night her mother died.

Even with all his good intentions, it was going to be tough to let her go. The way she put her whole heart and soul into her lovemaking created an experience that was more powerful, more erotic and far more memorable than those he'd known with other women.

"Please tell me that isn't the sun," she mumbled, rousing enough to speak but not enough to open her eyes.

He stroked her breast, admiring the sheer beauty

of it. The recent improvements to her body were dramatic. But her breasts were the same, and he was glad of that. He'd always liked them just as they were. "'Fraid so."

Her head popped up. "What time is it?"

The frantic note in her voice made him chuckle. "Relax. It's early yet, barely six."

"I have my grand opening today."

"When do you have to be there?"

"It starts at ten, but I have a lot to do before then."

The thought of Riley waiting eagerly for her doors to open threatened to ruin what was otherwise a great morning. "I hope you have a huge crowd."

"So do I." She scrambled out of bed without touching him.

"Where are you going so fast?" he asked.

"I've got to get showered."

"I told you—it's barely six."

"And I told *you* I have a lot to do."

"But you haven't had any sleep, other than thirty minutes here or there. Come back for an hour's nap."

"I can't. I need to make cookies and punch, and I have to print flyers."

"I'll help," he volunteered. "Just pull up the file on your computer."

"That's okay."

"Or I could start with the cookies. But having me bake probably isn't a wise choice. Not if you want them to taste right."

"I can manage. You're completely off the hook."

She could've taken a moment to consider his offer.... "You mean I've done my job."

"At least you did it well," she said with a smile.

Despite that smile, he couldn't tell if she was joking and had the uncomfortable feeling she wasn't. "So you're sending me off without breakfast?" He was hoping to lure her back, for a goodbye if nothing else. It was over too soon. There'd been no denouement, just a series of intense climaxes.

But she didn't return to him; she hurried into the bathroom. "You can have breakfast if you want to make it yourself."

Aaron remained on the bed, staring up at the ceiling. He'd gotten what he wanted last night; theoretically, he should be satisfied. He *had* been satisfied a second ago. But her dismissal, which seemed a little too pat, had ruined the afterglow. So did picturing Riley at her studio, waiting to prove his admiration and loyalty by bringing in a herd of his friends.

"Why don't I drive over to Nature's Way and buy a bunch of cookies?" he asked. Hopefully, Riley wasn't already doing *that*.

Her voice came to him above the sound of the shower. "I can't afford it."

"I'll pay."

"There's no need."

"You don't want my help? Why not? We're friends. We used to be, at any rate," he added. Since she'd moved back, he wasn't sure.

"Do you usually get up at the crack of dawn on Saturday and rush to the grocery store for your friends?"

"No, but none of my other friends has ever asked me."

"I'm fine. Really," she insisted. "Anyway, it's probably better if no one sees you at the store this early, especially with cookies that later show up at my grand opening."

He punched his pillow. "That's a guilty conscience talking."

She didn't reply.

"So you want me to leave?"

When he heard nothing but the water running, he assumed she wasn't going to answer him. But then she said, "I'm sure you have a busy day ahead."

That was essentially a yes.

Put out that she could go cold so quickly, he got up and jerked on his clothes. "Thanks for last night," he muttered and dug his keys out of his pocket.

She met him at the door, wearing only a robe. "Before you go, I just…I want to tell you how much I hope everything works out for you and…and that you'll always be happy."

The bright flash of optimism he'd felt when she stopped him winked out. She'd told him there was no "in between" for her; they couldn't be the kind of friends who hung out together. But what prevented them from being sociable when they bumped into each other? *Hello, how are you?*—that sort of thing. He liked her. He didn't want to lose her completely.

"Until I move to Reno, we'll still be living in the same town, Presley. Are you seriously planning to avoid me altogether?"

She hesitated as if she wanted to say yes but didn't have the heart to sound so unforgiving. "How much longer will you be here?"

"I can't say for sure. But that's fine. We don't need to have any contact if you don't want it."

To his surprise, she didn't backpedal. She nodded solemnly. "Okay."

Okay? After how hot she'd been for him mere hours ago? She'd nearly ripped off his clothes.

He was tempted to pull her toward him, to remind her what it was like when they touched. But he saw how rigidly she was standing there, holding her old robe closed, so he didn't. However misguided he'd been last night, he'd agreed to this.

"Goodbye, Aaron."

"There's no guarantee Riley will marry you," he blurted out. "You could be giving up months of great sex and a hell of a lot of fun—we always have fun, right?--for nothing."

She raised her chin in defiance. "The best way to guarantee I end up with nothing is to keep on sleeping with you."

He felt his jaw drop. "You want *him?*"

"Maybe I do and maybe I don't," she replied. "But I'd be a fool to lose such a great prospect just because I can't keep my hands off someone else."

"Off *me.*"

"Off you."

"God, you make me crazy," he said, and marched out.

Presley let her head fall against the door frame. Sex with Aaron had been more spectacular than she ever could have hoped. There was no feeling to compare with being head over heels in love. It was a far more intense high than any drug could provide. To enhance the experience, last night there'd been a new element: she'd felt powerful. Maybe she had power with Aaron only in the bedroom, but even that was unusual and somewhat liberating. She'd always been so eager for his attention, for his touch. There were isolated incidents when she'd gotten the impression that he'd made love to her just because she wanted him to. She'd felt those incidents had become more frequent shortly before she left town. But, like last Monday, the balance of desire hadn't been quite so uneven during this encounter. He'd wanted her every bit as much as she'd wanted him.

Regardless, their time together was over, and she refused to dwell on it. She had her future mapped out. Whether or not she ever found a man to share it with wasn't going to be something on which she hung her happiness. She had Wyatt and Cheyenne and Dylan in her life. She had her hopes and her dreams. And she now had a way to make them come true. She couldn't allow herself to be enslaved by craving the wrong man, especially when she'd done everything she could to assuage that craving last night—and found she was no better off than before. She had to move on and put him behind her.

Steam drifted into the living room. She was wasting hot water. Briefly squeezing her eyes closed, she took a deep breath, focused on the day ahead and hurried to get ready. She needed the opening to go smoothly.

Cheyenne called her once she had the cookies in the oven and was applying her makeup. "You all set?" her sister asked.

"Almost." She widened her eyes so she could finish her mascara while they talked. "How's Wyatt? Is he up? I would've called as soon as I rolled out of bed, but I didn't want to wake you before he did."

"He started jabbering a few minutes ago. So I took him into the living room, and now we're having scrambled eggs."

"I can't thank you enough for keeping him overnight." She paused to throw a frown at her reflection. *And look what you did with that time!*

"He just slept," Cheyenne said with a shrug in her voice.

Not quite. Presley knew he'd gotten Cheyenne up earlier than she normally would've climbed out of bed—and *she'd* spent the night with Aaron. Her sister wouldn't be happy to learn her sacrifice had made that possible. The fact that she'd, once again, broken her resolve not to get involved with him had Presley feeling she'd taken advantage of that kindness. "You're too good to me."

"You'd do the same for me. Are you excited about the grand opening?"

"More nervous than excited."

"I'm bringing a platter of sandwich rolls, and Eve's bringing her crab dip, so don't worry about having enough food."

"I was only doing cookies."

"This will give people something to do while they wait for their sample massages."

Presley began to apply mascara to her other eye. "Thanks. That's really nice of both of you."

"Did you get the new flyers printed?"

"I'm doing that next. One side will have my massage specials and the other my yoga schedule. I'll also have a sign-up sheet so I can schedule appointments right there."

"When will you be going over to set up?"

"In half an hour or so."

"Should I come and help?"

"Maybe after Dylan goes to work. There's no rush."

"Okay. I'll see you there."

As Presley finished the call, she received a text from Riley.

I had a great time last night. Thanks for the date, and good luck today. See you soon.

Her heart sank as she read it. She couldn't continue dating him, not after sleeping with Aaron. She didn't feel it was fair to Riley that she was still so fixated on her old sex partner.

Should she call him and tell him?

Not now, she decided. She had enough to worry about for one day. But she hated the thought that he was going to so much effort to bring her customers when things weren't quite as straightforward between them as he assumed.

With a quick, worried glance at the clock, she texted him back.

You don't have to come if it's inconvenient.

You kidding? No way would I miss a free massage.

She was tempted to say more but changed her mind. She'd just keep him and every other man at arm's length until Aaron was gone from Whiskey Creek and she could think clearly again.

OK. See you there.

When Dylan gave Grady, Rod and Mack some time off work to go over and support Presley's grand opening, he did it in such a way that Aaron knew he wasn't meant to hear. Dylan lowered his voice, said whatever he said and moved on. Then his brothers disappeared for an hour or so.

Aaron told himself he didn't care that they'd gone without him, even though appearing as part of the group would've been the most natural way for him to show up. If he went over now, he'd have to do it on his own.

But he couldn't help wondering what was going on. Was Presley getting the results she'd worked for? Were there lots of people enjoying the cookies and the massages—and scheduling future appointments or signing up for classes?

He didn't like to think of her sitting over there, mostly alone, worrying. She'd worked so hard to graduate from massage school, get moved and set up shop; this should be a triumphant day, a day of hope.

Finally succumbing to his curiosity and concern, he told Dylan he was taking off for lunch and drove over there.

As he parked, he saw a small crowd gathered inside her studio, and felt immediate relief. She had to be thrilled.

Since she obviously didn't need him, he nearly left. But then he saw Riley pull up.

"Shit," he muttered.

Still, he *would've* left—if only Riley hadn't grinned and waved.

Presley's lack of sleep began to take its toll sooner than she'd expected it to. So much for getting enough rest last night. She'd done the opposite. But she wasn't about to let her fatigue show. Cheyenne had come to the studio but already taken Wyatt home for a nap, so he was no longer fussing for her attention. And she had plenty of potential customers, probably the biggest group since she'd opened at ten. She had to make the most of this opportunity, needed to convert as many of them to paying clients as possible. So she smiled and explained what she had to offer—the benefits of yoga and massage—to everyone who walked in. They helped themselves to the food and punch as she massaged people in a steady stream.

Everything was going well. She could hardly believe her good fortune. Until Aaron arrived. Despite being focused on work, she spotted him the moment he strolled in, but he didn't speak to her. He took a cup of punch and a handful of cookies, then lounged on a chair in line. Clearly he planned to get his own free massage.

Presley wasn't looking forward to rubbing his back in front of a roomful of spectators. She was afraid that anyone who was really paying attention would be able to guess her feelings. But she didn't dread Aaron's impending massage as much as Riley's. Touching Riley under Aaron's watchful eye would be awkward, to say the least.

Maybe Aaron would tire of waiting and leave before she could get to Riley, she thought. As promised, Riley had brought several friends—Kyle among them. They were seated ahead of both Riley and Aaron. But as she worked her way down the line, Aaron didn't leave, as she hoped. She could feel his hazel eyes drilling into her as Riley removed his shirt and climbed onto her table.

Unable to stop herself, she glanced over. She was expecting Aaron to grin or do something else to tip her off that he was enjoying her discomfort. That had to be why he'd come—to rattle her cage. But he didn't smile. He seemed to be on edge throughout the massage, especially when it was over and Riley signed up for twenty future appointments.

"Are you sure you want to buy that many?" she asked in surprise. He'd selected her biggest package.

He pulled her close to answer. Although she saw Aaron's expression darken, he didn't move or speak up. For that she was grateful.

"If I buy a bunch, maybe other people will see it and do the same," Riley whispered.

She smiled despite her niggling concern over the hostility that seemed to be rolling off Aaron. "That's incredibly generous," she whispered back. "But I already owe you so much. I'll do them for free."

"This is the only payment I want." He brushed his lips across hers before she had any idea what he meant to do.

Aaron's chair banged against the wall, letting everyone know that he was no longer sitting. "I don't ~~think~~ that comes with the package," he said.

As soon as it dawned on Riley that Aaron wasn't

joking, Riley stepped up to him, and Presley's heart jumped into her throat.

Were they about to fight?

It certainly felt like it.

"Aaron, I'm sorry you're having to wait so long," she said, slipping between them. "But if you wouldn't mind coming back when I'm not so busy, I'll make sure you get your massage."

She held her breath as his gaze cut to her before returning to Riley. Riley looked every bit as strong and muscular as Aaron, but Presley had no doubt that Aaron could make quick work of him. To her knowledge, Riley had never had to fight for anything.

That didn't mean he was willing to back down, however. As far as she could tell—from the aggressive jut of his chin, his combative stance, even that kiss, which had suggested he was marking his territory—he seemed to be deliberately provoking Aaron.

"Temper getting the better of you again?" Riley spoke softly, but those words were intended as a taunt and there was no way to mistake that.

"Watch yourself," Aaron said, his voice low, muscles tense.

"Or what?"

Aaron's eyes flicked to Riley's fists. "It's hard to kiss a pretty girl when your jaw is wired shut."

"If you start something, I won't hold back," Riley warned.

"Then you'll have your ass handed to you."

Riley's eyes narrowed. "I don't know who the he[ ]you think you are. But you have no right to get i[ ]volved. Just because you once slept with a wom[ ] that doesn't give you any say over her life two years later."

She and Aaron hadn't last slept together two years ago; they'd slept together *last night*—so recently that Presley could understand why Aaron might be bothered by Riley's actions. But Aaron didn't betray her.

"I have more right than someone who's *never* slept with her," he said.

"I don't care about the past," Riley snapped. "I care about *now*. You don't have any claim on her. That's what I'm saying."

Again, Aaron didn't correct him about what was in the past and what wasn't. Thank goodness. Presley was embarrassed enough—or would've been if she wasn't too worried for that. She could sense Riley's friends gathering behind him, knew the odds were shifting in his favor but doubted Aaron would take that into account. He didn't walk out as she was hoping, which seemed to prove he'd take them all on, if necessary.

He stood glaring at Riley.

"Don't push this," she pleaded, grabbing Aaron's arm. "Neither of us needs this kind of trouble."

"He's an asshole," Aaron said.

"Why?" she asked. "He hasn't done anything that should bother you." Aaron had never cared enough to make a commitment to her or any other woman. Hormones and male ego had led him into this—and the same was probably true for Riley.

"Come on, Aaron," she said. "Go back to work. There's nothing to fight over here. Why end up in jail?"

Riley shot her a frown that told her he didn't like

that she was standing so close to Aaron. Appealing to him implied a level of intimacy beyond what she shared with Riley. But she and Aaron had a history. And she couldn't bear the thought of seeing him hurt if Riley's friends decided to jump in.

"Have it your way," Aaron said, but he forced Riley to back down enough to move aside, along with his friends, before he would leave.

"That guy has issues," Riley muttered as they watched Aaron go.

Presley wanted to defend him. What'd happened wasn't all his fault. Riley had been a bit smug, kissing her like that. It was almost as if he'd been *trying* to make Aaron jealous.

But maybe Riley could sense that there was more going on between her and Aaron than it appeared, and felt threatened. Maybe he instinctively wanted to stake his claim so there could be no confusion—and, hopefully, no challenge.

"Here, let's wipe off your back so you don't get massage oil on your shirt," she said to Riley, and after a slight hesitation, he turned to let her do it.

"Don't worry. He wouldn't really have done anything," she told everyone and took the next person in line.

14

When Presley was finally done at the studio and went to pick up Wyatt, it was after six but Dylan was still at work. Finding her sister alone wasn't entirely a good thing. It meant Cheyenne would be able to focus exclusively on her—and she did.

"So…how'd it go?" she asked as she held the door.

"Far better than I expected." As soon as Presley stepped inside, Wyatt squealed and came running.

Cheyenne waited as Presley swung him into her arms and planted a kiss on his chubby cheek, then she asked, "How many people did you have?"

"I lost count." She lifted her son's shirt and blew on his belly, smiling when he gave her the giggle she loved.

"How about a ballpark figure?"

It was so *satisfying* to have her son in her arms. The solid weight of him, that baby-soft skin, even the smell of his shampoo, made her feel as if the rest of the world could fall apart as long as she had him. But when he lifted the shirt himself so she could make him laugh again, she gave him a squeeze instead. She couldn't talk if they continued to play, and it was rude to keep Cheyenne waiting. "At least forty, judging by the massages I did," she said. "My hands are numb."

"And not everyone stayed for a massage."

"True. Some people had to leave when the line got too long."

Cheyenne clapped in excitement. "That's a *great* turnout. Was there enough food?"

"Almost. Your friend Callie came over after you left, saw that I was out of lemonade and low on all the rest and went to buy more. She wouldn't even let me pay her back."

"Callie's a wonderful person. So was it worth the effort? Did you book many appointments?"

"I did. I have a full week and then some. Not a bad way to start."

"What about the yoga classes?"

"They weren't quite as popular, but I handed out all my flyers. We'll see how many show up to the first class on Monday."

Cheyenne hugged her and Wyatt, too, since Presley was holding him. "That's fantastic, Pres. I'm thrilled for you."

"It's largely due to you and Dylan. I appreciate how you helped spread the word and got your friends and their friends to come. And thank you for looking after Wyatt, too. It would've been so distracting to have him there all day."

"No worries," she said. "I love this boy as much as you do."

Eager to get home, where she could rest and reflect on her day, Presley began to gather up her baby items. As far as her business was concerned, she was relieved and excited. But she felt less comfortable on the personal front. Riley hadn't stayed long after his massage, but he'd asked her to dinner tomorrow night and she hadn't been able to refuse because he'd done it in front of his friends.

"You got everything?"

At the change in Cheyenne's tone, Presley looked up. For some reason, her sister's enthusiasm had faded. "What's wrong?"

"You weren't going to tell me?"

"Tell you what?"

"That Aaron showed up and caused a scene?"

Presley swallowed a sigh. If Cheyenne had been testing her, she'd just failed. But she'd been hoping to avoid this conversation. It would include too much deception, and lying made her fear she was reverting to her former self, despite all the effort she'd put into growing beyond that. "How'd you find out?"

"Riley called."

"Was he upset?"

"Confused. He says Aaron acts as if he has some claim on you."

In a way, he did. He'd just spent the night in her bed, hadn't he? "Aaron didn't do anything. It was no big deal."

"*No big deal?* Riley said they almost came to blows!"

In those first few seconds after Aaron stood up, Presley had been afraid he might throw a punch. But the incident hadn't amounted to anything more than a tense moment, so she could downplay it and preferred to do so. "It was Riley who provoked the whole thing."

"How?"

She wished she hadn't said even that much. Because of Aaron's reputation as a troublemaker and Riley's as a model citizen, she doubted anyone else who'd seen what happened would perceive it the same way she did. But Riley had definitely tried to establish supremacy. Why let Aaron take all the blame? "It's hard to explain."

Recognizing her dodge for what it was, Cheyenne rolled her eyes. "Give it a try."

"Riley and I have only been on one date, and yet—" pausing as she finished collecting Wyatt's toys, she shifted him to her other hip "—he was sort of…acting as if we were together."

"That means he likes you!"

"He overstepped the bounds."

"So? What does that have to do with Aaron? Why would Aaron care if you were with Riley or someone else?"

"I'm sure he doesn't. Not really. He was just put out that Riley was making such a show of taking his spot."

Cheyenne scowled. "So you think it was Riley's fault."

"It was *both* of them. Riley got under Aaron's skin, and Aaron nearly taught him a lesson for it. That's all."

"That's enough." Cheyenne tied Wyatt's shoe, which had come undone.

"Let's not blow it out of proportion," Presley said.

Her sister sent her a dubious look. "I don't get what Aaron was doing at your opening in the first place."

"He showed up to support me like everyone else. It's not as if we were never friends, Chey."

"That's true, but…there are so many other women he could socialize with. I wish he'd forget about you."

"He did, for two years. But now that I'm back, and Riley's interested, he wants to be sure he's not missing out on anything. In time, he'll realize I'm pretty well the same girl he knew before, and that'll be the end of it."

Cheyenne twisted her lips to one side. "My guess? It's driving him crazy that you won't have anything to do with him. He's not accustomed to meeting with resistance from women."

He hadn't met much resistance last night, not in the end, which was why she couldn't look Cheyenne in the face. "There's probably an element of that, too."

"Having him buzzing around all the time makes me nervous. Wyatt's the spitting image of his father!"

Presley shouldn't have moved back until Aaron had actually left town, but she'd been so homesick, lonely and distrusting of anyone who watched Wyatt that she couldn't hold out any longer. Now she was in a tenuous situation.

She had other worries, too—like the fact that the pregnancy test she took last night might not have been one hundred percent accurate. Even if it was, she and Aaron had made love afterward. They'd used a condom every time, of course, but there was always the chance that one of them had failed, like last Monday. They must've had some type of failure when she got pregnant with Wyatt, too. She was living far too dangerously— and just when she was starting to do something with her life. *Foolish!*

"Like we've said before, he'll be leaving soon."

"Thank God," Cheyenne mumbled.

Presley scooped up Wyatt's diaper bag and walked to the door. "What's taking Dylan so long at work?"

Cheyenne helped her load the stroller. "They've been extra busy at the shop."

"That makes it even nicer that he sent his brothers over for my grand opening."

"He didn't send *Aaron*."

"He came separately."

"I know. Anyway, Dyl loves you like I do."

"You're lucky to have him."

"You'll find someone," she said. "And maybe that someone will be Riley."

Pretending she hadn't heard the last part, Presley said goodbye and pushed Wyatt home. Then, as soon as she got him settled, she called Riley and canceled dinner. Although he apologized for the incident at the studio, she told him it wasn't that. She said she wouldn't be dating for a while, that she had to concentrate on her son and her business.

As much as she'd enjoyed their time together on Friday, she felt a strange sense of release after she'd finished the call—and her relief grew later that night when she started her period.

Aaron didn't hear a word from Presley over the next two weeks; he didn't see her, either. He thought of her a great deal, and was often tempted to call. He was interested to hear how her business was going. Was she getting a good number of people in her yoga classes? Was she booking enough massages?

He would've checked in. He knew she was struggling to get by, and he worried about her. But afte letting his jealousy drag him into that pissing conte

with Riley Stinson at her opening, he decided he'd
do her a bigger favor by staying away. If she didn't
want his friendship, he needed to give her the space
to find something more fulfilling, even if he did want
to punch Riley in the face every time he remembered
that kiss at the studio.

Fortunately, he had his hands full with his own
life. From one day to the next, he wavered about
whether to open a franchise. He was concerned that
the letter he and Dylan had sent their father wouldn't
convince J.T. to move elsewhere. And when he wasn't
deliberating over those two things, he was trying to
figure out how to get Cheyenne pregnant without
doing anything that would make either one of them
uncomfortable with the process.

So far, she hadn't been able to find a local clinic
that would allow her to be artificially inseminated
without her husband's approval. So she'd asked him
to pose as her mate, but he was reluctant to go that
far. He was afraid the doctor or some nurse might take
him into the examination room—perhaps to show
him how the procedure would be accomplished—
and he'd see parts of his sister-in-law he was never
meant to see. He was willing to help, but those were
not the kinds of images he wanted imprinted on his
brain. Although he was trying to approach this in a
practical, even impersonal way, it still seemed too
intrusive and disrespectful of Dylan.

As an alternative they'd considered having her
claim to be a single woman, but she'd already approached all the clinics in the area and was nervous
that they might connect her new inquiry with her
old one. Many people still looked askance at a single

woman being artificially inseminated, anyway, which was why she'd initially admitted to being married.

The last time he and Cheyenne had talked, they'd still been wondering what route they should take. She'd said she would do more research. So when Dylan called everyone at Amos Auto Body to the front of the shop on a Thursday afternoon in early April, and he was wearing a broad smile and carrying a bottle of champagne, Aaron had no idea what might have made him so happy.

"What's going on?" Grady asked.

Aaron waited with his brothers for the answer, but Dylan didn't give them one. Instead, he had them each get a cup and ceremoniously poured the champagne.

Apparently, the best drinking device Rodney could scrounge up was the red Solo cup on the water cooler. "Are you going to tell us what we're celebrating?"

Last to join them, Mack pulled off his painting goggles and threaded his way through the others. "Don't tell me Dad's getting out of prison early!"

Aaron and Dylan exchanged a glance that said they would not be sharing champagne if that were the case, but Dylan said, "It's not quite *that* exciting."

Hearing the sarcasm in his voice, Mack bristled. "I don't understand why you don't want to see him, or even talk about him. It's been nearly twenty years. He's paid the price for his mistakes. Why can't we give him another chance?"

"The best indicator of future behavior is past behavior," Dylan said. "But we can talk about Dad later. Don't ruin this moment for me, little brother."

"Did you win the lottery?" Rod asked.

"I'd have to play the lottery to win it," Dylan replied.

"So what is it?" This came from Mack, who was intrigued enough to let the business about their father go.

"Cheyenne's pregnant." Dylan's smile stretched wide again, as if he simply couldn't contain it. "Can you believe that? We're going to have a baby."

Aaron caught his jaw before it could hit the floor. What was Dylan talking about? Last he'd heard, Cheyenne was still searching for a clinic. Had that changed? Did she not need him, after all?

He wanted to feel relief. Instead, a certain uneasiness crept over him. The fact that she was suddenly pregnant without even texting to let him know was… curious at best.

"I was wondering when you were going to get busy." Rod lifted his coffee mug. "Congratulations!"

Dylan's chest swelled. "I'm so happy I could die."

That was pretty happy, especially for his stoic brother.

When Aaron, too surprised to react, didn't perform the toast, Grady nudged him. "What's the matter with you?"

He cleared his throat. "Nothing. There's nothing wrong with me. I'm just…excited for Dyl, that's all." He held up his plastic Big Gulp cup. "Cheers."

"We're going to be uncles," Mack said.

Rod clapped Dylan on the back. "What do you want—a boy or a girl?"

"I'll take either. I just want the baby to be healthy." Dylan downed his champagne. "But if I *had* to choose? There are enough boys in this family. I'd like a sweet little girl."

"When's Cheyenne due?" Grady asked.

"Don't know yet," Dylan told him. "It's not quite official. She needs to see a doctor, but she took a home pregnancy test early this morning, and it was positive."

It's not quite official... Aaron stared into his drink. Was there a reason for that?

"Are those reliable?" Grady asked.

Dylan shrugged but was clearly more invested than that shrug made it appear. "They're supposed to be."

Aaron certainly hoped they were. He was relying on the results of the one he'd had Presley take. And he'd be thrilled to be let off the hook with Cheyenne.

Could this be for real?

"Here's to a girl who'll steal Daddy's heart." Mack raised his cup high.

Aaron joined the toast and pretended to enjoy the moment. But as soon as the champagne was gone and the others went to work, he slipped out back to call Cheyenne.

"It is true? Are you pregnant?" he asked the second she answered.

He was praying she'd say yes, but the hesitation that met this question only made the knots in his stomach worse. "Chey?"

"No. But I had to tell Dylan I was. He was planning to go to the doctor on Monday. He sprang that news on me late last night, just mentioned it casually. And then I tossed and turned for hours trying to figure out what to do. I had to give him a reason to cancel before it was too late."

"Oh, hell." Aaron pinched the bridge of his nose. "You've got to be kidding me." Now there was no way to back out—not that he was planning to, but at least he'd had the option. Worse, they were under increasingly more rigid time constraints. He had to help Cheyenne get pregnant and he had to do it before her next period, or his brother would be devastated.

"I'm sorry, Aaron," she said. "I didn't want to lie to him, but...I didn't feel I had a choice."

Aaron kicked a rock across the gravel that served as their overflow lot. "Cheyenne, I think we should tell him what we're doing. I mean...you haven't even found the right clinic yet." And was there any guarantee she would? Especially now that the procedure had to happen so quickly?

"That's just it," she said. "I may have a way around that snag, but..."

It was the "but" that made him nervous.... When she paused, he assumed she was gathering her nerve.

"How would you feel about doing the insemination ourselves?"

He straightened his spine. "*What?* How? And where?"

"Don't freak out. It'll basically be the same thing. We just won't be including a doctor. We can do it tonight, at Presley's."

"You're considering taking my sperm and...and inserting it yourself?"

"Yes. It's called the turkey baster method. For obvious reasons."

He tried to reject the image *that* presented. "I guess I'd rather not hear the details, after all."

"Got it," she said with a nervous laugh. "Sorry.

But…there'll be a lot of advantages. It'll be free, so that's one. And if it doesn't take, it won't be hard to repeat the process. We wouldn't have to wait for another appointment, and so on. What do you say?"

He rubbed his temples. What had he gotten himself into? "What's my alternative?"

"We could keep looking for the right clinic and hope to get in. But if it takes too long…"

"Then you'll have to tell Dylan you're not pregnant."

"Yes."

He imagined his brother strutting around the office pouring that champagne and knew he couldn't let it come to that. *Shit.*

"So what do you say?" she prompted.

When she first mentioned a fallback plan, he'd assumed he'd be opposed to changing course. But as uncomfortable as her proposal made him, on some levels he was relieved. Why not get this over with? Spending a few minutes in a private home instead of walking into a clinic, where he'd be faced with reams of paperwork and a slew of awkward questions, sounded fine to him. Maybe they'd get lucky and their do-it-yourself insemination would take the very first time. Then he'd be done with the whole business. Better yet, no one would know about it except the three of them. What they'd done wouldn't be listed on any medical charts, making the possibility of pulling it off far more plausible. Greater security. Less expense for Cheyenne. A local house that provided ease and convenience.

Damn, if it turned out to be as easy as it sounded, *he'd* bring champagne to work. As a bonus, agreeing to handle the insemination at Presley's meant he'd get to see her again. She was so close and yet so absent from his life, and that had been driving him crazy. "Done. What time?"

"I haven't asked Pres yet if we can use her place, but I can't imagine she'd mind."

He had to get back to work before one of his brothers came looking for him. "Text me yes or no and give me the time."

"I will. Today her last yoga class starts at seven, so she should be done around eight-thirty."

He'd been about to hang up, but at this he hesitated. "Dylan will be home by then. What will you tell him?"

"I'll say Presley needs me to watch Wyatt for an hour while she does a late massage."

"What if he wants you to babysit at your house?"

"I'll convince him that Wyatt will be happier in his own home."

"He could decide to go to Presley's with you."

"We'll have to call it off if he does and try again tomorrow or the next day."

She could always text him at the last second. That he could handle. He just didn't want Dylan showing up in the middle of it. "Fine."

"Thanks, Aaron," she said. "I really appreciate it."

He squinted at the sun. The cold front they'd experienced in March seemed to be gone for good. It was going to be a warm day. "You know he brought champagne to work, don't you?"

There was an awkward silence. Then she said, "Yeah. I tried to get him to wait until we could have the pregnancy confirmed by a doctor, but he was too excited."

Aaron sighed. "Let's hope he stays that way."

15

That afternoon Aaron had just finished painting a car and was busy washing out the stall when Dylan approached. Dylan didn't come into the paint bays that often. He ordered parts, maintained the books and manned the office, which kept him so busy he didn't have the chance to do much bodywork. He liked running the business. Aaron preferred doing the actual repairs. He loved taking a car that had been demolished and making it look new again, loved working with his hands. But unless he had some reason to go into the front—to grab a soda or cool off in the summer—he didn't see Dyl very often during the day. So he felt a little leery to be singled out by his older brother, especially since Dylan was wearing such a somber expression. Where was the unadulterated joy he'd been feeling when he came to work armed with the news that he was soon going to be a father?

Aaron turned off the pressure washer. "Something wrong?"

Dylan looked around as if he didn't want Grady, Rod or Mack to overhear. "I met Cheyenne for lunch."

The mention of Cheyenne did nothing to alleviate Aaron's concern. Had his sister-in-law decided to tell Dylan what they were planning to do? If so, Aaron hoped she'd left him out of the story. Dylan wouldn't be pleased that this had all been decided without him. "She okay?"

"She's fine, but…she brought the mail with her."

Feeling a measure of relief, Aaron hung up the wand he'd been holding. "You got a reply from Dad."

"He thanks us for our 'generous' offer, but he's not after money. He misses Whiskey Creek and wants to return."

"Damn."

"He also claims he wants to make up for lost time and get to know his sons."

"With him saying stuff like that, no wonder Mack's excited he's getting out." Aaron removed his goggles and let them dangle around his neck. "The poor kid thinks he's finally going to have a real father."

"He doesn't realize how difficult it might be, particularly now that Dad's remarried."

Aaron wiped his wet hands on his overalls. "Did you get the impression Dad was being sincere? Or does he believe he'll wind up with more if he comes back and inserts himself into the business?"

Dylan shook his head. "No way to tell. And… something else you should know."

"What's that?"

"I haven't wanted to say anything, even to Cheyenne, but his wife has been calling me for the past three days."

"No! What does *she* want?"

"She's asking if she could come out and meet us

next weekend. She says Dad would love it if we got acquainted. She'd like to take some pictures to give him when she visits him again."

"Having some woman we don't even know show up, some woman who probably feels we should welcome her with open arms, is not an appealing prospect."

Dylan puffed out his cheeks, then let his breath go. "I agree."

"So now what? Can we say no?"

"I don't see how," Dylan replied, "not if we want to maintain good relations with her, and that might be important until we see what kind of person our father's turned out to be."

"But I'd rather not have this stranger in my life! Hell, I don't even want *Dad* in my life."

There'd been times when Dylan had attempted to stick up for J.T. Recently, he'd stopped. Aaron believed that after the shank incident, they'd both come to the same conclusion: their father couldn't be trusted. "Like you, I'd rather leave the past alone," he admitted. "I'm finally free and clear of that time, that part of my life. Why would I want to look back? But…maybe we're being too closed-minded. Maybe it'll be a good thing for Mack and the others."

It probably *wasn't* fair to decide for their brothers. "So we take a vote?"

"Sure. We're all adults."

"If we do, they'll vote us down. They'll want to give Dad—and any woman he's married—a chance, but Amos Auto Body is our livelihood. We can't let Dad wreck our future like he did our past."

"They won't see it that way."

"So what are you going to do?"

"Put her off."

"Until…"

"As long as possible. If we're lucky, the situation will resolve itself. Somehow." With a sigh, Dylan headed back to the office. "But sometimes I'm afraid what happened all those years ago will never be fully behind us," he said over his shoulder.

Aaron's phone vibrated in his pocket before he could put his goggles back on. He pulled it out to see who was trying to reach him and found that a text had come in from Cheyenne.

Tonight won't work.

He checked to make sure Dylan was gone and wouldn't turn back before texting his response.

Presley can't do it?

It's not that. I wasn't thinking earlier. I have to be ovulating.

He could see why, after telling Dylan she was already pregnant, she'd be in a rush.

So do you have any idea when that will be?

I've been charting my cycle. Should be next weekend. I bought an ovulation test to be sure. It'll predict the two days this month when I'll be most fertile. We'll follow that. It'll improve our chances.

Because he wanted to have to do this only once, he was willing to wait until *every* indication suggested the optimum time. Have you told Presley what we have planned?

Yes. She's happy to help but knows we have to put it off for a week.

Great. Do I need to do anything to boost my fertility? Take some kind of vitamin or herb or...stand on my head? Anything?

LOL! I've read a little about the male side of it. Don't wear restrictive clothing. Don't let certain...equipment get too hot, which means you shouldn't get in any hot tubs between now and then. If you could hold off having sex a few days before the big event, that should help, too, by boosting your sperm count. But that's about it. Except I've heard that the clinics provide girlie magazines. Since I have no idea what turns you on, you might want to bring your own material, if necessary.

He could always think of Presley. These days, any sight or thought of her caused a spike in his libido.

I'll take care of that end of it.

He thought their exchange was over, but she texted him again

By the way, I found a site that sells in-home insemination kits. It's crazy what you can get online these days. It looks like it will have everything we need. And they have two-day shipping. As long as I'm home when the package arrives so I can hide it before Dylan sees it, we're gold.

Since he's always at work, that shouldn't be too difficult. Or you could ship it to Presley's.

Great idea.

So you'll let me know when the time is right?

I'll text you in a week or so.

I'll keep my phone handy.

"Hey, Aaron."

Startled by the interruption, Aaron whirled around to see Mack closing the distance between them.

"What's up?" he asked as he shoved his phone in his pocket.

"You almost done for the day?"

Some parts had come in that he needed for Malcolm Field's Toyota Land Cruiser. He needed to get them installed, or they'd never have it done by the time Dylan had told Malcolm they would. "I've got another couple of hours, why?"

"I was wondering if you want to go out afterward."

"Where to?"

"Sexy Sadie's?"

"There're other bars within a fairly short drive."

"Why leave town? We have to get up for work again in the morning."

But if they went to Amador City or Jackson he'd be less likely to run into Noelle Arnold. He hadn't talked to her since she'd hung up on him, and he liked the peace and quiet. "It might be nice to change things up."

"Next time. Lana's coming. If I send her somewhere new she might get lost."

Lana was Mack's cute girlfriend. Although she had a warm heart, from what Aaron had seen she wasn't the smartest girl he'd ever met. "You're not picking her up?"

"No." He grinned meaningfully. "She's bringing a friend to meet you."

Skepticism made Aaron less than enthusiastic. "So this is a blind date."

"Absolutely not. You hate those. It's just a group of people meeting for a drink at a local bar."

"Two *couples*."

"Two guys meeting two girls for drinks—arriving separately."

"You're splitting hairs."

When Aaron continued to act reluctant, Mack slugged him in the arm. "Come on, big brother. You haven't been out in ages. And Lana's sure you're going to like this girl."

These days he was almost as bad as Dylan used to be before he married Cheyenne. He just didn't go out much anymore. He was working too many hours, for one. And he'd lost interest. But he couldn't say no to the family favorite. "Fine, I'll go."

Two hours later, once Aaron was off work and showered, he managed to drum up a degree of interest in hanging out with Mack and his friends. But when they got to Sexy Sadie's, and Aaron saw that Presley was there *with Riley,* he wished he hadn't come.

Presley couldn't believe it. She hadn't accepted any of the invitations Riley had extended to her, not since she'd broken their last date. But two weeks of remaining strong and not seeing Aaron had boosted her confidence. Not only that, but Riley had caught her at the perfect moment, when she felt as if she were growing old before her time, living like a recluse at night, and that had made it difficult to say no. He'd promised he wouldn't keep her out late, because she had to work the next morning. He'd also lined up his son, Jacob, to watch Wyatt at his parents' house, so she'd feel comfortable that Wyatt was in a safe place and she wouldn't have to ask Cheyenne for yet another favor.

He'd overcome all her objections before she could even make them, so she'd agreed. She'd figured it couldn't hurt to have a drink and dance for an hour or so.

But she'd never expected to run into Aaron. Maybe if this had been a weekend, she would've been nervous that their paths might cross. They used to frequent Sexy Sadie's when she lived in Whiskey Creek before. But, according to Cheyenne, the Amos boys put in such long hours these days that they rarely went to bars during the week.

"You probably saw Aaron walk in," Riley murmured. "Is that going to be okay? Or would you rather leave?"

She didn't look in Aaron's direction, didn't want to make eye contact. She might've admitted to Riley that she'd prefer to go somewhere else, but they'd just arrived, right before Aaron and his youngest brother. It would be ridiculous to get up and walk out so soon. "It's fine. Of course."

"Great." He got up from the table. "I'll get you a drink. What would you like?"

"Cranberry juice?"

"That's it?"

She'd planned on having a glass of wine but now she didn't dare. The crowd, the sounds, even the smell of the place, took her back two years. So did seeing Aaron. And that had a powerful effect....

When she nodded, Riley went to the bar while she surreptitiously watched Aaron and Mack locate seats in the corner. She could tell Aaron knew she was there. She could sense it like she had at the bookstore. But he didn't approach her.

Although she felt a sharp pang of jealousy as two women, probably a decade younger than she was, joined the Amos brothers, she warned herself not to let it show.

Thankfully, Riley returned a moment later. Then she had her drink to concentrate on—little though it did for her.

"How're things going with your massage business?" Riley asked.

"Pretty well." She smiled as she spoke but couldn't help listening for Aaron's voice. Who was the girl? Presley had never seen her before. The blonde Mack had his arm around worked at Shearwood Forest. Presley had seen her there when she went in a week ago to have her hair trimmed.

"Which part of the business is doing better?"

She brought her attention back to Riley. "Definitely the massage, but my yoga classes are growing. The first day I had maybe ten people show up in the morning, and five at night. The Friday evening class is still struggling. I may have to cancel that one, but we'll see what happens."

"Is the massage side bringing in enough to get by?" He asked this with concern, which was nice of him.

"Fortunately, it is." She *was* earning enough to ease some of the worry that had plagued her when she'd been considering everything she needed to do in order to open. Since business could drop off suddenly, she couldn't be sure that peace of mind would last—but she hoped it would.

"Maybe you should advertise your yoga classes, try to draw from some of the neighboring towns," he suggested.

"I've thought of placing an ad in the various local newspapers. Maybe I will." When she had more money to invest.

A slow song came on—"In the Air Tonight" by Phil Collins—and he jerked his head toward the dance floor. "Would you like to dance?"

Bobbi, the girl Lana had brought to meet him, was attractive. And she seemed sweet. But Aaron had just met her and already he couldn't remember her last name. He found it hard to listen to her when Presley was snuggled up to Riley Stinson. That kiss Riley had given her at the studio kept playing in Aaron's mind, making him angry all over again—and embarrassed, too, because he'd let it get to him.

He tried to ignore that Presley was even there, but his eyes seemed to have a will of their own. He couldn't help watching to see if she was enjoying herself. If she was touching Riley anywhere she didn't have to. If Riley was keeping his hands where they should be—

"Hello? Aaron, are you in there?" Mack snapped his fingers in front of Aaron's face.

Aaron hadn't realized he'd missed part of the conversation. Blinking, he focused on his own table. "What did you say?"

Mack threw an irritated glance in the direction of the dance floor, but if he saw Presley, he didn't put two and two together. It was dark inside the bar and fairly crowded. "Bobbi is a welder. That's how she's putting herself through school. Isn't her job unusual? I've never met a female welder before."

"That's great," Aaron said, but his lack of enthusiasm earned him a kick under the table from his brother. Tossing back the rest of his beer, he stood. "I'm going to get another drink. Anyone else want one?"

They indicated that their glasses were still full. "We're good," Mack said with a note of "What the hell's gotten into you?"

"Gotcha. I'll be right back."

Once he walked away, Aaron felt a sense of relief. He wasn't happy to see Presley in Riley's arms, but at least he no longer had to watch them under the close scrutiny of his own party.

While he stood at the bar, waiting for the bartender to notice him, "In the Air Tonight" ended and "Have I Told You Lately" came on. Aaron hoped that Riley and Presley would sit down, preferably somewhere out of sight, but they didn't. They continued to dance, turning in a slow circle until Presley was facing him and, in that instant, their eyes met.

Aaron knew he should glance away, act as if it was no big thing. But it wasn't as easy to pretend as it should be.

She pulled her gaze away first.

"Can I help you?"

It was the bartender. Aaron nearly ordered another beer, but changed his mind. For the first time in a long while, he felt like getting smashed. "I'll have a straight scotch."

"Whoa, good thing I'm here to drive you home," Mack joked when Aaron returned to the table and finished his new drink almost as fast as he had the beer.

"Bobbi, you'd better get him out on the dance floor while he can still walk," Lana joked. Then she led Mack off, and Bobbi offered him a tentative smile.

"You okay?"

"I'm fine," he said. "Why?"

"I get the impression you don't really want to be here."

"Sure I do." It was a lie. To cover for it, he extended his hand to her. "Let's dance."

16

The dance floor wasn't that big, but there was enough room that she and Aaron shouldn't have had to dance next to each other. Presley could only assume that he was crowding her on purpose.

Riley ignored him entirely. And she and Aaron shot each other a few glances but didn't speak.

Finally, she closed her eyes and rested her head on Riley's shoulder. In response, he tightened his arms around her, but she wasn't trying to send him any signals; she was merely trying to avoid the sight of Aaron with that curvy brunette wrapped around him like a boa constrictor. She could remember every detail of how it felt to be in his arms, how confidently Aaron swayed to the music, his body against hers as if they were made for each other. Riley was just as good a dancer. Some might even find him as attractive. But it wasn't the same.

For a second, Presley even believed she could smell Aaron as if he, rather than Riley, was holding her. That was when she stepped away and said she had to use the restroom.

"Don't let him chase you off," Riley whispered.

She smiled. "He's not. I'll be back in a minute."

Riley didn't seem convinced, but he accepted the excuse without further argument. "Okay, I'll be over at the table."

With a nod, she fled to the deserted hallway behind the bar, where she dragged in a great gulp of air before hurrying into the ladies' room. Fortunately, it was empty; she needed a few minutes to regroup.

She was leaning over the sink, trying to slow the pounding of her heart, when the door opened. She looked up, expecting a woman to head toward the stalls—and saw Aaron. "What are you *doing?*" she asked. "You can't come in here!"

"I won't stay long. I just… I wanted the chance to tell you…" He seemed to struggle for words. "I'm sorry about how I acted at your opening. I didn't mean to ruin it for you."

She curled her fingernails into her palms, afraid she'd reach for him. If she did, it would be all too easy to get carried away and end up making love in the bathroom. Even as the thought crossed her mind, her eyes flicked toward the dead bolt, and he seemed to register a similar impulse.

But she'd never do something like that to Riley, or any other date. Not these days, thank goodness.

With effort, she held up one hand in the classic stop position. "You didn't ruin it. Besides, it wasn't just you. I know that."

He seemed relieved. "But you're still seeing Riley? You like him, then?"

"Sort of."

"Sort of?"

"I don't know who or what I like right now." She

forced another smile. "But it looks as if you've found a cute girl."

"Who?"

Her eyebrows went up. "Aren't you here with someone?"

"Oh, Bobbi. She's a friend of Mack's."

"She seems eager to be your friend, too." Weren't they all? She'd seen it so many times.

He shrugged. "She's too young for me."

"There are a lot of other attractive women here tonight."

"I haven't noticed."

"You'll have to take a look around."

"Why should I bother? I can't keep my eyes off you."

Lorna Mae, who worked at the bakery, charged in before Presley could respond, nearly hitting Aaron with the door.

"Oops!" A drunken giggle followed. "Am I interrupting?"

A muscle flexed in Aaron's jaw, and Presley could tell he was frustrated that they'd already lost what privacy they'd had. "No, I was leaving, anyway," he said, and stepped out.

By the time Presley returned to the dance floor, he was gone from the bar. But Riley was where he'd said he'd be, at the table, waiting for her.

He stood when he saw her. "You okay?"

She nodded.

"What'd Aaron have to say? I saw him go after you."

"Not much. What'd he do when he came back?"

"Whispered something to his brother. Then they all got up and left."

"I'm sorry, Riley," she said. "I should have been straight with you about Aaron before now, but…I'm not over him. After two years, I thought…I thought I'd be able to cope with the occasional sighting. That I'd keep my distance and there wouldn't be much contact. But since I came back, it just… It hasn't been the way I imagined it."

Riley scowled. "Because he keeps coming around, showing you that he's still interested. But there are other women he could see, women who don't have as much to lose. Don't let him use you, Presley."

"He's not the type to use people, Riley. He's too sensitive for that, too independent."

If anything, he grew even more skeptical.

"You might not believe this," she added, "but when we slept together before, it wasn't because *he* instigated it. It was me."

"So he was doing you a *favor?*"

She heard the wry note in Riley's voice. He'd never understand because he didn't know Aaron the way she did. But she was telling the truth. She'd been both needy and desperate when she'd latched on to Aaron. He'd befriended her out of the goodness of his heart, and then he'd let her push that friendship further than he should have. She wasn't dumb enough to believe he didn't enjoy the physical pleasure. There was no question that he did, especially once they both became so good at fulfilling each other's needs. But that didn't change the fact that he hadn't instigated a sexual relationship. *She had, and* she'd been the one to keep it going. When she showed up at his house the night of her mother's death, he'd finally run out of patience, which was why she left Whiskey Creek. She'd been expecting it to happen some day.

"He cares," she told Riley. "He just doesn't want the same things I do." And there was no self-respect in that type of obsessive love.

"I'm not trying to villainize him, Presley. But so what if he cares? It's obviously not enough or your situation would be different."

"You mean he'd want to marry me."

"Why not? Why wouldn't he want to spend the rest of his life with you? Be a father to your son?"

He *was* her son's father, which made it even harder to let go. "Dylan used to be the same way," she argued. "He was very noncommittal—until he met Cheyenne. That didn't make him a bad person."

"No, it didn't. I haven't wanted to marry every girl I've dated, either. I'm sure Aaron will fall in love eventually—when he meets the right woman. *If* he meets the right woman. But…"

He let his words trail off, and Presley guessed it was because he feared he'd taken honesty too far. "But if that woman was me, I'd know it by now," she finished.

He sighed. "That's what I think. It's what your sister thinks, and it's what Dylan thinks, too."

"Did Cheyenne warn you that I might have some… residual feelings for Aaron?" She imagined them discussing her and her situation during any number of calls, and it rankled. Her sister was *her* confidante. She didn't want to feel that Cheyenne was giving information to Riley.

"She did," he admitted. "I didn't come into this

blind, so you have nothing to worry about there. If friendship is all you can offer me, I'm fine with that. Maybe our relationship will progress someday, and maybe it won't. I'm not pushing you. But you're going to have to get over Aaron sooner or later." He winked at her. "Far as I'm concerned, it might as well be sooner."

"Sometimes I fear I'll *never* get over him," she said.

He took her hand. "It might not be me, but you'll find *someone* who can fill the gap. So—" he stood "—do you want to go back out on the dance floor?"

Slipping her fingers through his, she nodded.

"Wow, you were a barrel of laughs tonight," Mack said once they left Lana's, where they'd gone after Sexy Sadie's. "And you were willing to stay out for what…a whole hour and forty minutes?"

Aaron threw his brother a disgruntled look. "I'm tired, okay?"

Mack slung an arm over the steering wheel. "You wouldn't even talk to Bobbi!"

"She's still in college! What was I supposed to say? 'What do you want to be when you grow up?' Welding can't be her future or she wouldn't still be in school."

"She didn't care that you have a few years on her. She thought you were hot."

"Ten years is more than a few," he said dryly.

"Since when did you get so picky about who you party with? She wasn't planning on *marrying* you. She was just looking for a good time."

Aaron loosened his seat belt. "I guess I'm a little past the one-night-stand stage."

Mack stopped at the light. "So that means you're planning to get serious? You? The biggest partier in the family?"

He avoided the first question by answering the second. "In case you haven't noticed, I don't party all that much anymore."

"Because…"

"After a while, it all begins to feel very…repetitive—as if you're going to the same party over and over."

"Great. *That* gives me something to look forward to."

Mack would be married by the time he reached twenty-five. He always had a girlfriend. "Happens to the best of us."

His brother scowled at him. "But did you have to grow up *tonight?*"

Aaron knew Mack was disgruntled that he hadn't been a more enjoyable date for Lana's friend, but he couldn't help laughing. "Better late than never."

When the light turned green, Mack gave the truck some gas and drove the rest of the way in silence. He broke that silence only after they pulled into the drive. "Is that why you're still talking about moving away?" he asked. "You're bored and searching for new experiences, new challenges?"

"Maybe." He had to admit he was looking for… *something,* whatever was supposed to come next in his life.

"I don't see how Reno will be any improvement over Whiskey Creek, not when *we'll* be *here*." Mack had lobbied against the idea of Aaron moving from the start. Mack held those he loved very close. But he was also Dylan's favorite, and that had once caused Aaron a bit of jealousy. Aaron had always been the odd man out. Not that he'd ever held it against Mack. He couldn't. He loved Mack too much himself. But he couldn't expect Mack to understand.

"Chances are it won't be," Aaron admitted. "But I've decided I will move. I've got to strike out on my own at some point."

"Why?"

"It's…time." He'd finally made up his mind, he realized. The uncertainty was gone. With their father returning, and his stepmother badgering Dylan for the opportunity to be welcomed into the family—he preferred to sidestep all of it.

Mack frowned at him. "That sucks."

"I won't be far."

"Three hours isn't exactly close. Everything's gonna change." Mack didn't even know he had a stepmother. *There* was some change. But he and Dylan hadn't told anyone about that yet. They were hoping to put Anya off long enough that J.T. would be released by the time they had to meet her. Actually, they were hoping she and J.T. would divorce before then, but if they couldn't have that…

Of course, there was the slight possibility that Anya might help improve J.T. That would be the best of all scenarios, but the way they'd met—the fact that they didn't really even know each other—didn't give them a lot of hope.

Mack shoved the gearshift into park and cut the engine. "How much longer will you be here?"

Aaron opened his door. "Maybe two months."

17

Presley was much happier by the time Riley took her home. She'd always feel sad that she couldn't be with Aaron. But having that candid conversation with Riley, admitting she was still in love with Aaron, had helped to lower her guard. Now Riley couldn't expect anything from her that she wasn't prepared to give, including her heart, and that made her far more open to his friendship. Maybe she could be friends with him just like Cheyenne was. She'd always been envious of the closeness within her sister's group.

They went to Just Like Mom's after leaving Sexy Sadie's and had a late dinner before the place closed. Then they picked up Jacob and Wyatt and brought them to her house, where they watched a movie. All was going well until midnight.

Then Aaron began to call....

Although Presley stopped her phone from vibrating three or four times, Riley never commented on it. Perhaps he'd said all he was going to say about Aaron while they were at the bar. Or he was pretending not to notice because they had Jacob with them. What-

ever the reason, Presley didn't volunteer who was trying to reach her. She didn't want to ruin the evening.

Once Riley and Jacob had gone home, however,
she felt the same old compulsion to see Aaron, to
touch him, to hear his voice. But she didn't call back.
She remembered Riley telling her that she had to
get over him sooner or later and agreed. She saw so
many couples break up and get back together in what
seemed like an endless cycle. She and Aaron had
never been "official," but why let the undertow of her
emotions drag her backward? Seeing him would only
risk her precious secret and make her look foolish in
front of Cheyenne and Dylan and everyone else in
Whiskey Creek. So she closed her bedroom door as
if she was shutting him out and went to bed.

But just before she fell asleep, her phone vibrated
again and this time she couldn't stop herself. She answered it, using the excuse that she needed to find out
why he was so determined to reach her.

"It's about time," Aaron said, obviously exasperated.

She pulled a pillow over her face. "Time for what?"

"Time Riley went home. Doesn't he have to work
in the morning like the rest of us?"

"As a matter of fact, he does. He and Jacob will be
building a garage in six or seven hours. I hope they
can get enough sleep." She tossed the pillow aside.
"How'd you know he was here?"

"I'm assuming you would've taken my call otherwise."

She'd just proven him correct. "What do you want,
Aaron?"

"To tell you that I'll be moving to Reno the first

of June if I can make the arrangements that soon. I'm going to settle on a location and go ahead and sign a lease."

That was only a little over six weeks away. "I'm sure your brothers will hate to see you go."

"And *you?* How will you feel about it?"

She hated the thought of his leaving. But it would be easier to quit obsessing over him if she didn't have to run into him all over town, so she figured it was for the best. "I'll miss you."

"I want to make a suggestion," he said.

Suddenly wary, she scrambled out of bed and crossed to the window, which looked out on her narrow side yard. "What?"

"I'd like to date you while I'm still here."

"No."

She spoke fast but he came right back at her. "It's just for a few weeks!"

"I can't."

Silence. Then he said, "You'll date Riley but you won't date *me?* Are you guys exclusive already?"

"Of course we're not ex—"

"So you can see other men."

"Yes, I—"

"Then why can't I take you out once in a while, too?"

Because she'd just recommitted herself to getting over him! And Riley was going to help her by giving her someone to talk to and do things with. She planned to take the hand she was being offered.

"It wouldn't be a good idea."

"You're serious? You won't go out with me?" He was justifiably shocked. Two years ago she would've burst into tears of gratitude and relief if he'd tried to legitimize their relationship like this.

"Come on, Aaron. We don't date. We never have."

"We *sort* of dated," he said.

"They call that fuck buddies."

"Wow. I'm surprised you said that. You don't even swear anymore."

"The truth isn't always pretty."

"I say potato, you say po-tah-to."

No, there was a difference between dating and what they'd had and the distinction was an important one. "Aaron, our relationship was lopsided. Why would I ever go back to that? Why would *you?* It was difficult enough for you to tolerate my adoration the first time."

"I don't think this'll be the same."

"Of course it will. We'll go right back to what we're used to." Her body yearned for him even now, when she was feeling some conviction. How much stronger would that desire be in the moments she wasn't?

"So what if we end up in bed together again? That wouldn't be the worst thing in the world. We're very compatible in that regard. But first I'll take you to dinner, dancing, a movie—whatever you want. That's dating, right?"

She gently bumped her head against the glass, although she felt like doing it much harder. "Not exactly."

"Fine. I won't touch you. We'll just…date and see where we're at in six weeks."

"And Riley?"

"What about him?"

"I won't stop seeing him."

"Then date him, too," he said grudgingly.

"But you don't like it when I'm with him."

"Just give me six weeks, damn it!"

She pivoted and started to pace. "Why? What's convinced you it'll be different this time around?"

"*We're* different, Presley. Both of us. Don't you feel it? The changes may be subtle. Once you dig under the surface, we're still basically who we've always been. But…it might be enough."

"Enough for what? To make you care more than you did two years ago?"

"I'm not making any promises, but I am asking for one last chance."

To what? Destroy her heart for the second time? And what about Wyatt? "Sorry, I wish you well but… we have to move on."

"We can move on in six weeks as easily as we can now!"

Not if he fell in love with her son and began to wonder about him. The more time she spent with Aaron, the harder it would be to guard every word, every look.

The thought that he might discover the truth terrified her enough that the answer became absolute. "That doesn't change my mind," she said, and ended the call.

"Hey, got a question for you."

Aaron was putting a new front panel on a souped-up Camaro when Mack poked his head into the repair bay. He didn't want to be interrupted. He'd gotten very little sleep and hadn't started the day in a good mood. He kept replaying the conversation he'd had with Presley last night, kept seeing her in Riley's arms as they danced at Sexy Sadie's. "What is it?" he snapped.

Mack's eyebrows shot up. "Did I catch you at a bad time?"

Aaron tossed his wrench into his toolbox, where it landed with a solid clang. "I'm frustrated with this," he said as if getting that part in place had been giving him fits. But work wasn't the problem.

"Presley was at the bar last night with Riley Stinson."

Mack had noticed, after all. "And?"

"Is that what's wrong with you? Why you were so preoccupied?"

Aaron began organizing his tools. "Is that your question?"

"No, that's a perception."

"Then get to your question."

"Lana just called me."

Mack still hadn't asked a question, but something about his demeanor caught Aaron's full attention. "What'd she have to say?"

"You remember she does hair at Shearwood Forest?"

"You dragged us all down there when she got her license and she butchered our hair. How could I forget? Go on."

"She's gotten better," he said with a defensive scowl. "Anyway, she hears a lot of gossip at that place."

Gossip? "Forget it." Aaron raised a hand. "I'd

rather not hear what people are saying about me. I don't give a damn."

"You're going to care about this."

Aaron studied him. Then he nodded. "Go on."

"Riley's mother came in this morning."

"She still complaining about how I treated her son at Presley's grand opening?"

He shook his head. "She helped Jacob watch Presley's little boy last night so Presley and Riley could go out."

Back to that sore spot? "Are you ever going to get to your point?"

Mack clasped Aaron's arm in genuine concern. "Aaron, she said Wyatt looks *exactly* like you did at his age. She said the moment she laid eyes on him, she thought she was looking at you all over again. She also said she'd bet her bottom dollar he's yours."

Aaron stood in stunned silence. Wyatt *wasn't his.* Presley had said as much. Dylan and Cheyenne both believed her. Wyatt belonged to some man in Arizona....

Some man for whom they didn't have a name...

Some man she told Dylan it would be impossible to find...

Some man who'd given her no help whatsoever...

But she'd gotten pregnant *after* she left Whiskey Creek—hadn't she?

That had to be the case. He'd always been conscientious about birth control. The only time he'd known about a malfunction was that night nearly a month ago.

"You have nothing to say?" Mack pressed.

Aaron wasn't sure he could speak. His heart was

pounding so hard he was afraid it might leap right out of his chest. Presley wouldn't lie about something *that* important, would she? He managed to form two words. "That's crazy."

"The way you've always harped at me to be careful, to use protection, I thought…I thought it *couldn't* be true. But…birth control can fail. I mean, you've seen her kid, I haven't. He doesn't look anything like you, does he?"

Aaron hadn't seen a resemblance. But he hadn't been looking for one. Now that the issue had been raised, however, he could see where someone might think Wyatt favored him. Wyatt had his mother's eyes, but…

Presley says his father was tall…

He was just some prick who took advantage of her… But she doesn't have contact with him, doesn't know how to reach him.

Those snatches of conversation immediately came back to him, as well as one other detail. For several months before she left, Presley hadn't been sleeping with anyone else—at least as far as he could tell.

Mack lowered his head to study Aaron's face, since Aaron was staring at the concrete beneath his feet as he tried to piece it all together. "I'm sorry, man. I hope I didn't upset you."

When Aaron met his brother's gaze, Mack hunched over and shuffled his feet. "You look like you've seen a ghost."

"What you said a second ago, it's not true," he said. "It *can't* be true."

"I'm sure you're right. I just… I felt you should know. Not only that, but people are speculating. I figured you'd hear it from someone else if you didn't hear it from me."

"Does Dylan know what Mrs. Stinson is saying?"

Mack shrugged. "I haven't mentioned it to him, and he hasn't brought it up to me, so I'm guessing he doesn't."

Forgetting the Camaro, Aaron stalked past his youngest brother in search of his oldest.

"Something wrong?" Dylan asked when the door slammed against the inside wall of the front office.

Aaron had planned to question his brother about Presley's baby, to see if he was keeping Wyatt's true paternity from him. But the moment he opened his mouth, he realized he might be pouring gas on a rumor that had no merit to begin with. Why create doubt?

"What is it?" Dylan prompted.

"I have to go somewhere," he replied.

Dylan came out from behind the counter. "Right *now?* Jason Peel's hoping to get his Camaro back today."

Aaron pictured Wyatt in his mind's eye and felt his stomach muscles tighten. Could that be *his* baby? His *son?* "Jason will have to wait."

Aaron was glad Presley wasn't home when he arrived. Before he confronted her and demanded reassurance that Mrs. Stinson was in no way correct about Wyatt, he wanted to see the child in question, wanted to study him with a more discerning eye.

Alexa, daughter of Sophia DeBussi, Ted Dixon's fiancée, was babysitting. Only fourteen or so, she was a sweet, pretty girl. They'd met at Ted and Sophia's Valentine's party a couple of months ago so, thankfully, she recognized him and didn't seem to be frightened by seeing him at the door.

He stood back so he'd appear even less threatening. "Hello."

A shy smile curved her lips. "Hi."

"I take it Presley's still at work?"

"Yeah." She checked her phone. "She won't be home for another hour. She had a massage at three."

"No yoga tonight?" he asked conversationally.

"There weren't enough sign-ups so she had to cancel Friday's class."

"That's too bad." He pretended to be sympathetic, but he was too rattled to feel much empathy over a canceled class. "How's Wyatt doing?"

Her smile broadened. "Great! He's *so* cute, isn't he?"

No question. But was there also an Amos family resemblance? "He awake or…" In the afternoon, there was always the chance he'd be napping. Even Aaron knew that.

"He got up half an hour ago. We've been playing." She opened the door wider to show him Wyatt sitting amid a sea of toys.

When the toddler looked up and grinned, Aaron suddenly felt as if he had a thousand pounds of sand sitting on his chest. He'd swung by his house to get a picture of himself as a baby; he planned on pulling that out for comparison as soon as he had the opportunity.

"I'm meeting Presley here when she gets off," he told Alexa, "so I'll take over for you."

"Really?"

"Is that okay?"

"I guess, but…Presley never said anything."

"We could call her, but I'd hate to interrupt her massage."

"No, that wouldn't be good. So…should I go ahead and call my mom?"

"If you don't mind having her pick you up a little early, that'd be great."

She hesitated, but he took out his wallet to pay her, and that seemed official enough that she didn't voice whatever question might have been on her mind.

When he handed her the money, she looked up in surprise. "This is more than I usually make. I've only been here for a few hours."

He'd estimated what he considered to be an appropriate amount, but he wasn't worried about the extra. "Consider it a bonus."

With a blush, she shoved the bills in her pocket. "Thanks. Come on in. I'll call my mom. If I do it right away, I can probably catch her before her nail appointment."

Aaron couldn't take his eyes off Wyatt as he and Alexa waited for Sophia. They made small talk, and he pretended to watch TV with her, but he wasn't really paying attention. When they heard the honk that was Alexa's signal, he breathed a sigh of relief.

"That's her," she said, and stooped to kiss Wyatt before slinging a backpack over one shoulder and hurrying out.

Then Aaron was alone with Presley's baby, who was dragging around a plastic bat and using it to smack a plastic ball.

"I'm going to have to teach you about baseball,"

Aaron told him, but even saying that, thinking like that, frightened him. Was this child *his?*

Wyatt's eyes lit up when Aaron spoke. "Ba!" he said, pointing to the ball.

A hard lump sat heavy in Aaron's stomach as he got out the picture of himself and crossed the floor. He was afraid Wyatt would be unhappy if he tried to pick him up. What if the kid started crying and wouldn't stop? Aaron didn't have Cheyenne here today, or anyone else, to pass him off to, and he'd never taken care of a small child. But Wyatt hadn't been afraid of him when they first met at Cheyenne's. It was possible he'd be brave here, too—and he was, as long as Aaron didn't try to touch his bat.

"Where did you come from?" Aaron asked him.

"Ba!" He proudly held out his toy.

Aaron examined his baby picture, searching for similarities and differences.

Presley's coloring was darker than her son's. Wyatt had chocolate-colored eyes, but his hair was more of a sandy blond like Aaron's. His father was definitely a white man, Aaron concluded. That fit. And no doubt he was tall, as Presley had told Cheyenne. At six-two Aaron wasn't short. But hair color and size? That certainly wasn't conclusive evidence when it came to offspring.

Neither did it rule him out, however.

Aaron carried Wyatt to the couch and sat down. At first, Presley's son seemed surprised and a little intrigued by the stranger who'd suddenly appeared in his home. But that didn't last. After a few seconds, he grew bored with Aaron's fixation and tried to get down. Then Aaron's cell went off, and the ringtone got the tyke's attention.

"Pone!" He waited for Aaron to take action, but Aaron left the phone in his front pocket. It was probably Dylan, wondering when he'd be coming back to finish the Camaro, and Aaron didn't have an answer for him.

"Pone?" Wyatt poked a finger at the noise, but that didn't change Aaron's mind. Nothing else mattered in this moment; he couldn't quit staring. He was hoping to see *something,* some trait or expression that would answer his question.

Wyatt was so distracted by the noise and what it signified that he dropped his bat and tried to get to Aaron's cell himself. "Pone!"

Aaron had to admit the kid had personality, and he seemed smart. His determination and insistence might've made Aaron laugh—if he wasn't so terrified of what he was going to find out when Presley got home.

18

Presley was excited as she hurried to her rental house from her studio. She hadn't had too many massage appointments this week. They'd been tapering off since the opening. But she'd expected that, since people who weren't true candidates lost interest. The clients who did return tipped well, so she was still generally on track. Bill Hunsacker, who owned the jewelry shop down the street, had just given her an extra twenty dollars.

While she was mentally adding up how much she'd made this week and deciding which bills the money would cover, she put her key in the door—and realized it wasn't locked.

Whiskey Creek was a safe place, but Alexa was only fourteen. Presley didn't believe in taking chances, not after living in a questionable part of Fresno.

"Hey, why's the door unlocked?" she called out as she let herself in. "Did you guys go for a walk and forget to lock up when you came back?"

The stroller was on the front porch, where she usually parked it. So she knew they weren't gone now.

The TV was on, too. But Alexa and Wyatt weren't in the living room, and Alexa didn't answer.

"Hello? Lex, I'm home!"

Footsteps sounded in the hall. Presley dropped her canvas tote on the coffee table before glancing up—and then froze. Aaron stood in the hallway, holding her baby.

"You couldn't have come home ten minutes ago?" he asked dryly.

Wyatt's pants were off, and his diaper was askew. Although Aaron looked funny standing there, his expression harried after attempting his first diaper change, Presley didn't laugh. She couldn't. Fear welled up, nearly sealing off her throat.

Why was he in her house? And where was her babysitter?

"I didn't see your truck."

"It's out there, big as life."

"Not in the drive…"

"Across the street."

She nodded. She'd been so focused on her budget that she hadn't been paying attention. "Where's Alexa?"

"Her mother picked her up an hour ago."

"Because…"

"I was here. I figured you didn't need both of us."

The fact that he'd taken such a decision on himself let her know she had reason to worry, and that brought tears to her eyes. She blinked quickly, trying to stem them, but they slipped over her lashes and ran down her cheeks.

"Why are you crying?" he asked. Despite her effort to hide her guilt and terror, she was reinforcing his suspicions, and his suspicions made him angry. Justifiably so. But she'd heard the accusation in his voice from the moment he first spoke, knew why he was here. Fear of this encounter—and its outcome—nearly overwhelmed her.

"I—I don't know."

"Really?"

"Aaron—"

"Mama!" Wyatt leaned forward, trying to climb into her familiar arms, but Aaron wouldn't let her have him.

"Is it true?" He held Wyatt but kept him just out of reach. "Is this child mine?"

There'd been times, usually late at night, when she'd imagined such a confrontation. But never had she imagined a scenario that started with her being so teary and tongue-tied.

For a brief moment, she was tempted to shore up her lies, to stand by them, but it was futile. She'd always known that once Aaron began to suspect, the game would be up. All he had to do was demand a paternity test. Within three or four weeks, DNA would remove all doubt.

"I was trying to do you a favor." Her voice fell to a whisper because she was struggling just to breathe.

"A *favor?* Having my baby and pretending he belongs to some…some asshole in Arizona who supposedly used you for an hour or two? That's doing me a *favor?*"

If only he knew what'd happened in Arizona, how close she'd come to being swallowed up by the quicksand of her drug abuse, maybe he'd have an ounce or two of understanding. "It's not like I got pregnant on purpose, Aaron. It's not like I *wanted* to be put in that situation."

"Then how'd it happen?"

"I have no idea! When my period didn't come, I was as surprised as you are now. We always used birth control so…maybe you're not his father."

If she could create enough doubt, would he walk away? Why not? He didn't *have* to open this Pandora's box.

"Who else could it be?"

She didn't have any candidates to offer him. He knew everyone she knew around here, and he wouldn't believe it was someone from Arizona if she brought that up again. It wasn't as if she could point a finger at someone without expecting him to demand verification, and there was no chance she could give him that. When she found out she was pregnant, it had been at least six months since she'd had sex with another man. Filled with panic and despair, she'd behaved badly in that short time after her period didn't come—and she'd decided in retrospect that she'd done it just to prove how unlovable and unworthy she was. But that didn't change Wyatt's paternity. "I didn't get his name."

He stepped closer. "*When* did it happen?"

"I can't tell you that, either."

With a curse, he raked his fingers through his hair. "So you were pregnant before you left? There's no chance it happened after?" When she hesitated, he raised his eyebrows. "I'm going to get a paternity test, so you might as well tell me the truth."

She'd guessed as much. She wiped her cheeks.

"That's partly why I left. But if it helps to think he *could* belong to someone else, then think it."

"Helps?" he echoed. "How is that supposed to help if it's not true?"

"It doesn't matter if it's true! I've taken full responsibility. I haven't asked you for anything and I never will. Just walk away!"

"How? The fact remains that you lied!"

"I knew you wouldn't be happy with the news," she snapped, finally rallying enough to come back at him. "I did what I thought was best for all of us at the time."

"You thought it was best for my son to grow up without his father?" He seemed wounded, which surprised her. "I'm not perfect, Presley, but am I really that bad?"

"I could have aborted him. I almost did. If I'd gone through with it, we wouldn't be having this conversation. So how is it a major crime that I kept him a secret? You wouldn't have wanted him even if I'd told you about him!"

Wyatt had had enough. Fussing and squirming, he fought to escape Aaron's hold.

Aaron set him on the floor, but when she crouched to pick him up, Aaron intercepted her. "No way. Leave him where he is."

"Why?"

He handed Wyatt his bat. "Because I won't have you cuddling him and staring at me as if I'm some kind of ogre. I have a right to be mad, damn it."

Wyatt peered around one of his legs, uncertain now that he'd been released whether or not he should be upset. He didn't continue to cry, but his lip quivered as he glanced from one adult to the other.

"You have every right to be mad," she agreed. "But what were my options? Was I supposed to drop him off on your doorstep? Take care of him myself but ask you to help feed and clothe him even though you had no voice in my decision to keep him? Or should I have put him up for adoption? Would that have made you happier? I told you I almost terminated the pregnancy. I went to an abortion clinic in Arizona, you know." Her voice broke as Wyatt managed to navigate around Aaron. When he reached her, he seemed pleased with himself, but she didn't dare pick him up. She was too busy trying to make Aaron understand, too busy struggling with the strong emotions Wyatt—and Aaron—evoked.

Aaron looked at her for several seconds. "What stopped you from going through with it?"

That had been her darkest moment, but it was also the turning point, when she'd decided to fight for a better life. Wyatt had been her motivation. It didn't hurt that he was part of Aaron, a part she could keep. But there was no reason to go into all that. A man who'd never been in love wouldn't understand.

"I couldn't," she said. "And I can't tell you how glad I am that I didn't."

Whether it was that close call or the tears in her eyes, *something* cracked Aaron's hard, angry exterior. She felt him soften as, with a sigh, he stopped scowling and began to pace. "You could've communicated with me, damn it. You could've *told* me. We should've decided together! I would never have encouraged you to get an abortion or give him up if you didn't want to."

"So you would've offered to…what? Coparent? Or would you just have sent me a check every month?"

"I would've done whatever we agreed I should do!"

She shook her head. "Let's face it, Aaron. You weren't ready for a child. You might have helped out financially, but you would've been glad to see me go, along with your new responsibility. So, you're mad that I *didn't* charge you?"

He sent her a disgruntled look. "You didn't have a crystal ball. Stop acting as if you knew how I would've reacted."

"I didn't need a crystal ball. I knew how you felt about me, how tired you'd become of our one-sided relationship. So I let you go on with your life completely unfettered. I wanted our baby, even if you wouldn't. It seemed fair at the time."

"There you go again, saying I wouldn't have wanted him. But you didn't give me the chance to decide. *That's* why I'm upset—not to mention that you flat-out lied! I would rather have known the truth!"

He was right, of course. It was fear, more than anything else, that had caused her to do what she'd done—fear that he would somehow try to take control of the situation. What if he sued for custody? If not now, later? Since he didn't particularly care about *her* that was a very real possibility.

She reached down to smooth Wyatt's hair from his forehead. "What made you suspect?"

Pivoting at the far side of the room, he shoved his hands in his pockets but didn't protest when she lifted her son into her arms. "Riley's mother has been blabbing her big mouth all over town."

"Mrs. Stinson? But how—"

"She went to get her hair done this morning and told everyone at Shearwood Forest that he's the spitting image of me."

Did *he* see the resemblance? He didn't indicate one way or the other.

Too exhausted, physically and emotionally, to continue standing while holding her son, Presley sank into her favorite chair. "That was all it took?"

"Once I started wondering—" he dropped onto the sofa "—I just…knew."

The fatalism in his voice made her wince. "I'm sorry, Aaron."

When he didn't answer, she set about fixing Wyatt's diaper so it would do the job it was intended to do. Trying to refasten the tabs gave her something to concentrate on besides Aaron's shell-shocked demeanor. But adjusting it only ruined the diaper. She might've teased him about his inability to properly change a baby, but doubted that would go over very well at the moment. At least he'd made the effort.

"So now that you know, what are you going to do?" she asked.

He lifted his gaze from the carpet. "Was Dylan in on the secret?"

"No. He believes the same thing you did."

Suspicion entered his eyes. "What about Cheyenne?"

Presley thought of the favor he was about to do her sister and prayed her answer would be credible cnough that he wouldn't change his mind. "I didn't tell *anyone*."

He shot to his feet. "Bullshit!"

Presley felt terrible that she wasn't better able to defend Cheyenne's interests, but nothing she said would convince Aaron now. She and Chey were too close. "You're right. But…she wanted to tell you. She begged me to do it."

"Before or after she asked me to donate sperm? Neither of you cared that I would have *two* children?" He rubbed a hand across his face. "Shit. For someone who's always been so careful about birth control, now I'm fathering babies all over the place."

Wyatt wriggled out of her lap and went over to get his bat. "You won't have two children, Aaron," she said. "Dylan and Cheyenne will have one, and I'll have the other—with whoever I eventually marry."

His eyes narrowed, so she tried to win him over, to bring about the solution she'd held in reserve against this day. "You could sign away your parental rights. Then you'll have *no* responsibility for Wyatt. None."

"Oh, and *that's* such a tempting offer."

She hadn't expected him to be so sarcastic. "You'll be free to move on, to relocate and live your life as you see fit, a single man with no responsibilities."

"I understood what you were offering the first time," he said.

"Why does it make you so mad?"

"You think, now that I know, I could do that?"

Her pulse, which had begun to race when she first saw him, spiked again. Aaron might have softened somewhat, but this was not going as she'd hoped.

"Why not?" she asked. "You could always have

a family later, when you're ready. With a quick signature, there'd be nothing lingering in your past that you'd have to worry about. No one who could lay any claim on you."

A muscle moved in his cheek; he was struggling with as much emotion as she was. "While someone like Riley raised my son."

"Maybe. Him or someone else." Taking a deep breath, she got to her feet. She *had* to persuade him. It felt as if she was fighting for her life—and in a way she was. She was fighting for life as she knew it, where she had full custody and control of her child. "I have the form in my bedroom. I'll get it."

He didn't protest, but when she came back, his lip curled. "You just happened to have that handy?"

She put it in front of him and handed him the pen she'd also retrieved. "I've considered telling you before."

"So you got prepared, just in case."

"Wyatt means the world to me," she said softly.

When he didn't respond, she pushed a little harder. "I'll take good care of him, Aaron. I promise. Whether I ever marry or not, you won't have to worry about me hitting you up for support. You've seen how hard I'm working, what I've done to change my life."

He tossed the pen onto the document without signing it. "Yeah, I've seen how you cut me out of it. I guess this is where I'm supposed to thank you for that, too, huh?"

"It's what you wanted!"

He was leaving. Why? She couldn't let him go. She had to have some reassurance, even a hint, that he wouldn't threaten to take Wyatt away from her.

"Aaron?" As she followed him to the door, she managed to hold fresh tears at bay, but it was all she could do not to plead with him to understand, to move on as if Wyatt had never been born. She *would* have resorted to begging if she'd thought it would help. "What are you going to do?"

"Beats the hell out of me." He paused long enough to look back at Wyatt. Then he shook his head and slammed the door behind him.

"What's wrong?"

Cheyenne had heard the tears in her voice. Presley would've preferred to make this call once she'd pulled herself together, but she couldn't allow her sister to be blindsided. For all she knew, Aaron was on his way to their place right now. "Are you alone?"

"Not quite but…give me a minute."

Presley heard some rustling, then the sound of a door closing. When her sister spoke again, there was an echo, as if she'd just locked herself in the bathroom. "What's going on?"

"He knows."

"*Who* knows? Not Dylan. He seems fine…."

"Aaron!"

"About Wyatt?" She was whispering, but her voice rose in spite of that.

Hot tears rolled down Presley's cheeks. "Yes."

"No! How did he find out? *You* didn't tell him…,."

"He guessed. He was waiting here for me when I got home from work."

Silence fell, a silence that stretched for several seconds. Then Cheyenne said, "Are you okay?"

"I'm sick to my stomach."

"I can understand why. How'd he take the news?"

"Pretty much as we expected." She blew her nose and dried her eyes. "He's not happy. He feels cheated and betrayed, by both of us."

Cheyenne let out a small squeal of alarm. "You told him *I* knew Wyatt was his?"

"I told him you *didn't* know, but he didn't believe me. I'm sorry."

She groaned. "I was afraid this wasn't going to end well. Now *Dylan* will find out I've been lying to him about Wyatt, too."

"You're going to lie to him about something much bigger."

"That's for his own good. This can't be construed the same way. This was for you. I put you above him."

Presley slumped on the couch. Wyatt was playing with his blocks in the middle of the floor, but he could tell that something was wrong. He kept coming over to pat her leg before wandering off again. "It was a mistake for me to move back to Whiskey Creek," she said. "I should've waited. But I didn't think it would make any difference. In the two years I was gone, Aaron didn't try to contact me once."

"Actually…" Cheyenne cleared her throat.

"What?"

"He asked for your number a few times. Maybe… several times."

"Why didn't you tell me?"

"Why would I? You were doing so well. I didn't want to weaken your resolve. And he could've tried a lot harder. He would have if he'd really wanted to reach you."

Stung that Cheyenne had kept this from her, Presley sat up. He'd let her go so easily, and that had been a painful thing to cope with.

But she might've settled for continuing the relationship if she'd known. Maybe Cheyenne had done her a favor. Aaron cared. He'd *told* her he cared. He'd just never cared enough. "Either way, I thought he was relieved to be rid of me, that he wouldn't pay any attention to the fact that I was back. I never dreamed he'd fight for our...friendship."

"I don't mean to be rude, Pres, but I think he's bored with the women he's been seeing. Noelle's not exactly good company. And you've been trying to keep away from him, so you're a new challenge."

Presley dropped her head in her hands. She'd brought that up before, but... "That's not very flattering to either of us, Chey. It makes him look shallow and me like an infatuated fool."

Her sister didn't respond immediately. "I shouldn't have said it. I just don't want to see you get hurt again."

Presley didn't want to *be* hurt. She'd barely been able to navigate the dark labyrinth of the past two years; she definitely didn't want to start that journey over.

"Thanks. I think." She didn't believe Cheyenne truly understood what it was like when she was in Aaron's arms. The way it felt as if she mattered so much more to him than she really did. But what was the use of insisting she wasn't merely a challenge to Aaron? She had to accept the fact that they were never going to be together.

Cheyenne quickly steered the conversation into safer territory.

"I still don't understand how he guessed about Wyatt."

"All it took was for someone to point out the similarities," she said. "Then it clicked, and something he'd never thought to question seemed obvious. I would've tried harder to convince him he was wrong, but he could prove the truth too easily."

"He plans on getting a paternity test?"

"That's what he says."

"He wouldn't go that far unless he really wants to know."

"Apparently, he does. Aaron might have his flaws, but he's not afraid of facing a challenge."

"Does that mean he plans to participate in Wyatt's life?"

"I can only guess it does. I gave him the chance to sign away his rights, told him if he did, Wyatt and I would never bother him again."

"And?"

"He didn't take it."

Presley waited for her sister to digest this information. "So where'd you leave it?" she asked at length.

"Up in the air."

"Just a minute…"

Presley could tell by her sister's inflection that this was a separate concern. "What is it?"

"He's here—*Aaron's* here." Her next words came as a whisper. "You don't think he'll tell Dylan about the artificial insemination, do you? Just to get back at us?"

"He's not vindictive enough to do something like that out of spite or…revenge. But even if he does, we haven't performed the insemination yet, so Dylan can't get *too* mad."

"Aaron could tell Dylan I'm not pregnant."

Presley jumped to her feet. "Dylan thinks you're *already* pregnant?"

"That's why I tried to call you earlier," she said. "But never mind that right now. I've got to go."

There was no chance to say anything else. Her sister was gone.

19

As Aaron stood on Dylan's front stoop, asking his brother if he had a second to talk, he could see Cheyenne hovering in the background, near the kitchen. It wasn't hard to see that she was nervous. But he couldn't bring himself to say or do anything to relieve her anxiety. While he understood that her loyalty to Presley would be stronger than her loyalty to him, this wasn't a small matter. They were talking about a *child. His* child. She'd kept Wyatt's paternity a secret from him for two years. And she'd had the nerve to come to him when *she* needed help, to tell him she trusted him more than anyone else. How did she expect that to make him feel?

Used? Because that pretty much summed it up.

"Sure," Dylan said. "Come on in."

Aaron shook his head. "I'd rather we took a ride, if you don't mind."

Dylan blinked at him. Aaron had never dragged him out of the house like this before. Generally, if they had something to discuss they could handle it at work or over the phone. But he didn't hesitate. "I'll be right back," he said to Cheyenne.

"What's going on?" he asked as they both climbed into Aaron's truck.

Aaron started the engine, drove two blocks and pulled over at the park. They didn't need to go far. He merely wanted a few moments of privacy. "I just came from Presley's."

Dylan managed to keep his expression neutral. "You've made it perfectly clear that you're going to do what you want where she's concerned, so…why are you telling me?"

"Because I didn't go there for the reason you think."

"Then why *did* you go there?"

He drew a deep breath. "I went there to see my son."

The placid mask on Dylan's face cracked. "Your *son?* Are you saying what I think you're saying?"

"Wyatt is mine."

"And you haven't done a damn thing to support him? Or Presley?"

"How could I?" he snapped. "I found out today."

"Holy shit." Dylan kneaded his forehead. "Are you *sure?*"

"I'll order a paternity test to verify it. But it's easy to believe, wouldn't you say?"

"Now that you've told me, it is, but…we talked about this once before, when we first learned she was pregnant. You told me the baby couldn't be yours, that you used a condom every single time you were with her."

"I did." And as far as he'd known, they'd all worked. Until recently…

"So how…"

He shrugged. "Nothing's foolproof. You took health classes in high school. Even the pill isn't one hundred percent effective in every situation."

"But you believed her...."

"Completely. Thanks to what happened after she left here—or what you guys hinted at—and what she said about the father of her child, I accepted it without question."

Dylan turned off the radio; Aaron hadn't even realized it was on. "Okay, but Presley's had a rough go of it. There were months when she lived on noodles so Wyatt could have everything he needed. Why would she lie when she could've had your help? You've always had more money than she has."

Aaron shook his head. "That's what I don't get. She said she was doing me a favor. That I wouldn't have wanted him, anyway. But why wouldn't she give me the chance to decide for myself?"

"She wasn't in a good place back then."

Although it was true, that was difficult to acknowledge. He was too angry.

"Maybe she thought you'd give her too much trouble," Dylan said. "That she'd have to take you to court to get you to step up."

He scratched his cheek. "But I'm equally responsible for creating Wyatt, so I would've been willing to do my part."

"And now?"

"I'm *still* willing. But she doesn't want my help. She just asked me to sign away my parental rights."

Understanding suddenly dawned in Dylan's eyes. But he didn't react the way Aaron had expected. "Oh! *Now* I get it."

"Get what?"

"It's not that she was afraid you *wouldn't* want Wyatt. She was afraid you would."

"What?"

"She knew you'd help, Aaron. Maybe nobody else saw it, but I was living with you. I remember how you used to look out for her. No doubt that was part of what made her fall in love with you. But think about it—a man who participates financially is much more likely to insist on being involved in his child's life."

"Isn't that how it's supposed to go?" Aaron asked. "Isn't that what's best for the child? Why would my participation be a bad thing?"

"That's not the point. You've always had more resources than she has. Maybe two years ago you weren't quite where you are now, but you were still a lot more stable than she was. You had a reliable job, a house, close family. Her mother had just died. Cheyenne, her only sister, was planning to marry. And you didn't want to be with her in the way she wanted to be with you. She had nothing but her baby when she left here. Not even a way to earn a living."

Aaron rubbed his temples. Dylan described a pretty sad picture, but Aaron had wondered about Presley and where she'd been at that point in her life many times. He'd agonized over how he'd treated her when she came to the door that night, wished he could go back and be kinder. But somehow she'd gotten through it. She'd gotten over him, too. And these days she didn't want to risk associating with him. What options did that leave him now that he knew about Wyatt?

"So what do I do?" he asked.

Dylan took a moment to answer. "Wyatt's a great kid, Aaron. I'd think long and hard before giving him up."

"If I don't give him up, Presley and I will have to figure out some way to share him. She won't be happy about that."

"It'll scare her. But you can handle it fairly."

Aaron shifted in his seat. "I thought you wanted me to stay away from her."

The beard growth on Dylan's chin rasped as he ran a hand over his face. "That was before."

"You were feeling a great deal of loyalty to her just a few days ago."

"I still feel that loyalty. She's my sister-in-law. But you're my brother. I guess that's why Cheyenne didn't tell me."

"So you realize she knew all along? And you're not upset about that?"

"No. I'm glad she didn't put me in the position of having to choose. She must've known I'd tell you."

Aaron smiled. Of course Dylan would tell him. Dylan had always looked out for his best interests. "I admit I was hard to raise. And we still bump heads now and then. Sometimes I don't even know where the anger inside me comes from. But…" He wanted to tell his big brother that he appreciated everything he'd done, that he loved him. He'd never come right out and said it. There'd been a lot of times when he hadn't shown it, either—and yet Dylan was still there after all the years, ready to stand between him and any threat.

"But what?" Dylan asked.

Somehow the words seemed to get trapped in Aaron's throat. He couldn't speak without breaking down, and there was no way he was going to do that. He swallowed hard, struggling to curb his emotions before he embarrassed them both—but as soon as Dylan clued in to what was going on, he bailed him out.

"It's okay. I know," he said, and squeezed Aaron's shoulder before getting out. "I'll walk back."

The tears came, anyway, but at least he was alone.

Cheyenne fidgeted nervously as she heard the door open and close. Dylan was back, but was he mad? She'd never kept anything from him before— just Wyatt's paternity and, in the past few weeks, the plans she'd been making—so she had no idea how he might react. She hoped he wouldn't assume that she'd lie for any old reason. Or that she didn't love him.

"I'm sorry, Dyl," she said, meeting him in the hallway. "I'm *really* sorry. I got mad at *you* for keeping the news about your stepmother from me, and now you find out that I kept something much bigger from you, but…I didn't know what else to do."

He looked more thoughtful than angry. But she didn't touch him; she wasn't sure he'd welcome it. Knowing how protective he was of his brothers, this could be their first serious fight. She'd broken the rules of loyalty, and loyalty was more important to the Amoses than love.

"Are you upset with me?" she asked.

"No."

"Disappointed?" She winced because that would be even worse. He'd always made her feel so good about herself, as if he accepted her and loved her just as she was and always would no matter what. That she'd done this put her at risk of losing something very precious to her.

"Do you think I betrayed you by keeping Presley's secret?" she asked. "I would've told you, but…she begged me not to. And I…I couldn't take the chance that it would wreck everything if Aaron found out. I couldn't *begin* to guess how he'd react. You know how her life has gone. Not only that, but I believed her when she said that Aaron wouldn't want the baby. It made sense considering where he was two years ago, but…"

"But?"

She clasped her hands in front of her. "The more time passed, and the more I came to understand Aaron and see him gain control of his life, the harder it was for me to keep my mouth shut. So I did the wrong thing, but it was for the right reasons—for Presley's sake. I hope you'll believe that. It's been terrible to feel so torn. I've almost told you a million times."

The words poured out but, by the end, he was smiling. "Shush," he said, and gathered her close. "It's okay."

Filled with relief, she wrapped her arms around him. "Really, Dyl? You understand? Because I've been so scared of how you'd react if you found out."

"How could you be scared of *me?*" he murmured into her hair.

"Not *of* you—of what you might feel about me."

He pulled back far enough to look into her face. "Nothing could ever make me stop loving you."

"But I know how you feel about Aaron and the boys—"

"Which is exactly why you did the right thing. I

wouldn't have wanted to be in your shoes—knowing the truth but feeling I couldn't tell. You saved me from being in that spot, from having to betray one or the other."

She rested her head on his shoulder and breathed in his comforting, familiar smell. "That's it. I couldn't be true to both of them, and it was so difficult, because I love Aaron, too."

He gently massaged her back. "I know you do."

Now that she could think beyond how the secret might damage her marriage, her thoughts turned to Aaron and what his reaction might mean for her sister and nephew. "How's Aaron taking the news?"

"He feels blindsided, as you might expect. It'll take him some time to come to grips with this."

"But do you have any idea whether he wants to be part of Wyatt's life?"

"Not yet."

"If he signs away his rights, Presley won't ever ask him for anything."

"I think she made that clear."

"And?"

"It was a direct hit."

She drew him into the living room so they could sit. "What does that mean?"

"It hurt his feelings, Chey. Just because he's never wanted to marry Presley doesn't mean he doesn't give a shit about her. He cares, just on a different level. For her to reject even his participation in their son's life...that would sting, right? So he seemed rattled."

"I'm sorry about that. I realize Aaron's sensitive under all that male bravado."

"He's particularly sensitive to this issue because,

for all intents and purposes, we lost *both* parents. He wouldn't walk away from a child of his."

That sent a chill through Cheyenne. "If he can't care about Presley, too, it would be better for him to let her have Wyatt."

"I'm not convinced of that."

"Do you understand how hard she'd find it to have to see Aaron on a continuing basis? She's still in love with him, Dyl."

"That's unfortunate for her, but at this point our concern needs to be for Wyatt. If he has a father who's willing to be part of his life, he deserves that."

"In other words, the adults will have to muddle through."

"Exactly."

"So you do think he'll want to be involved."

"I don't know my brother as well as I thought I did if he gives up his son."

"You know him." Cheyenne released her breath in a long sigh. "Poor Presley. I pray she'll be able to cope."

"We'll do all we can to offer her the support she needs. Maybe, in the end, this will wind up being for the best."

She managed to smile despite her worry. "I can't believe I married such a wise man."

He leaned over to peck her lips. "Your luck had to turn some time, babe."

He was teasing, but she was serious when she responded. "I'd go through ten more childhoods like the one I had in order to reach the happiness I've found with you."

He pressed a hand to her stomach. "We have only good things to look forward to."

A fresh dose of guilt ruined everything. He'd taken the news about Wyatt in stride. He'd understood her dilemma, as only Dylan could. She should've had more faith in him.

Should she strip away *all* the lies? Tell him she'd been to the doctor and that she'd tested his sperm? She could explain she'd already researched artificial insemination, offer that as an alternative. But she no longer had any idea whether Aaron would still be willing to help. She couldn't blame him if he'd changed his mind.

Maybe Grady or Rod or Mack would do it if Dylan knew and was okay with it....

If she told him, she'd also have to admit that she wasn't really pregnant, but she had no more appetite for secrets. "Dyl?"

A text from Grady, something about work, had come in on his phone and he was looking down at it. "What?"

"Did you cancel your appointment with the doctor?"

"Of course. Why would I keep it if we're already pregnant?"

She closed her eyes. "I was just...wondering." How could she say what she had to say? She couldn't come up with the right words.

She decided to launch into it, but as soon as he finished with his phone, he pulled her close.

"I can't tell you how happy I am about the baby," he said. "There might be some crazy days ahead with Aaron and Presley, but we've got that. There's no way

I can be upset about anything when I think of my baby growing inside you."

The words she'd been about to say—about how, if he wasn't able to be a biological father, they could try other options—congealed in her throat. She tried to force them out, anyway. If she was going to tell him, now was the time. Once they performed the procedure—in the unlikely event that Aaron was still game—they'd be past the point of no return.

But then he said, "Maybe we had screwed-up childhoods, but we've come out of it just fine. We have each other, and we'll soon have our baby."

After that, Cheyenne couldn't destroy his happiness. "The future will be everything you want it to be," she promised instead.

"So what's Aaron going to do?" Presley had called Cheyenne twice, but it wasn't until the third try that her sister answered.

"We don't know, Pres. He didn't tell Dylan. He's just trying to come to grips with it, right, Dyl?"

Presley hugged her legs tighter to her chest as Dylan murmured in the background. After putting Wyatt to bed, she'd been sitting on the couch, unmoving. She hadn't eaten any dinner, but she wasn't hungry. She needed sleep more than food, if only she could unwind. But since she didn't dare call Aaron, she was hoping for some reassurance from Cheyenne and Dylan. "Let me talk to Dyl," she said.

"Just a sec."

The phone changed hands and her brother-in-law came on the line. "No wonder that kid of yours is so cute. He's a blood relative of mine," he joked.

She appreciated that he wasn't angry with her. Cheyenne had already told her that, but she felt she owed him a personal apology. "I hope you don't hate me now, Dyl. I would've told you, but I was too afraid you'd tell Aaron."

"He *is* my brother."

"So can you see why I thought it would be best to keep it to myself?"

"I'm not sure I agree with 'best.' But you weren't in the greatest place emotionally, and that makes it possible for me to understand."

"You're saying you don't condone it."

"Being a guy, and seeing it from a guy's perspective, I'm afraid I can't, no."

She hugged her knees that much tighter. "But can you forgive me?"

"Of course."

"How upset was he?" she asked, her mind immediately switching to Aaron. "I mean…he'll be reasonable, won't he?"

"Are you asking if he'll sign away his parental rights? Because I doubt he will, and I can't encourage that."

"He wouldn't have wanted Wyatt two years ago."

"Things change. People change. You've both proven that."

"But I think we should go by what we both wanted when I had to make the decision. Aaron often mentioned that he wasn't ready for children."

"What about Wyatt?" he countered.

"What about him? I'm taking care of him. And I'll find him a good dad someday."

"He already has a good dad—if you'll let Aaron have a role in his life."

She felt her hopes wilt. "I can't have Aaron in *my* life. How will I ever get over him? How will I move on if he's there as a constant reminder? How will that be beneficial to Wyatt?"

"Other people deal with this sort of thing all the time, Presley."

Then other people were stronger or smarter than she was. Maybe those bad genes of hers were getting in the way again. "You can't expect too much from Anita's daughter," she said bitterly.

"You don't have to be like your mother if you don't want to be," he told her. "You have control of your life. Look what you've been able to do in just twenty-four months. Imagine what you could do with more time."

But giving up Aaron had been harder than giving up drugs. "We've slept together since I've been home," she blurted out. "I haven't been with anyone since Arizona. But I didn't last a week back in Whiskey Creek, not with Aaron around."

He didn't respond right away.

"Dylan?"

After a muttered curse, he said, "I've never seen anyone so stuck on another person, which makes me mad at him."

"He's not trying to hurt me. It's just… I don't know. We seem to be…sexually addicted to each other."

"Then he needs to exercise some restraint."

"We both do. But I've *tried* to stay away from him. My stubborn heart won't let him go."

"Stubborn is right," he said. "Does Cheyenne know about the two of you?"

"No."

"Good. I won't tell her."

Presley could hear Cheyenne complaining in the background.

"It'll be my revenge secret," Dylan joked.

Presley hardly felt like laughing. "I wish you could tell me how to get over him," she said.

"You just got to make up your mind, little sister. Demand that whatever man you get with gives you his whole heart. And if he doesn't? He's not worth your time."

"I don't think I have the confidence," she admitted.

"That's your background talking," he said. "Don't listen. It's lied to you before. You're worthy of *any* man."

Her sister was back on the line. "What did you tell him?" she asked. There was a bit of a ruckus, as if they were wrestling over the phone. But Presley wasn't paying much attention. *Make up your mind....* Somehow she'd let her old doubts and insecurities creep up on her again, and it had happened so quickly and smoothly that she hadn't even noticed.

"You're right," she said.

"Who's right?" Cheyenne asked.

"Dylan."

"About what?"

Presley stood up. "I have a choice."

"I don't understand."

"I can choose what I'll accept and what I won't."

It was Dylan's voice she heard next.

"Now you've got it," he said.

20

After she'd waited anxiously for nearly twenty-four hours, Presley's phone rang at seven-forty the next evening, and the caller ID identified Aaron's number. She hadn't known when she'd hear from him, but she'd assumed he'd contact her at some point. He'd had a day or so to mull over the fact that he was a father. Now he was apparently ready to discuss the situation.

Presley preferred not to handle such a sensitive issue while she was at work. She had a client who would be showing up in less than ten minutes, expecting an hour-long, full-body massage, so she had limited time. It wouldn't be professional to greet her client with red, swollen eyes—which would happen if she started crying during her conversation with Aaron. But she was so anxious to learn her fate, and so afraid that any misstep might antagonize him further, that she couldn't help answering.

"Hello?" Hearing the breathy quality of her own voice, she wondered if he could tell how terrified she was. But he gave no indication. He didn't even respond. *"Hello?* Aaron?"

"I'm here." *Finally* he spoke, but his voice was flat and hard.

She rubbed the sudden chill bumps from her arms. "Why wouldn't you answer? Couldn't you hear me?"

"I heard you just fine. I wasn't sure if I was actually ready to have this conversation."

"You're still angry."

"Don't I have a right to be?"

"You do. But…I did what I thought was best, Aaron. What I thought you'd want."

"You decided what to do with our baby without even asking me."

"Once you knew, there'd be no going back. I saved you from having to decide! I let you go on your way unfettered and unbothered!"

"That's bullshit," he snapped. "You didn't keep Wyatt a secret for *my* sake. You did it for your own."

She threw a nervous glance at the clock. She didn't have time to let this blow up in her face. "Look, I'm sorry. But we're here now. So what do you want to do?"

"You think I can get over it that easily? Maybe I could if you were *really* sorry, but you're not. You're only sorry I found out. It's not as if you were going to tell me."

What could she say? She'd expected this. Some might even claim she deserved it. But she'd been in such a dark place when she first learned about her pregnancy, with her mother dying, and her own addiction and her confidence so low. There had seemed like only one way out after she'd decided to keep the baby—and that was to go away, start over. She doubted she would've been capable of putting herself back together if she'd stayed in contact with Aaron, even if it was just to have his help with Wyatt. He was too much of a temptation for her. "Probably not," she said.

"And then you had sex with me, knowing we already had one child together!" he said, pointing out how that made the whole thing worse. "I could've gotten you pregnant *again*."

"The fact that pregnancy can result from sex is a surprise to you? You're saying I owed you some… some sort of disclaimer? 'I already have a child by you so you'd better move on.' I don't remember inviting you over in the first place. The whole encounter was an…accident, a slip-up."

"You wanted it as badly as I did."

"Old emotions and desire got ahead of us. But it's in the past now, and it doesn't pertain to this."

"How do *I* know that? You could've been lying when you took that pregnancy test. You wouldn't let me in the damn bathroom."

"Stop it! You're acting like I've been *trying* to have your babies. Wyatt was an accident, Aaron. Just like that broken rubber we had recently. I got pregnant in spite of birth control, and I certainly haven't been knocking on your door, asking for more babies since. Do you think it was easy having a baby on my own? You know where I started out, how little I had to work with."

"That's your fault!" he nearly shouted. "It didn't have to be so hard. I would've helped you."

She lowered her voice. "You would've told me to get an abortion."

He didn't deny it.

"Maybe I didn't want to hear that, okay?" she went on. "Maybe I decided, since I was very likely the only one of us who wanted the baby, that I should be responsible for him."

"That's what enrages me! How do you know what I would've done? You never gave me the chance to decide for myself."

"Am I wrong about how you would've reacted? Would you have been excited? Would you have said you were ready to become a parent?"

"I probably wouldn't have said I was 'excited.' But I wasn't any less ready than you were, and you managed it. I wouldn't have forced you to get an abortion, so quit making it sound like I wouldn't have taken your feelings into consideration."

"You wanted me out of your life! The night my mother died, you told me to go home and you shut the door in my face as I stood crying. You think I was going to tell you about the baby after that? Hell, no! You would've assumed I was trying to trap you, or rope you into being part of my life. I chose not to become a debt, an obligation. Don't you get that?"

"I get that you knew I didn't want *you,* so you weren't going to let me have him."

Those words hit her like a physical blow. She'd always intuitively understood that Aaron didn't return her feelings, but he'd never spelled it out quite so bluntly. Stunned that this acknowledgment could still bring her pain, even after all the time they'd been apart, she opened her mouth to refute the accusation. That had nothing to do with the reason she'd gone away and decided to raise Wyatt on her own.

But then she caught herself. She'd just told *him* to

be honest. Maybe she should do the same. That might not have been the reason when she left, but what about since then? What about *after* she returned to Whiskey Creek? Now that she had Wyatt and loved him so deeply, she *didn't* want to be the only one Aaron couldn't love. She also didn't want to compete with someone like Aaron, someone so charismatic, for her son's love.

"That wasn't how it all started," she said softly. "But…it might be why I continued to keep the secret."

The way she'd suddenly stopped protesting and acknowledged that he could be right seemed to take the fire from his anger. "Wait, I'm sorry," he said. "I didn't mean that to be as harsh as it sounded."

She saw her client pull to the curb outside and knew she had to somehow find the strength and mental fortitude to get to work. And she wasn't going to do that by continuing to talk to Aaron. "Of course you did. But I need to go. I'll give you visitation rights, if that's what you want. Just text me if you'd like to take Wyatt some weekend. I'd rather we communicated that way from now on," she said and greeted her client while disconnecting.

Aaron dropped his phone on the couch, fell back against its cushions and closed his eyes. He wasn't sure what, exactly, he'd just done, but he knew it wasn't good. He felt sick inside, as if he'd taken something beautiful and smashed it on the ground. Presley had always struggled with her self-esteem. Now that she'd finally developed some, he hadn't meant to knock her flat by making it sound so unbelievable that he could ever love her. Over the course of her life, there'd been enough people tearing her down. He'd prided himself on being different, on being able to see who she *really* was. That was why he'd reached out to her that day at Sexy Sadie's; that was how he'd come to know there was a lot to admire. He liked how unpretentious she was, how grateful for the slightest kindness, how flexible and easy to please. He also enjoyed her street smarts and her sense of humor.

So why had he just cut her to the quick?

Because he'd been angry and frustrated and he'd let his temper get the best of him. Again. "Shit!"

"What's wrong?"

Aaron opened his eyes to see that Grady had walked in. "Nothing."

"Is it what we talked about yesterday? Wyatt?"

His brother had cornered him at work early this morning to ask if the rumors about Wyatt were true. Aaron had admitted they were. Then he'd heard from his other brothers, who were shocked but tentatively excited. Dylan was the only one who hadn't made a big deal about his having a kid. He'd understood that Aaron needed some space to cope with such a bombshell.

"Yes."

"Won't she let you see him?"

It wasn't that. Presley had *offered* visitation rights. She'd told him to text her if he wanted to arrange a time to see Wyatt. But that was as upsetting as all the rest of it. She'd just taken another giant step away from him.

"We'll see. I'm going to ask if I can have him tomorrow."

"You think she'll agree to that?"

"Why not? I'm off work. And she's had him for eighteen months. I should have the chance to get acquainted."

Grady rubbed his hands together in eagerness. "That means *we'll* be able to get acquainted, too. I can't wait. Dylan says he's cute."

"You haven't seen him?"

"Not yet."

"He's *definitely* cute."

His brother said something else, but Aaron didn't hear him and he didn't stop to find out what it was. He scooped his keys off the kitchen counter, hurried out to his truck and drove over to Presley's. To hell with texting; they lived in the same small town.

No one answered the door, so he decided to try the studio.

She was in the middle of giving a massage when he walked in. There was a sign on the door that said Massage in Session. A paper clock hung below, indicating the time she'd be available. It read nine.

He checked his watch. He'd have to wait forty-five minutes, but he wasn't going to leave and come back. If he missed her, she'd very likely go to Cheyenne's, because Cheyenne probably had Wyatt. And once Presley went there, he'd have to wait even longer to speak to her in private. So he sat in the reception area until he heard the door open. Then he stood.

The moment she saw him, she tensed up. It looked like she'd been crying, which made him feel even worse.

"I have a client here," she whispered, her words rushed as if she feared he'd start an argument before they were alone.

Hoping to ease her anxiety, he nodded and sat down again and, before long, Joe DeMarco, who owned the Gas-N-Go along with his father, appeared. Although Aaron didn't know him well, they'd seen each other around town plenty of times.

Joe said hello before paying Presley. Then he thanked her for the massage and walked out.

As soon as he was gone, Aaron tried to approach her again. "I'm sorry," he began. "I didn't mean to be such an ass on the phone." He tried to draw her to him, to soften her up so he could fix the damage he'd caused, but she jumped out of reach as if he intended to slug her instead.

"It's okay," she said. "Like I told you, there's probably some truth to what you said. I've never known exactly what makes me do what I do. Anyway, I can't change the past. So I'm going to stay focused on building a good future."

"You're well on your way. I admire you for the changes you've made."

She didn't seem to take that compliment to heart. She certainly didn't thank him. Maybe she thought he was just trying to be nice to compensate for how he'd acted before. "I have a long way to go, but at least I've started. One day at a time, right?"

"That's all anyone can do."

"So…back to Wyatt," she said. "We'll get a paternity test. I wouldn't want to move forward without proof, any more than you would. But then you're going to be faced with a choice, so you might as well be thinking about it now. Like most fathers in this situation, you can choose to pay child support and have visitations, or you can choose to sign away your rights and never hear from us again."

He felt some of his anger return. "You're still pushing for that?"

"It should be an attractive option. I can't guarantee that Wyatt won't try to contact you when he's older, of course. But I can take certain steps to make that unlikely."

He already knew he wasn't interested in bowing out. He was, however, curious about what she'd just said. "And those steps would include…"

"Being careful not to reveal your name or any other details about you."

"God," he muttered.

She lifted her chin. "I'm just saying it's up to you. I've never tried to force you into anything. And I'm not trying now."

"But it's perfectly clear what you'd prefer."

"I'm looking down the road, trying to imagine what the future might be like for both of us when we eventually find partners. If we do…" she added.

He didn't like what she'd said. Neither did he like that she sounded so remote. Her response frightened him. It showed him that he no longer held much power where she was concerned. And now she had his son.

"I know you've been generous with your love and kindness from the beginning, Pres. That's just who you are. I also know you didn't get pregnant on purpose. I feel bad that you had to go through it all on your own. Chances are that I've been reacting out of guilt as much as anything else. I should never have let our relationship develop into what it did." He sighed. "Everyone seems to think I was using you. That was never my intent, but…maybe I *was* doing it and then justifying it by telling myself I was giving you what *you* wanted."

She laughed mirthlessly. "You *were* giving me what I wanted. No question about that."

And yet she didn't seem interested anymore. Somehow, he'd taken it for granted that he'd always be able to have her if he wanted her. "There were enough good things about what we had that I let it go, I guess."

"That's understandable, since I made it so easy for you."

She had a way of looking at the harsh truth without flinching. He'd always admired that, too. "But I should never have been as oblivious as I was those last few weeks," he said. "I basically turned a blind eye to what was happening with your mother, tried to ignore it. And after that, once I learned you were having a baby, I should've wondered about it more than I did. If we hadn't been so careful about birth control, I think I would have."

She clasped her hands behind her back. "You know, or probably guessed from the parts of my ordeal you heard about from Chey or Dylan, that I ran into some…problems with other men after I left, even if you never learned all the details," she said, and immediately winced as if she was shying away from the memories even as she spoke. "The timing was only off by a month or so, and you weren't marking the days of my pregnancy off on a calendar."

"We both made mistakes. I say we let the past go and focus on what's best for Wyatt from here on out. Can you do that?"

She managed a weak smile. "Of course. So...do you want me to figure out how to get a paternity test?"

"I will. But I already believe Wyatt's mine, and that means I want to be part of his life. As tempting as you've tried to make it sound to walk away, I could never do it."

For a second, she looked like he'd just shot her. Then she rallied, but he knew she was barely holding herself together. "Okay."

It bothered Aaron that she wanted him out of her life so completely. He was going to try and stand up and do the right thing—and she was acting as if her worst fears had been confirmed. "That disappoints you?"

"I'm sure we can work out something that'll be fair to both of us."

Her words were measured and polite—nothing like the impulsive, passionate woman he'd known who'd always worn her heart on her sleeve. He hated the transformation. But he was determined not to cause an argument now that they'd made some progress toward an amicable solution.

"Great," he said with a nod. "So is there any way we can start by letting me take him for a few hours? I'm off work tomorrow and...I'd like the chance to become more familiar with him."

She avoided his gaze. "I guess that would be fine."

"You could both come over, if you're worried." He hoped she'd say yes. He knew it would be a lot more fun that way. Surely she'd loosen up once they spent some time together and he'd find his friend again.

But the bell over the door rang before she could answer, and they both turned to see Riley walk in.

Riley took one look at Presley's swollen eyes and hurried to her side. "You okay?"

Aaron was back to wanting to punch him. Riley was behaving as if Aaron was some kind of bully, as if she needed someone else's protection.

"Good as ever," she told him. "We're just…settling some details. Could you wait for me out in the car? It'll only be a few minutes. Then I'll explain everything."

"Are you sure?" he asked, and it was all Aaron could do not to show him how little they needed his presence.

She nodded. "I'm sure."

With a final condemning glance for Aaron, Riley stalked out.

Aaron stepped closer to Presley and lowered his voice. "You can't be serious about that guy."

"Don't," she said. "Let's decide right now that we won't comment on each other's romantic interests."

"*Romantic* interests? You're not *sleeping* with him!"

"Aaron—"

He raised one hand. "I'm sorry. You're right. That was out of line."

"Thank you."

"So what about tomorrow?"

"You can pick Wyatt up at ten. But before you take him anywhere, I need to teach you how to change a diaper."

"You won't be joining us?"

"No."

He scowled. "Why not?"

"Riley's taking me on a picnic."

Aaron breathed in through his nose and let the air go out his mouth. "Fine. I'll see you tomorrow, then."

"Goodbye."

It was definitely time to leave, but the situation felt so surreal he couldn't seem to move his feet. Presley had always been singularly devoted to *him*. Now she was the mother of his son, and they would be dealing with each other for the next two decades or more, but she was determined not to even *like* him?

"Where are you and Riley going tonight?" he asked.

"To get something to eat."

And then what?

He knew better than to ask.

21

"So it's true?" Riley asked. "Wyatt belongs to Aaron?"

Presley forced herself to swallow the salad she'd put in her mouth. She hadn't been hungry, not since Aaron had confronted her at the studio. But Riley had asked Cheyenne to keep Wyatt for an extra hour so he could take her out to eat, and Cheyenne had happily agreed. "Yes."

Judging by the grim set of his mouth, he wasn't pleased to hear this news. She could understand why he wouldn't be. Aaron would continue to be part of her life—and the life of any man she got involved with, especially if that man became a permanent fixture.

"Why didn't you tell him when you found out you were pregnant?" he asked. "You didn't think he'd stand up and be a father?"

"It was my decision to keep the baby. I figured it should be my responsibility to raise him." She stuck another bite of salad in her mouth. They'd made small talk until their meals arrived, carefully avoiding the subject of Aaron but, apparently, the pleasant part of the conversation was over. She lamented that. After all the angst and worry she'd been feeling since Aaron learned about Wyatt, she wanted to relax. But that would be impossible. Word would spread and everyone who knew her would have an opinion—questions, too.

Riley had ordered a burger and fries; he wiped his mouth with his napkin. "It takes two to make a baby, Presley."

Everyone said that. But no one understood the nuances of their relationship—the gratitude she owed Aaron for befriending her. For giving her someone she liked so much to hang out with during those lonely years. For the attention and fun. Even for meeting her physical needs so expertly and completely. "It's kind of hard to explain, but the pregnancy was more my fault than his."

Such a lame explanation only elicited another grimace. "That makes it sound like you *tried* to get pregnant."

"I definitely didn't *try*," she said ruefully. "I was in no state to raise a child and terrified of failing as a mother." Like *her* mother had failed. "I just mean that…I knew he wasn't in love with me and yet I kept seeing him, kept sleeping with him. I guess you could say I deserved what I got."

"A lot of people have lopsided relationships. That doesn't release the uninterested party from all responsibility."

She didn't think the relationships he referred to were quite as lopsided as hers had been. "Is that how it was with Jacob's mother?"

This subject couldn't be any more comfortable for

Riley than Aaron was for her, but he didn't seem reluctant to talk about it. Maybe he'd expected her to broach his own past at some point.

"Not at first. Phoenix was…different. She had a…darker quality than any other girl I'd been with. My friends thought I was crazy to be attracted to her. They didn't get her. But I saw her as quirky, intriguing."

Suddenly the fact that Riley, who came across as so mainstream, could be interested in dating someone with a few rough edges didn't seem so unusual. "Like me?"

"Sometimes you remind me of her," he said. "A little."

She added more dressing to her salad. "How long were you two together?"

"Maybe three months."

"That's not long."

"No. And yet the relationship progressed really fast, considering we were both virgins when we started talking."

Presley had been about to take a sip of water. Distracted, she set her glass down. "You got the first girl you ever slept with *pregnant?* How's that for shitty luck?"

He was chewing, so he just gave her an ironic smile.

"You were so young!" she exclaimed.

"Young and stupid," he added when he could speak

"Was it the news of the baby that came between you? Did the thought of having a kid put too much pressure on the relationship?"

"It wasn't that. I didn't know she was pregnant until *after* the...incident."

The incident. He was talking about Phoenix running down his next love interest with her mother's Buick. But Presley could see why he might not want to say *that*. The death of Lori Mansfield had been tragic and horrifying. There was still a sad echo in the community today. Lori's family wasn't about to let anyone forget. They held a candlelight vigil on the anniversary of her death each year, and every time Phoenix was eligible for parole, they gathered as many people as they could to appear before the parole board and lobby against her release. Presley had seen articles about it in the *Gold Country Gazette,* which she'd followed religiously once she'd left town. That had been her only taste of home, besides hearing from Cheyenne.

"So why'd you break up with her?" she asked.

"It was too intense a relationship for seventeen. We wanted to be together 24/7. My grades and sports were starting to suffer, and my parents were freaking out. They didn't want me getting married right out of high school. So they told me I couldn't have a steady girlfriend, that I needed to date a number of girls."

Presley felt her eyes widen. *"And you listened?"*

He shrugged. "I knew they were right—that I could get locked into a life that wouldn't make either of us happy if I didn't put some distance between us. We'd met at the wrong time."

"And I'm guessing your parents didn't want you marrying *her*. Cheyenne and I aren't the only ones around here who come from poor white trash."

"It may be grossly unfair, but that's true," he ad-

mitted. "They tried to say they weren't being judg-
mental. They *still* say that. They call it being 'realistic'
instead. But I'm sure Phoenix's situation and family
played a role. I don't know how much you remember
about her, but her mother was almost as bad as yours."

"I remember." In some ways Lizzie Fuller was
worse than Anita. While Anita had been selfish and
neglectful, and had often walked on the wrong side of
the law, especially when it came to drugs and prosti-
tution, Phoenix's mother was physically abusive and
mentally *disturbed*. Presley honestly couldn't say
she'd had a more difficult childhood.

"Social services were always showing up at her
house," Riley muttered.

From what Presley could recall, the Fullers had
lived in a run-down mobile home on what amounted
to a patch of dirt a couple of miles out of town.

"Where's Mrs. Fuller now?" she asked.

"Still in the same place."

"And her sons?"

"Who knows? They don't live around here and,
far as I can tell, they never visit."

"I've heard of them but don't think I've ever met
them."

"Because you and Cheyenne weren't living here
when they were. All three left home by the time they
were sixteen. One even got himself emancipated at
that age. The other two just ran away. Now Lizzie
lives alone and is basically a recluse."

Presley sipped more of her water. "That explains
why I haven't seen her in town."

"She can't get around too easily these days. She
weighs nearly four hundred pounds."

"I feel bad for Phoenix." Presley wasn't sure she should reveal that. She knew it wasn't politically correct to say that kind of thing about a *murderer*. But it was true. Her own past made her sympathetic. She'd made her own share of bad decisions. There was no excuse for taking a human life, but a broken heart, jealousy, fear, obsession—those were strong emotions and could lead to very poor decisions. Turning the wheel of that Buick the wrong way when she was seventeen had in effect taken *two* lives, since she'd never be the same or have the same prospects.

Fortunately, Riley didn't seem offended. "In some ways, I do, too," he said. "The girl I knew would never harm anyone. She was tough, a force to be reckoned with, which was part of her appeal. But she wasn't evil."

With one last bite, Presley pushed her plate away. This was a great deal more interesting to her than talking about *her* problems. It also gave her some insight into who Riley was beyond what she'd seen of him so far. "What made her do it? What really goes through someone's mind before something like that?"

"She was seventeen, pregnant and afraid to tell anyone. I was the first boy she'd ever loved, the first boy to show her any love in return, and I moved on rather...abruptly." He pursed his lips as he stared at his plate. "I guess you could say it was a perfect storm."

"That's heartbreaking."

He shoved a fry into his mouth. "What's crazy is that Jacob is nearly as old as we were when it happened. I was so young. At least, that's what I keep telling myself." He grew thoughtful again. "Still, I could definitely have handled it better, and I wish every day that I had."

"It sounds like you feel partly responsible."

"I do. I don't think there's any way to escape that. I keep wondering if I'd been wiser, kinder, more willing to remain friends with Phoenix, would Lori be alive today?"

"Hindsight is always twenty/twenty."

"She'll be getting out soon," he said.

"But Lori's parents—"

"Can't keep her in prison forever. It was second-degree murder, not something she'd planned. And even though they tried her as an adult, she was only seventeen. She's lost the opportunity to raise her child, as well as nearly sixteen years of her life and what friends she had here."

Presley peered at him more closely. "I'm not sure if you're saying she deserves a second chance or she doesn't."

"She paid the price for what she did. I just hope she doesn't come back *here*."

"Where else would she go?"

"That's the problem. She doesn't have anywhere else."

Despite knowing they weren't good for her, Presley tried one of his fries. "Do you ever hear from her?"

"She sends Jacob letters and whatever money she's able to earn making a dime an hour or however much she gets paid working in the laundry."

"Won't she need that money when she gets out?"

"I'm sure it would come in handy. But she wants something to give him."

"Does he write her back?"

Riley didn't answer; he stared pensively into his coffee.

"Riley?"

"I've never given him her letters and I've been saving the money for his college fund—not that it amounts to much."

"Because…"

"I don't dare encourage a relationship between them." He seemed tortured by this decision but committed to it. "With Lizzie the way she is, and everything Phoenix herself has been through, she can't possibly be normal."

But Presley wasn't "normal," either. Did he realize that?

"Jacob will be confronted with her at some point, Riley. You said yourself that Lori's parents can't keep her in prison forever."

"She thinks she's getting out this summer."

"But even if she is released, she won't really come back to a community that hates her—and a mother she'd be better off without, would she?"

"Like I said, she has nowhere else to go. And she insists that getting to know Jacob is the only thing that matters to her."

"Is she interested in seeing *you* again?"

"No."

"How can you tell? Maybe the obsession has grown instead of diminished. What else would she have to think about in prison?"

"She's never said anything that leads me to believe she still has feelings for me. Her letters are all about Jacob."

"That's got to make you nervous about the day she'll be released."

He sighed. "I'll admit I'm concerned."

The waitress came to collect their plates. Presley asked for some coffee, and Riley indicated he needed a refill, along with a piece of banana cream pie.

"I guess we all have our problems," she said with a chuckle.

Leaning back, he stretched out his legs. "So...what are you going to do about Aaron?"

Since he'd confided in her, she felt more comfortable discussing her own situation. "What can I do?" she asked. "He's Wyatt's biological father. He's got rights."

"He also has obligations."

"I'm sure he'll be fair when it comes to finances, if that's what you mean. Aaron has always been generous with money."

Riley seemed to be studying her extra closely. "So maybe it'll be a blessing that the truth came out."

"The financial help will be nice," she said. But seeing Aaron all the time? "Too bad that isn't all there is to it."

"You're afraid he might be difficult in other ways?"

"It's not necessarily Aaron I'm worried about." He could be stubborn. But she couldn't talk badly about him, not to Riley. It just felt too disloyal. "When he eventually marries, I'll be dealing with another woman, a woman I haven't met. What if the two of them decide I'm not doing something the way they think I should? Or they believe Wyatt would be better off living with them?" She smoothed the napkin on her lap. "Things could get rocky then, especially when you consider that Aaron will likely have more resources than I do. So…I don't know. The lack of control, the possibility of conflict. It all frightens me."

"The balance could shift in your favor when *you* marry. Maybe you'll be the one with plenty of resources and support."

She nodded and let it go at that. The future would bring whatever it brought; she didn't want to borrow trouble. But even if she did find a husband, she doubted she'd ever *want* to fight Aaron.

She could only hope he never forced her into that position.

Thanks to the knowledge that Presley was out with Riley, it took Aaron forever to get to sleep. So he wasn't pleased to be awakened when Cheyenne called him.

"It's got to be after midnight," he grumbled into the phone as soon as he heard her voice. He knew it was that late because he'd watched the clock until then, trying to resist the urge to drive by Presley's.

"I'm sorry. I had to wait until Dylan fell asleep before I could slip out of bed. Can you meet me at the graveyard?"

"The *graveyard?* Isn't that a little macabre in the middle of night?"

"What's going on?"

"I just want to talk."

He generally avoided the cemetery. His mother was buried there, and he preferred not to revisit the past. "About the insemination?"

"And a few other things. Can you come?"

Hauling in a deep breath, he rubbed the sleep from his face. "Okay. I'll be there in fifteen minutes."

She hung up without saying goodbye, and he made himself roll out of bed and get dressed.

By the time he reached for his keys, he almost felt human again. He only hoped Cheyenne didn't have any more surprises for him. Agreeing to father a child for her and Dylan, and then learning he was already the father of Presley's child, was enough excitement for one spring.

As he walked out of the house, he was eager for the cool breeze. But the air felt heavy with rain. He frowned at the sky as he started his engine. The uncertain weather, and the dark clouds that scuttled across the moon, would make standing in the graveyard seem even creepier. What a place to meet....

It was close to Cheyenne's house, however, and should give them some privacy.

Cheyenne was waiting for him when he arrived. He could see her sitting on a bench under the old oak tree not far from her own mother's burial plot and wondered how she felt toward Anita these days. She hardly ever talked about her.

When he'd asked once, she said it was complicated, and Dylan had sent him a look that suggested he not push.

"Don't you find it disturbing to sit here alone?" he asked as he approached. "Most women would be terrified of coming here at this hour."

"To me it's peaceful," she said with a shrug.

He was slightly embarrassed that it bothered him. "If you say so."

"Anita tied me to this tree once, as punishment for

staying out too late," she explained. "Made me spend the whole night—until Eve's parents rescued me the next morning. At first I was out of my mind with fear, but it forced me to make peace with this place, to realize there's nothing here that will hurt me."

When he came closer he saw that she was actually sitting closer to Little Mary's grave than Anita's. Six-year-old Mary had once lived in the Victorian next door, now Eve Harmon's B and B, where both Eve and Cheyenne worked. Mary was killed in the basement back in the 1800s, not long after Whiskey Creek was founded. No one had ever figured out who her murderer was, and there'd been sightings of her ghost ever since.

"The stories I hear about the woman who raised you and Presley never cease to amaze me," he said.

She pulled the sleeves of her sweatshirt down over her hands as a chill wind stirred her hair. "She was not your average mother."

"No," he said, and sat beside her. "So…why are we here?"

She glanced at his face but quickly looked away. "I wanted to apologize to you, first of all. I didn't get the chance when you came by to talk to Dylan last night."

"For keeping Presley's secret?"

"You understand why I did it, don't you?" she asked imploringly.

He leaned forward and propped his elbows on his knees, trying to avoid the sight of his own mother's grave in the far corner. "More or less."

"I felt terrible about it from the beginning, Aaron. But Wyatt was all Presley had, all that was keeping her off drugs and moving in the right direction.

You remember how she was when she left here two years ago."

"Of course."

"You've asked me where she went during that time when...when we couldn't find her."

"It wasn't Arizona?"

"It was. But when she finally called me, she was at an abortion clinic. I left that part out. I also left out the part about the guy who'd driven her there and was planning to take her home afterward. You should've seen what he did to her—the cuts, the bruises."

Aaron didn't even like thinking about it.

"Deciding to keep the baby was what motivated her to turn her life around," Cheyenne continued. "That's easy to say, of course. But if I hadn't gone to that abortion clinic, if I hadn't seen how close I'd come to losing my sister for good, I never would've gone along with hiding what we did. I know I can't expect you to believe that, but it's the truth, Aaron. I didn't even tell Dylan, and you know how much I love him."

He let his hands dangle between his legs. "You didn't have to come out in the middle of the night to tell me that. And I'm sorry for what Presley went through. I'll admit I feel partially to blame."

"*She* doesn't blame you."

"I know." She was forgiving. She'd never blamed him for anything, never expected anything. She'd just loved him.

Cheyenne reached into her purse and pulled out a photograph of Wyatt. "I brought this for you. Presley will probably give you one, or you can take some pictures of him yourself, but...I thought it might be nice to have while you're in the midst of making the hard decisions you have to make."

Still barely able to believe he was Wyatt's father, Aaron stared down at the cherubic-looking toddler. When he finally pulled his gaze away, he raised his head to meet Cheyenne's eyes. "I can't imagine you'd hand me this right now if you wanted me to give him up."

She put her arms around him and leaned her head on his shoulder. "I'm sure he could use a good father, and I'm equally sure you'd be one."

He felt a flash of hope but couldn't avoid what Presley had made so plain. "I doubt your sister would want you to encourage me. I get the impression she's hoping I'll sign Wyatt over."

"She might be hoping that, but *I'm* hoping she's underestimating her ability to adjust to having you in the picture. That's *all* I can hope for, at this point."

He couldn't help smiling. "Thanks."

He got up to leave, but she wasn't finished. "I also wanted to tell you that…that you don't have to worry about doing the artificial insemination. There's too much going on right now for you to make a decision about something that…far-reaching. It was really nice of you to be as willing as you have been, but…I can't feel good about it after…all this."

So *that* was why she'd called him in the middle of the night. Everything else could've been said in front of Dylan. "If we don't move ahead, Dylan will be really disappointed when he discovers you're not pregnant."

"I'm sorry about that. I definitely didn't mean for it to come to this." She shook her head. "My timing's been terrible. It's not just Wyatt, although that's enough. I know you're stressed about your father's release and his new marriage, and what that'll do to your life and your brothers' lives. There's a lot going on."

He pulled her to her feet. "Cheyenne, I haven't changed my mind."

A doubtful expression appeared on her face. "You can't mean that."

"Yes, I can. Let's do it."

Her eyebrows shot up. "Even after what's happened?"

The memory of Dylan squeezing his shoulder before getting out of his truck last night convinced Aaron that he couldn't say no. He owed his brother too much. "It's the least I can do."

22

Riley hadn't tried to kiss her. He'd helped her get Wyatt from Cheyenne's and drove them both home. Then he'd brought the car seat inside because Wyatt had gone right back to sleep. But Riley hadn't asked to stay. He'd given her a hug and told her to sleep well.

Since he'd left, Presley had been wandering around her house, keyed up and restless for no particular reason. Otherwise, she wouldn't have been awake when Aaron's text came in at two-thirty.

Are you in safe?

Why would he care?
She blew out a sigh and keyed in, Yes.
How was it? came his response.

Fine. Riley's a nice guy.

So you keep saying.

It *was* what she kept saying—probably to cover for the fact that she felt no sexual attraction to Riley.

She made no reply, but that didn't stop Aaron from texting her again.

I want to see you.

It's too late to talk about anything tonight, Aaron.

I don't want to talk.

Closing her eyes, she rested her head against the wall. She'd known better than to answer him after *Are you in safe?* So why had she?

Because she wanted to see him, too. Badly. She yearned for him. But she wasn't going to succumb to that weakness ever again. It was more important than ever that she maintain her self-respect and not lose power in the relationship.

I'll see you when you pick up Wyatt, she wrote back, then turned off her phone.

Presley was freshly showered when Aaron showed up at her place at ten the next morning. He could tell by the way she smelled. He liked that scent, which reminded him of all the times he'd had his nose pressed into her hair as he made love to her.

"You look nice," he said. He'd never really tried to win anyone over, but he was trying now. He couldn't help hoping he could get her to cancel her picnic with Riley and come with him instead. He still wanted to reestablish the camaraderie they'd once enjoyed.

He was also more than a little anxious at the thought of being alone with the child he believed to be his son for an extended period. His brief babysitting stint the day he'd learned the truth hadn't gone smoothly. He'd never seen—or smelled—anything worse than what was in that diaper he'd had to change. Just the memory of it made him gag.

Presley didn't thank him for the compliment. She smoothed the cotton print of her sundress and, again, he got the impression that anything flattering he said would be discarded with the assumption that he couldn't mean it.

He'd taught her not to expect too much of him, and taught her well. But she *did* look nice—soft, the way he liked his women, with plenty of golden-brown skin showing. She also looked tired, however. Dark circles underscored her big eyes, and she wrung her hands with anxiety whenever he came around.

"I've packed everything you should need," she told him, and picked up a plastic-covered diaper bag that had been waiting by the door. "There's food and snacks in here. A change of clothes. Extra diapers. Wet wipes. Diaper rash ointment. And a bottle of milk."

"Got it." He glanced at the toys on the floor, but didn't see the baby. "Where's Wyatt?"

"In his high chair. I'll get him so I can show you how to change a diaper."

"Diaper changing isn't rocket science," he said, following her into the kitchen.

She turned around to give him a questioning look. "Oh, really? I couldn't tell from the way you did the last one."

"That wasn't my fault. He had a blowout. And then he didn't want me to change him. He kept crying and squirming, and I didn't know how hard I could hold him down. I didn't want to hurt him."

"I'm grateful for that," she murmured.

"You *know* I'd never hurt him, right?"

She nodded. "I do know that."

That acknowledgment made him feel slightly better but, the way she'd been treating him left a lot to be desired.

"Anyway, that wasn't a good one to start with," he said. "We got shit everywhere. On the table. On me. On another diaper I had to throw away."

When she laughed, he grinned at her, hoping to reach the woman he'd known so well. But the warmth fled her face the second she met his eyes and she turned away. "We'll go over it just so I can feel I've done my part as a mother."

As he accompanied her down the hall into Wyatt's bedroom, he glanced into hers. He wasn't sure what he expected to see. He remembered the night he'd stayed over, and wondered how it would feel to be welcome to stay again, especially now that he was at such a crossroads in his life. He'd just decided to move to Reno—and now *this*. Should that change his plans? Should he remain in Whiskey Creek and co-parent? Or drive back whenever he could get a manager to cover for him?

He craved the familiar, craved *her*. But, looking into her room, he was also afraid he'd see some sign that Riley had taken his place in her bed.

"When you change him, sometimes it helps if you distract him by giving him a toy," she said. Aaron needed something to distract *him*.

As she went through a quick demonstration, he

stood behind her, barely resisting the urge to slide his hands around her waist and up over her breasts.

"See how easy that was?"

"He was hardly even wet."

She rolled her eyes. "Practice will make perfect—eventually."

"When do I feed him lunch? At noon? Or did he just have breakfast?"

"He woke up at seven. Breakfast was at seven-thirty."

No wonder she was tired. She wasn't getting much sleep.

"He was in his high chair when I got here."

"Having a snack. You can feed him at twelve-thirty or one. He'll act fussy and let you know."

"Got it." They stood in Wyatt's room, staring at each other for several seconds. Then she kissed her son's cheek and reluctantly handed him over.

"I'll send along a couple of his favorite toys. And you can call me if you have any trouble. Don't hesitate. I won't think badly of you if you want to give him back after an hour or so."

"Come on, I'm not that big a wimp."

"It's that kind of thinking I'm trying to prevent. Don't hang in there because you feel you have something to prove."

"I wouldn't," he said. "But I don't want to interrupt your picnic, either."

She narrowed her eyes. "That sounds as if you'd actually enjoy it."

"I hate the idea of you being with him," he admitted. "I don't know why you won't date *me*."

"We've been over this."

"You're making me the bad guy and giving Riley an unfair advantage!"

He thought she might argue with him, but she didn't. "Riley has never rejected me. I have nothing to fear from him."

"So you're being a chicken shit?"

"That's easy for you to say. It's not your heart on the line!"

"I'll be more careful with it this time." He was as sincere as he could be, but she didn't seem to take his promises any more seriously than she did his compliments.

"It's pointless! I don't have what it takes to make you fall in love with me, and I don't want you to date me just because of Wyatt or because we're good in bed together. There's no need to confuse everything again now that we have it sort of figured out."

"I'm only here for a short time." If he stuck with his plan. "I'm asking for six weeks! How could that leave you any worse off?"

She glared at him, but he could tell there was no real anger behind it. He got the impression she was showing him that tough face, hoping he'd back off before she could give in.

"Come on," he said, taking her hand. "How about one more chance?"

For a second, he was sure she was going to agree. But then she straightened her shoulders, raised her chin and flatly refused. "No, but thanks for making the effort."

When he swore, she seemed a little shocked. "What's going on with you?" she asked.

"Are you having fun turning the tables on me?"

"I wish." She marched out to get Wyatt's diaper bag. Then, a few minutes later, he found himself in his truck with a baby in his backseat—for the first time *ever*.

"Wow, she let you bring him home," Mack said.

Aaron held Wyatt, still strapped in his car seat, in one hand, and the diaper bag in the other. "That's right."

Mack watched as he set both on the floor and released Wyatt, who squealed with excitement as soon as he saw the dogs. "Gog!" he cried, and pointed as Aaron picked him up. "Oooh, gog!"

Mack started laughing. "Look at the expression on his face. That's pretty damn cute."

"It's all fun and games until you have to change a diaper," Aaron grumbled.

"Yeah, but that's *your* job, big brother."

"What kind of uncle are you, anyway?"

Mack didn't answer. Wyatt was fighting to get down, which surprised Aaron. He'd thought he'd be frightened by Shady and Kikosan. A chocolate Lab and a golden retriever, they were a lot bigger than he was.

"Let him go," Mack said. "Let's see what he does."

Aaron put Wyatt on his own two feet and they both laughed as he stomped and shrieked in pleasure when the dogs licked his face.

Mack rested his hands on his hips. "I'm impressed that he's not scared."

Aaron gave him a "get real" look. "My kid would never be afraid of a dog that's wagging its tail," he teased, but he'd expected the same reaction Mack had.

"I bet he hasn't been around many dogs."

"He obviously knows what they are."

They both watched Wyatt pull Shady's tail. Then they laughed as he stumbled and fell on his diapered behind when the dog circled around to see what was going on.

"Gog!" Wyatt repeated, pointing.

"He has no fear," Aaron marveled.

"He's too awestruck." Mack crouched down. "Hey, little guy." He tried to pick Wyatt up, but Wyatt wasn't having any of it. All he cared about was his new four-legged friends. So they gave up trying to hold him and let him play for an hour while they watched him and a football game at the same time. Then Grady and Rod came in.

"Hey, look who's here!" Grady said the moment he saw Wyatt.

At that point Wyatt seemed ready to focus on something other than Shady and Kikosan, who were tired of being mauled and kept moving away when Wyatt toddled toward them.

"This is great!" Rod sat down next to him. "You have a kid. I can't believe it."

"Neither can I," Aaron said.

"What does he do?"

"What do you mean…what does he do?"

"I'm guessing he can't play catch. And he doesn't seem too interested in watching the game. So…what can we do with him at this age?"

That was a fair question. Aaron had been wondering the same thing. There didn't seem to be many options yet. "Don't ask me. I'm new at this."

"He plays with the dogs," Mack volunteered.

"And he loads up his diaper." Aaron hoped he wouldn't have another experience like the last one. "But we'll get to the good stuff eventually."

"Wouldn't it be cool if he turned out to be a professional baseball player?" Grady asked.

"Hey, we'd get free tickets." Mack clearly liked that idea.

"Maybe he won't be athletic," Rod chipped in.

Aaron scowled at him. "Of course he'll be athletic."

"I'm just saying he might be smart instead—a brain surgeon."

The possibilities that lay ahead were exciting. Aaron sure hoped Wyatt had a better childhood than either he or Presley had endured. He decided to make sure of it, and was grateful to Presley for trying so hard to outdistance her past. "You're going to be smart *and* athletic, right, Wyatt?" He grinned at his brother. "And let's not forget handsome."

When Aaron said his name, Wyatt toddled over, and let Aaron lift him into his lap. Aaron suspected that Rod, Mack and Grady, who were watching to see how the two of them interacted, were wondering if Wyatt was going to tolerate this. But the kid seemed perfectly content, as if he'd *wanted* Aaron to hold him.

Then something extraordinary happened, something Aaron had thought would take much more time. The look or the feel of this child, or some magical quality, some chemistry between father and son, evoked a poignant and unfamiliar emotion that swept through Aaron so suddenly it took him by surprise.

"Wow," he breathed as he gazed down at Wyatt and Wyatt gazed back at him, unblinking.

Grady spoke from the chair to his left. "Wow, what?"

Aaron hadn't realized he'd spoken aloud. He glanced over at his brothers but returned his attention to Wyatt. "That was easy."

"We have no clue what you're talking about," Mack complained.

Of course they didn't. And Aaron couldn't find the words to explain. Or maybe it was just that he didn't want to admit how, deep down, he'd been afraid he wouldn't be able to love his own son. Been afraid that not being part of his life from the beginning would somehow rob him of what other dads felt naturally.

But now he knew those fears had been unfounded. He'd only known he had a son for a few days, and he'd had minimal contact since then. Yet the little guy had already stolen a piece of Aaron's heart.

Presley was trying to enjoy her picnic with Riley. The Sierra Nevada foothills were gorgeous this time of year, so she should've been enjoying the scenery, if nothing else. But she was too preoccupied thinking of Wyatt and Aaron. She couldn't imagine what they were doing. She'd never seen Aaron around children. To her knowledge, they'd never even discussed kids, besides the throwaway statements when he'd indicated he didn't want any —certainly not yet. And there was that diaper incident, which had emphasized his lack of experience....

She surreptitiously checked the time on her phone. She'd thought Riley hadn't noticed. He was busy packing up the picnic basket. But when she glanced up, she saw him frowning at her.

"Are you that worried?"

Worry wasn't the right word, not *exactly*. Perhaps regret, since she wasn't where she really wanted to be. Even though her brain insisted she'd made the correct choice when she'd turned Aaron down, her heart and her body weren't so sure. It felt more like she'd missed a prime opportunity to be with the people she loved most.

"He's never been around children."

"But you trust him to be kind."

"Of course. He'd never *purposely* hurt Wyatt. It's just that he's a fish out of water right now."

"Do you want to call and check in?"

She was about to say no, but then broke down. Why not put her mind at ease?

"We don't have a very good signal," she said.

"We're heading back. Wait until we get closer to town."

They didn't talk much on the drive. Had Riley figured out, once and for all, that their relationship would never evolve into anything other than what it already was? Perhaps he was looking at it practically: he'd been attracted to her, investigated the potential and eliminated the possibility. Now he could move on to someone else.

"I'm sorry I've been so quiet today," she said.

He adjusted the volume on the radio. "With everything that's happened recently, it's understandable."

"Aaron is asking me to see him."

"When?"

"I mean, go out with him."

His eyebrows went up. "And you're considering it?"

"He'll only be around for six more weeks."

"And then?"

"And then he'll be leaving, and I won't have to see him as often. Maybe then I can get over him."

He rubbed his chin. "You'll still have contact. Now that he knows about Wyatt, you'll have contact with him for at least the next eighteen years."

"But he won't be right...*here,* right around the corner."

"That makes a difference?"

Presley shrugged. "It's driving him crazy that I'm hanging out with you."

"Then you should be leery of his interest. If it's all about the competition, it won't last. Don't let him fool you."

"Thanks for that."

He'd heard her sarcasm. "What?"

"Is it so impossible to think he might be able to care about me?"

"You have to face the truth or you'll never get over him."

She didn't want to hear it, but Riley had a point. Her sister would say the same thing, which was why she hadn't brought up the subject. And with Cheyenne she couldn't attribute that reaction to male rivalry. Cheyenne loved Aaron and *still* warned her to keep her distance.

"You're right," she said. *Burn me once, shame on you; burn me twice, shame on me.*

23

Once she and Riley returned to town, Presley had tried to check in with Aaron. She hadn't reached him, which worried her—and now that she was home alone she could obsess without distraction. So it was fortunate that he called her back after only thirty minutes.

"Why didn't you answer my call?" she asked.

"I didn't hear my phone," he said. "What's up?"

"I wanted to see how it's going."

"It's fine."

Fine? That was it? "Are you bringing Wyatt home soon?"

"Not *real* soon. Can I have him for another couple of hours?"

"This is turning into a pretty long stay for the first visit. What are you doing?"

"Shopping."

"That's not easy with a baby. Wouldn't you rather I watched him?"

"He's asleep in the stroller I just bought."

"Why did you buy a stroller when you could've used mine?"

"This one is much nicer," he said. "It's the Cadillac version. You're going to love it."

"But strollers are expensive."

She'd gotten hers secondhand, just like all her baby equipment and most of Wyatt's clothes.

"It wasn't too bad. So what do you say? Can I keep him longer? It'll take us an hour to get back, anyway. We might as well go to a few other places while we're here."

"Where's here?"

"Sacramento."

"You took my son all the way to Sacramento?"

"He's my son, too, remember?"

"That means you've done the DNA test?"

"We swabbed, and I've put the samples in the mail for the lab, but we won't have the results for a few weeks."

"Is that what took you out of town?"

"No. There's no Toys "R" Us in Whiskey Creek."

She'd expected him to be overwhelmed and eager for her to take Wyatt off his hands, but it didn't sound that way. "Fine. Go ahead and finish whatever you're doing."

"Maybe you can grab some shut-eye while Wyatt's gone. You sound tired."

She *was* tired. She hadn't been getting enough sleep. Juggling a business, a baby and an obsession with the wrong man—it wasn't easy. If one wasn't keeping her up at night, the other was. "That's tempting. But I have a few things I need to do at the studio. I should go over there while I've got the chance."

"Sleep," he insisted. "You'll feel a lot better if you do. I've got Wyatt, and I'm taking good care of him."

"We're having fun," someone in the background called out.

Presley had assumed Aaron was alone. "Who's that?"

"Grady came with us."

"What exactly are you shopping for? Besides the stroller you already bought, of course."

"More kid stuff. What else?"

"But there's no need to double up. You don't even know what I've got."

"I've seen what you've got."

The sexual innuendo was unmistakable. He was teasing—that took her by surprise, too. It told her he was enjoying himself and wasn't feeling harried or pressured or angry with her. "I can't believe you said that with Grady right there."

"You and I have a son, Pres. I'm sure my brother can figure out that we slept together."

"He'll think we're still sleeping together!"

She thought he'd remind her that it hadn't been all that long. But he didn't. When he spoke again, he asked, "How was the picnic?"

Not particularly exciting. She'd spent most of it dwelling on how badly she wanted to be with him and Wyatt. "Really fun," she lied.

The way he dropped his voice led her to believe he'd turned away so that Grady wouldn't hear him. "How much fun?"

"None of your business," she replied, but she couldn't help feeling a measure of satisfaction that he didn't like thinking of her with another man.

"Is he gone?"

He seemed reluctant to use Riley's name. "Yes."

"Good. Get some sleep. I'll see you in a few hours."

She was already climbing into bed. It felt like forever since she'd had an afternoon to herself without *something* putting pressure on her—fear that Wyatt would wake her too soon, the knowledge that she had to pick him up from Cheyenne's or an evening of massage appointments or yoga classes ahead. It was a mellow spring afternoon and she was all alone and confident that Wyatt was safe.

For the moment, all was well. She refused to think of the future....

"That's what I'm going to do," she told Aaron. Then she must've dropped off, because she didn't remember saying goodbye. The next thing she knew, it was three hours and twenty minutes later, and he was knocking on her door.

"Hey, so you did get a nap," he said when she finally opened up.

Struggling to collect her faculties, she covered a yawn. With the sun setting behind him, it was difficult to see much more than his outline, but she could tell he was carrying Wyatt, still strapped in his car seat, in one hand. He clutched her diaper bag in the other. She wished it was that effortless for *her* to tote Wyatt and all his stuff around.

"I didn't mean to sleep so long." She bent to release her son from the car seat's restraints as soon as Aaron put him down. "But I have to admit it felt good."

"Maybe having me involved in Wyatt's life won't be so bad, after all, huh?"

She would've kissed Wyatt, but his face was sticky. "Mama!" he said, clapping until he could get his arms around her neck.

"Not if you're always as nice as you are now," she said to Aaron.

He gave her an exaggerated scowl. "When have I ever been anything *but* nice?"

"You've had your moments."

"I apologized for being a jerk the night your mother died. You know I feel bad."

"I'm not talking about that. Anyway, the past is the past. It's the future that concerns me. What will you be like later, when you get married and have a wife to please?"

"*That's* what has you so concerned?"

She patted Wyatt's back as he hugged her. "Of course it is. It's the possibility that frightens me the most."

He put the diaper bag in the empty car seat. "So it's not necessarily *me* you don't trust."

"Not as long as you're on your own."

"Presley, I've never even told a woman I love her. How do you know I ever will?"

She sensed that he wasn't being flip; he was looking for reassurance from someone who knew him well. But he didn't have anything to fear. He attracted women, and one day there'd be someone. "With my luck you'll fall in love with a woman who can't have kids, and she'll want Wyatt."

He caught her arm. "I would never take Wyatt away from you."

"Is that a promise?" she asked, studying his face.

His gaze moved to her lips. "Yes."

Her heart was suddenly beating in her throat. He was too close, and so were the memories of their night together. She stepped back. "I hope not," she managed to say. "He means everything to me."

Although he was no longer touching her, he was still close enough to rub Wyatt's knee. "I can see why."

"Da!" Wyatt said, pointing.

Presley blinked in surprise. "Did he say what I think he did?"

The pride that showed on Aaron's face delighted her. The fact that he seemed so happy made *her* happy, too. Whether he was with her or not, at least he seemed to be doing well these days. She liked seeing that, believing it. They'd *both* come a long way.

"Grady and I taught him that."

"How?"

His lips twisted into an endearing smirk. "We gave him an M&M every time he got it right."

She gasped. "You fed him *sugar?*"

He held up a hand to calm her. "Just a little. I knew we shouldn't, but…" That boyish grin appeared again. "God, it was hard to stop. He liked them so much."

Occasionally she, too, fell prey to Wyatt's excitement over certain things, so she could hardly get angry with Aaron. It was too easy to picture his pleasure at hearing Wyatt call him Da for the first time.

"It's okay," she said. "He's had a sucker every now and then, when I've needed him to behave in his car seat and he was fussy. But if we're both going to overindulge him, he won't turn out too well."

"I think he will," he said. "You've done a great job with him, Pres. He's happy, well-adjusted. Grady and Rod and Mack couldn't believe how unafraid he is."

She hadn't expected the compliment. "Thank you."

His hand moved from Wyatt's knee to her chin, which he cupped as he lowered his head. He was going to kiss her. She knew what was coming and yet she didn't have the willpower to stop him.

When their lips met, the charge that ran through her stole her breath. She felt the same tension in him, but he just gave her a soft kiss. Then he pressed his forehead to hers. "Go out with me," he murmured. "I won't push you into bed. I promise. Whether or not we ever make love again...I'll leave that entirely up to you. We'll go out and have fun."

"Aaron—" She tried to step back, but he clasped her arms.

"Don't say no," he said. "Let me be part of your life until I move. That's only six weeks."

But if she lost all the ground she'd gained, would she be able to recover it when he was gone?

When she continued to hesitate, he said, "Think how much fun we could have with Wyatt."

"And Riley?" Truthfully, Riley wasn't much of a reason to refuse. She cared for him as a friend, nothing more, and he understood that. But Aaron didn't, and she was desperate for something or someone she could put between them.

He grimaced. "You can go out with him, too, if you want. I've told you that before. I'm just asking you to quit getting defensive every time *I* come around."

Wyatt was wiggling to get down. Presley crouched to set him on the floor so he could reach his toys— which gave her a few more seconds to think. But the extra time didn't make any difference. She knew when she was beaten. "Fine. I guess we could go out to dinner once or twice before you move."

Now that he'd achieved his goal, Aaron's expression lightened. "Are you hungry? I'll take you out right now. Wyatt can go with us."

She ran a hand through her hair. "No, I just woke up, and I'm a mess."

"You look great to me."

Sure she did. She rolled her eyes while she considered whether she could repair her appearance.

"You never believe me when I tell you how beautiful you are," he complained.

Because she *couldn't* believe him. He'd befriended her out of pity. He'd barely been able to tolerate her affection. And he hadn't acted as if he'd missed her much. If he really thought she was beautiful, she'd know it by now. Besides, most of her actions in the first thirty years of her life had left her feeling anything *but* beautiful. *Cheyenne* was the beautiful one. Presley had always paled by comparison. "Give me a minute to brush my hair."

"You're not going to say anything about what I told you?"

She had him wait in the living room as she hurried down the hall. "Just watch Wyatt, okay?"

When she came out of her bedroom, she found Aaron carrying in what looked like a heavy box. Several other boxes already littered her living room. "What is all this stuff?" she asked.

"Baby furniture."

"You bought a *crib?*"

"I figured we could move his old crib to my place, and you could have this nice one." He turned the biggest box so she could see the picture on the side. "I also got him a bed for when he outgrows the crib."

"I see." She looked from one box to the next. Besides the furniture, which included a set of drawers and a changing table, there was a swing-set, a trike, a batting tee and— "Is this a *trampoline?*" she asked.

He hooked his thumbs in his pockets. "Yeah. Fun, right?"

"But…he's not old enough for a trampoline. He's only been walking for four months."

"There's a net that goes around it."

"He could still fall off!"

"Not if I'm there to make sure he doesn't. And he'll grow into it."

She glanced through the window at the weed-strewn patch of earth between her rental and the back fence. "I don't think I have room in my backyard for something like that."

"Then we'll keep it at my house. There's definitely room on five acres. It can go by the barn."

She opened a shopping bag that contained more sports equipment. All of it was brand-new, the best money could buy. "How much did you spend?" she asked in amazement. Talk about a shopping spree. All this stuff must have cost more than her monthly rent!

"Don't know." He shrugged. "Didn't add it up."

Which meant he didn't have to worry about the amount.

When she didn't seem excited, he gave her a questioning look. "What's wrong?"

Aaron could provide Wyatt with so much more than she could. How would she ever be able to compete with him, especially once Wyatt got older?

"Nothing," she said, and forced a smile. "Let's go."

* * *

"Are you upset?" Aaron asked.

Presley poked at the lettuce in her salad as they sat in a booth at Just Like Mom's. "No, why?"

He slid some condiments around, trying to make more room on the table. "You're quiet. I thought you'd be excited about all the things I bought."

"You got some nice stuff."

He leaned over and brought her face up with a finger under her chin. "You can keep any of it you want. Did you think I lugged it in just to show off? I figured it would make you happy."

She knew he was trying to cheer her up, but giving her all the things she couldn't afford didn't help. She was too jealous of what he could give their son. Aaron and Wyatt were already smitten with each other. She'd expected that to happen eventually. Who could resist Aaron *or* Wyatt? But…she'd also expected to be the center of Wyatt's universe for a little longer. He and his father had only been together one afternoon!

"I have enough baby furniture and toys," she said. "I don't need anything."

He held his fork midway to his mouth. "You're kidding, right? What I bought is a lot better than what you've got."

"I'm sure it is."

"Da!" Wyatt was trying to get Aaron's attention, but the way he relished his new word —and what it represented—made Presley feel worse.

When Aaron glanced over, Wyatt opened his mouth wide, wanting another spoonful of Aaron's tomato bisque soup.

Aaron complied, then used his own napkin to wipe Wyatt's chin as if he'd been feeding Wyatt since he could eat solid food.

"I can't believe he likes that soup," Presley muttered.

Aaron laughed when Wyatt smacked his tray. "He loves it."

"I can see that." As she watched Aaron continue to feed their son, it felt as if Wyatt was already defecting. But that was nothing compared to a few minutes earlier, when they'd walked in and Wyatt had leaned over so *Aaron* could carry him. That had taken Presley by complete surprise—and heightened her worst fears. Once again, she'd been pushed out into the cold.

She put down her fork.

"Whoa, you've hardly touched that," Aaron said.

She pushed it toward him. He'd always finished whatever she left. She used to save part of her meals for him, just because she knew how much he liked to eat. "I'm not very hungry."

"Do you want a massage?" he asked. "I realize you're the professional, but that means you probably never get one yourself. And I could give you one tonight while we watch a movie."

"I have a class first thing in the morning. I'd better get home."

He stared at her as if he couldn't quite figure out what was going on. But then the waitress came with the check.

The workweek passed with agonizing slowness for Aaron. Maybe that was because he didn't want to be at the shop. He didn't want to be traipsing all the way to Reno, either, doing everything necessary to open the new business. He'd finally found a location he liked and was currently in negotiations on the lease, but he preferred to spend his time with Wyatt. As soon as he got off at night, he'd hurry home to shower and drive over to Presley's, where he'd either watch Wyatt so she could work, or play with him while she was there.

Wyatt had grown familiar with him—enough that he came running the second he heard Aaron's voice. That was especially gratifying. But Presley had gone in the other direction. She'd become very withdrawn. Sometimes he'd catch her standing in the hallway, watching as he gave Wyatt a piggyback ride or tossed him in the air, but when he invited her to join them, she'd say she had to clean the kitchen or the bathroom or pay bills.

One night when Aaron was there, Riley showed up and Aaron actually watched Wyatt while they went out. That was on Thursday. He thought he was handling the whole thing okay until he put Wyatt to sleep. Then he spent the next three hours pacing in the living room, wondering when she'd be back. There wasn't much in Whiskey Creek, other than Sexy Sadie's, that stayed open after eleven on a weeknight.

When he finally heard voices at the door, he hurried over, planning to yank it open. He didn't want Riley kissing her on the stoop or anywhere else. But he caught himself at the last second and returned to the couch.

"How was it?" he asked when she came in—thankfully, alone.

"Fun. Sorry we were out so late. I know you have to get up early."

"I don't mind helping out."

"I appreciate it."

She obviously expected him to leave, but he was tired of the strain between them. He'd been trying his best to be friendly. He'd even asked her out for Friday or Saturday, but she'd turned him down—said she'd probably have to work late both nights. He'd then reminded her that they were supposed to be doing the artificial insemination this weekend, if Cheyenne's projections proved accurate, and she'd said she'd be available, which made him feel she'd just been making excuses.

"I bet he liked that dress."

She glanced down as if she couldn't remember which one she'd put on. "Oh, I've had this for a while. Cost me four bucks at the secondhand store."

"Looks good on you."

"Thanks." She dropped her keys in her purse.

"I mean it," he said. She'd always had a nice body, but these days she could stop traffic—not that she seemed to notice or trust the extra attention.

"I appreciate that," she replied, but those words were as empty of conviction as the initial thanks. "How'd Wyatt do tonight?"

"Grady came over. We taught Wyatt to say Uncle." The one subject they should be able to discuss was their son. Wyatt had been such an incredible addition to his life, had given him the purpose he'd been lacking. But instead of drawing Presley closer to him, any mention of Wyatt and the fun they had or the things Aaron had taught him only seemed to push her further away.

"It's great that he suddenly has so many men in his life," she said.

Aaron stood. "Really?"

She didn't look at him as she put her purse on the coffee table. "Of course."

"I'm not getting the impression you honestly feel that way." She'd asked him to take almost everything he'd bought over to his place.

"What are you talking about?" she asked. "I've let you see Wyatt every night. I've put no restrictions on your time with him. None."

"And I'm grateful for that, but…something's wrong."

"No. I understand that you've only got…what? Five weeks? I'm trying to let you have as much time with him as possible."

"I'm not talking about Wyatt, damn it!"

Her eyes widened. "What else could you complain about? What else do I owe you?"

Not quite sure how to explain his frustration, he advanced on her. "You don't *owe* me anything. I don't want you to owe me anything. It's just…sometimes you look at me as if…as if you still want me. But the second I try to respond, you do whatever you can to avoid me."

"That's not true."

"It's absolutely true. When we went out the other night, you wouldn't let me within two feet of you."

Her gaze shifted to her favorite chair, but sitting there meant she'd have to walk past him. "I didn't want anyone to get the wrong idea."

"The wrong idea about what?"

"That we're seeing each other!"

"*I* thought we *were* seeing each other!"

"Not in the way they might assume."

"Meaning we haven't been to bed. But that was the agreement. I'm giving you what I believed you wanted—something official and respectable."

"Official?" she scoffed. "You never see *any* woman in *that* way."

"There's always a first."

"And why would that first be with me?"

"Maybe you don't want to acknowledge it, but there are still a lot of…feelings between us."

She backed up as he came closer. "Aaron, there've never been any feelings on your side."

"How do *you* know?"

"Trust me, I'd be able to tell."

"Then why does it drive me nuts when you go out with Riley?"

Her mouth fell open. Obviously, she was surprised by the anger in his voice. But she couldn't move any farther back. "I don't know what you want from me," she said.

"Yes, you do." He'd promised he wouldn't touch her, not unless she asked him to, but he missed her too much, missed her more than ever now that he was seeing her every day.

Slipping his hands around her waist, he lifted her up to meet his mouth. He expected her to shove him away. But once their mouths met and their tongues touched, she made a sound of submission, and his body instantly reacted.

"There you go, Pres. Let me touch you," he whispered. "I'm dying to touch you."

He wasn't sure she believed that, either. She seemed suspicious of everything he said or did, but when she unbuttoned his shirt and pulled it off, he knew she was going to take what she wanted—and that meant he'd get what he wanted, too.

24

He'd be gone in five weeks; she needed to take advantage of this opportunity. That was all Presley would let herself think—until she'd dragged him down the hall and into her bedroom. She'd wanted to join their bodies as fast and hard as that first encounter after she'd come home, when they'd been carried away by a tsunami of desire. But he insisted they slow down so he could take his time and make love to her "right."

That was when she started to have second thoughts. As long as he got what he wanted, why would he care about slowing down? He'd never troubled himself before. He'd always been a good lover, always made sure she was as fulfilled as he was by the end, but he'd do that for any woman he was with.

Tonight he was taking their encounter so seriously that she could easily get the wrong idea, easily believe that it might be more significant than it was, and that frightened her. It was a delusion. Somehow she had to keep from falling into the same pit of false hope she'd escaped these past two years, and she didn't see how she could do that with the emotions that were pouring through her.

She would've stopped him. She sensed the danger and had finally regained the presence of mind she'd momentarily lost. But she'd waited too long. She didn't want to be a tease, someone who'd get a man this excited and then bail out at the last second. She'd always delivered before; of course he'd feel he could depend on her. So she tried to detach her mind instead. This couldn't mean anything to her. She couldn't hang on every kiss, every sigh, every touch.

It's just physical sensation. Mutual pleasure. There's no meaning behind it.

But he noticed the change in her right away, and forced her to look up at him.

"What's wrong? Where'd you go?"

She wouldn't explain, *couldn't* explain. Revealing her conflicted emotions would make her that much more vulnerable. So she gave him a devilish smile, urged him onto his back and made sure he couldn't think of anything except her tongue moving over the most sensitive part of his body.

Despite that, he tried to stop her at the last second. He held her head and gasped that he wanted to finish inside her. But she told him that would be too risky, that it could result in another pregnancy even if they used a condom, and pushed him over the edge.

After that, she had no compunction about sending him home. He couldn't complain that she'd somehow misled him, since she'd given him what he'd been hoping for. So she got up immediately and retrieved his clothes.

"Thanks for watching Wyatt tonight," she said.

He made no move to take the articles she held out to him. "That's it?" he said. "What about you?"

"Don't worry about me. I'm fine."

"It's not like getting you off is a chore. And leaving you unsatisfied is not how I want this to end."

"I'm fine, like I said. I'm just…not in the mood, that's all."

"You were in the mood a second ago."

"I'm tired."

He seemed completely baffled. "But you wouldn't have to do anything!"

"You've got to be tired, too. And you have to work in the morning."

Still, he didn't move. "Have you decided you'd rather be with Riley?"

Usually when he spoke of Riley she could detect some jealousy, even a little arrogance—Aaron's competitive nature coming out. But when he asked this question, he sounded like a hurt little boy. Was there some fear, or maybe shock, in there? Or was she imagining things again?

He was probably just trying to make sure she couldn't later accuse him of being a poor lover.

"I haven't slept with Riley," she said.

"That's not what I asked."

"I don't *know* who I'd rather have in my bed. I'm not in that type of relationship with anyone."

He took his clothes, but tossed them back on the floor. "Come here. If you're tired, we'll just sleep."

She didn't want him to stay. She'd have to be on her guard for the rest of the night if she had him in her bed. But he pulled her down next to him, and even though she faced away to sleep on her side, he wrapped his arms around her.

"You can't stay overnight! Riley might see your truck here when he drives to work in the morning," she said, fighting her natural inclination to sink into him and cuddle.

"Relax." His hand was already sliding down her stomach. She stopped him before he could reach his target, but when she woke up the next morning, he held her arms above her head and worked such wicked magic with his mouth and fingers that she was gasping his name and begging him to take her.

"I thought you weren't interested," he said.

She stared helplessly up at him but refused to speak. She'd always been interested, but why give him the pleasure of admitting it?

"Come on, tell me what you want," he coaxed.

Pursing her lips, she shook her head, and he frowned.

"You don't play very nice these days."

"I let you into my bed." Although she was trying to sound as if she was in control of herself, her voice was thick with desire. "What I gave you last night was pretty nice."

"I can't argue with that, but I've never been one to settle for less than I want. So let's see what we can do to make you a little more…pliable." Lowering his head, he brought her to the brink of climax—then stopped and grinned up at her. "I'm asking you again. What do you want?"

Her body was quivering with anticipation. He had her so worked up it was impossible to deny him. "I want you," she admitted.

He raised his eyebrows. "You could've said that less grudgingly."

She swallowed hard but added nothing else. Although it was a small rebellion, to her mind it was an important one. But she knew he wasn't going to settle for that when he licked his finger and ran it over the tip of her breast. "How badly?" he breathed in her ear.

She glared up at him. "Quit torturing me."

"I'm more than willing to give you anything you want. As soon as you tell me how much you want *me*."

"You know how much."

He covered her but didn't take it any further. "More than Riley?"

She closed her eyes. "Yes."

"About damn time you admitted it." He made a show of putting on a condom. Then he paused to stare down at her, and she thought she saw something unusual in his expression, something far more possessive than she'd ever seen there before. But she couldn't rely on anything that happened in the throes of passion, when emotions were often exaggerated or distorted. She knew that from experience. She was too far gone to correctly analyze what he might be feeling, and he didn't give her much time before he finally drove inside her.

"That's it," she breathed.

His teeth flashed in a smile. Then he brought her to climax again and again and again.

As each new wave of pleasure hit, the satisfaction on his face increased, but he wasn't as in control as he was trying to pretend. Every muscle grew taut as he fought harder and harder to stop himself from reaching his own climax. "Again," he told her, his voice ragged.

From that point on, their lovemaking grew even more intense. They were in the middle of a wordless war, where pleasure was their most powerful weapon, one they could each wield with skill and accuracy. She was battling to hang on to her heart, and he was battling to show her just how easily he could reclaim it. But that struggle made every sensation much more acute. Every nerve seemed to be carefully attuned to Aaron's touch, his voice, even his scent.

"You've become stubborn," he muttered when he stopped long enough to tell her she was beautiful, perfect, and she merely scowled at him. She wasn't being stubborn; she was learning from the past. She would *not* allow him dominance. No way. Not like before. And because he could sense her resistance, he kept trying to overcome her skepticism and entice her into submission.

Nothing but their power struggle seemed to matter—until they heard Cheyenne's voice from the living room.

"Pres?"

Aaron rolled away and dove for his clothes. Presley scrambled off the bed, too, and hurried to dress. But it wasn't easy to pull her clothes over her sensitized, sweat-dampened skin. Weak and shaky, she called, "Hang on, Chey. I'll be right out."

"What's going on?" her sister called back.

"I'm, uh, running late."

"But you're okay? Wyatt's okay?"

"I'm fine. Wyatt's still asleep."

"Mama!" Wyatt called from his crib. "Mama!"

"Or he was," she added.

"You haven't even gotten him up?" Cheyenne asked. "What happened to arriving at the studio early? You were supposed to have him at my house half an hour ago."

Presley pressed a finger to her mouth to signal that Aaron shouldn't say anything. Obviously, her sister hadn't seen his truck or she would've mentioned it. There was still a chance he might escape her notice. "I overslept."

"You're going to miss your class if you don't hurry. You have maybe thirty minutes. I'll take care of Wyatt's breakfast and get him packed up. That should help."

"Okay, thanks."

Presley could hear her sister talking baby talk as she got Wyatt out of bed. "Just stay in my bathroom until we're gone, okay?" she whispered to Aaron. "You can lock up and leave after that."

"Why do I need to hide? We're both consenting adults. We're both unattached. We even have a kid together, for crying out loud. Why can't I say hello and let it go at that?"

"Because I don't want her to know what a damn fool I am!"

She hadn't meant to offend him. That comment had been an extension of her inner dialogue and the way she was berating herself for falling back into bed with him. But when he looked as though she'd just slapped him, she realized how he'd taken it. "I'm sorry. I didn't mean that like it sounded."

He stabbed a hand through his hair. "Yeah, you did," he said, and walked out.

The house shook as he slammed the door and, a moment later, Cheyenne poked her head into the room. "Was that who I think it was?"

Presley released a gusty sigh and dropped onto her bed. "Yeah."

Riley showed up for Presley's Friday morning yoga class. She thought that was so nice—given his resistance to trying it every other time she'd mentioned it—that she agreed to go for coffee with him when the class ended. Apparently, he was between jobs, and her next appointment wasn't until noon so they both had time. And because he'd come to her class, he'd missed his usual get-together with his friends at Black Gold.

Rather than leave her sister babysitting during the interim, she called to invite Chey, too. Chey had also skipped out on Friday-morning coffee, since she'd come to get Wyatt, so she pushed him over in his stroller.

"Isn't it a gorgeous day?" she asked as she joined them at an outdoor table.

Presley slid the cappuccino she'd purchased for her sister closer to Cheyenne. Then she unfastened her son's seat belt and pulled Wyatt into her lap. Until now, she hadn't even noticed the weather. She hadn't been feeling particularly energetic since Aaron left. She'd wanted to call him ever since, to apologize, but she hadn't had a chance. She'd been in a rush to get to the studio. Then she'd led her class. And now she was entertaining Riley.

She glanced at the street, searching for Aaron's truck in the traffic flowing by. She doubted she'd see it. He was probably at work. But she looked for him whenever she was out and about in Whiskey Creek. It was a habit she'd formed when she'd first fallen in love with him.

"Did you have a good turnout this morning?" Cheyenne dropped her wallet and house keys on the table before taking a seat.

"Not bad." Presley smiled at Riley. "I had my first guy."

Cheyenne looked appropriately impressed. "Wow, Riley. Breaking the gender norms here in Gold Country, are you?"

"You couldn't tell by my yoga clothes?" he joked.

"I saw the shorts, but I assumed you were playing basketball or tennis."

"Nope." He swelled out his chest. "I was doing the lotus and the… What was that other pose? The full owl?"

"The full pigeon," Presley corrected.

"I hope you got a picture of that," Cheyenne said. "Maybe we'll be able to blackmail him with it someday."

Presley might have enjoyed the banter if she wasn't so preoccupied with the way Aaron had left. But those last few seconds, and the look on his face, kept replaying in her mind. "Next time," she mumbled, and gave Wyatt a piece of biscotti.

Riley dug through the packets of sugar looking for a Sweet'N Low; he couldn't find one, so he went inside.

"I'm worried about Riley," Cheyenne said, the shade from the table's umbrella dividing her face into light and dark.

Presley leaned back. "Why?"

"He really likes you. And after what I saw this morning…"

"He knows I'm still in love with Aaron."

"But does he know you're still *sleeping* with him?"

Did she need to tell him? She and Riley had exchanged a few chaste kisses, but they'd never even made out. She wasn't sure their relationship had reached the stage where she owed him that kind of information. She wasn't sure it ever would. "Riley and I are just friends."

"He wouldn't show up for your yoga class if he wasn't trying to impress you."

Presley shrugged. "Did you suggest it?"

"No."

"I know you were coaching him."

"Not anymore. Not since Aaron found out about Wyatt."

"Aaron will be leaving in five weeks, anyway."

"You think your…infatuation will end there?"

"It'll have to, won't it?"

Cheyenne didn't seem convinced. "The way he walked out this morning…is it going to be okay to have him over again tonight?"

"Why would I have him over again?" she asked, shifting in her seat.

With a sound of impatience, Cheyenne lowered her voice. "For the artificial insemination. What else?"

"That's *tonight?*"

"I told you it would probably be this weekend."

"But you never confirmed it."

"Because I'm waiting for him to answer my text to make sure he's still on board."

"How long have you been waiting?"

"A couple of hours." Cheyenne was obviously concerned.

"Can't we put it off?" Presley asked.

Her sister gave her an incredulous look. "Are you kidding? Dylan already thinks I'm pregnant. And I'm ovulating. I took a test to prove it. We have to act as soon as possible."

Riley was on his way back, so Presley bent over the stroller as if she was searching for something. "I'll get in touch with him."

Cheyenne didn't have time to respond.

"I broke down and bought a piece of the coffee cake," Riley announced. "I know you don't eat a lot of sugar," he added in an aside to Presley, "but you two have to try this."

Presley managed a smile, accepted the fork he handed her and took a small bite. He was right—she wasn't interested, in the coffee cake or the conversation that followed. But she soldiered on, smiled and made small talk until they split up. Then she canceled her next massage and walked over to Amos Auto Body. She didn't really want to show up at Aaron's work. She knew it would attract too much attention from his brothers. But she was afraid that if she didn't talk to Aaron before the big "procedure" tonight, he might feel justified in bowing out.

When Dylan used the PA system to call Aaron to the front office, Aaron twisted around to look at Mack, who was helping him fix the hydraulic lift in one of the repair bays. "If he wants me, why doesn't he just walk his ass back here?"

Wiping the grease from his hands, Mack stretched his back. "Beats me."

Aaron scowled at the parts lying all over the concrete. This wasn't a good time to take a break. "You okay here?"

"Hell, no," Mack said. "You're better at putting this back together than I am. I'll wait. I need a drink, anyway."

They walked to the front, and as soon as they passed through the door, Mack veered off to the vending machine and left Aaron standing in the middle of the lobby, staring at Presley, who was wearing a simple white cotton dress that set off her dark skin.

Since when did she get so damned pretty?

She was sitting in one of the plastic chairs along the front window but got to her feet when she saw him. "Hello."

It was almost impossible to keep his gaze from sliding down her body. These days she did something to him he couldn't explain, and that dress only made it worse.

To avoid temptation, he glanced outside, thinking that maybe Cheyenne had driven her over, or that she'd borrowed a car. The shop was at least a mile from Presley's studio. But he didn't see any evidence suggesting she had a vehicle. "How'd you get here?" he asked.

"I walked."

He noticed the leather sandals on her feet, the nail polish that matched her lip gloss. Pink? She'd grown so conservative—but her tattoo reminded him that she wasn't as conventional as she appeared. It was the combination of that wild streak, the hard-luck beginning and what she'd made of herself since that appealed to him. "That's a hike."

"It's a nice day. I didn't mind."

She'd never been one to complain. He liked that about her, too—liked that she was willing to make the most of any situation. No question her background had left some scars, but it had also created a woman who was happy with the simple things in life.

He could feel Dylan watching them from where he stood behind the counter, working on the computer. "What's up?"

Had she come out here to drive him crazy, like she had last night and during every other encounter since she'd returned to town? Even when he was making love to her, he couldn't really reach her. He'd *never* been so off balance with a woman. She used to be consistent, predictable, always there waiting for his attention. But now…she was determined not to get caught in the same trap and was withholding what she'd once given so freely.

He couldn't be happy when he was with her, and he couldn't be happy when he wasn't, because…

He wasn't sure exactly. All he knew was that he no longer felt as ambivalent toward her as he had two years ago. No doubt it would surprise her to learn that Wyatt wasn't the only thing that drew him to her place each night. He looked forward to seeing her just as much. But she wouldn't believe it if he told her. She wouldn't believe he cared about her, wouldn't even believe he found her *attractive*.

At this point, he wished he didn't. He was done trying to overcome the past. He *couldn't* overcome it—not if she wouldn't let him. He was just going to be Wyatt's dad and leave Presley alone. That was what she wanted, wasn't it?

"Can we talk?" she asked.

"About..."

She cleared her throat and shot Dylan a covert glance. "Wyatt. What else?"

He had a feeling this had nothing to do with their child, but she wasn't the only one eager for some privacy. With a nod, he held the front door and they walked outside and around the building.

"I'm sorry about what I said this morning." She bit her lip as she looked up at him, and the frustration he'd been feeling since she returned to town welled up again. One minute he thought nothing had changed between them; the next it felt like everything had.

"I didn't mean to offend you," she added when he didn't respond. "And I didn't realize what I said would do that."

"Because I have a heart of stone."

"Not stone." Her normally smooth forehead rumpled as she cast about for the right words. "You can be sensitive and...and kind. And you always—"

"Stick up for the underdog," he broke in. "You've told me that before."

"You don't sound like you're taking it as the compliment it's intended to be."

"I don't want praise for protecting the weak. As far as I'm concerned, that should be expected of any man. Anyway, you can't be considered an underdog anymore. You're on your feet and you're doing great. So why do you think I keep coming around?"

"You're Wyatt's father," she said. "Why else? You

already love him and you want to be with him as much as possible before you leave."

"But *you* play no role in that?"

Her eyes slid away from his. "I'm sure you'd like me to be supportive of your relationship with Wyatt."

"So *that's* why I keep trying to get in your pants."

She shifted from one foot to the other. "If you can get a piece of ass in the same place, why not?"

"Shit." He shook his head. If, after the past few weeks, she still believed he was using her, there was no convincing her. He'd burned her in the past and, although it was unintentional, it had been traumatic enough that she couldn't get beyond it. Maybe he'd been a fool to even try—but there was something there, something he'd never felt for any other woman. "And you've put out for me so much since you got back," he said dryly.

"I have!" she retorted.

They'd been together three or four nights in the past two months, but not nearly as often as he would've liked. She tried to push him away every time he got close. It was only after he'd gone to a great deal of effort to overcome her resistance that she became compliant. At least, that was the case last night. And then, as soon as they got out of bed, she reverted to the person she was right now. No matter how much fun they had together, no matter how eager he was to see where his feelings might lead, she cut him off and built an even higher wall.

"A few nights are hardly a lot. And you've turned around and spit in my face every time."

"You'd rather I fell swooning at your feet? Because you liked that so much before?"

"We're not talking about before. That was then, this is now."

"Never mind." She waved him off, and he was glad. Although he blamed her for his frustration, he wasn't entirely sure that was fair. He couldn't identify exactly what he wanted or what he needed. He just knew it was more than she was giving him. And maybe, because he'd been so stubborn before, he deserved it.

"I'd rather not talk about us," she said. "I can't. I don't have the time."

"Why?"

"I have a massage at four. I have to get back. I already canceled one to come here. I don't want to lose another appointment."

"You canceled— Wait. Why'd you do that?"

"To make sure what I said this morning isn't going to keep you from showing up tonight."

What was she talking about? He eyed her dubiously. "Showing up where?"

"At my house."

"I don't remember being invited over. You've been too busy trying to shove me away."

She glanced around again and lowered her voice. "You have a date with Cheyenne."

"Don't call it a date," he said with a grimace. "We're talking about my sister-in-law."

"You know what I mean."

"So she's ovulating?"

"Yes. She's been texting you, but she hasn't gotten ten a response."

He thrust his hands in his pockets. "I was in such a hurry this morning that I left my phone at home."

She tucked her hair behind her ears. "Does that mean you'll go through with it?"

If only he didn't have to... But he couldn't set Dylan up for that kind of disappointment. "What time?"

"Late. After Dylan's asleep and she can slip out. She'll have to text us both. He could watch TV until midnight or later."

"Okay."

"You'll get back to her?"

"I told her I'd do it, didn't I?"

She took a deep breath. Apparently, she'd been nervous that she'd screwed things up for her sister. "Okay. Good. Thanks for that."

"There's just one catch."

At the change in his voice, she turned around and clasped her hands in front of her. Maybe she could tell from the way he was looking at her what his "catch" would involve.

"What's that?" she asked.

"It'll cost you a kiss."

"Why?"

"Because I finally have some leverage."

"Stop it." She knew he wouldn't bail, regardless of what he said. "The only reason you want to kiss me is because you know I don't want you to."

He almost laughed. "Since when?" he asked. "You might say that, but your body tells me something else."

She folded her arms, assuming an even more defensive posture. "Fine. Make it fast."

He folded his arms, too, and leaned against the cinder-block wall. "*You* have to kiss *me*."

"Why are you playing these games?" she asked.

"It's not a game."

Looking irritated, she came closer, rested her hands on his shoulders and stood on tiptoe so she could press her lips to his. At first he thought it was going to be the worst kiss they'd ever shared. But once he slid his arms around her, she melted into him as she always did. Then she parted her lips, allowing him exactly what he wanted—a way to say goodbye that might actually show her how he felt.

Not that he expected her to be convinced.

At least she wasn't the one to pull away. When he broke off the kiss and lifted his head, she actually seemed a little dazed.

"You win," he said, presenting her with his best smile.

She stared up at him. "What do you mean?"

"I'll come over and give Cheyenne what she wants. And then I'll leave you alone in the future."

"What?"

"That's what you want, isn't it?"

"But…what about Wyatt?"

"We'll make a schedule so I can see him."

Instead of offering her a ride to her studio, as he normally would, he walked back into the shop. He hoped she wouldn't let him go that easily. He wanted her to fight for what they had the way he'd been fighting. But if she wasn't willing to forgive and forget and try again, to have some faith that he could love her, there was nothing he could do.

25

Presley had been anxious all day. She told herself that her unease had nothing to do with her encounter with Aaron at the auto body shop. She didn't care if he was backing off. That was what she'd wanted him to do from the beginning, wasn't it? If he wasn't there at every turn, tempting her, maybe she could get over him.

She was just nervous about the insemination and her role in it. Fortunately, Wyatt was down for the night so they didn't have to worry about him. And they had the kit Cheyenne had ordered online. Each tool was lined up on a piece of waxed paper on her dresser, which she'd cleared off for that purpose. She'd removed the syringe and the insemination catheter from their separate packages and attached them. She'd also read all the paperwork. She was supposed to insert a speculum in Cheyenne's vagina and widen it, find her cervix with a flashlight and use the catheter to deposit Aaron's sperm at the opening.

The procedure sounded simple enough—except that Presley was afraid she wouldn't recognize the cervix even if she saw it. Not only that, but what if she was shaking too badly to deposit the semen in the right place? To force it from the catheter as slowly as she'd been instructed so it would pool correctly?

"You okay?" Cheyenne asked as they sat in the living room staring at each other while they waited for Aaron to join them.

"Fine," she replied. "You?"

Her sister nodded, but they both watched the clock with frequent glances—then jumped to their feet when they finally heard Aaron's knock.

"He's here," Presley breathed.

Cheyenne tightened the ties of a robe Presley had lent her. "Want me to answer it?"

"Actually…I think it would be better if he didn't have to see you. You might want to wait in the bedroom."

Her sister didn't have to be asked twice. As she hurried down the hall, Presley hauled in a deep breath and opened the door. "Hi."

Aaron inclined his head but didn't answer. Although she'd left the porch light off, in case someone saw him arrive, she could tell by the set of his jaw, and the stiffness of his bearing, that he was as tense and nervous as they were.

"Would you like a drink or…or something first?" she asked as he came in.

"No."

He wasn't carrying anything. She'd thought he might bring a *Playboy* or some other magazine to help get him excited. "You ready, then?"

"Ready as I'll ever be."

She handed him the sterile cup he was supposed to use.

He accepted it without another word and went into the bathroom.

Presley had expected him to take maybe ten minutes. When it went past that, she began to wonder if he was having trouble. After twenty minutes, she slipped into the bedroom to wait with Cheyenne, who kept sending her worried glances. If Dylan woke during the night to find her gone, the gig would be up, and they all knew that.

"Do you think he's having trouble?" Cheyenne whispered.

He *had* to be, or he would've emerged by now. But Presley didn't want to add to the pressure they were all feeling. "I'm sure he's okay."

"Maybe he's too upset or reluctant or—"

"His body works great. He'll be fine."

"This has as much to do with his head as his body. If his head's not into it, we could be in trouble."

Presley understood that, which was why she was fidgeting, too. "He didn't bring any magazines," she confided.

"Why not?"

"How should I know?"

"Should we get him some?"

That was a thought. "I guess I could offer to run to the store, but it could take a long time to find a place that's open and far enough away that I'd be anonymous," Presley said. Still, she was about to go knock when she heard the bathroom door open. "There he is."

She rushed out to meet him and almost asked how it had gone, but the expression on his face told her he wasn't in a good mood. He simply handed her the cup and left without even peeking in at Wyatt.

Presley wanted to go after him, to soothe him. Giving Cheyenne and Dylan the chance to have a baby was so generous. She didn't want him to feel bad about it. But Cheyenne was waiting in the bedroom and nervous about being out of her house for so long.

Besides, Presley figured they'd have a better chance of conception if they used Aaron's sperm while it was fresh.

Trying to forget about Aaron and the jumble of feelings he always evoked, she carried his sperm into the bedroom.

Her sister's eyes flicked to the cup, then to Presley. "He okay? I heard the door close."

"He already left."

She sighed. "That's probably just as well. I'm sure he doesn't want any part of what we're going to do next."

Presley was a little grossed out herself. She was using the sperm of the man she loved to impregnate her sister. That was difficult to start with. But she was doing it for the best of reasons. And she was trying to keep the mechanics in perspective, too. This was a medical procedure, nothing more than what was done in fertility clinics across the country. It just felt strange that it would be happening in her house—and that she would be playing the role of doctor or nurse.

"All set?" she asked.

Cheyenne gave her a tortured look. "This is awkward, isn't it?"

"Definitely. Reminds me of when you were fourteen, and I had to teach you how to insert a tampon."

"Thanks for reminding me."

"We're sisters. We do these kinds of things for each other."

"I wish our roles were reversed."

"*I'm* glad they're not!" Presley drew up the sperm in the syringe. "Let's get it over with."

Cheyenne squeezed her eyes shut for a second, as if she was praying for the nerve to go through with it. Then she removed her robe and climbed on the bed, situating the pillows under her hips as the literature suggested.

Aaron didn't text or call to see how the procedure went. Presley didn't hear from him for the next several days. Cheyenne told her she'd texted him a thank-you, but received no reply. He didn't even come over to see Wyatt that week. Presley was beginning to wonder if he was going to ignore them both until he left for Reno. But she woke up early the following weekend to find him in her yard, fixing the fence.

"What are you doing?" she asked as she stood in the doorway, squinting out at the source of the noise that had awakened her.

He glanced over his shoulder but didn't answer.

"Aaron?" she prodded.

"What does it look like I'm doing?" he asked.

"It looks like you're repairing my fence."

"You've been wanting this done for a while, haven't you?"

But she hadn't asked *him* to do it. She hadn't mentioned it since the night she saw him at Ted Dixon's book signing nearly two months ago. The fence was something she'd been meaning to take care of when she had the money to hire Riley or someone else. She hadn't tackled it herself because she knew she wouldn't be capable of digging out the large chunk of concrete that supported the broken post. "I didn't expect *you* to do it. It's not your responsibility."

He didn't look back at her again. He was too busy wielding that shovel, which made a terrible scraping sound every time he pushed it into the ground. "You're the mother of my child, aren't you? And Wyatt lives here, too."

She tightened her robe. Just seeing Aaron, even when he was hot and sweaty, made her want to touch him. "I thought maybe you'd forgotten about Wyatt."

"I haven't forgotten about either of you."

How was she supposed to take that? The way he said it didn't sound as if he considered it a *good* thing.

"So I can count this as…part of your child support?" she asked uncertainly. They hadn't agreed on a monthly amount. He'd spent so much on toys and furniture, all of which he'd offered to her. And when he'd been coming over regularly, he'd brought groceries and diapers. So Presley had let it go at that. As long as he was being thoughtful and generous, she didn't feel they had to settle on a particular sum. She'd never wanted to become a financial burden to him, never wanted what they'd had to be reduced to a dollar figure.

"The paternity test came back yesterday," he told her.

"And?"

"It was positive, of course. I have a check for you, too."

She clenched her hands in the pockets of her robe. "I don't want your money."

"Now my money's not good enough, either?"

"You can see Wyatt whenever you want. This isn't how I imagined it would be when I came back."

"I know. You weren't even going to tell me about him. You wanted me out of your life completely. But you're not going to get that. I have the right to see my son."

"I said I'd never stop you. You don't have to fix the fence or anything."

"Shit." He threw down the shovel. "I'm not arguing about Wyatt. I know you'll let me see him."

"Then what has you so mad?"

"What do I have to do to see *you?*"

"Don't ask," she said, but that didn't put him off. He covered the ground between them in three long strides.

"You still care about me." He stared down at her as if searching for some sign of it. "I know you do."

She couldn't deny that, especially when her eyes suddenly welled with tears.

"Stop shutting me out," he whispered.

"Why are you doing this?" she asked. "How will this time be any different?"

"I've got a month left in this town—one lousy month. Give me a chance, Pres. Give me that long. If we can't establish what you want—if I'm…incapable of it, as you seem to think—I'll move on and we'll get through the breakup the best we can."

"While arranging visitation for Wyatt." She could only imagine how much more difficult that would make everything.

"Of course. Divorced people do it all the time."

"But we already know—"

"We know nothing," he interrupted. "Maybe I can't say I love you. Maybe I'll never be able to say it. But I can tell you this. These days you're all I think about—you and Wyatt."

Would that be enough? Or was she being tempted into making another painful mistake?

History would certainly weigh against him. Cheyenne and Dylan would probably discreetly do the same. But her heart begged her to soften, regardless of the risk. What if there was a remote chance that they could actually become a family?

It was too good to be true. Presley couldn't count on this—but then he kissed her, and she was lost. She didn't care about the sweat or the dirt that clung to him—or even that they were standing in her front yard for anyone to see. She wanted to kiss him back, to get as close to him as she possibly could. Despite all her efforts to escape the hold he had on her, *nothing* had changed.

"I'll paint your porch, too," he promised her. "And buy you jewelry, if you want jewelry."

Consolation prizes, she thought—gifts to replace the commitment he couldn't quite give her. But he was trying so hard to make his offer appealing that she melted all the same. She was even tempted to tell him that she loved him enough for both of them. Those words sat on her tongue, but she choked them back. What was wrong with her? She couldn't be *that* stupid. She'd give him the month. But she wouldn't let her hopes soar too high, and she certainly wouldn't smother him with protestations of love.

"Okay," she said, and went in to get Wyatt, who was awake and calling for her.

When Cheyenne felt her husband's hands on her body, she struggled to cast off the last vestiges of sleep. If she didn't, Dylan would get up and head to work. He usually left early.

"Hey," he whispered when she opened her eyes.

"What are you doing?" she asked, but it was obvious. He'd lifted her nightgown and was kissing her belly. He anticipated the baby, relishing the knowledge that she was pregnant—and she prayed she was. It'd been a week since they'd performed the artificial insemination, but she didn't know if it had worked. She'd been trying to give her body time to produce the hCG she hoped would show up in her next pregnancy test.

"Wishing our child would grow faster," he said.

"It'll take several months for me to show."

"I can't wait to feel him or her moving inside you."

"You're already afraid to make love to me for fear you'll hurt the baby. Is that going to get worse?" she teased.

"I can't resist you for long." He kissed her as he slipped his hand between her legs, and she closed her eyes.

"I'd like to stay in bed with you all day," she told him. "Tell me you can take the time off work."

He kissed her neck. "Sorry, babe."

"But you're the boss."

"I'd love to stay home, but Aaron asked for the day off, and we can't both be gone."

"You said yes?" She infused her voice with sufficient disappointment.

"I couldn't say no. He put in twice as many hours as the rest of us this past week. He was there when I left at night—he was there when I arrived in the morning. I almost wonder if he ever went home."

"Why would he be working that hard?"

"He said he wanted to get us caught up before moving to Reno."

"That's nice of him."

"Except I don't think that's all there is to it."

"What more could there be?"

He didn't answer right away. He was too distracted by what he was doing to her breasts.

"Dyl?"

"Something's bothering him."

She felt a twinge of guilt as she wondered if it was the artificial insemination. Aaron had never responded to her thank-you text. He hadn't called to see if the insemination had worked, either. She hadn't heard from him at all, and Presley said the same. "Like…"

"Who knows? It could be that Dad's getting out of prison soon. Or that Dad's married to someone he's spent very little time with, which is almost guaranteed to complicate our lives. It could also be the move. We're all sad to see him go."

She caught his face so he couldn't keep kissing her. She wanted a second to concentrate on the conversation. "Even you?"

"Me probably more than anyone. He can be difficult. You know how determined he is when he makes up his mind about something. That's frustrating if you're the one in charge. But he's also insanely talented, and someone I can absolutely rely on at the shop—now that he's quit partying."

Cheyenne was secretly glad Aaron was leaving town. Having his baby would be much easier if he wasn't there, watching her carry his son or daughter into the auto body shop whenever she dropped in to see Dylan. But she felt selfish for even thinking that way. It wasn't fair to Aaron. So she hoped he'd be happier in Reno. "Did he tell you what he has planned for today?"

"No." He gave her a funny look. "Should I have asked him?"

"Just curious." She pulled Dylan to her and ended the conversation. Talking wasn't what he'd had in mind to begin with, and she was feeling so hopeful she was definitely in the mood to enjoy him. Maybe these few minutes with her husband would bring her good luck, because she planned to take one of the two pregnancy tests she'd bought and hidden in her drawer as soon as he left for work.

Aaron had never had a better day, at least not in recent memory. Once Presley returned from teaching her morning yoga class and taking two massage appointments, she spent the rest of the day with him and Wyatt. They didn't do anything most people would consider particularly fun. He tinkered around her place, fixing things while she cooked and cleaned and looked after their son, but helping out made him feel useful. He liked the appreciation she showed him—and he especially enjoyed how excited his little boy was to see him. Every time they encountered each other, even if Aaron had merely walked outside for ten minutes, Wyatt acted as if he'd just shown up.

Because Aaron considered the day to be far more successful than he'd dared hope, he couldn't be mad at himself for approaching Presley when he'd promised only a week earlier that he wouldn't. He wasn't used to playing the role of supplicant, but at least his persistence had worked. She'd stopped backing away when he touched her. From what he could tell, she'd stopped closing off her heart and mind, too. Finally, she snuggled comfortably against him, meshing her body with his as she'd always done before—and that was as enjoyable as he'd expected. They'd already made love twice, once in the shower and once when Wyatt was taking his afternoon nap. Although Aaron was the aggressor—she never reached for him—the fact that she was still holding back was a small quibble. They'd just barely worked out their differences. Maybe, in time, she'd fully engage with him again.

"So this is how you eat these days?"

She'd made a vegetable stir-fry for dinner and was feeding Wyatt some of the softened vegetables. "You don't like it?"

He'd be hungry again in an hour. "It would be great…as a side dish."

"I'd offer to add meat, but I don't have any," she said with a laugh.

"We can go over to Just Like Mom's later. I'm just surprised that you've turned into such a health nut. So…are you a vegetarian?" She'd never mentioned that but everything she'd eaten today—nuts and berries and yogurt and a whole-wheat bread and cucumber sandwich—certainly suggested it.

"Not completely. But I don't eat a lot of red meat, or processed foods, for that matter."

"That's it. I'm taking you out for a big steak this week before you put me on the same diet."

They were interrupted by a knock at the door, and a hint of apprehension entered Presley's expression. "That's got to be Chey."

"Are you expecting her?"

"She's sent me a few texts—says she has 'news.'"

"She hasn't told you what that news is?"

"I haven't given her the chance. Since you didn't ask how things went after you kindly donated what you donated a week ago, I thought you were trying to forget about it for the time being…maybe forever. I was going to respond when I could focus on her."

Some of the contentment he'd been feeling faded. He'd gone through with the insemination, but he wasn't sure how he felt about it. "She doesn't yet know if it took?"

"I'm guessing she does now. What else could her news be?"

He pushed a piece of zucchini around his plate. "Why would she wait so long to take a pregnancy test? I assumed it was a go, that she'd call me if it wasn't."

"You can't check right away." She started across the room. "It's probably still a bit early for total accuracy, but I know she was having a hard time waiting. She wants to be pregnant so much—before Dylan can find out she isn't."

He remained at the table but braced himself in case it was Cheyenne. He wasn't sure which answer would be worse. That he'd helped her create a baby without Dylan's knowledge, which was a secret he'd have to live with for the rest of his life. Or that she hadn't conceived and they'd have to try again.

But it wasn't Cheyenne. Aaron might've considered that fortunate, except Presley's visitor was even higher on the list of people he'd rather not see.

"Riley," she said awkwardly. "I wasn't expecting you."

Riley's eyes cut to him, to Wyatt sitting in his high chair, to their plates, and Aaron knew it looked like they were in the middle of a family dinner. "Sorry to interrupt, but when I saw Aaron's truck and realized he was here visiting Wyatt, I thought maybe he'd be willing to babysit so I could take you out."

Aaron had watched Wyatt for them once before, but he hadn't liked it. He'd spent the evening imagining all sorts of things that made him want to punch Riley. But he wasn't convinced that Riley really believed he'd do the same thing again. He'd probably been driving by, noticed the truck and stopped to see what was going on. So when Presley seemed uncertain about how to respond, Aaron got up and walked over. "Actually, Pres and I have plans this evening."

"You do?" Riley said, but he kept his attention on her. "What kind of plans?"

Aaron answered even though he wasn't the person who'd been asked. "Plans that will last until I leave town in a month."

Presley opened her mouth as if she had something to add. Maybe she was going to tell him they weren't exclusive. They hadn't agreed not to see other people, and he'd told her before that she could. But he was feeling far more possessive and far less generous now.

Anyway, he didn't get to hear what Presley might've said. Riley spoke first.

"Is that true? Are you seeing him again?"

Even Aaron could hear the accusation in that question, as if she was making the dumbest mistake in the world. It angered him that Riley was acting so superior. However, Presley was trying to be polite, and *he* was trying to show some respect. "Yes, but...we're not making any big commitments."

"Of course not," he said with a bitter laugh.

She blinked at him. "Excuse me?"

"I could've guessed that. Aaron's not the type."

"You have no idea what type I am," Aaron snapped, but Riley, clearly unhappy with this turn of events, couldn't seem to control his emotions.

"Are you sleeping with him?"

At that point, Aaron couldn't restrain himself. "What we do or don't do is none of your damned business."

Again Riley ignored him. "Are you?"

When Presley didn't answer, he laughed mirthlessly. "He won't ever be what you want him to be. I thought you'd finally figured that out."

Aaron felt his hands curl into fists. He didn't want to let his temper get the better of him. He was still embarrassed about the way he'd behaved at her opening. But Riley seemed to be itching for a fight.

"I'm sorry you're so upset." Presley gently pushed Aaron back. "It's not as if you and I were exclusive, Riley. Or...or that there was any expectation of that."

"Expectation," Riley repeated. "I guess that's it. I expected too much."

Presley spread out her hands. "How could I have

been any clearer?" she asked, but Riley had already stalked off.

Jealousy often brought out the worst in people. Ever since Presley had returned to town, Aaron had felt his share. Still, he was surprised that Riley had gotten so angry. And he felt bad that Presley had taken the brunt of it. He would have shielded her from that if he could. She was taking a leap of faith in trusting him again—she didn't need Riley or anyone else creating doubt.

"Don't let him upset you," he said, slipping his arms around her. "How can he say what's best for you? He hardly knows either of us."

"Maybe he knows us better than we think," she said.

She'd stiffened again, grown worried, but he turned her around and held her face between his hands. "I can't promise you the moon," he said. "But neither can he."

He never got to hear how she might have responded. Cheyenne and Dylan drove up just then. He heard the car engine, could see them through the open doorway.

26

Aaron sat on Presley's couch, feeling uncomfortable for a number of reasons. After what had happened with Riley, he was sensitive to how people were going to react to him and Presley getting back together. Cheyenne and Dylan would certainly be skeptical, especially since he'd be leaving town soon. They'd think he was hanging around just long enough to interfere with her progress. So he preferred that the subject not come up. He wasn't going to allow Presley to be lambasted again, which meant they could easily get into an argument.

As if those concerns weren't enough to strain relationships, there was a strong possibility that Cheyenne was pregnant with his child, and Aaron knew Dylan would *not* be happy if he discovered the details. So what if he'd merely been trying to help? That wouldn't be much of a defense. The fear that their secret wouldn't remain a secret forever would linger, and it could affect his relationship with his older brother—not to mention Cheyenne and even Presley.

Aaron could sense that Cheyenne was equally uncomfortable. Probably frightened that she'd make

Dylan suspicious in some way, or that *he* would if she gave him the opportunity, she wouldn't address him directly or meet his eyes. She and Presley exchanged a few significant glances, but he had no idea what they signified. Was she pregnant or not?

If she wasn't, he was getting out of the arrangement while he could.

"So you'll do it?" Dylan asked. He and Cheyenne had dropped by to see if he'd take over the running of the auto body shop while they went to Hawaii. Apparently, they'd received some kind of travel brochure in the mail this morning and, on the spur of the moment, decided to take a vacation.

"It'll be a lot harder to get away after the baby's born," Dylan added. "You'll be in Reno by then, anyway, so we'll be shorthanded."

His brothers would have to hire someone to replace him, but there wasn't anyone with his experience in or around Whiskey Creek. That meant they'd be in a weaker position than they were now, at least until they could train someone.

"Of course. No problem." Aaron was more than willing to take on his brother's responsibilities for ten days. Dylan deserved a break. But they were going to celebrate their baby, a celebration that could end very badly if Cheyenne wasn't pregnant.

"And you'll be able to line up babysitting for Wyatt?" Cheyenne asked Presley. "I hate leaving town when you're counting on me. But like Dylan said, we may not get another chance."

"I'll be okay," she said.

"How?"

"I'll try to shift my standing massage appointments and schedule the rest for evenings and weekends, the hours Alexa is out of school."

Aaron had given her enough to cover the rent, so that should help.

"And Eve said you can leave Wyatt with her at the B and B when you have your yoga classes," Cheyenne told her.

"That's nice of her."

"We'll only be gone ten days," Dylan reiterated.

Presley smiled. "I'm sure we can muddle through."

They talked for another half hour, mostly about the baby and their plans for the nursery. Presley did a better job of entertaining them than Aaron did. He focused on playing with Wyatt while waiting for them to go, but Presley seemed even more relieved when that happened than he was.

"Is she or isn't she?" Aaron asked as soon as he heard them drive off.

Presley perched on the arm of her orange chair. "She is. She whispered it in my ear when she hugged me goodbye, and you were talking to Dylan."

With Cheyenne's obvious excitement about the nursery, he'd guessed as much.

After Aaron left and she'd put Wyatt to bed, Presley tried calling Riley. He didn't pick up, which made her sad. She liked him, but even if he decided he was no longer her friend, it wouldn't change the situation. She was planning to apologize if she'd somehow misled him, despite their conversations about Aaron. She was also hoping to explain that whether or not it was a mistake to let Aaron back in her life, she had the right—maybe even the obligation—to try to make things work with the father of her child.

Riley would probably have insisted that Aaron was only going to disappoint her—and he'd probably be right. Aaron hadn't been able to give her what she wanted when they were together before. But things had been different with him today, different enough to show her what life *could* be. And if she gave up too soon she'd be the one walking away from that possibility. Why be defeated so easily? No one ever won a boxing match hiding behind their gloves. She had to drop hers, be willing to take a hit, because trying to stay out of the ring certainly hadn't worked. She'd walked away two years ago. It'd been the right decision then. She'd been fighting for far more basic things—her health, her survival, her future. But now?

Now she was back where she'd begun. There had to be a reason. There *had* to be more for her here in Whiskey Creek than heartbreak.

So maybe it was time to quit doubting, time to push past the fear. If she and Aaron ended up together, she'd be the happiest woman in the world.

And if they didn't? She'd make the best of it. She wouldn't go back to drugs under any circumstances. She had control of her life at last, and that gave her options.

As he was lying in bed, trying to sleep, Aaron received a text from Cheyenne thanking him again, but he couldn't make himself respond. Instead, he erased her message. He wanted to pretend he'd never had any involvement in her conception, that she'd gotten pregnant just as Dylan thought. Dylan was going to love the child she had regardless, so maybe it would all work out.

At the moment, Aaron was more worried about his relationship with Presley. Riley's visit had spooked her. He knew because she'd been so reserved after Cheyenne and Dylan had left, and she hadn't argued with him when he mentioned heading home for the night. So much had changed in one day that they needed time to think. Aaron hadn't set out to hurt her, but everyone was so damn certain he would that he was beginning to doubt himself.

Maybe he was being selfish to knock down her defenses and try to stir her interest. Would she be better off with someone else? Someone like Riley, who considered himself such a great family man?

Aaron couldn't say for sure. He needed a trial period. Was that too much to ask?

His phone rang. When he saw that it was Presley, he almost didn't answer. He was afraid of what she might say. Earlier, she'd given him the impression that she was already changing her mind.

But just in case it had to do with Wyatt—in case he was sick or something—Aaron picked up.

"'Lo?"

"Did I wake you?" she asked.

He tried to prepare himself for whatever was coming next. "No."

"It's late. And you have a big day tomorrow."

Pressing a thumb and finger to his eyes, he wondered where she'd go from here—and surprised himself by trying to head her off with the truth. "I'm having trouble sleeping without you."

"Good," she said. "Come back here."

He dropped his hand in surprise. "You heard Riley. I'm a womanizer out to break your heart."

There was a slight pause. "Maybe he's underestimating me."

"*You?* How?"

"Maybe this time I'll break yours."

He laughed when she hung up, then got dressed and hurried over. He wasn't worried. But once he climbed into her bed, he could tell that she was no longer as tentative as she'd been before—and he liked it.

The days that followed were heaven for Presley. May was filled with long, sunny days that were neither too hot nor too cold. Cheyenne was ecstatic over her pregnancy. Presley's business was growing and so was Wyatt, and she spent almost all her free time with Aaron. The only negative was Riley, who was still put out enough with her defection that he barely spoke to her. She didn't let that bother her, however; she didn't have any time to give him, anyway.

Determined to simply enjoy what Aaron offered and leave it at that, she refused to become obsessed with what he was or wasn't feeling. So she never brought up their relationship or asked him to talk about his emotions. Besides going to work and shopping for baby things with Cheyenne, she played with Wyatt and made love to Aaron, and they had fun as a family in other ways—eating at Just Like Mom's, going hiking, having picnics and touring the Kennedy Gold Mine. They even visited Moaning Caverns, which weren't far, although they couldn't go spelunking since they had Wyatt.

Everything was wonderful, until he took her to Reno for the first time to see the location he'd settled on for his Amos Auto Body franchise. It was a corner lot that had once been a small dealership and seemed to have plenty of potential. But she felt a niggle of concern because he made no mention of the role she and Wyatt would play in his life once he moved there.

Still, she said nothing. She'd promised herself she wouldn't press him, and she wasn't going to. When he was ready to make the commitment, he would.

"You've changed, you know that?" he said once they were driving back home.

They had the windows down at her request. They could've used the air conditioner, but she liked the feel of the wind on her face. "How?"

"You've become so responsible. And you have a lot more confidence in your own abilities."

"Haven't you changed, too?" she asked.

He shrugged. "Maybe. But you're more flexible than I am. I love how much fun you are, how easy to be with."

She smiled as he took her hand. That was the closest he'd come to any type of declaration. She was happy he was thinking positive thoughts. But it was a little harder to take the following week in stride, because that was when he found the housing accommodation he'd been looking for.

Presley sat outside Black Gold Coffee, stirring sugar into her chai tea. Wyatt was in his stroller on one side, with Cheyenne across the table. Presley knew her sister met friends here every Friday, but this wasn't Friday. It was a Wednesday, the day before

Cheyenne and Dylan were set to leave for Hawaii, and it was just the two of them.

"I saw Aaron at Nature's Way with Wyatt," Cheyenne said. "He's so smitten with this boy." She gave Wyatt's chin a little tweak. "They're darling together."

Wyatt adored his daddy as much as his daddy adored him. Sometimes that made Presley nervous, maybe even jealous—when the doubt and insecurities of her past welled up. But she did her best to force those concerns into the back of her mind. She'd deal with whatever came up, and she'd do it with class. That was her goal. "He's a good father. Much more interested in Wyatt than I expected him to be."

"Yeah, he seems to have Wyatt with him a lot."

She offered her son another drink of his milk. "I think he's taking him as much as possible, since it'll be harder once he moves."

Aaron's relocation loomed larger with each passing day. It sent a pang of anxiety through her now, but she suppressed that, too.

"What happens then?" Cheyenne asked, sipping her orange juice.

Presley added another packet of sugar to her tea so she wouldn't have to look up. She'd released all her fear, stopped trying to second-guess what might come next. She'd decided that living in the moment was the only way she and Aaron would have a chance. They'd had a lot of fun, but he hadn't said the three words she longed to hear, hadn't asked her to marry him, either. With his departure getting so close, her hopes were beginning to dwindle.

You saw this coming. You've had most of May with

him, which is more than you would've had before. At least you were brave enough to take the risk.

"He'll have to drive back here if he wants to visit us, I guess," she said, lowering her eyes in case they revealed her true feelings.

"He hasn't mentioned the possibility of you going to Reno with him?"

Trying to be the picture of poise and confidence, Presley leaned back, crossed her legs and took a sip of her tea. "Why would he? My business is here."

But he could have asked her to relocate. She would have done it, for him—if not immediately, then in time, when she could make the arrangements.

"But you're a couple now, right? I mean…from what Dylan and I can tell, you're basically living together. Grady says Aaron hardly ever comes home. He can't remember the last time Aaron did laundry there."

Aaron had seemed less and less interested in staying at the house with his brothers. But nothing made their "togetherness" official. He'd been moving forward with the franchise and, most recently, he'd secured living accommodations. "Like I said, I'm letting him spend time with Wyatt."

Cheyenne wiped the table with a napkin. "You mean, when he's not in your bed."

"I might be enjoying the perks that go along with that, yes."

"Presley, I hope— "

She raised a hand. No way would she allow her sister's empathy to make her falter. "Don't. It's okay if Aaron moves without me. I'm not the fragile person I used to be. I can take it."

Cheyenne didn't look too convinced. "What will you do?"

"I'll keep building my business, like I'm doing now. And someday maybe there will be someone else." That was hard to imagine, but it was the classic line, what she was supposed to say when putting on a brave face. She'd made this decision. She wasn't going to drag her sister and brother-in-law through whatever she might experience as a result. They'd done enough for her already.

She and Chey sat in silence for several seconds. Then Cheyenne said, "Has he mentioned the baby?"

"The baby?" Hadn't they just been talking about Wyatt?

"*My* baby," she clarified. "I've texted him a few times, but he's only responded once."

"What'd he say?"

"He's happy that I'm happy and he wishes me luck. That was it. I get the feeling he doesn't even want to talk to me."

"It's not that. He wants to put some distance between himself and you and your pregnancy. It's actually a good thing that he doesn't expect you to keep acknowledging his contribution, right?"

"I guess. But I feel bad. I don't want this pregnancy to cost me my brother-in-law. I didn't go into it thinking there'd be that kind of sacrifice."

"He just needs some distance, like I said. He feels guilty for keeping it a secret, and yet he can see why everyone's better off that way."

"We *are* better off," Cheyenne insisted. "Dylan is, anyway. He's so happy."

Presley certainly hoped so, because it was too late to turn back. "Have you heard from Riley?"

"Here and there. He was at coffee last Friday. Why?"

"I've tried to reach him a few times, but he hasn't replied."

Cheyenne finished her drink and tossed the container in a nearby wastebasket. "He had high hopes where you were concerned."

"I don't see why."

Her sister gave her arm a slight tap. "Don't say that."

"I'm not putting myself down. There wasn't any chemistry between us."

"On your side, maybe. But you were already in love, so I'm not sure you would've felt it even if it had earthquake proportions."

"He hasn't been coming in for his massages," she said. "I feel like I should give him his money back. I sent a text to that effect, but no answer there, either. I guess I'll have to call him again."

"Don't bother returning his money. I love Riley, but it's his choice whether he gets the massages he bought. You haven't done anything wrong." She slipped Wyatt another of his organic juice-sweetened animal crackers. "I'm guessing he'll schedule an appointment in a few months, after Aaron's gone and he thinks you've had a chance to forget him."

If she could forget Aaron, she would've done it already. "Maybe you're right."

A honk drew their attention, and Presley glanced over to see Aaron parking his truck.

"Speak of the devil," Cheyenne murmured.

"He knew I was going to be here. I told him. I hope you don't mind."

"Of course not. Maybe he'll finally have something to say to me."

Presley pulled a chair from the table closest to them so he'd have a place to sit. "You didn't reply when I texted you to see if you wanted me to order for you," she said as he walked up. "I was afraid maybe you weren't going to make it."

"I was driving. But that's okay. I'll grab something." He paused long enough to take Wyatt, who was giddy with happiness at the sight of him, into the coffee shop.

As the door swung shut behind them, Cheyenne winked at her. "He looks good."

She grinned. "He always looks good."

When Aaron returned carrying an iced coffee, he bent to kiss her before taking his seat. "What'd you get?" he asked as he positioned Wyatt on his lap.

"My regular."

"Chai tea? I should've known." He smiled at Cheyenne. "This girl won't eat anything that's bad for her anymore."

Cheyenne moved her purse to give him more room. "I know. Makes it difficult to have dinner at Just Like Mom's, right?"

"Speaking of Just Like Mom's. You guys are on for tonight, aren't you?" Aaron asked.

"To meet your new stepmother?" Cheyenne whistled under her breath. "Of course. I'm dying of curiosity."

"I'm glad *you're* excited about it, because I'm not," Aaron said.

Cheyenne slid the sugar toward him. "It should be less awkward if there's a group."

He ripped open one of the packets. "My thoughts exactly."

According to what Aaron had told her, Anya Sharp had been trying to get the Amos brothers to have dinner with her for weeks, and they'd finally run out of excuses. "I'll make an exception with my diet," she said, "even though you've been taking me to that restaurant too often as it is."

"Are you nervous about meeting her?" Cheyenne asked Aaron.

"Not nervous," he replied. "Apprehensive. Who knows what this woman will be like?"

Cheyenne waved as someone called out to her from across the street. "Maybe she'll be pleasant. Haven't you talked to her on the phone? Dylan told me you're the one who set this up."

"She's been calling me ever since Dylan gave her my number. You'll have to thank him for me."

She laughed at his sarcasm. "He couldn't put her off any longer and figured you'd have better luck."

"Apparently, I'm a softer touch than I like to believe. Or I got her after she'd run out of patience. She wasn't taking no for an answer. I was afraid she'd just show up at our house."

"She's that aggressive?"

"Absolutely. She's so damn eager to meet us, but I don't get why she's in such a rush. Why not wait until my father's released?"

"I agree," Presley said. They'd talked about this before.

"We're all adults," he added. "It's not as if we need a mother."

"Maybe she's lonely," Cheyenne said. "She married a convict, after all."

Experience had taught Presley that Aaron didn't enjoy talking about his stepmother, so she changed the subject. They'd find out exactly what Anya was like tonight. Conjecture was getting them nowhere. "So how'd it go this morning?" she asked Aaron. "Did you sign the lease on the cute little house you found in Reno?"

He'd asked her to go with him, but she had yoga class and three massages.

"I did. Handed over my security deposit and first and last month's rent."

"Nice." She managed to keep her smile in place.

Cheyenne looked from him to Presley and back again. "So you've rented something? It's official?"

"Nothing too fancy," he replied. "But it's comfortable." He nudged Presley for confirmation. "Wouldn't you say?"

"I love it," she admitted.

Cheyenne scooted her chair back so she could stay in the shade of the giant umbrella. "When will you be moving?"

"The lease starts June 1."

"That soon? That's only a week away."

"June's always been my goal once I decided to do this."

Cheyenne frowned. "But Presley's birthday is at the end of the month, and I'm planning a big party. You'll drive back for it, won't you?"

Presley spoke up before he could. "If he has time. It'll be hard work to get the shop going."

"If I have time?" he echoed.

"You'll be busy." She checked her phone. "I've got to run or I'll be late for my next massage. Chey, are you okay with Wyatt?"

"I can keep him with me," Aaron said. "I've got some calls to make, but I can do that at the house."

"Great. I'll see you later." Aaron had kissed her when he sat down, but she was always careful not to lay any claim on him, especially in public. So instead of touching him, she gave her baby a quick hug and waved goodbye.

27

Cheyenne watched her sister leave. "She's doing so well."

Aaron handed Wyatt to her while he folded up the stroller. He kept a child's seat in his truck, which was something Cheyenne had never thought she'd see. It made her smile every time she saw it peeking up over the window. "Here in Whiskey Creek?"

"In life. Generally."

When he narrowed his eyes, she knew he recognized that as the lead-in it was.

"Sounds like you're getting philosophical."

"I'm just glad she's happy!" she said, trying to backpedal.

"And that's it? Tell the truth," he retorted. "You have something else on your mind."

Aaron wasn't letting her get away with anything.

Cheyenne scowled at him. "Come on, Aaron. I just need to know that you care about her. You do, don't you?"

"I've told you before that I do."

"And yet you're going to move to Reno and leave her behind?"

His expression held a not-so-subtle warning. "Stop. Don't get involved."

She didn't dare push him any harder. At least he was being a good father. She couldn't fault him there. And he treated Presley really well. It was only his lack of commitment to the relationship that worried her. She knew how difficult that had to be for Pres.

With a sigh of frustration at his hardheadedness, she said, "Can we talk about the baby, then? At last?"

He drilled her with another level stare. "*Which* baby?"

"*My* baby." She put a hand to her stomach. "The one you gave me."

"I don't want you to ever talk to me about that again," he said. "As far as I'm concerned that night at Presley's—what we did—it never happened."

"Fine. Wonderful. There's just one problem."

He grimaced but asked, anyway. "What's that?"

"I don't want it to cost me my relationship with you. You matter to me, as my brother-in-law. And you matter even more to Dylan. When I made the decision to ask for your help, I wasn't consciously trading you for what you could give me."

Fortunately, he didn't say that was a trade she'd make without a second thought. He could've accused her of it, considering how desperate she'd been. But he seemed to understand that she was trying to get everything to go back to normal. "It hasn't cost you anything, Chey. Just forget it, okay?"

"I can't forget. You treat me like a complete stranger these days, and that makes me feel it was a mistake to involve you. It's not as if we can ignore each other indefinitely, Aaron, even if I was willing to settle for that. We'll continue to see each other at events like the one tonight, when we have to meet the new Mrs. J. T. Amos. I'd rather those events not be awkward."

After glancing around to find the sidewalks clear, he lowered his voice. "I treat you the way I do because I don't want you to acknowledge what happened. I don't want you to thank me. I don't want you to be grateful. I don't want us to be any different than we were before because of our little secret. The idea that what we did would bring us close feels wrong to me, do you understand? Just be happy and make my brother and your baby happy. That's the only way I can feel good about the situation."

"Then I'm sorry."

She could tell that wasn't the response he'd been expecting.

"What? *Why?*"

"Because I *am* grateful. I could never explain how much. And I will never mention it again, to you or anyone else. But how could I ever forget that you're the one who made it possible for me to be a mother and Dylan a father?" Although she held Wyatt, and he held the stroller, she stood and gave him a brief one-armed hug.

"I appreciate the sentiment," he mumbled as she pulled away. "But that's all that needs to be said, okay? No more thankful smiles or 'are we okay' glances."

She laughed. "Got it."

"You promise?"

"Yes."

"Thank God." He strode to his truck and put Wyatt's stroller in the bed.

"There's just one more thing," she said, following him.

He turned to face her. "I'm almost afraid to ask what it is," he said dryly.

"If you hurt my sister again, I'll make you sorry you were ever born." She nodded as if that was the end of it, and he finally seemed to relax into his old self.

"Glad we're back on familiar ground," he said, taking his son.

Anya Sharp-Amos was nothing like Aaron had expected. He'd thought she'd have to be unattractive and well past her prime to settle for a prison inmate. But she was neither of those things. Maybe thirty-five, she had an excellent figure and was doing everything possible to flaunt it—hardly a challenge since she was dressed in a pair of shorts that practically showed her ass. The addition of a leather vest and army boots made her look like a true biker chick. The tattoos on her arms and legs, and the fact that she reeked of tobacco smoke, completed the stereotype. But Aaron could suddenly understand why his father had married a woman he didn't even know. After twenty years in the slammer, the promise of conjugal visits could probably tempt him into anything. To a regular man, however, all she had to do to ruin her appeal was open her mouth. She was far too pushy for Aaron's taste; he'd experienced just *how* pushy when she wouldn't let him postpone tonight's dinner.

"Look at all these handsome men." She stood as

they filed in, then she motioned for a teenage girl, who was apparently with her, to show some enthusiasm. Whoever the girl was, she didn't seem happy to be included in this little get-together. She rolled her eyes as if she was sick of her mother, and gave them a brooding glare.

"This is my daughter, Natasha," Anya announced. Aaron had already guessed from the teen's large almond-shaped green eyes that they were related. But Anya had never once mentioned a daughter when they'd spoken on the phone, so Natasha came as a total surprise.

"She's got a bit of an attitude problem, as you can tell," Anya went on. "She needs some big brothers to set her straight and look out for her. Because if there's trouble, she'll find it," she added with a smoker's raspy laugh.

They were meeting at the steakhouse in Sutter Creek. At the last second, Aaron had called her to change the location. Anya had argued, said she really wanted to see where they lived. But he hadn't been too excited about having this meeting at Just Like Mom's, where the whole town could watch. Now he was glad he'd insisted they eat here, where they could maintain a degree of anonymity. This was going to be quite an interesting—interesting as in *horrifying*—meal, and he was pretty sure the girl, Natasha, understood that even better than he did.

"You must be Dylan," Anya cried, picking him out immediately. "I recognize you from the picture your father showed me."

Aaron wanted to ask what picture. They certainly hadn't sent J.T. anything recent. But he had no idea what Grady, Rod or Mack had provided. They were a lot closer to J.T.

Dylan nodded and suffered through an enthusiastic embrace before managing to extricate himself and introduce Cheyenne, who was staring at her stepmother-in-law in stunned disbelief.

"My God, you're gorgeous!" Anya grabbed Cheyenne next. "Look at you."

Her too-loud voice caused several other diners to glance over, but she didn't seem to notice. Or maybe she didn't care. Cheyenne didn't even get a chance to respond before Anya turned to Aaron. "And you! Tell me your name. No, wait. Are you Aaron? You are, aren't you?"

"I am." He saw that her daughter had propped her chin on one fist and was sunk in on herself, as if she wished she could shrink into oblivion.

"So you're the one I've been talking to for the past two weeks," Anya said. "I hear you're a bit of a troublemaker. Your father has so many funny stories about you, like that one where you jumped off the roof because you thought you could fly and nearly broke your back."

Aaron was glad he had Wyatt in his arms. That made it difficult for her to plaster herself against him as she had Dylan. She fussed over Wyatt next and then sized up Presley.

"I see you've met your match with this stunning creature. And you are?"

Presley cleared her throat as if she was suppressing laughter, but Aaron was too overwhelmed to find this funny. "Presley Christensen," she replied.

"Named after the King. God, that's rich. Aren't

you cute!" She nudged her daughter so hard, she knocked her chin off her hand. "Well, Natasha, if you had your eye on Aaron, you're out of luck."

"Mom!" The girl's disgusted expression indicated that she understood how completely inappropriate *that* was, even if her mother did not.

"How old are you?" Presley asked, focusing on the girl.

Folding her arms, she leaned back in her chair. "Sixteen. I'm also sixteen years younger than my mother." She smiled sweetly. "In case you were wondering."

Aaron *had* been wondering. He'd guessed thirty-five. But Anya was a year younger than he was?

This situation just kept getting more bizarre. In all the letters they'd received from their father, and the calls they'd received from Anya, there'd never been any mention of her daughter, let alone a daughter who was still in high school.

At least…he hoped Natasha was in school. She seemed ready to flip off the whole world—a sentiment he could identify with from his own angry years but one that didn't produce the best results. So maybe she'd dropped out. If not for Dylan, he probably would have.

Aaron quickly introduced Rod, Grady and Mack so she couldn't regale them with stories about each one of them. Then they took their seats, ordered and ate. The conversation was stilted; none of them had much to say. But Anya kept it going, babbling on and on about how much their father had changed, and how he looked as young as they did. It wasn't until Dylan had paid the check—she didn't even attempt to pay her way—that she got to the real reason she'd been so eager to meet them. Apparently, she was being evicted from her place in Los Banos, had no money to rent elsewhere and was hoping they could help her get a place in Whiskey Creek, so she'd be all moved in when J.T. returned.

Aaron almost started laughing when this came out. Finally, all her calls and effusive compliments made sense.

Fortunately, Dylan took the lead on their response. If Aaron had had to talk right then, he might've told her she was exactly what he'd been afraid she'd be—a parasite.

"How much do you need?" Dylan asked.

"Just a couple thousand," she replied. "Your father told me to tell you he'll pay you back as soon as he can. He's worried about us."

"My father said *he'd* pay us back?" Dylan asked.

Aaron knew what his brother was thinking—J.T. didn't have a pot to piss in.

"We're a bit down on our luck now, that's all," she said. "Once we get moved, I'll find work, and we'll be fine."

If she could find work. Otherwise, what would happen? Would she expect them to continue taking care of her?

Aaron suspected she would.

"I'm sorry, I'm afraid we can't help," Dylan said, but Anya wasn't willing to let it go at that. She'd gotten them all out here for a reason, and she wasn't going home empty-handed.

"Look, if it was only for me, I wouldn't ask," she responded. "But I've got Natasha to think about. She needs a roof over her head, the poor girl. I mean…if you don't have the cash to lend us, maybe we could move in with you guys. J.T. said there should be plenty of room. He said maybe she and I could take your old bedroom, since you moved out," she told Dylan.

Natasha had remained silent throughout the meal. She'd ordered only a side salad and picked at it, and the way she flushed when her mother pleaded their case gave Aaron the impression she'd known this was coming and hated every word of it. She hadn't been the least bit friendly, but she was the one he felt sorry for. She reminded him of Presley and Cheyenne when they were younger, completely at the mercy of an irresponsible mother.

"I'm afraid that wouldn't work." Aaron spoke up to support Dylan. "But my father will do what he can for you when he gets out, I'm sure."

"It'll be too late by then," she cried, grabbing Cheyenne. "Can't *you* talk to them? I know this isn't the best introduction, but we're family now."

Cheyenne looked startled that Anya had chosen her for this appeal, and the fact that she'd laid hands on his wife didn't sit well with Dylan.

"I'm sorry if we seem coldhearted, but we barely know you," he said. "It's my father's place to see to your needs."

Aaron ground his teeth. They'd be fools to let her start using them. But…what would happen to the girl? They'd come into this feeling leery, afraid that Anya would try to get away with something, but they hadn't expected the complication of an innocent party.

"J.T. gets out in less than three months," Anya went on. "We wouldn't be there long. What's three months if you can save two people from becoming homeless?"

The girl looked so disheartened that Aaron was tempted to say they'd take her and her alone. Dylan was wrestling with the same uncertainty; Aaron could see it on his brother's face. But, in the end, it was Grady who spoke up.

"What if we take Natasha? Do you have a friend you could live with until Dad gets out?"

Anya rocked back, obviously insulted that they'd try to exclude her. "I can't let my teenage daughter move into a houseful of men! Not without me there to protect her."

"It wouldn't be a household of *men*," Aaron pointed out. "It'd be a household of brothers—to set her straight and look out for her, remember?"

Her lips pursed at his sarcasm but it was Natasha who responded. "I don't need anyone. I can make it on my own." Tossing her napkin on the table she got up and walked out.

Anya didn't follow. "Don't listen to her. We don't have anywhere else to go," she pleaded. "If you're willing to take Natasha, you can let me live there, too, can't you? Why would you want to split her up from her mother?"

Aaron was willing to bet Natasha would love nothing more than to be separated from Anya. He was also convinced she couldn't make it on her own at all, that she had no real options, or she wouldn't have accompanied Anya here today.

When Presley squeezed his hand, he guessed she felt the same.

"Maybe it wouldn't matter if they stayed for a few

months," Rod said. "As long as they share a room, like she said."

"We could do that." Anya pounced immediately. "That'd be perfect. And think how great it would be to have a woman around. Wait until you see how I can cook. I'm good at a lot of other things, too."

She didn't elaborate on that, and Aaron was afraid to ask.

"Grady, Rod..." Dylan began, but could say little more. Although they must have heard the warning note in his voice, Grady sighed and shrugged it off.

"Everyone needs a break now and then, Dyl," he said. "And this could make a big difference in Dad's life, give him a break, too, since he can't help her at the moment. But I can only speak for myself. Rod's weighed in. Mack, what about you?"

As all eyes turned to him, Mack hesitated. It was rare for him not to side with Dylan. But, ultimately, he nodded. What else could he do? He was the most excited about J.T. getting out, about finally having a father. But chances were good that their father would put this woman first, and Mack would wind up with nothing—like always.

Aaron glanced at Presley. He could tell that Anya was taken aback that she hadn't managed to gain a warmer welcome, but she wasn't going to let what they thought or felt stand in the way.

"You'll see that I'm not hard to live with," she said and quickly made arrangements to arrive the very next day.

"Holy hell," he muttered as, a bit shell-shocked, they slowly made their way to the exit after she'd left. "I knew that wasn't going to go well, but…shit. I don't think it could've gone any worse."

Presley was carrying Wyatt, but she propped him on one hip and looped her arm through Aaron's. "Tell the truth. You felt as sorry for the girl as the rest of us did."

"Of course," he admitted. "Anya had a secret weapon. She completely disarmed us, just as she set out to do."

They paused in the shade of the overhang and watched the two drive off in a rattletrap car.

"I think we're in for trouble," Grady said.

They sure were. But Aaron wasn't going to let his father ruin his life again. If he'd ever had any doubts about moving to Reno, he didn't now.

28

Presley hardly saw Aaron the following week. Dylan and Cheyenne had left for Hawaii, so he was running the shop, as well as trying to keep up with his own share of bodywork after hours. He called her whenever he took a break, and slipped into bed with her late at night—he refused to go home, where he could run into Anya or Natasha—but he was gone again before she got up. She missed him, but she knew these lonely days were only a sample of what it would be like when he was no longer living in town.

Once Dylan and Cheyenne returned, Aaron started moving into his new place. Presley went with him when her schedule allowed it and helped him clean the house and unpack. He didn't ask for her help, but he seemed to like having her and Wyatt with him whenever possible, and she figured it would be reassuring, a way to prove to herself that he'd be comfortable and happy in his new home.

He talked as if he'd be visiting Whiskey Creek often, as if the move wouldn't change a thing between them. But Presley didn't believe that. A three-hour drive was a significant obstacle. As soon as he got busy—and he'd be extremely busy launching the new shop—he'd stay in Reno for longer and longer periods of time. And she had no car, so she couldn't drive herself.

She supposed that was for the best. Then the amount of their interaction would be up to him. She was tired of caring more than he did, hated that it seemed as if that would never change. If he wanted to be with her and Wyatt, he knew where to find them. It wasn't like he'd *had* to make this move. Dylan and the others would've been fine with his staying. *He* was the one who'd wanted to branch out on his own. Sure, he wasn't happy about Anya and Natasha inserting themselves into his life, but his brothers were tolerating it. As recently as just a few weeks ago, he could've chosen to stay in Whiskey Creek, but he'd signed both leases after they'd started seeing each other almost every day.

The first night they spent at his place was three weeks before her birthday. "What do you want me to get you?" he asked. They were wrapped in each other's arms and had been talking about the party Cheyenne was planning to throw for her, which was how the subject came up.

Presley had to admit she was disappointed that he'd ask. She would've preferred that he pick out something on his own and surprise her. But maybe she was being too sensitive. He'd had a lot on his mind and his schedule, and that was only going to get worse.

"I don't need anything in particular," she said. "Maybe some yoga mats so I can provide them to students who don't have their own."

"That's pretty practical."

"It would still be a good gift. I want to be success-ful." Besides, practical gifts were about the only kind she'd ever received, so she was used to it.

"What you need is a car."

"Not in Whiskey Creek," she said. "And I'd rather not have the payments."

"Then how will you drive up here?"

"I won't. You'll have to visit me." Even if he found other friends, other women to date, he'd come back for Wyatt, wouldn't he? That gave her some secu-rity—but also made it impossible to build a life that didn't include him.

He kissed her bare shoulder. "Don't worry. I'll visit often."

"Are you coming to my party?"

"Of course," he said. "What was that you said to Cheyenne, anyway? 'If I have time'? What kind of guy do you think I am? I wouldn't miss your birth-day."

"You have a lot to do here. That's all I was think-ing."

"None of it is more important than you."

She didn't argue with him, but if that was true, he wouldn't have moved. Or…he would've asked her to come, too.

Just as she'd feared, Presley didn't see much of Aaron in the days leading up to June 26. He called her daily, but the drive was too long to make very often. She couldn't go to Reno herself because, be-sides the fact that she didn't own a car, she had early yoga classes and massage appointments. He couldn't come down because he was already paying rent on his new location and needed to get the renovations finished as soon as possible so he could open.

She missed him more with each passing day, but she refused to dwell on it—or show her sister, who was obviously concerned, how much it hurt that he could move on so easily.

"Aaron told me he'll definitely be here for your birthday," Cheyenne told her when they were addressing the invitations one afternoon.

"He hasn't been able to come back as often as he thought," she said, "but…hopefully he'll make it."

"He will."

Presley hated that he'd ever left. Even Wyatt seemed sad. When he called, Aaron always asked to talk to his son if Wyatt was up, but nothing was the same. She knew Riley believed it was over between them because he came in for one of the massages she owed him and flirted with her as if they'd never had that encounter at her house.

By the time her birthday rolled around, she was so homesick for Aaron that she didn't care about cake or presents or even the friends who might come to her party. It was more about seeing him. So she splurged on a new dress—a brand-new dress, not one from the secondhand store—gave her fingernails and toenails a fresh coat of polish and sprayed on his favorite perfume, all in anticipation of the moment he'd walk through Cheyenne's door. She'd put so much effort into her appearance that when he texted to let her know he'd be late, she couldn't help feeling let down.

Although she smiled and talked and pretended to have a great time, it was easy to tell that Cheyenne and Dylan were just as upset with Aaron. As the minutes turned into hours, she began to wonder if he was going to show at all.

"It's time for Presley to open her presents," Cheyenne announced.

They'd already stalled as long as possible. Cheyenne couldn't put it off any longer without ruining the party. People were starting to leave. So Presley sat down and let Wyatt play with the discarded wrapping paper as she opened each package.

Cheyenne and Dylan gave her an expensive painting of the foothills surrounding Whiskey Creek, one she'd been fixated on since they'd seen it at a local gallery. Grady, Rod and Mack gave her a sizable gift certificate for Amazon. Ted Dixon and his fiancée, Sophia, gave her an e-reader. From Anya and Natasha she got a handmade certificate for some "free" babysitting for Wyatt—not that Presley would ever let Anya be alone with him. She didn't trust Aaron's new stepmother but she liked Natasha. Other than that, she got various items from her yoga and massage clients—movie tickets, a houseplant, a pretty necklace.

She managed to hold back the tears that lurked just below the surface long enough to thank everyone. Then she couldn't wait to escape her own party so she wouldn't have to try so hard to keep up the act, but Cheyenne told her there was one package left.

Dylan brought it out of one of the bedrooms and said, "This is from Aaron."

Aaron had a gift for her? How, when he hadn't even arrived?

She didn't ask. Too many people were looking on, feeling sorry for her. She could sense their sympathy,

hear the whispers. *Isn't she with Aaron anymore?...
Why didn't he come to the party?...I heard he was
supposed to. Cheyenne said so...Did they break up?*

She'd been seen all over town with the father of
her baby just three weeks earlier. Happier than she'd
ever been. Now he wasn't even at her birthday party.

She didn't want to open Aaron's gift in front of
anyone, especially Cheyenne and Dylan because they
were most privy to her disappointment. But Cheyenne
had Dylan bring it in, and if she refused to open it,
the hurt she was feeling would be that much more
apparent.

Swallowing hard, she told herself to hang on a bit
longer. "Wow. It's big."

"Don't get your hopes up," she heard Cheyenne
mutter, and unwrapped it to find forty yoga mats.
He'd gotten her the practical gift she'd suggested—
but at least he'd gotten her a lot of them.

"This is wonderful," she said. "I really...need
these." She looked at Catherine, one of her yoga students, who sat nearby playing with Wyatt. "Won't
having so many of my own mats be handy?"

Catherine nodded, but even her smile seemed
forced.

Presley got to her feet. "Thanks a million for coming," she told everyone. "And for all the lovely gifts.
This has been the best birthday ever."

It was a pretty transparent lie, but they all hugged
her, wished her a final "happy birthday" and drifted
off to their own homes.

"You okay?" Cheyenne asked as they started to
clean up.

"Of course," she replied, and promised herself that soon she'd be able to crawl into bed.

Cheyenne grabbed her arm when she moved toward the kitchen to throw away some paper plates. "You can go now, if you want. It's past Wyatt's bedtime, anyway."

"He'll be fine for a few more minutes. I don't want to leave you with this mess," she said, but she wished she'd taken Cheyenne up on her offer when she heard Dylan, his voice low and angry, talking to Mack.

"Where the hell is he? He has me go buy yoga mats and thinks he's covered?"

Mack saw her standing nearby and cleared his throat, which caused Dylan to turn.

"Shit. I'm sorry, Pres," he said when he realized she'd overheard.

Tears sprang to her eyes, but she blinked them back. "Don't worry about it. I appreciate you getting the mats. They'll…they'll come in handy."

"He would've done it himself, but he didn't have time. He said today was crazy. He's still coming, by the way. At least he was the last I heard. He called a little while ago."

"It's a long drive." She'd been saying that all night, but no sooner had those words come out than her phone buzzed.

It was another text from Aaron.

I'm finally here, babe. I'm so sorry. I just need a quick shower. Then I'll be over.

It's okay, she wrote. Everyone's gone.

So you're coming home now?

Yes.

Good. I'll meet you at your place.

Presley let her breath seep out as she stared down at his words. What was she going to say when she saw him? She wasn't sure she could pretend it hadn't hurt that he'd been so cavalier about her birthday.

"I guess he's here," she told Dylan when she saw him frowning at her.

"Great. Where?" he muttered. "I'll kick his ass."

"Don't be mad at him," she said. "I was warned, right?"

He gave her a hug. "If that brother of mine had a brain in his head, he'd know what he has in you."

"You can't make your heart love someone it won't. I think that's a line in a song, isn't it? Or something like that." She chuckled mirthlessly. "Who can argue with such wisdom?"

There was nothing he could say to that, nothing anyone could say.

"We'll keep Wyatt here while you go talk to him," Cheyenne said.

She allowed that because Wyatt was still so wound up she had no idea how long it would take to get him to sleep. And she had to tell Aaron that he was off the hook, that he didn't need to return to Whiskey Creek anymore, not to see her. They'd given a relationship their best shot, but he obviously didn't care about her very much. He hadn't even offered an excuse for missing her birthday party. That was what stung the most. If he'd had a good reason, maybe she could've forgiven him. But even Dylan was mad.

It was hot outside, one of those rare nights that brought no reprieve from the summer heat. But Presley's house was close enough that she wouldn't have to be outside for long.

She'd barely rounded the corner before coming to a halt. She'd assumed Aaron would be inside, having a shower, as he'd said in his text. He had his own key. But he stood waiting for her, leaning up against the side of a big U-Haul truck. His pickup was hooked to the back via a tow dolly.

What was this?

So surprised that she forgot to be upset, she hurried over. "What's going on?"

He wiped a bead of sweat from his temple. "Sorry. I'd hug you, but I'm filthy."

"From…"

He indicated the truck behind him. "What does it look like? I've been moving."

"But…I don't understand. You rented that house in Reno. You signed a lease for the shop. You just moved up there three weeks ago!"

"And I just figured out that it was all a mistake, Pres." Shoving away from the truck, he stepped closer and rested his hands on her shoulders. "The past three weeks have shown me that I can't live without you."

Presley couldn't believe her ears. "What are you saying? You're moving back?"

His lips twisted into a wry grin. "I already did. Everything I want is right here."

In the truck. Her mind was reeling. "But you—you paid rent on the business and your house. You're locked in for a year. You'll lose thousands of dollars if you walk away."

He winced as he scratched his head. "Yeah. Not the smartest move I've ever made. I'll do what I can to salvage it—maybe hire a manager and some techs to run it. If that doesn't work, I deserve the financial loss for being so slow on the uptake. Somehow I thought we could carry on pretty much the way we were, that I could escape my past and start over without losing you. I even thought that maybe you'd be willing to move up there at some point." He gave her a rueful smile. "But I just couldn't see you leaving what you've established here. Which meant I needed to be the one to make the sacrifice."

"But…that's such an expensive decision!"

"You're worth it. The past three weeks have been the most miserable of my life, Pres. I go to work. I come home. Nothing has any meaning without you and Wyatt."

Presley was still so shocked she couldn't even speak. She stood there, gaping up at him and that big truck behind him.

"Tell me you're glad I'm home," he said. "Because it's been a long, hard day and it was this moment that kept me going."

She finally found her voice. "Of course I'm glad! But…I would've helped you. You didn't have to pack and move by yourself."

"I thought I could do it quicker than I could," he explained. "I wanted to surprise you at your party, but—" he wiped his hand across his face "—that was easier said than done."

"So what are you going to do with the real estate you've leased?"

"If I decide not to have someone else run it for me. I'll see if I can sublease it. That's all I can do."

"And your brothers will be okay with that?"

"Any loss will be my loss alone, since I'm the one who took the risk. I'm just glad I negotiated a good price and the right to sublet if I want. That might make it possible."

"But…your brothers. I just saw them. They can't know you've changed your mind, or they're the best actors in the world!"

"No one knows. I was afraid it would spoil the surprise if everyone was smirking and whispering when they ran into you."

The tears she'd been holding back for most of the night began to slide down her cheeks, only now they were happy tears. "So you're really back? For good?"

He leaned down to kiss her lips. "That's right. And I won't ever leave you again."

When she threw her arms around him, he muttered another quick warning about how dirty he was, but she didn't care. She would've hugged him even if he'd been covered in mud. She'd never been happier in her life. *I won't ever leave you again.* Aaron had said that, and he didn't make promises lightly.

"I was so mad when you missed my party," she whispered.

"I'm sorry about that, babe. If I'd realized that I was going to blow it this badly, I wouldn't have bothered with the surprise. But once I decided to come back, I couldn't leave my stuff behind. I wanted to pack up and get out of there as soon as possible."

"It's fine. Having you here, in my arms, that's all I care about. You'll be okay with Anya and Natasha... and your father, when he gets out?"

"I'll have to be," he said. "Did you like the yoga mats?"

She nodded. He could've given her a bucket of water from the hose and she wouldn't have cared now that she had him home for good.

"I'm glad. I'm hoping you might like this even better."

He pulled away long enough to extract a small wrapped box from his front pocket. When she glanced up to meet his eyes, his smile was slightly crooked. "Another reason I was late. I had the plan laid out so perfectly in my mind, and this was part of it."

Presley's heart pounded as she accepted the gift. She told herself not to get excited, that it *couldn't* be a ring. But it certainly felt like one.

She drew a calming breath, trying to prepare herself in case it was a necklace or earrings instead.

"Aren't you going to open it?"

Her eyes were burning again. She didn't want to cry, but she felt so hopeful and vulnerable and in love. She prayed he couldn't tell that her hands were shaking as she ripped off the wrapping paper and opened the velvet box.

Her breath caught in her throat. It was a diamond, all right: a huge solitaire, bigger than anything *she'd* ever dreamed of owning.

"Do you like it?"

"It's gorgeous!" she said. "The most beautiful ring I've ever seen. But...it must've cost you a fortune. And with moving back, and having to pay on those leases until you can find someone to take over, I'm afraid we should return it."

She heard him chuckle. "No way. You deserve to come first for a change. I wanted you to think it's the most beautiful ring you've ever seen. That's why it took me so long to decide. It's not easy for a guy. There were hundreds to choose from," he complained, as if the whole process had been harrowing indeed.

She laughed. "You did well. I love it."

"Will you marry me, Pres?"

A ripple of pure excitement ran through her. She'd gone from opening yoga mats to a stunning engagement ring, complete with wedding proposal. While she'd been moping around her party, she'd thought this might be one of the worst nights of her life. Now she knew it was the best.

"Are you *sure* you want me?" She knew that probably wasn't the usual question a prospective bride asked her groom. But Aaron had been so wary of commitment.

His lips curved into a confident smile. "Would I have asked if I wasn't?"

She laughed again through the tears that were slipping over her lashes. "No."

"There you go. I wanted to be sure I was doing it for the right reasons, not out of a sense of guilt or obligation but because we were good together, right for each other. I had to screw up my whole financial picture to finally realize it, but…I'm there now. And we'll recover eventually."

We'll recover. That had a nice sound to it.

She gazed down as he slid the ring on her finger.

"Wow. Would you look at that! It's so big I'm afraid I might get mugged."

"No one had better hurt you, ever, or they'll answer to me," he said. Then he cupped her face in his hands and wiped her tears with his thumbs. "Presley?"

For a moment it seemed as if her little-girl self, the grimy waif who'd had to steal food from Dumpsters to survive, was watching her from one side—watching her adult self step into a fairy tale. "What?"

He kissed her, tenderly. "I love you."

* * * * *

An irresistible new installment in the
Swift River Valley series from
New York Times bestselling author

CARLA NEGGERS

**Unlikely partners bound by circumstance...
or by fate?**

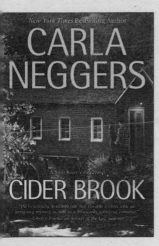

Rescued by a sexy bad-boy firefighter isn't how Samantha Bennett expected to start her stay in Knights Bridge, Massachusetts. Now she has everyone's attention—especially that of Justin Sloan, her rescuer, who wants to know why she was camped out in an abandoned New England cider mill.

Samantha is a treasure hunter, returned home to Knights Bridge to solve a three-hundred-year-old mystery. Justin may not trust her, but that doesn't mean he can resist her....

Available wherever books are sold.

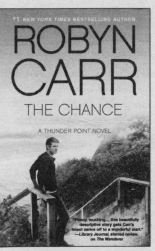

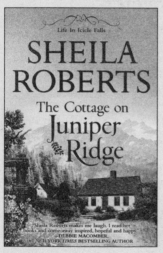

REQUEST YOUR FREE BOOKS!

2 FREE NOVELS
FROM THE ROMANCE COLLECTION
PLUS 2 FREE GIFTS!

YES! Please send me 2 FREE novels from the Romance Collection and my 2 FREE gifts (gifts are worth about $10). After receiving them, if I don't wish to receive any more books, I can return the shipping statement marked "cancel." If I don't cancel, I will receive 4 brand-new novels every month and be billed just $6.24 per book in the U.S. or $6.74 per book in Canada. That's a savings of at least 22% off the cover price. It's quite a bargain! Shipping and handling is just 50¢ per book in the U.S. and 75¢ per book in Canada.* I understand that accepting the 2 free books and gifts places me under no obligation to buy anything. I can always return a shipment and cancel at any time. Even if I never buy another book, the two free books and gifts are mine to keep forever.

194/394 MDN F4XY

Name   (PLEASE PRINT)

Address   Apt. #

City   State/Prov.   Zip/Postal Code

Signature (if under 18, a parent or guardian must sign)

Mail to the Harlequin® Reader Service:
IN U.S.A.: P.O. Box 1867, Buffalo, NY 14240-1867
IN CANADA: P.O. Box 609, Fort Erie, Ontario L2A 5X3

Want to try two free books from another line?
Call 1-800-873-8635 or visit www.ReaderService.com.

* Terms and prices subject to change without notice. Prices do not include applicable taxes. Sales tax applicable in N.Y. Canadian residents will be charged applicable taxes. Offer not valid in Quebec. This offer is limited to one order per household. Not valid for current subscribers to the Romance Collection or the Romance/Suspense Collection. All orders subject to credit approval. Credit or debit balances in a customer's account(s) may be offset by any other outstanding balance owed by or to the customer. Please allow 4 to 6 weeks for delivery. Offer available while quantities last.

Your Privacy The Harlequin® Reader Service is committed to protecting your privacy. Our Privacy Policy is available online at www.ReaderService.com or upon request from the Harlequin Reader Service.

We make a portion of our mailing list available to reputable third parties that offer products we believe may interest you. If you prefer that we not exchange your name with third parties, or if you wish to clarify or modify your communication preferences, please visit us at www.ReaderService.com/consumerschoice or write to us at Harlequin Reader Service Preference Service, P.O. Box 9062, Buffalo, NY 14269. Include your complete name and address.

ROM13R

BRENDA NOVAK

(limited quantities available)

TOTAL AMOUNT	$ _____
POSTAGE & HANDLING	$ _____
($1.00 for 1 book, 50¢ for each additional)	
APPLICABLE TAXES*	$ _____
TOTAL PAYABLE	$ _____

(check or money order—please do not send cash)

To order, complete this form and send it, along with a check or money order for the total above, payable to Harlequin MIRA, to: **In the U.S.** 3010 Walden Avenue, P.O. Box 9077, Buffalo, NY 14269-9077 **In Canada:** P.O. Box 636, Fort Erie, Ontario, L2A 5X3.

Name: _____

Address: _____ City: _____

State/Prov.: _____ Zip/Postal Code: _____

Account Number (if applicable): _____

075 CSAS

*New York residents remit applicable sales taxes.
*Canadian residents remit applicable GST and provincial taxes.